THE SON OF GOD

SHARON LINDSAY

Unto Us

THE
SON
G OF OD

Series: Book 1

TATE PUBLISHING
AND ENTERPRISES, LLC

Published by Tate Publishing & Enterprises, LLC
127 E. Trade Center Terrace | Mustang, Oklahoma 73064 USA
1.888.361.9473 | www.tatepublishing.com

Tate Publishing is committed to excellence in the publishing industry. The company reflects the philosophy established by the founders, based on Psalm 68:11,
"The Lord gave the word and great was the company of those who published it."

Book design copyright © 2015 by Tate Publishing, LLC. All rights reserved.
Cover design by Nino Carlo Suico
Interior design by Jomel Pepito

Published in the United States of America

ISBN: 978-1-68028-096-8
1. Fiction / Religious
2. Fiction / Historical
15.03.23

To the Spirit-led leadership
and members of B'rit Hadasha
Messianic Jewish Synagogue
They welcomed my husband
and me at a very low point
in our lives and ministered
God's healing to us.

Contents

Introduction

The purpose of this book is to breathe life into the plastic characters of the nativity so that the reader can identify with the flesh-and-blood people who lived and were associated with the birth of Jesus. Their experiences with each other and with the beings who dwell in the spiritual realm are not unlike the experiences of people today.

A great deal of research has gone into this book, but it does not contain the definitive answers to controversial questions. It does attempt to follow the biblical narrative and the chronology of historical events; the rest is theory or imagination. All direct quotes from scripture are italicized and referenced at the end of the book. An index of characters will help you recognize biblical, historical, and fictional characters. *Unto Us* is the first book in the *Son of God Series,* five novels which cover the life of Jesus.

So let the story begin.

In the beginning was the Word [Yeshua the Creator] *and the Word was with God* [the Eternal Father and his Holy Spirit], *and the Word was God. He was with God in the beginning. Through him all things were made; without him nothing was made that has been made. In him was life, and that life was the light of men.* (John 1:1–4)

Prologue I

CREATION

So God created man in his own image, in the image of God
he created him, male and female he created them. God blessed
them and said to them, "Be fruitful and increase in number;
fill the earth and subdue it."

—Genesis 1:27–28

In the beginning

Like a fiery wind, the Spirit of God moved back and forth over a patch of bare soil, waiting for the moment.

"Let us make man in our image!" the voice of the Eternal Father boomed from his Holy Sanctuary. From the sapphire throne on the backs of cherubim, his all-powerful voice instantly cut a path through the vast void of space. It reached the ears of Yeshua the Creator, who was kneeling in the dirt he had created three days earlier.

Responding to the voice of that part of the Godhead which maintained order in the universe, Yeshua thrust his hands deep into the black soil, pulling from it elements with which to form cells, the building blocks of flesh. Skillfully, he packed various types of cells together. Bone tissue—one by one, he formed and laid out over two hundred bones to shape the skeletal system.

"Father?" the Creator's voice traveled through space unimpeded by time or distance. "Man is smaller than the angels."

"Only for a time is he less than the angels. He will grow into companionship with us," the Eternal Ruler replied. "All he needs is the potential to grow more and more into our likeness."

Nodding his head in agreement, Yeshua continued to work. He knew his Father omnisciently watched from the throne room, pouring himself into this unprecedented event. Never before had such thought, such personal tenderness gone into an act of creation.

Heart tissue—the Creator packed it together into an irregular ball about the size of a fist, then he created chambers and attached a system of veins and arteries through which life would surge.

"Make it big enough to hold more than blood," the Spirit urged. "Man's heart must hold love, compassion, patience—all the emotions we share. He must feel deeply about righteousness and justice. And he must need companionship"—the Spirit sighed such a long deep sigh that the trees bent as his breath went forth with the words that completed his thought—"like we need companionship."

The Godhead, a single omnipotent being who had divided himself into three separate beings with specific roles, now focused on the creation of a being more like himself than anything previously created—not equal, not an exact replica, but very similar in many significant ways.

Nerve tissue—painstakingly, the Creator threaded the sensory paths, linking each one to the center of intelligence that was protected by the skull. "The capacity of man's brain, like ours, is infinite," Yeshua commented to his coregents as he placed centers of language, speech, and creativity in the brain. "For now, I am giving him the basic information for life. As he experiences life and as we share with him, he will grow to be more and more like us."

Reproductive tissue—from the throne room, the Eternal Ruler shouted with excitement! "We are going to be a father many times over! This man is only the beginning. He will reproduce and fill the universe with beings that are our children, each one like us in many ways and still unique created beings. I can hardly wait!"

At last the Creator straightened up. "The form of man is finished!"

At that moment, all eyes focused on that one spot in the Garden of Eden. Like a beautiful clay statue, the first man lay lifeless on the ground.

Throughout the universe, not a note was sung, not a word was uttered as slowly the Creator bent over. Pressing his lips to the mouth he had formed, he blew into the man his own life.

Immediately, the man warmed and then took his first shuddering breath. His lungs filled with air. His cells began functioning according to the design of their Creator. He opened his eyes.

"Adam," the Creator said his name as he reached out with both hands to help the first man to his feet and bring him into a welcoming embrace.

Instantly, the Spirit wrapped himself around the man, enshrouding him in a mantle of light, his only clothing.

"It is good!" Father God shouted from heaven.

Lucifer, the prince of the cherubim, sang a perfect pitch, and suddenly all seven angelic choirs burst into song. Their anthem could be heard in every corner of the kingdom that was ruled by the Eternal Father, Yeshua the Creator, and the Holy Spirit.

Throughout the entire choral anthem, Yeshua held his newest creation close to his chest. As newly awakened flesh pressed against the spiritual being of his Creator, they bonded. "I love you," the Creator whispered, tears of joy running down his glowing face. "The experience of having you alive in my arms is more joy than I have ever experienced before! We will spend time together." As the last musical note sounded, Yeshua released Adam and took him by the hand. "This world is for you! Let me show you!"

Dazzled, overwhelmed, Adam began to look around. His nervous system began feeding and storing information. Suddenly, he was animated, running from forest to meadow, from seashore to mountain. Hand in hand with his Creator, he explored the garden. Then at the command of Yeshua, the animals presented themselves, coming forward in pairs, and Adam named each kind.

When the last pair of animals had passed, Adam continued to look around.

"What are you looking for?" Yeshua the Creator gently asked.

"My partner," Adam responded. "Every kind of animal that has passed by me has come with a mate, another like itself. I am looking for another like myself."

"We made you to need companionship," the Spirit commented.

"We did," Yeshua concurred, "and now that you have felt that need, I will fill it." As he spoke, Yeshua led his creation to a mossy bed near a flowing stream. "Lie down," he directed.

Adam stretched out on the ground, and Yeshua the Creator knelt beside him. With one hand, he reached out to touch. It was a tender touch, repeatedly brushing the golden curls back from Adam's forehead until sleepiness made his eyelids close and his breathing became slow and shallow.

Then while Father God watched, the Spirit tenderly glowed, causing warm breezes to engulf the first man. With one finger, the Creator opened up Adam's side. Skillfully, without spilling any of the blood that carried life throughout Adam's body, he removed one of Adam's ribs, sealing the incision immediately.

While Adam slept, Yeshua worked with the genetic material he had placed within each cell in the rib. From it, he generated new cells which he formed into another being, a being like Adam in most ways but significantly different—a compliment, a companion, a being capable of bearing the offspring that would populate the earth and spill over into the other solar systems and galaxies that had been spoken into existence on the fourth day.

"She is beautiful," the Holy Spirit whispered. "Her heart is tender and capable of holding tremendous love."

Once more, the Creator pressed his lips against the cold clay lips of his creation, breathing steadily into her mouth. Color bloomed in her cheeks, and as she turned her head, rays of sunlight caught the movement of her long dark tresses.

"Eve," Yeshua spoke the name of the first woman. She took a breath and slowly opened her eyes.

"It is good!" Father God announced, and once more, the angelic choruses burst into song while Yeshua pulled the first woman to her feet and into his arms, welcoming her, pouring himself into her. The Holy Spirit also caressed her, dressing her in a garment of light.

As the angelic chorus ended, the Creator took Eve by the hand and showed her Adam as he slept. "You were made to be a companion and a coregent with this man."

"Adam!" the Spirit called the man out of his sleep.

Adam opened his eyes, reaching up and accepting the hand of his Creator.

"This is your partner, your mate for life," Father God announced from the throne room as the Creator placed Eve's hand in the hand of Adam.

As flesh touched flesh, an electric thrill surged through both the man and the woman. Joyfully, the Spirit swirled around them, knitting them together heart and soul.

"Together, you are to rule over the Earth, the plants, and the animals. Make all flourish, and then bear children so this planet will be filled," God commanded.

In response, both Adam and Eve bowed to the ground, accepting the mandate of the Eternal Triune.

With an outstretched hand, Yeshua the Creator brought them back to their feet. "Come, I will show you more of the garden." Grabbing each by a hand, Yeshua began to run, taking them from quiet ponds to cascading waterfalls, from golden fields to majestic forests.

Time passed. Earth rotated away from the sun, and darkness filled the sky. Throughout the night, Adam and Eve sat with their Creator, naming the stars and wondering at the brightness of the moon. At dawn on the seventh day, Yeshua led them to an orchard where they enjoyed the sweet produce of the trees. Then he took them to a field where they plucked the ripe grain, chewing handfuls as they walked along.

They drank water from a stream and then sat on its mossy bank with feet submerged. "This day, the seventh day of every week, will be our day," the Creator said. "I will come to you in the evening as the sixth day ends. For the entire seventh day, we will celebrate the creation of this world. *For in six days* I *made the heavens and the earth, the sea, and all that is in them, but* I *rested on the seventh day. Therefore* the Eternal Father, the Holy Spirit and I have *blessed the Sabbath day and made it holy.*[1] It will be our eternal celebration."

Then the Creator led Adam and Eve to a grassy hill. At the top, he paused, pointing to the sunset. "Our day is ending. I have so much more to tell you, and you need time to make your own discoveries. For now, I will leave you to explore, to taste, to experience. All has been created for your pleasure. There is only one restriction, the Tree Of Knowledge of Good and Evil, which is planted in the center of the garden. Do not eat from it. The fruit of that tree causes sorrow, separation, and death."

Before parting, the Creator pulled each one close. Then as the sky began to lose its light, his bodily image became a fiery spirit enveloped in clouds, and he ascended into the twilight.

High atop the golden walls of the celestial city, Lucifer, prince of the cherubim, looked down on the Creator's most recent achievement. "The Creator actually gave dominion of the planet and all the creation associated with it to those inferior beings," he muttered. "They are so immature in the ways of the kingdom! Why couldn't the Creator have given that world to me? I am qualified for greater responsibilities than supporting the sapphire throne and directing the choirs."

One of the angelic watchers soared to the top of the wall, stopping in front of Lucifer to make a quick sweeping bow.

Lucifer nodded, enjoying the recognition of his superior rank within the angelic hosts.

"Gabriel sent me to take this position on the wall where I can watch over Adam and Eve. If they appear to have any need, I am to report it immediately," the watcher relayed his assignment.

Concealing the resentment he felt, Lucifer stepped aside, allowing the angelic watcher to take his place. After a brief hesitation, he flew off to take his position, walking among the fiery stones while supporting the sapphire throne of the Eternal God, Three-in-One.

"He is coming!" Adam pointed toward a tiny glowing point of light in the early evening sky. He took his wife's hand, and together, they watched as the golden ember in the heavens became a giant ball of fire streaking toward Earth. As it appeared to increase in size, clouds formed at the base of the fireball, cushioning and slowing its descent through the atmosphere.

Hand in hand, the first man and woman ran through the grassy meadow to the top of a flower-strewn hill, to the place where the Creator usually met them. Breathless with anticipation, they raised their hands in welcome. A deliciously warm breeze enveloped their bodies. Like the kiss of God, it sent warm shivers through their souls.

"The Holy Spirit is with him," Eve said, acknowledging the presence of that part of the Godhead that moved like the wind, burned like fire, and flowed like oil throughout the kingdom of the Eternal.

As the fiery cloud touched the ground, it suddenly transformed into a towering man clothed in shimmering white light. A smile covered his glowing face, and he stretched his arms out in a welcoming gesture. "Adam my son and Eve, my daughter, I am so eager to hear what you have been doing with the Earth and the creatures I have placed under your authority." Before the Creator could say more, he engulfed both of his unique creations in his arms and pulled them firmly against his chest. "I can feel your excitement! I know you have so much to tell." Releasing them, the Creator stepped back. Then with an arm around each, he led them to a bench-shaped boulder, where they sat together while the Spirit swirled around them.

For a few moments, everyone was silent, just enjoying the physical closeness and the beauty that surrounded them.

"You know, the angels do not understand what it is to enjoy the results of a creative effort. They are incapable of experiencing the satisfaction and pleasure that we are feeling at this moment," Yeshua commented quietly, as if he were speaking to himself. Then he turned to Adam. "You've named the creatures and assigned each to a region suitable to its physical and temperamental needs. Now in what other ways are you ordering and expanding upon my creation?" Yeshua asked.

"I am learning to communicate with the dolphins, and they are helping me explore the underwater regions. Coral fascinates me. It provides a habitat for so many sea creatures. I was wondering if it could be made to grow above the waterline, providing a habitat for flying creatures?"

In response to Adam's question, the Creator waved his hand, and a giant illustration filled the sky. "You have to make a basic change at the intracellular level." Yeshua pointed to a tiny point on the spiraling chain of genetic material located in the core of the cell. "A change here will allow the tiny creatures that build the coral to adapt to a dry environment."

Adam studied the illustration intently, his face breaking into a big grin as he began to understand how to apply the information the Creator was sharing with him.

"Do you know how happy you make me?" the Creator asked. "For so long, I have desired to have someone with which to share the secrets of creation, someone who would be able to come up with original ideas and implement them! I am looking forward to seeing coral rise out of the sea! And what about you, Eve?" He turned to the beautiful woman he had made to be a companion to Adam and mother of the human race.

"I have been cross-pollinating fruit trees with fruit-bearing vines."

"And I have had to taste the results," Adam quipped. "Today she was perfecting sour." Adam's mouth puckered as he spoke.

"Sometimes a pure sour taste is exactly what is needed when you are working with food combinations," Eve good-naturedly defended her project. Laughter rolled off the hilltop as Adam, Eve, and Yeshua appreciated the humor of the moment.

When their laughter died away, Yeshua asked, "Have you found a place to make your own special dwelling, a place to begin your family?"

Adam answered, "We found a place near the river. Together, we planted grapevines, which we are going to train to arch, forming a roof."

"I've put lily of the valley near the base of the grapevines and transplanted moss and ferns," Eve added. "It will be a cool, comfortable place, our own dwelling that we do not share with the animals."

"We will always share our dwelling with you," Adam hastily added, including both his Creator and the Spirit in his invitation.

"I hope that is always true," the Creator replied with an unusual note of wistfulness in his voice.

Prologue II

THE FALL

You were anointed as a guardian cherub, for so I ordained
you. You were on the holy mount of God; you walked among
the fiery stones. You were blameless in your ways from the day
you were created till wickedness was found in you.

—Ezekiel 28:14–15

Like fiery oil, the Holy Spirit made a glowing circuit of the room before flowing into the shape of a flaming hand and filling his place on the throne. "Eternal Ruler," the Spirit addressed his coregent, "Lucifer is spreading sedition again."

Before the Spirit could communicate his thoughts on the activities of the highest-ranking and most beautiful cherub ever created, a seraph named Ophaniel soared into the throne room. He made a sweeping bow before the trifold rulers of the universe. As this beautiful angel prostrated himself before his God, one pair of his shimmering wings covered his face, and another pair of wings covered his feet while a third set of wings slowly beat the air and whispered, "Holy, holy, holy! Wonderful Creator, Eternal Ruler, and Bountiful Spirit!" For a long time, the high-ranking seraph remained in that position.

Ever watchful, Michael, one of the archangels on the Mount of God, stepped to the side of the kneeling seraph to gently urge him to take his post above the throne. But at that moment, the

Eternal Ruler held up a restraining hand, and Michael, with a respectful bow, returned to his place beside the throne.

"Your heart is heavy," the Eternal Father observed.

"Speak," Yeshua the Creator urged. "Unburden yourself before you take your place above the throne."

Without commenting, the Spirit flowed from his place on the throne and engulfed the now-trembling angel. His sweet aroma, mercy mingled with compassion, filled the holy chamber.

Ophaniel breathed deeply, allowing the fragrance of genuine comfort to fill his nostrils. It broke through his respectful reserve and allowed him to confess, "My heart is breaking over the accusations of Lucifer, your wisest and strongest cherub. With his body, he supports your throne, but with his words, he tears it down!"

"We have heard him, and we have seen the dark places in his heart," the Father responded.

"Then please, speak out! Refute Lucifer's claim that he and not man should have been given dominion over your newest creation, Earth! Silence him now before it is too late! Many of the hosts of heaven are convinced that you have treated the royal bearer of your throne with undeserved disdain. Some ministering spirits have stopped praising your name and have become obsessed with judging and condemning your actions. Your kingdom is being divided. The spiritual beings that you have created to minister in the heavenly courts and sing praises before your throne are now taking sides. You must take action!"

"Do not be troubled," the Creator responded. "We have a plan. As Lucifer continues to build a wall that separates himself from us, our plan will unfold."

"Forgive me," Ophaniel cried. "I have listened to his divisive words."

"There is nothing to forgive," Father God responded. "You have chosen us, and that choice brings some rejoicing to this dismal situation."

"It is all about the choice," Yeshua the Creator asserted. "We are the rulers of created beings who choose to submit to our authority." He gestured toward the Archangel Michael and to the guardian cherubim on whose backs the throne floated. "They, along with many others, have turned their backs on Lucifer and have pledged their allegiance to us." Yeshua pointed above the throne toward Gabriel, who had joined the seraphim to fill the throne room with praises. "Each time one of the heavenly hosts comes freely into this room to declare allegiance, there is rejoicing."

"I do pledge my allegiance and submit to the authority of the Eternal God, Yeshua the Creator, and the Holy Spirit," Ophaniel declared.

In response, Yeshua extended his hand toward Ophaniel. "Accept this white stone. It bears the mark that identifies those who are with us."

Ophaniel extended his hand and received a pure white stone, on which two intersecting lines were engraved: one long and one short. He placed the stone in his breastplate among the other gems that had been given to him at his creation and on the occasion when he received the honor of singing praises above the throne.

"Some of the heavenly beings are still deciding. For now, we will wait until all of our created beings have affirmed their loyalty. Allegiance cannot be forced," Father God added.

Satisfied and comforted, Ophaniel rose from his kneeling position and flew to his station opposite Gabriel above the crystal-blue throne. Their shimmering wings arched like the dazzling emerald bow above them, and together, they sang their love and loyalty to the Trinity.

Simultaneously, Father God and Yeshua looked at the Holy Spirit, waiting for him to complete the thoughts he had begun to share.

"Lucifer is on the walls attempting to convince the watchers and the heralds. Many other heavenly beings are also with him." The Spirit had stated what the other members of the Godhead knew. Sadly, the three rulers turned their attention to the gathering near the jasper watchtower on top of the golden walls of the celestial city.

Lifting his chin a little higher, Lucifer, the prince of cherubs, observed his glorious reflection in the polished jasper of the corner tower. "I am an astoundingly beautiful creature!" He then spoke to a cluster of angels and heavenly beings who had been drawn almost irresistibly to the top of the towering walls of the heavenly city, "You came to see the Creator's wisest and most wonderful creation." Lucifer's melodious voice pulled his audience closer while his eyes remained fixed on his own reflected beauty.

He stared at himself. Like all cherubim, he had four faces: a man, a lion, an eagle, and an ox. Each was magnificently regal, and each glowed like polished gold. Deliberately, he pulled his gaze away from his own dazzling reflection and turned his manly face toward his audience.

The promenade on top of the golden walls continued to fill with every rank and kind of heavenly being. Lucifer waited. The air became heavy with anticipation. Finally, with a voice as clear and resounding as a perfect musical note, he trumpeted, "When you see my wings, woven with strands of silver and gold and set with diamonds, are you not awed? And when you see my breastplate filled with precious stones, are you not amazed at the honors I am worthy of! Each of these stones represents a position in the kingdom." Then he paused, slowly turning so the gems the Creator had placed in his breastplate could catch the rays of light that emanated from the throne room of the Eternal Trinity.

"When you observe the Creator's newest addition to his kingdom—man, ruler of Earth..." The royal cherub's intonation signaled his disdain. His pause allowed anticipation to build. Then dramatically, he arched his wings and shook his head so his golden tresses caught the breeze and floated like a shimmering halo. Suddenly, he turned his eagle face on his audience. For a spellbinding moment, he swept the crowd of heavenly beings with his piercing sapphire gaze. Only when he was satisfied that he had the attention of every celestial being within the range of his voice did he revert to his manly face and finish his sentence, "...and you see the plainness of flesh with a mere covering of light that is Adam and his partner, Eve, are you not aghast that they were given dominion over the planet? Did you see what the man was made from? Dirt! Not precious stones filled with light and set in gold! Man cannot transform himself into energy and move faster than light. He cannot even change his form, yet God expects us to minister to him! There is nothing about man that commands my respect. Adam and his partner, Eve, are inferior creatures who should be ministering to us!"

In response, a cacophony of voices filled the air as some voiced their agreement and others their amazement.

"You heard me!" Lucifer repeated. "Adam and his partner, Eve, are inferior creatures who should be worshipping and ministering to us! A mistake! Yeshua the Creator surely made a mistake in setting the hierarchy of his new domain!"

"Mistake!" A subordinate cherub vehemently protested as he turned a brilliantly glaring ox-like face toward his superior. "The Creator does not make mistakes! Adam and his partner, Eve, are made in the image of God, with unlimited potential and the ability to procreate! They are destined to rule with the Godhead. That is truly awesome! You should not speak against your Creator and his plans without cause."

"I have cause!" Lucifer shouted back as he turned his lion-like face toward the protesting cherub. Shaking his beautiful hair like a magnificent golden mane, he roared, "Injustice!"

Lucifer smiled to himself in satisfaction as his audience gasped. "How could the Trinity be accused of injustice?" they asked.

Returning to his most serene face, man, he responded to his listeners, "Since the moment of my creation, I have demonstrated the ability to rule. I have become more than a mere cherub, supporter of the throne." He pointed to his breastplate, to a shimmering piece of topaz cut so it appeared to have an eye within its center. "I organize the watchers and send them to their posts." Next, his finger touched the pulsating ruby set near the center of his breastplate. The living stone sang a perfect scale. "I compose the music and conduct all seven choirs of morning stars." As he enumerated the positions he flawlessly maintained, he pointed to the corresponding stones in his breastplate. "Jasper—I direct the heralds to announce every movement of each member of the Godhead. Because I understand the needs of the Godhead, I make sure there are always two guardian cherubim and numerous seraphim in the throne room." He pointed to the royal sapphire, then to the onyx stone, black as the uncreated voids at the edges of the kingdom. "I also oversee the keepers of the records of heaven." With a sneer, he added, "Adam, lord of the Earth, has named the animals and is now attempting to communicate with them!"

Within the heavenly audience, there were a number of responsive chuckles, but many of the heavenly host remained uncomfortably silent.

Encouraged by the positive responses, Lucifer continued, "Justice demands that I take dominion of Earth, that Adam and his offspring submit to my authority and honor me."

From the center of the audience, a beautiful winged creature rose in a shimmering mist that condensed into a brilliant fireball. Like a comet, he soared into direct confrontation with the Prince of Cherubim. "Do not give the false impression that you have been treated unfairly! Yeshua the Creator made me to spread his beautiful qualities throughout the kingdom. He is the source of all that I am, and my loyalty is with him!" Turning on his glowing tail, the outspoken creature soared off the city walls into the celestial clouds. Other shimmering creatures rose from the crowd, condensing into brilliant balls of fire as they flew away toward the Sea of Glass in front of the Sanctuary of the Most Holy. Many cherubs, seraphs, watchers, and heralds also followed, leaving Lucifer with those heavenly beings whose thoughts and allegiance he had captured.

"Can't you show the Trinity that they made a mistake?" a prince from the heralds voiced his suggestion.

"The Godhead is fair. If you show them the error of their ways, they will have to correct their mistake," another seraph offered support for the herald's suggestion.

"I have considered a demonstration." Lucifer nodded thoughtfully before he continued. "I want to show the Creator that Adam and Eve are of inferior intellect. They should be ministering to the heavenly host. The host of heaven should not be ministering to them.

"Yeshua has spoken with the man and woman frequently, and still they are simple beings incapable of ruling Earth. I have observed them closely and know for a fact that they spend much of their time trying to communicate with the animals. They are very slow to accomplish the things we are all able to do. The Godhead will thank me for making their ineptitude clear."

"Do you really think the Creator will give you dominion over the Earth just because they have not mastered communicating with the animals?" a doubting herald asked.

"I am counting on the objectivity that the Trinity has always boasted," Lucifer answered in a challenging tone.

"Nearly one-third of our ministering spirits agree with Lucifer," the Eternal Father said, stating what the Triune Rulers omnipotently knew.

"When we created beings with the ability to reason and make choices, we always knew rebellion was a possibility," the Creator asserted with resignation.

"But we did not know it would hurt so much." Father God wiped a crystal tear from his face, and a little of his physical brilliance seemed to fade with the emotional pain of accusation and rejection. "My heart aches for Lucifer, our wonderful creation."

"I will go to the Garden of Eden and warn Adam and Eve once more," the Creator stated. "They must understand their vulnerability."

"And they should be advised to stay away from the place where they are most vulnerable," the Spirit added.

"The Tree of Knowledge of Good and Evil," Father God breathed the name of the element of choice that, after much conferring, had been placed in the garden.

"At Earth's twilight, I will meet them," the Creator said.

"You may be too late." As the Spirit spoke, each member of the Trinity was simultaneously aware of Lucifer's presence on Earth.

"Winged serpent?" On Earth, the Prince of Cherubs approached the most intelligent and dazzling creature that Yeshua had placed in the garden.

Gracefully, the iridescently scaled reptile raised its magnificently sculptured head. With quizzical onyx eyes, it looked directly into the face of the most beautiful and intelligent angel ever created.

"I speak your language, and I have authority over the animal kingdoms," Lucifer announced.

The beautiful winged serpent stared uncertainly, then he spread his wings and started to soar away into the treetops.

Quickly, Lucifer interposed his dazzling body into the creature's flight path. Flaunting his position, he said, "I'm sure you recognize that I am a very high-ranking emissary from the

Most Holy Sanctuary of the Trinity. Adam is not the only being who has dominion over you!"

Immediately, the serpent responded as he would to his Creator. Submissively, he folded his wings and lowered his gold-and-silver patterned head.

Lucifer read the creature's body language and nodded to himself in satisfaction. The serpent was going to cooperate. Making his voice as nonthreatening as possible, he continued, "Yeshua has asked that you allow me to inhabit your body so I may speak to Adam and Eve through you."

The serpent's high-pitched song of consent softly floated on the air as Lucifer transformed himself into a stream of high-energy living matter that flowed into the body of the winged reptile. As soon as he had possession of the beautiful creature, he soared to the top of the Tree of Knowledge of Good and Evil to wait for his opportunity.

It was not long before Eve wandered by. The early afternoon sun caught her long black tresses, reflecting the colors of the rainbow. Enviously, Lucifer fixed the hypnotic eyes of the serpent on his prey. Hidden in the silver foliage of the forbidden tree, he watched every movement the woman made.

As she walked from tree to tree, gathering fruit, the translucent light that clothed her body revealed the silhouette of her exquisite feminine form. Lucifer had to admit that there was primitive beauty in this newest creation, so much beauty that he could not tear his eyes from the graceful movements of the creature called woman. She was alone, and her arms were loaded down with the fruit from several species of trees. Through the serpent, Lucifer called to her, "Eve, daughter of Father God!"

Immediately, the beautiful female paused and looked around, astonished that someone other than Adam or Yeshua had called her name.

"Over here," Lucifer called. "Come over to the tree so I can talk with you."

Wide-eyed and curious, the woman created from Adam's rib turned to see a winged serpent speaking to her from within the branches of the Tree of Knowledge of Good and Evil.

"I have been trying to learn how to communicate with you. How did you learn my language?" Eve asked.

"I ate the fruit of this tree," Lucifer responded through the serpent.

"I have never touched that fruit," Eve thoughtfully replied. Then as an afterthought, she added, "The Creator told us never to eat from that tree."

"Hasn't God said, 'Every tree that bears fruit is good for food'?" the serpent countered.

"God has given us every tree for food but this one," she answered as she moved a little closer. "You are a winged serpent! I did not know the Creator had made any other creatures with language like ours."

Lucifer chuckled to himself. He could see the way her eyes widened with curiosity and the way her body leaned toward his own. "You are intrigued by my ability to speak." He spread his shimmering wings and soared to a lower branch, stretching his long body so Eve could get a better look.

"Yes." Eve started to take another step but hesitated. "I really should not touch the fruit from this tree, for the Creator has said if we eat the fruit of this tree, we will die."

"Die! Surely not!" The serpent took a bite from a nearby piece of fruit. "Look at me! I am not dead. Come close and touch my living scales," he invited.

"Oh, I couldn't," Eve protested, "but a talking serpent, it is so fascinating." She took a few steps closer to the tree.

"I obtained the ability to speak after only two bites of this fruit. After a few more bites, I gained unbelievable wisdom. I now know things that are only known by the Creator, God the Father, and the Holy Spirit. They fear you will also gain their knowledge."

"That is not true!" Eve objected. "I think I had better go find Adam." She started to turn away.

"Adam? What do you need him for? Is your mind so befuddled that you cannot think for yourself?" the serpent taunted.

"I can think!" Eve protested with an emphatic toss of her head. "I am a very intelligent being."

"Then show your husband just how intelligent you are. Take two pieces of this fruit: one for yourself and one for him. Eat, and you will both have the wisdom of the Three-Gods-in-One." Lucifer slithered along the branch until he reached several pieces of ripe fruit. With his nose, he nudged them until they fell to the ground. "Just pick them up," the Tempter suggested. "Take a bite and see. You will have as much wisdom as you have beauty. You are very beautiful, you know."

Basking in the glow of the serpent's flattering words, Eve stood in stunned contemplation, and Lucifer remembered the first time he had felt the overwhelming emotions of pride and covetousness. It was a moment to savor. He could see that she was deeply moved by those sensations. "There is so much to experience on this Earth. Don't let the Creator hold you back."

Immediately, Lucifer could see that his words had moved the woman to action. Eagerly, she picked up one of the two pieces of fruit he had dropped to the ground. She took a bite, savoring the sweetness, then exuberantly, she reached up to gather more. She could not get enough. He chuckled to himself as he watched her discard her previously gathered fruit, fill her arms to overflowing, and then run to find Adam.

Then still in the body of the winged-serpent, he followed, soaring from treetop to treetop, all the while keeping a discreet distance.

"Adam! Adam!"

From beneath the sea where he was diving with the dolphins, studying their precision swimming and communication skills, Adam heard the sound of his wife's voice. Slowly exhaling, he swam to the surface and looked around. He could see Eve on the beach, her arms overflowing with fruit. With strong easy strokes, he swam toward shore to see what was causing his partner such excitement.

How wonderful the Creator was to have made such a perfect partner for me, Adam mused as he swam toward the beach. He remembered that short period of loneliness when it had seemed that every creature had a mate except him, and then he relived his joy and excitement when the Creator had introduced him to Eve.

Nearing the shore, Adam was almost close enough for his feet to touch the sandy bottom. Eve came wading toward him. Her arms were still full of fruit. As Adam's feet touched the smooth sand of the seabed, he got a closer look at the fruit Eve was carrying. It was…no, it could not be! But it was—the fruit from the Tree of Knowledge of Good and Evil!

"What have you done?" Adam cried as he ran toward his wife, splashing through the knee-deep water. "You know what the Creator said, *'You must not eat from the tree of the knowledge of good and evil, for when you eat from it you will certainly die.'*"[1]

Eve met him. Blithely shrugging her shoulders, she ignored his words and held out a piece of golden fruit. "I have brought you wisdom. Here, taste and see! You will feel wonderful and know so much! I met a winged-serpent who could talk—"

"Eve!" Adam interrupted her excited babbling. "This is the forbidden fruit! Now you will die! What can I do?"

"If you eat the fruit, you will be as wise as the Creator, then you will know what to do," Eve asserted.

"I am not even certain that I know what death is." Adam was pacing back and forth in the calf-deep water. "But it must mean that you will be separated from me!" He threw his hands up in despair. "I cannot bear it!"

"Adam," Eve coaxed, "just from eating this fruit, the winged serpent has gained the ability to speak. He knows everything the Creator knows. He knows what death is and how to avoid it. The serpent is not dead, and look, nothing has happened to me!"

"I must know what to say to the Creator. I must know how to stop him from taking you away from me!" Adam stopped pacing and looked his wife directly in the eye. "Are you sure you feel exactly the same as before you ate the fruit?"

"Everything is the same," Eve assured her husband, "except I am sure that I am now much wiser than ever before."

Deliberately, Adam reached out and took a piece of fruit from her hand. He ate it, tossing the core into the water where they both stood.

From the top of a nearby tree, Lucifer, still possessing the body of the serpent, observed his complete triumph. Man had chosen to reject the authority of the Godhead. He could no longer occupy an elevated position in the heavenly kingdom. The ministering spirits of heaven could not possibly be expected to minister to him. Man must now minister to angels. Lucifer pushed his reasoning to what he considered the ultimate conclusion: man must minister to his new Lord, Lucifer. The Prince of Cherubs would become Lord of Earth. All that remained was to wait for the Creator to arrive and make the inevitable declaration.

Adam noticed that a sober demeanor had suddenly come over his wife. She dropped the rest of the fruit. It splashed, floated momentarily, and then sank beneath the gentle wavelets. With downcast eyes and a heavy heart, Adam took his wife's hand, and together, they walked out of the water toward the grass beyond the crystal sand of the beach.

When they reached the shade of a large oak, Adam paused. "Eve, I ate the fruit, and I still do not know what we are going to do or say when the Creator returns." At that moment, he lifted his eyes from the ground and looked at his wife. "Eve!" he gasped. "You are naked!" The light that had always provided an ethereal translucent covering was gone, and for the first time, bare flesh presented itself.

Eve began to sob. Tears ran down her cheeks.

Adam had never seen such a thing, and he reached out with one finger to touch the drops of water that were streaming from his wife's eyes.

Between sobs, Eve choked out, "Oh, Adam, your beautiful light is also gone."

Adam looked down and felt repulsed by his nakedness. He could not look at it. Forcefully, he grabbed Eve's hand and pulled her into a waist-high cluster of ferns. For the moment, they were partially covered, but it was not enough. Desperately, he looked around until his eyes fell on the broad leaves of a nearby fig tree. From those, he fashioned a garment that covered his wife from her neck to her thighs and one for himself that covered his flesh from his shoulders to the tops of his knees. Then they huddled together, for the first time experiencing shame and fear.

As Earth's twilight filled the sky with dazzling colors, Lucifer sensed the royal holiness of Yeshua and knew the Creator was approaching the garden. The Prince of Cherubs felt a tingle of anticipation run along his serpentine spine. Ever since the creation of man, he had been waiting to show the Creator his error. The obvious wisdom that he, the most honored member of the heavenly host, had shown in pointing out this mistake would have to be rewarded. This time, the reward would be greater than another stone in his breastplate. It would be a crown on his head. In his mind, he imagined approaching his Creator as an equal and reasonably stating the undeniable facts, "Man has rejected the authority of the Godhead and has submitted to my angelic authority. Earth is now rightfully my kingdom."

The first man heard the familiar footsteps of Yeshua as he walked through the garden. Unfamiliar waves of apprehension ran along Adam's spine and sent him, along with his wife, scurrying deeper into the foliage.

"Adam? Eve? Where are you?" The Creator's voice followed them. His footsteps stopped very close to the spot where they crouched.

Sensing their Creator's presence and realizing there was no place to hide, Adam answered a little evasively, "*I heard you in the garden, and I was afraid because I was naked; so I hid.*"[2]

"*Who told you that you were naked?*" the Creator asked. "*Have you eaten from the tree that I commanded you not to eat from?*"[3]

Squirming under his first experience with guilt, Adam replied, "*The woman you put here with me—she gave me some fruit from the tree and I ate it.*"[4]

"Eve," the Creator addressed the woman, and she cowered, covering her face in shame. "What have you done?"

The need to escape blame was so overwhelming that Eve answered, "The serpent spoke to me, so I ate."

"Serpent?" The Creator's voice echoed through the garden.

Hoping that the serpent would carry the blame, Adam and Eve looked up and around to see if the serpent would appear.

In the body of the winged-serpent, Lucifer spread his glittering wings and soared to the top of a nearby tree.

The Prince of Cherubs knew the Creator had recognized his presence. He could feel Yeshua's righteous gaze penetrating the glossy scales and searching his mind, his heart. Resentfully, Lucifer tried to cloak his thoughts, but it was impossible, so he threw out a challenge, "I have earned the right to be Lord of the Earth!"

The Creator answered Lucifer's challenge. "Serpent, you are cursed above every creature on Earth." Yeshua's voice seemed to split atoms as he continued, "From this day on, all serpents will crawl in the dust."

Adam and Eve were shocked to see the winged serpent suddenly fall from the top of a nearby tree. Its long thick body hit the ground with a resounding thud. Its beautiful wings had completely broken off from its scaly body. Awkwardly, the serpent writhed, trying to find a way to move through the dust. The glorious flying creature had become a pitiful snake.

With all his might, Lucifer tried to extricate himself from the body of the earthbound serpent, but he was trapped. The heat of the Creator's gaze sealed him in the body of the squirming snake. Dust clogged his nostrils and made him choke.

"I will put enmity between you and the woman, and between your offspring and hers,"[5] the Creator announced.

"No! No!" Lucifer tried to voice his objection, but the serpent was no longer able to make a sound. Silently, the Prince of Cherubs railed, "They are my subjects. They have to love and adore me! They have to worship me, like the other ministering spirits, and I have always worshipped you!"

"He will crush your head!"[6]

Who? An offspring? Eve's offspring? Lucifer struggled to comprehend.

Deliberately, the Creator's heel came down on the head of the wriggling serpent, applying steady pressure.

Suddenly, it became perfectly clear to Lucifer. Yeshua the Creator was going to somehow do the crushing! Painfully pinned under the weight of the Creator's heel, Lucifer could only grind his jaws in impotent rage.

In horrified amazement, Adam and Eve watched. It was the first act of violence they had ever witnessed. Without mercy, their kind Creator kept bearing down on the serpent's head until its beautiful onyx eyes protruded unnaturally and its forked tongue lay limp in the dust. Suddenly, Yeshua lifted his foot, and instantly, the serpent struck at it, almost touching, but just missing, the Creator's heel.

"You will strike at my heel," Yeshua admitted. "Your fangs will draw blood."

"Read my thoughts," Lucifer retorted. "I'll do more than strike at your heel! One-third of the hosts of heaven have already abandoned you. I am their commander! Together, we will seek out this offspring of Eve, thwart his appearance, and strike a deadly blow. I have the allegiance of your son Adam and your daughter Eve. All the generations within their reproductive organs belong to me. Earth is mine!"

Refusing further communication with the angel who was now his enemy, Yeshua turned his attention to the created beings that he loved, the ones made in his own image for his personal companionship. "Eve." The Creator's voice revealed the heaviness of his heart. "I will greatly increase your pain in bearing children. For your protection, you will desire your husband and submit to him in all things."

In reverent submission, Eve dropped to her knees, bowing her face to the ground.

"Adam, because you listened to your wife and ate from the tree that I commanded you not to eat from, I curse the ground! Through backbreaking toil, you will grow the food that you need, wrestling it from thorny ground."

In the dust at the feet of the Creator, the serpent continued to writhe as Lucifer struggled to extricate himself from the body of the cursed reptile. Exhausted, the Prince of Cherubs paused and looked up at Yeshua. The Creator was completely absorbed in man, his inferior creation! At that moment, anger and resentment exploded in Lucifer's mind. It rushed through every fiber of his spiritual being, fusing itself to the living energy that was his life.

Burning with rage, the Prince of Cherubs refocused his energy and pushed to escape the fleshly confines of the serpent, only to find that he was bound by its rigid ribs and constricting muscles. How could the Creator do this to him! He was a royal angel of light, a bearer of the throne. His power had never been so restrained!

Unfettered rage quickly turned to anxiety when he realized that the serpent was dying. This confrontation with flesh and death was a shocking experience. Gradually, the movements of the snake slowed. Its body temperature dropped. The scales and flesh of the serpent now weighed heavily on Lucifer, making him fear that he would never again soar through the heavens. On the verge of panic, loath to accept the embarrassment of calling on his Creator, Lucifer consolidated all his energy and finally burst through the imprisoning corpse.

Seething under the stinging humiliation of the curse and the confinement, the Prince of Cherubs returned to the celestial city with plans to consolidate his forces and confront the Trinity.

Weeping and bent under the weight of their newly gained knowledge of good and evil, Adam and Eve left the garden. It would no longer be their home. A few paces past Eden's gate, Adam turned his head and looked back over his shoulder. A sword-wielding cherub stationed at the entrance effectively killed all hope of ever returning to the only life he had known.

As if reading her husband's thoughts, Eve offered, "We have the promise that through a son, we will be restored."

"Lucifer is waiting for an audience." The Archangel Michael bowed before the Triune Rulers. "A third of the heavenly host has gathered with him."

"They will never enter this throne room!" The Eternal Father raised his right arm in a gesture of defiance.

Forming a flaming beam of light into a sword, Yeshua the Creator placed it in the hand of Michael. "Gather those who are with us and give them swords."

Without hesitating, the Creator descended from his throne. The train of his regal robe shimmered and floated around him. On his head, a jeweled crown radiated like the suns of the solar systems he had created.

Like a wall of fire, the Holy Spirit followed.

In the Most Holy Sanctuary of the Trinity, praises ceased, and awesome silence filled the throne room.

Sword in hand, Michael soared past his Creator to gather the loyal hosts of heaven.

As Yeshua the Creator moved past the altar, he could see Lucifer and his followers gathered on the Sea of Glass. "What brings you to the Mountain of the Lord and the Court of the Almighty?" Yeshua asked in a voice that shook the foundations of heavenly Zion. Behind him, the flames of the Holy Spirit flared and roared.

"I have come to receive the deed to Earth and official lordship over mankind," Lucifer responded with unwarranted confidence.

"I am the Creator, and Earth is mine!" Yeshua announced. "You are no longer Lucifer, prince of the cherubs. You have become Satan, a thief and my adversary!"

"I am your coregent!" the deposed Prince of Cherubs protested. He gestured to those who stood behind him. "I am recognized by one-third of the heavenly hosts, and mankind has chosen to obey me."

From the clouds that enveloped the Most Holy Sanctuary, the voice of God thundered, "You will never enter my throne room again!"

The sapphire in Satan's breastplate, symbol of his position as guardian of the throne room, suddenly fell from its gold mounting. In a moment of shocked dismay, the former Prince of Cherubs stared at the blue gemstone. It was disintegrating at his feet. "I am your equal! Angels and creatures do my bidding," Satan shouted.

Yeshua thundered in response, "You deceived my creation. They were not given an honest choice!"

"Nevertheless, they belong to me!" Lucifer retorted.

In the cloud-filled expanse above the confrontation on the Sea of Glass, Michael and his warrior angels gathered. High-intensity beams of light from their burning swords flashed through the glowing canopy of clouds.

"They will be mine again!" Yeshua shouted. "They will be given an honest choice, and all who choose my kingdom will be restored to me. As for you"—anticipatory silence reigned as all of heaven held their breath—"I strip you of every position in my kingdom!"

The rest of the stones in Lucifer's breastplate began to fall from their mountings, leaving only the gold frame.

"Leave! Leave my kingdom! Take your followers with you!"

"You have no right!" Satan protested.

"I am your Creator, and I have every right," Yeshua answered.

At that moment, the Holy Spirit exploded into a shower of flaming arrows. Satan and his forces fell back.

"Go to Earth, Satan, my enemy. Pretend to be prince of that world until I come and take it from you!" Yeshua announced as Michael and his host of warrior angels swooped down from the clouds.

Confusion and panic broke out in the ranks of the fallen host. Overwhelmed and outnumbered, the ministering spirits who had given their allegiance to the ex-Prince of Cherubs fled poured over the golden walls of the celestial city in a cascade of chaos.

With as much dignity as he could muster, Satan followed. Soaring to the top of the city walls, he turned his lion face toward Yeshua the Creator and roared in defiance.

"You will be defeated," Yeshua announced as his face took on the appearance of a lamb.

Like lightning, Satan, the deposed prince of cherubs, fell from the heavenly city to Earth.

Chapter 1

An Unbelievable Story

This is how the birth of Jesus Christ came about: His mother Mary was pledged to be married to Joseph, but before they came together, she was found to be with child through the Holy Spirit.

—Matthew 1:18

"This is the time, and this is the place." The fallen angel Raziel urged the dark spirits who accompanied him to slip under the roof of a humble home in the Galilean town of Nazareth. "Watch their body language." Through the cracks in the wooden gate to the courtyard, Raziel could see Heli the scribe of Nazareth and his wife talking to their daughter, Mary. "Listen to their words and try to weasel your way into their thoughts, but be careful! You will have to work from a safe distance." He pointed to the glow from the Holy Spirit, which surrounded the young girl seated in the center of the courtyard.

The spirits of Doubt, Fear, Condemnation, and Judgment trembled and held back.

"Go in," Raziel urged, pushing them through the spaces between the stone wall and the mud-and-thatch roof. "Do what our master has taught you to do," he admonished before soaring off to report to his immediate superior, Satan, the prince of evil.

"Now, Mary," Heli raised his hand in a gesture meant to silence his daughter. "I know you love Joseph and he is eager to take you into his home and make you his wife. You two have waited a little longer than usual, but that is only because Joseph is such a fine craftsman and won't settle for anything less than the best. The bridal chamber and cooking area that he is attaching to his shop are almost complete. No girl living anywhere in the region of Galilee will have two rooms with finer craftsmanship, even if the rest of her home is a carpenter's shop." Heli paused, stroking his beard, taking a few pacing steps on the hard-packed dirt floor of the courtyard as he contemplated the situation.

"Sometimes the waiting is just too difficult," Mary's mother suggested as she comfortingly put her arm around her fourteen-year-old daughter. She spoke to her husband as much as to her daughter. "There are feelings and physical drives between men and women that are difficult to say no to." Looking directly at her daughter, she sternly admonished, "Mary, you don't have to make up a story about an angel and the Spirit of God coming upon you. Your father and I understand those desires." The very married Jewish couple exchanged affectionate knowing glances. "I have to admit, I am surprised at Joseph. I thought he was a man more bound to the law than the desires of his flesh," Mary's mother added, as if trying to shift some of the responsibility from their daughter to their future son-in-law.

"Now, Mother." Heli stopped his pacing directly in front of his wife and daughter. "Don't pass judgment on Joseph. He is a man of the Torah, just like my ancestor, King David. And you know the stories about him!" Heli's eyebrows lifted, and his eyes became big with suggestion.

"Heli, this is not a light matter!" Mary's mother scolded.

"Yes, I know." Heli composed himself and turned a solemn face on his daughter, who sat on a small stool, head respectfully bowed and eyes on the well-trampled dirt of the small courtyard, as was the custom for children who were being reprimanded. Heli wiped the sweat from his forehead, walked over to the water jar, and dipped himself a cup of water. "It is too hot a day for such a story! Mary, the mother of the Son of God? You mean the Messiah?" Mary's father shook his head in disbelief. "It is unnecessary to go to such extremes. Joseph is an honorable man. He will do the right thing. He will take you into his home right away. I will speak to him."

"But, Father, you don't understand. I have not been with Joseph." Mary looked up. Her eyes, a serious dark brown, met the horrified eyes of her parents. All levity left the room.

"Oh, Mary! Then how?" Her mother's hand slipped from Mary's shoulder and went to her mouth in a gesture of unspeakable horror. "What have you done?"

"Nothing! I have done nothing!" Mary protested. She stood and looked her parents squarely in the eyes. "I know what you are thinking, but I have not been with any of the men of our village."

"Then how can you be sure you are with child?" Mary's mother asked.

"My body is going through all the changes Cousin Hannah told me about, and you have seen what is happening to my breakfast every morning. Even you began to suspect and ask questions. That's why we are having this conversation," Mary replied.

"It wasn't a Roman soldier, was it?" Heli spit the question through clenched teeth.

"Oh no!" Mary responded with equal horror.

But her mother started weeping as if she had not heard her daughter's reply. "Remember your cousin Deborah? Poor child. She had no choice, and no one dared come to her assistance. Oh, Mary, you can tell us."

Heli looked tenderly at his beautiful daughter while placing a comforting hand on his wife's shoulder. "Mary, you do not need to fear being stoned. If this child that you carry was forced upon you by our oppressors, you can expect mercy. We cannot take the bodies down from the crosses that stand by our highways, but we can spare the women they molest."

Mary looked up and raised her arms in exasperation. Then she began repeating her story, measuring each word. "Father, I tell you, the angel of the Lord appeared to me in this courtyard. Mother, you know I have never told an untruth. I am speaking the truth to you now. He stood in that corner next to the water jars." She pointed, hoping her parents could visualize the scene. "He was dressed all in white, and his skin glowed like the coals of a fire. His head was higher than the roof on the surrounding rooms. When I saw him, I was frightened and speechless, but he spoke to me. He said, *'Greetings, you who are highly favored! The Lord is with you.'*[1] He frightened me so much that I was about to flee, but he spoke again, and the tone of his voice was so gentle that I wanted to run to him instead of away. He said, *'Do not be afraid, Mary. You have found favor with God.'*"[2]

"Child," Mary's mother interrupted, "you should have run away. You should have run into the street and screamed for assistance."

"Who is this man you are talking about?" Heli raged as he paced around the tiny open courtyard, peering into each adjacent room as if he were looking for the stranger his daughter was describing. "How dare he enter my house and molest my daughter! Didn't you cry out? Didn't anyone hear?" He stopped pacing in front of the partially opened drape separating his daughters' sleeping area from the courtyard. "Where was your sister, Salome, when this was taking place?" With one hand, he swept the drape open and glared down at the young girl who sat on the floor listening.

"She was working in the garden," Mary answered.

"Salome can go to the garden now," her mother sternly insisted as she quickly strode over to place a basket in the hands of her youngest child. "This is not a conversation you are involved in," she rebuked. "Go to the garden and pick all the cucumbers that are ripe. If any of the neighbors come by, do not speak to anyone regarding this matter!"

Obediently, Salome stood, accepting the basket and walking toward the gate, but not without catching Mary's eye and silently mouthing, "I believe you!"

Once more, Heli turned to his daughter. The sadness, the pain in his eyes, Mary could hardly stand it. "I taught you the Torah, the sacred laws that we live by." He began to quote, "*If a man happens to meet in a town a virgin pledged to be married and he sleeps with her, you shall take both of them to the gate of that town and stone them to death—the girl because she was in a town and did not scream for help, and the man because he violated another man's wife. You must purge the evil from among you!*"[3]

"Heli," Mary's mother spoke up, "the Romans do not allow us to carry out death penalties."

"The Romans are not everywhere," Heli argued. "They are seldom in small towns like Nazareth. In Jerusalem, they regulate the religious courts, but in small towns, tradition often prevails."

"We must protect our daughter," Mary's mother insisted. "We love her, and she has always been our most obedient child. But, Mary"—she turned to her daughter—"you must tell us the truth!"

"He never touched me," Mary insisted. "He just said, '*You will conceive and give birth to a son, and you are to call him Jesus.*'[4] The angel told me this child would be great and he would be called the Son of the Most High."

The Holy Spirit drew near. "Speak, Mary. Say the exact words of the heavenly messenger." The beautiful anointing that accompanies the presence of the Spirit of God fell upon the girl.

Mary stood and quoted from the heavenly being that had visited her, "*The Lord God will give him the throne of his father David, and he will reign over Jacob's descendants forever; his kingdom will never end.*"[5]

Entwined in the thatch and clinging to the rafters, the demonic observers trembled. "She is speaking of the promised Messiah, the very prophecy that our lord, Satan, has sworn will never be fulfilled.

For a few moments, both of her parents were struck by the power of their daughter's words. They stared at her, not knowing how to respond. Finally, her mother broke the silence with a practical statement. "Mary, you cannot have a child without knowing a man." She looked at her daughter skeptically. "I thought you knew how God ordained that men and women come together to have children."

"I know," Mary rushed to defend herself. "I asked the angel how this could possibly be since I am a virgin. I am still a virgin to this day! I have never known a man!" Her voice pleaded with her parents to understand and believe. "As the angel continued to speak, my whole body began to tingle and shake." Again under the power of the Spirit, she repeated the exact words, "*The Holy Spirit will come on you, and the power of the Most High will overshadow you. So the holy one to be born will be called the Son of God.*"[6]

Mary continued, "I replied, '*I am the Lord's servant. May your word to me be fulfilled.*'[7] At that moment, I lost all strength. No one touched me, but the presence of the Holy God was so overwhelming that I could not stand. It was like the Shekinah that once filled Solomon's Temple. It filled me at that moment."

"We must do something!" Spirits of Doubt dropped from the ceiling, landing like unnoticed insects on the shoulders of both parents.

Mary looked at her parents who stared back at her, speechless. Doubt and horror seemed to be written on their faces. "You do believe me, don't you? Father, say you believe me. Mother?"

"Well, Mary"—her father continued to shake his head while he groped for words—"this is quite a story! In this story, there are elements of many prophecies. I taught you those prophecies, but I did not intend for you to use them to get yourself out of an unlawful situation." There was a painful pause while doubt and belief struggled. "I just don't know what to say." Worriedly, almost under his breath, he finally said, "What will I tell Joseph?"

"The angel gave me a sign," Mary added, hoping to bring her parents confidence in her truthfulness.

"A sign?" Both parents leaned forward, their bodies and minds begging for reassurance.

"The last thing he said was, *Even Elizabeth your relative is going to have a child in her old age, and she who was said to be unable to conceive is in her sixth month. For no word from God will ever fail.*"[8]

"Elizabeth? She is my mother's sister!" Mary's mother gasped. "She could not possibly carry a child at her age!"

"I have been inquiring in the town, trying to find someone who is going to Carem in the Judean hills just west of Jerusalem. Father, I need to go and see Elizabeth for myself," Mary pleaded. "I have found no one going all the way to Carem, but Hur the silversmith and his wife are going to Jerusalem in a few weeks. He needs to sell the jewelry he has been making. I could travel that far with them."

"Carem is only a little further," Heli commented. "You could walk from Jerusalem to Carem in just one more day."

"I don't see that we have any choice but to let her go and see if this miracle has taken place," Mary's mother offered.

"I will speak to Hur, but I don't want you to tell him or anyone the story of the angel. It's just too hard to believe," Heli stated. The slow side-to-side movement of his head indicated his own struggle to accept his daughter's story. "If what you say is true…" His voice trailed off in contemplation.

"I want to see with my own eyes," Mary softly stated. "I must know without a doubt."

"Yes, my daughter. You must travel to visit Elizabeth and Zechariah the priest," her mother quickly replied.

Heli agreed. "Stay only a few weeks and bring a letter back from Zechariah confirming the word of the Lord to you. When you return with the letter, I will speak to Joseph."

A shofar sounded in the village of Nazareth. Heli turned toward Jerusalem and pulled his prayer shawl over his head, but not before Mary got a good look at the pain and anxiety in his eyes. As he began to chant the ancient prayers of her people, his body swayed back and forth in the traditional davening prayer of the pious. She watched him and felt a pang of regret.

For a moment, the spirits of Doubt united in the air, swarming in consultation before separating and coming down to crawl under the head coverings of each person in the house. Like annoying flies, they swarmed around the ears, whispering worry and attempting to nibble away at faith and experience.

"Your father is a devout man. Look how you have hurt him. You should have resisted the stranger." A spirit of Doubt clung to Mary's ear and whispered, "If you had not come into agreement with the messenger, then you would have never have had this conversation with your parents. There would be no problem to bring to Joseph. Your life would not be in danger."

In her mind, Mary protested, It was an angel. I submitted to the will of God for my life.

"Are you sure you were visited by an angel and not a clever stranger who had his way with you?" Doubt persisted.

"What I felt, what I experienced, it was supernatural and pure." Mary relived her encounter with the angel.

The words of the angel seemed to ring in her head as the Spirit whispered, *"Do not be afraid, Mary; you have found favor with God."*[9]

The voice of Doubt intruded, sweeping aside the whisperings of the Spirit, "Maybe you submitted to Satan, the Prince of Darkness. Maybe you had relations with him? Were you aware of everything that happened after you collapsed? After all, your knowledge of the ways of men and angels is very limited. Even your knowledge of procreation is very limited. You could have been deceived like Eve in the garden. You could have had relations with that being without understanding what you were doing."

No! Mary protested mentally. And once again, the words of the angel filled her mind, *"So the holy one to be born will be called the Son of God."*[10]

The spirits of Condemnation and Fear chimed in, trying once more to shake God's chosen vessel, "Look at your mother. See how she pauses to worriedly wring her hands between each lamp she trims. She is the daughter of a Levite, married to a scribe from the tribe of Judah. She knows the law regarding these matters. She knows how the people of a small town can become uncontrollable, rock-throwing zealots. She is fearful. And there is reason to fear. You could be pulled from the safety of your parents' home and taken to the cliff just outside of town. Unless Joseph, a man known for his truthfulness, claims the child, you will be stoned and your body tossed over the precipice. Joseph will never tell a lie. He is a man of the law. *'You shall not give false testimony.'*"[11]

Mary shivered involuntarily. Once, she had seen the people of the town in a rage, chasing a loose woman to the cliff just outside the village and there stoning her to death. Now she saw the scene again, only this time she was the woman. No one would listen to her story or her protests that she was innocent. In her mind, the townspeople were screaming curses at her family and pelting her with rocks. Imagination played like reality. She kept backing away from the angry mob, closer and closer to the cliff until she stepped over the edge, falling, falling. Horror caught in her throat, and she nearly gagged on it.

"I know it was the angel of the Lord. I was not deceived. I was not physically touched." Under her breath, she kept repeating, *"Don't be afraid... You are highly favored of God."*[12]

But who would believe it? If she told them how the Spirit of God filled her, how her soul seemed to burst with intimate knowledge of the love of God for his people, no one would understand. To some, it might even sound like the physical union of man and wife. Even though she had no words to describe such an overwhelming spiritual experience, it was burned in her memory forever. She raised that memory like a protective shield.

The voices wouldn't quit. "Mary, Mary, you need this problem to go away. You are breaking the hearts of your parents, and Joseph will despise you. You don't have to have this child. Remember? One time at the well, you heard about an Egyptian woman who lives on the outskirts of town. She knows how to make unwanted pregnancies go away."

Mary covered her ears with her hands and cried out, "In the name of God Almighty, be silent! I will not listen!"

At her outburst, both parents turned, unable to disguise their looks of alarm. "Are you possessed?" her father asked.

"No, Father. Only the Spirit of God fills me," Mary calmly replied as she picked up a water jar and walked out the door toward the village well. The cooler evening air seemed to have cleared all the voices from her head. How was it, she wondered, that one minute she could be in complete mental turmoil and the next in such tranquility?

The Spirit of God Most Holy rose and went with her, only to be confronted by the ugly demonic spirits who had been forced into submission by her words. "You shouldn't have stopped us!" a spirit of Doubt shouted his accusation from a safe distance.

In response, the Holy Spirit seemed to expand and glow like fire. "Mary commanded you to be silent in the name of the Lord Almighty. She is a favored daughter of God. When she speaks his name, you are to submit."

The one outspoken spirit drew back into the dark clustering of his evil cohorts. Together, they stood their ground, feebly resisting the Holy Spirit.

Glowing with righteousness, the Spirit stared them down and spoke a slight variation of the words he had given to David five hundred years before, *"For the LORD God is a sun and shield; the LORD bestows favor and honor; no good thing does he withhold from those whose walk is blameless.*[13] Blessed is his daughter Mary, who trusts in him."

With a scream of rage, all the evil spirits retreated to the outskirts of Nazareth. Then, undetected by humans, the Holy Spirit spread himself over the entire village while specifically taking residence in the home of Mary. He spent the night ministering to the fears of her godly parents.

It was an unusually peaceful evening in all the homes of that little village on that summer night.

"Shalom and good morning to the house of Heli!" It was Joseph's voice. Mary would know it anywhere.

"Father and mother of my betrothed, are you home?" His deep voice penetrated the wooden gate and rang through the courtyard into every part of the house.

Mary looked up from the figs she was peeling and cleaning. She loved the sound of Joseph's voice. She loved this swarthy man who worked with his hands and rippling muscles.

Working beside her, Salome took the figs from Mary's hands and nudged her. "Hurry, go to the gate! Tell him you will be leaving in a few days, going to visit Elizabeth."

Mary shook her head negatively at her sister and called, "Joseph, my parents are not here!"

Normally, she would have run out to greet him, to feast her eyes on his suntanned face and dark curly beard, but since the visit from the angel, she had avoided encounters with her betrothed. Not to explain all that had happened to her seemed so uncomfortably dishonest; she just couldn't face him. It would be easier to leave it to her parents to explain her journey to see Elizabeth.

"Mary!" Joy seemed to fill Joseph's voice when he said her name. "Come to the gate and get the fish I brought your mother." He rushed to add, "Let me tell you about the bridal chamber and the cooking area. I just need to finish the lattice and the trim on the windows."

"Go!" Salome pushed her toward the courtyard.

Feeling trapped, Mary wiped her hands and walked quickly through the courtyard. "Oh, Joseph, you don't have to bring us things," she spoke as she passed through the tiny courtyard toward the wooden gate that opened onto the street. "We have plenty."

She lifted the latch and swung the sturdy gate open. Immediately, her eyes feasted on Joseph's well-muscled body. He took a step forward and filled the entrance to her parents' home, and Mary's heart danced like the maidens at their betrothal feast. It had been at least four weeks since she had spoken to him, such a long time, and so much had happened.

Silently, Salome came up behind Mary, giving Joseph a little wave so he knew they were not alone and it was proper to speak with his betrothed.

"I know I don't have to bring things to your family, but I am going to be a good son-in-law to your parents and a great husband to you." He grinned at his bride-to-be. If he could take her into his home at this very moment, he would, but he restrained himself with the knowledge that in just a few weeks, he would get his friends together and they would come to her father's house shouting and singing. He would carry her, light as a feather, to his own home and into the wedding chamber he had been laboring on for more than a year. Even though his mind was full of desire, he properly remained on the threshold of her home and spoke of safe, mundane things like fish. "Zebedee was peddling his dried sardines from Galilee. I brought your mother a basketful for her wonderful fish stew." Joseph lifted the lid of his basket to show a pile of dried miniature fish.

The odor of dried sardines filled the entrance, and without warning, Mary found herself gagging. There was nothing she could do but clamp her hand over her mouth, push past Joseph, and run for the garden, where she heaved up and splattered her morning meal beside the ripening melons.

"Mary?"

She sensed Joseph's strong body behind her.

"Are you ill?"

His carpenter's hands grasped her shoulders and steadied her until her stomach stopped heaving. Turning her to face him, he asked, "What is wrong? Do you need a physician? Your mother?" His face was filled with worry. "Where is your mother? I'll go get her!"

"I'm all right, Joseph." She didn't want to tell him now. She needed the letter from Zechariah.

Joseph's eyes were staring into hers, demanding an honest answer. Over his shoulder, she could see Salome running to the neighbor's, where she knew her father was discussing the Torah.

"It was just the warmth of the day and the smell of the fish," Mary replied while wiping her mouth with a rag she had pulled from the folds of the belt that encircled her waist. "It turned my stomach," she added with unconvincing honesty.

"I don't understand. It never bothered you before." Joseph was not satisfied with her answer.

What could she say? The man she had pledged to marry was waiting for a better explanation for her strange behavior. "My father is going to talk to you." Mary was trying to choose her words carefully.

"Your father? What does he have to say to me?" Joseph dropped his hands from her shoulders and took a step backward. Confusion and worry played across his face.

"Joseph, my son." Heli and Salome had come up behind them.

Immediately, Joseph turned and asked, "What is wrong with Mary?" He glanced at his betrothed, who was bent over as if she were going to vomit again.

Heli took in the scene with a sigh of resignation and said, "Mary believes she is with child." He took an unsteady breath before adding, "I was going to tell you soon."

"With child?" Joseph repeated the words in agony. "Mary, how could you?"

Heli placed a hand on Joseph's shoulder. "We must sit down and talk." He gestured toward the wooden bench at the back of the house. "There are special circumstances. My daughter has told us a most unusual story."

Joseph took another step backward, and Heli's hand fell from his shoulder.

"Joseph, listen!" Mary pleaded. Salome ran to her sister's side.

"No! I will not sit down and talk!" Joseph continued to back away. "Mary," he groaned. "You know the child is not mine." He turned to Heli. "There is nothing you can tell me. She has broken her vows, and now I cannot take her to be my wife under any circumstances!"

"Mary." He turned once again to the girl he loved. She was kneeling in the dirt of the garden. In a hoarse half-whisper, he spoke, "I cared deeply for you. I thought you cared for me. We had plans. We had a legal contract." Joseph's face contorted as he struggled to control his grief and rage.

"Joseph, I have not been with any man. I have not broken our contract," Mary said, pleading with him to believe her. "This child that I carry is from God. I was visited by an angel."

"She is telling the truth!" Salome loyally inserted.

"Don't, don't say such things." Joseph held up his hands as if to shield himself from such evil words.

"You know the prophecies of a Messiah, a son of David," Heli interjected.

Joseph turned to Heli, gesturing angrily. "I have heard enough. Send her away. I will divorce her quietly." He shook his head in sad disbelief. "This one untruth I will tell. I will say that she no longer pleases me, and based on that alone, I will go before the elders and dissolve our betrothal."

"But, my son," Heli tried, "you could just take her into your home. She does please you, and you do care for her. It may even turn out that she is mistaken and she is not with child."

Joseph ignored Heli's pleas and continued asserting the unwavering righteousness that Mary had so admired in him. "There is only one reason that a young woman would suspect that she is with child, and that is, she knows she has been with a man!" Joseph composed himself and looked squarely into Heli's eyes. "I will not demand to know the name of the father or bring her before the local council, but I do not want to see her face or hear her name again."

"No!" Mary dropped her head to the soft ground, sobbing. Her hair fell from its loosely tied knot and spilled around her face like a black mourning veil hastily thrown over her head. Salome threw her arms around her weeping sister.

Righteously, Joseph turned and strode away. After a few steps, he looked back, throwing a solemn warning over his shoulder, "Get her out of town, Heli, before her condition becomes obvious and the matter is taken out of my hands."

Chapter 2

THE ROAD TO CAREM

Once when Zechariah's division was on duty and he was
serving as priest before God, he was chosen by lot, according to
the custom of the priesthood, to go into the Temple of the Lord
to burn incense. And when the time for the burning of incense
came, all assembled worshipers were praying outside, then an
angel of the Lord appeared to him standing at the right side
of the altar of incense.

—Luke 1:8–11

"This is certainly not the way you imagined things would turn out." Spirits of Doubt clung to Mary's mantle. Like flies around a festering wound, they irritated the painful rejection Joseph had inflicted.

Mary hung her head and watched her feet move one step at a time toward the little Judean town of Carem. In a matter of weeks, she had gone from betrothed maiden to scorned woman. She hardly noticed the voices, but they were all around her, whispering hopelessness.

Invisible to the human eye, demons from the kingdom of evil had taken this opportunity to close in with their formidable emotional weapons. A spirit of Abandonment spoke, his words cutting like a sharp knife, "Joseph never wants to see your face again, and your parents were so eager to get you out of the village, they insisted you begin this six-day journey alone. They would not even allow you to wait two more days so you could travel with the family of Hur."

Spirits of Fear slithered up from the ground. "The road to Carem is dangerous, you know. Roman soldiers, highwaymen, foreign traders, wild animals…"

Purposefully, the fallen spirits worked together to create a knotted web of binding fear, cutting abandonment, and weighted discouragement.

"Mary has nothing to fear. She is deeply loved!" The Holy Spirit, a presence never far from Mary, touched the evil web while it was in progress. Instantly, it became ashes and dropped to the ground. Like scattering worms, the demons fell to the packed dirt and crawled to the side of the road, creeping from rock to rock, waiting and watching for another opportunity.

Incensed, one of the spirits protested, "Mary has a right to her feelings. She has not asked for your help!"

"My daughter will ask," the Spirit of God replied.

Splitting the air with sharp mocking laughter, another dark spirit responded, "She thinks she is alone on the highway that runs almost the entire length of the land." Then just to flaunt his right to hurl lies like lethal darts, that evil spirit announced, "Mary, you are alone with this problem. God has burdened you with this unwanted child, and now even he has deserted you."

As the Holy Spirit watched, he saw their darts penetrate Mary's emotional skin. He knew she was cut and bleeding.

"No," Mary protested, pushing her emotional pain aside, "I am the servant of the Most High God, and I will serve him." With each word Mary spoke, the Spirit poured his soothing oil into her wounds. "He will protect my life because I am with child—a son—and I will call him Jesus." Mary continued to shield herself with her statements of faith. "*He will be great and will be called the Son of the Most High. The Lord will give him the throne of his father, David, and he will reign over the house of Jacob forever; his kingdom will never end.*"[1] The words the angel had spoken seemed to give her strength. She straightened her back and walked with more determination.

"She is rejecting you, turning her back on your lies," the Spirit hotly retorted. "I know she does not comprehend the spirit realm, but that part of me that lives in her discerns the voices of Satan and the voices of the Eternal Rulers. She has hidden the words of the angel and the prophets in her heart. She cannot be overwhelmed by your lies."

In frustration, a spirit of Fear crawled into the middle of the road. Facing the young Jewish girl, he shouted, "Mary, this may cost you your life."

Mary's foot kicked a fist-sized stone out of her way, and it rolled into a pile of stones by the side of the road.

"God sure filled this land with stones." Fear continued by quoting from the Law of Moses, *"You must purge the evil from among you!"*[2]

"I am not evil or immoral," Mary countered under her breath.

"Mary, remember," the Spirit urged.

Once again, in her mind, she relived the incredible experience of being overshadowed and filled with the Spirit of God Most Wonderful. Words from the prophets were suddenly running through her head, *"Therefore the Lord himself will give you a sign: The virgin will be with child and will give birth to a son and will call him Immanuel."*[3] She remembered sitting at her father's feet while he copied those words and explained them to her. The memory warmed her and anchored her to a lifetime of security in the traditions and hope of her people and also to her parents' love.

Discouragement could not find a place to attach himself. So he projected another thought. "No one is going to believe your story. Everyone will think you are a fallen woman. Even Joseph, who loves you with all his heart, has turned his back on you."

"Fear not, favored child of heaven. Your God is with you, and the battle is the Lord's." Compelling and warm, the voice of the Holy Spirit ended the demonic onslaught.

Mary looked around, almost expecting to see the angel again. Instead, some distance ahead, she saw a family: four children, a father and mother, and one other adult. They were stepping onto the road and beginning their journey in the same direction that she was traveling.

"Go, child, catch up with them," the Spirit whispered encouragement. "I do not want you to travel alone."

And Mary responded, breaking into a run, sprinting up the road to join the travelers. As she decreased the distance between them, she could hear them singing. It was a familiar psalm.

> *Give thanks to the LORD,*
> *for He is good;*
> *his love endures forever.*
> *Let Israel say:*
> *'His love endures forever.'*
> *Let the house of Aaron say:*
> *'His love endures forever.'*
> *Let those who fear the LORD say: '*
> *His love endures forever.'*[4]

A little out of breath, Mary joined the travelers. They smiled and nodded their acceptance. She matched her pace to theirs and joined in their song. The words were like a message from God.

> *In my anguish, I cried to the LORD,*
> *and he answered by setting me free.*
> *The LORD is with me;*
> *I will not be afraid.*
> *What can man do to me?*
> *The LORD is with me; he is my helper.*
> *I will look in triumph on my enemies.*
> *It is better to take refuge in the LORD*
> *than to trust in man.*[5]

The song ended, and before Mary could introduce herself, the older woman asked, "Where are you from, and what is your destination?"

"I'm from Nazareth. I'm going to visit relatives in Carem," Mary replied.

"Carem!" everyone exclaimed. "We're traveling to Carem! We've been to Nain for a marriage celebration, and now we are returning home."

I'm traveling with people who actually live in Carem! Mary marveled at the coincidence. "I wonder, do you know Zechariah the priest?" she asked. Could the coincidence extend further?

"Everyone knows Zechariah," the younger woman responded, adding, "My name is Rivkah. This is my mother, Hadassah."

"If they don't know Zechariah personally, they know about him," the older woman added.

Mary looked puzzled. "What would everyone know about Zechariah other than the fact that he is a priest who is very close to the age of retirement?"

"Don't you know the story?" Rivkah asked. "After the Feast of Dedication, the people in Carem could talk of nothing else, and even Jerusalem was abuzz."

"What story?" Mary replied, knowing that there was always small-town gossip, some worth listening to but most nothing more than the stories of old women with too much time to speculate and exaggerate.

"Zechariah and I are in the same division of priests, the division of Abijah. We serve together in the Temple two times a year and on all the high feast days," Rivkah's husband joined the conversation. "During the Feast of Dedication, our division was on duty in the Temple. Since we live in the same town, I always go up to Jerusalem with him."

Mary's ears perked up. The priest had a story to tell! The women of small towns frequently engaged in idle talk, but the men were rarely taken in by such nonsense. This must be a very important story if a priest was telling it!

"Zechariah is an older man, so my Joram"—Rivkah nodded toward her husband—"loads and leads Zechariah's donkey each time they go up to the Temple. He was soon to be fifty years old, so this was his last time to actively serve in the Temple. That is the law that God gave to the Levites."

"For Zechariah, how could I do any less?" her husband exclaimed. "Ever since I began my duties as a young priest, he has taken me under his wing and treated me like a son. I have never experienced the shame of being unprepared for any of the many complicated rituals that go on in the Temple because Zechariah has always had the foresight to prepare me."

"He is a good man," Hadassah asserted, "a humble and quiet man who only wants to live to see the salvation of Israel."

"He does not like to feel rushed, so of course we arrived at the Temple two days before we had to be on duty," Joram tried to continue the story.

"Zechariah always needed to rest before he begins officiating at the altar," Rivkah explained.

"There is a lot of physical labor to cutting up the lambs and carrying their parts to the altar," Hadassah seemed compelled to add. "And the cleanup! Yes, Zechariah always needed to refresh himself between the journey to the Holy Mount and the beginning of his duties."

Hadassah paused for breath, and Joram jumped in, "It was on the second day of the Feast of Dedication. After the morning sacrifice had been slain, we assembled in the Hall of Polished Stones to cast lots for the third time that day. Praise be!" Joram raised his hands in solemn thanksgiving. "The lot fell on Zechariah, making him the priest who was to burn incense in the Holy Place that morning. He chose me to be one of his assistants."

"My Joram got to go into the Holy Place," Rivkah proudly chimed in. "It was his first time to go beyond the Court of the

Priests." Her eyes fixed on her husband with such a look of admiration that Mary felt the pain of her own loss. She used to look at Joseph with that same admiration. His rejection, how it hurt!

Silently swallowing her private pain, Mary responded, "I'm sure Zechariah wanted your husband to have the experience, and that's why he chose him." Then addressing Joram, she asked, "What was your role?"

"I carried a golden bowl filled with coals from the altar of burnt offering."

Mary could hear the pride in his voice as he started to describe his duties.

"I was there in the Court of the Women," Rivkah interrupted, "standing on the circular steps at the entrance to the Court of the Israelites. From there, I could see the altar of burnt offering and, beyond that, the steps leading up into the Holy Place. It's an awesome sight! Have you ever seen it, Mary?"

"No." Mary felt a little awkward. It was embarrassing to be a small-town girl who had never been to the big city. "My father goes three times a year, and often my mother accompanies him, but my sister and I have always had to stay home to take care of the animals and the garden."

"Just imagine, Mary," Rivkah continued her description. "You arrive at the Temple gates just before sunup. As the first streaks of light break on the horizon, the gates open, the people enter, and at that moment, the lamb for the morning sacrifice is slain."

"The blood is caught in a golden bowl, and then some is sprinkled on the altar before the rest is poured out at the base of the altar," Joram said. "I have often done that."

"Before the lamb is prepared and placed on the altar, a gong sounds, and from every part of the Temple, barefooted priests scurry to assemble between the altar and the Holy Place. On the steps just outside the gate to the Court of Israel, the musicians gather for the morning hymn while designated Levites line up those who have come with their own sacrifices. You must see it, Mary. It is breathtaking," Rivkah encouraged before continuing, "I stood on the top step peering in through the open gate. You know women cannot enter the Court of the Israelites, but from the gate, I could see my Joram on the right side of Zechariah slowly walking up the stairs. Then I couldn't see him anymore. I thought my heart was going to pound right out of my chest."

"Then?" Mary asked Joram.

"In the Holy Place, there is only the light of the seven branched candlesticks, although it reflects off the golden table of showbread and the golden altar of incense. Two priests had gone ahead of us to tend to the lamps. When we entered, I spread the coals on the altar of burnt incense. The other assistant left the incense ready to be burned. All of us then bowed and backed out, leaving Zechariah alone facing the veil which separates the Holy Place from the Most Holy Place."

"It gives me shivers and bumps all over my arms," Mary responded.

"But Zechariah wasn't alone!" Hadassah interrupted Joram's story, waving her hands in the air as she spoke. "An angel came and stood on the right side of the altar and spoke to him!"

An angel! Mary felt her heart beat faster. Zechariah had also seen an angel!

Rivkah began speaking. Mary hung on every word. "Elizabeth told me it was the Angel Gabriel, who stands before the throne of God Almighty, the same one who spoke to the prophet Daniel."

"Gabriel," Mary whispered the name. The angel who had spoken to her had told her his name. It was the same angel. She shivered with the thrill of confirmation, and in her mind, she saw the angel again: tall, brilliantly white, and glowing.

Joram tried to pick up the story again. "Outside the sanctuary, we all prepared for the morning prayers. At the signal, all of the priests and all of the people in the Temple area fell facedown before the Lord. The smoke from the incense was supposed to ascend to heaven even as their prayers were going up to the Holy One, but there was no white smoke for a long time. Some of the priests were beginning to confer even while they were flat on the ground with their faces pressed against the stone floor. They feared that Zechariah might have been struck dead because of some unconfessed sin. Finally, we saw the white smoke and began to chant, 'True it is that thou art Jehovah our God...' When the prayers ended, the priest who was to complete the lighting of the oil lamps entered the Holy Place and escorted Zechariah out to bless the people."

"That is when everyone knew something had happened," Rivkah interrupted her husband again.

Excitedly, Mary asked, "Did he speak to the people? Did he say what the angel looked like?"

"Who knows what an angel looks like!" Hadassah exclaimed as she threw her hands in the air in a gesture of exasperation. "What an angel looks like? It is too much to comprehend!"

Rivkah interjected, "It must have been awesome because Elizabeth said Zechariah was terribly frightened."

"The angel said, 'Do not be afraid,'" Joram said in a tone meant to convey that this was his story and the women should not interrupt again.

"I want to know every detail," Mary declared, hoping that the man would allow his wife and mother-in-law to add any little bits of information they had.

"Anyway, the angel said to Zechariah, 'Your prayer has been heard. Your wife, Elizabeth, will bear you a son. He will be a joy and delight to you, and many will rejoice because of his birth.'"

"I can tell you that Elizabeth is overjoyed," Joram's mother-in-law broke into the story, flashing an I-dare-you-to-silence-me look toward her son-in-law. "Elizabeth and I are the same age. She has been with me for the birth of each one of my children, and each time, I could see how much she wanted a child of her own. Well, it never happened. It was just a few years ago that she told me she had finally stopped hoping and praying for a child. She had accepted God's will for her life."

"Just when Elizabeth submits herself to the will of God and accepts the sorrow of being childless, she receives the desire of her heart," Mary commented in whispered awe.

With obvious impatience, Joram cleared his throat, signaling all the women that he was ready to take over the story. "The angel gave instructions about raising the child. The child is never to drink wine or any fermented drink. He is never to cut his hair."

"A Nazirite," Mary stated under her breath, "a holy man whose life is totally dedicated to God." The awesomeness of this thought reverberated through every fiber of her body.

"From birth, he will be filled with the Holy Spirit of the God of Israel."

"It's wonderful to be filled with the Holy Spirit," Mary commented with such a knowing tone in her voice that all three adults stopped walking and stared at her for a few moments. Immediately, she felt the awkwardness of the situation and said, "Continue with your story. I didn't mean to interrupt."

It was so exciting. Mary felt like the Spirit was filling her again. She could hardly contain herself. As she listened, her feet were dancing on the hard-packed dirt road. She could hardly keep herself from interrupting their story with shouts of hallelujah! The angel of the Lord had visited her and had visited Zechariah! It was all so wonderful!

"The angel even said that it will be like he has the Spirit and power of the prophet Elijah!" the older woman had interrupted her son-in-law again, and Joram's shoulders slumped in silent surrender. "Elizabeth told me her baby is to grow up and turn the people back to serving our God wholeheartedly."

"And," her daughter added, "he is to prepare the way for the Messiah."

"May it please the God of our fathers to send the Son of David to restore the land to holy sovereignty," Hadassah shouted.

"And rid this nation of the heathen dogs of Herod and Caesar," Rivkah added, punctuating the comment by sending an unladylike wad of spit flying into the dust.

"Be careful, wife." Her husband's back had stiffened, and his hand was raised to signal silence.

Both women stopped talking, and Mary's feet stopped dancing. All three women responded immediately to the warning and soberly looked to Joram for direction.

Silently, he nodded toward the road ahead.

Immediately, Mary and the other two women pulled their mantles over their faces. Without being told, the children stopped chasing each other and found a place to walk within the circle of somber adults.

At this point on the road between Nain and Beth Shan, everyone in the little band of travelers turned their backs toward the right side of the road and walked in grieved silence. They would not give their oppressors the satisfaction of staring at the symbols of their tyrannical occupation.

No matter how hard Mary stared at the tiny ocher clouds of dust around her sandaled feet, she was painfully aware of the strangled breathing that came from the side of the road. Out of the corner of her eye, she caught a flash of red and knew that Syrian mercenaries, part of the Roman army, lounged on the rocky hillside, laughing and waiting for the final gurgling breath. Before covering her face, she had seen two crosses heavy with courageous Jewish men. Her heart ached for the men, for their families, for her country.

The band of travelers hung their heads, averted their eyes, and walked by in silence. When they had covered a sufficient distance, the husband commented, "There was an incident on this road a few days ago. A tax collector, Thaddeus of Nain"—the husband spit as he said the man's name—"had unfairly taxed a small village."

"Actually, he stripped them of every coin and every piece of livestock," his mother-in-law angrily interjected! "He's a traitor! A Jewish traitor!"

"The elders of the village followed him and begged him to reconsider. Tempers flared. The men began roughing Thaddeus up a bit."

The mother-in-law interrupted again, "A squad of Roman soldiers was traveling along this road, and Thaddeus called for help."

"The elders of the town were accused of stealing from Rome. The trial was taking place while we were at the wedding. Everyone was talking about it, and now we see the outcome." Joram shook his head and sorrowfully said, "May the Son of David come quickly and free his people from this awful oppression."

The Spirit who was traveling with them breathed on Mary.

Suddenly, Mary heard herself repeating the words of the prophet Jeremiah, "*'The days are coming,' declares the* LORD, *'when I will fulfill the gracious promise I made to the house of Israel and to the house of Judah. In those days and at that time I will make a righteous Branch sprout from David's line; he will do what is just and right in the land. In those days Judah will be saved and Jerusalem will live in safety. This is the name by which it will be called: The* LORD *Our Righteousness.'*"[6]

The words of the prophet seemed to lift the cloak of oppression that had settled over the small band. In response, a chorus of amens went up from the travelers. The flame of their national and spiritual hope burned in their hearts again.

"Nathan, Gershom, run ahead and find a good camping spot for the night," Joram instructed his sons. Then turning to Mary, he asked, "You will spend the nights with us until we reach Carem, won't you?"

"Oh, yes, I do not want to be alone on the road," Mary responded.

"Whom did you say are you going to visit in Carem?" his wife asked.

"My mother's aunt, Elizabeth, the very one we have been talking about. She may need some help during her time of waiting," Mary replied.

"So you knew the story," Rivkah stated.

"No. I had only been told that Elizabeth was with child," Mary said. "I was expecting to hear any special details from Zechariah and Elizabeth when I arrived."

"Oh, you won't hear anything from Zechariah," the mother-in-law announced. "He has not said a word since he saw the angel."

"When he came out from the Holy Place and stood on the steps ready to bless the people, all he could do was raise his arms and gesture with his hands," Joram said. "After a few minutes, the priest standing next to him intoned the blessing over the people."

"Oh?" Mary was surprised. "Then how do you know what happened?"

"Before he left the Temple, he wrote a complete account of his encounter with the angel."

"Gabriel," Mary whispered the name and once more felt the thrill of confirmation rush through her body.

Rivkah's husband continued, "Some people in Jerusalem and in the village think what Zechariah has written is just the confusion that comes on men and women of advanced years, that even his lack of speech can be attributed to declining health."

"I believe him," Mary stated emphatically.

"And so do I," chorused each adult in the group of travelers.

The sun was touching the rocky summit of a distant hill when the band of travelers stepped off the road to make camp near a small stand of fig trees. Mary, now almost a member of the family, helped with the evening meal and then sat by the fire singing psalms with the family until the flames became coals.

In the Most Holy Sanctuary of the Eternal, there was silence. Ever since the moment Yeshua the Creator had transformed himself into the genetic material of procreation, Ophaniel and the other seraphs had been too overcome to sing. The entire focus of heaven was on that tiny half-God embryo. The life of Yeshua the Creator had been entrusted to the Holy Spirit, who had transported the transformed genetic material into union with a human egg.

Now the entire existence of Yeshua the Creator was so entangled with humanity that he was more vulnerable than the first humans he had created. Only the life processes of a young Jewish girl separated him from the inevitability of fleshly death.

Ophaniel could barely move his wings as he watched God, the Eternal Ruler, and waited to hear the next report from the watchers on the walls of the celestial city regarding activities on Earth.

Omnipotently aware of the movements of the agents of Satan, Father God observed the length of the road on which Mary traveled. Demonic agents lined the highway from Nazareth to Jerusalem. Only the presence of the Spirit of God, third member of the Godhead, prevented an all-out attack.

"Michael!" God summoned his archangel, commander of the warrior hosts. "Take a legion. Back up the Holy Spirit. Guard Mary and Yeshua within her womb."

Drawing his glowing sword from its silver scabbard, Michael saluted God.

"It is not time to defeat our adversary," God cautioned. "Just maintain him and his agents at a safe distance until Yeshua is able to confront him."

Before Mary spread her cloak on the ground and rolled her bundle of clothing into a pillow, the Archangel Michael stationed warrior angels with drawn swords on the perimeter of the camp. Like a canopy, the Spirit spread himself above their heads, pressing his presence into the sleeping travelers beneath him. Outside the heavenly perimeter, agents of Satan pulled back, lurking at a distance, waiting for their next opportunity.

Chapter 3

IN THE HOME OF ZECHARIAH AND ELIZABETH

*At that time Mary got ready and hurried to a town in the
hill country of Judea where she entered Zechariah's home and
greeted Elizabeth. When Elizabeth heard Mary's greeting,
the baby leaped in her womb, and Elizabeth was filled with
the Holy Spirit.*

—Luke 1:39–41

With a tired little sigh, Mary shifted the cumbersome bundle that contained her change of clothing and a packet of cooking spices, a gift for Great-Aunt Elizabeth. This morning's walk over the mountain then up and down several hills had been the most difficult part of the journey. Knowing that the town of Carem lay just ahead, at the top of the next hill, Mary pushed herself to continue.

She was alone now; Joram, his wife, and his mother-in-law had given her precise directions to the home of her relatives before they left the road, heading across the fields to their own home just outside of town. One foot in front of the other, Mary climbed the last rocky hill. A soft breeze drifted through the olive orchard that flourished on one side of the road while the steep side of a mountain threw a welcome shadow across her path. Only a little further, and she knew she would break out of the shade into the sunshine of a clearing near the summit. She would walk past a spring that gushed from the rocky mountain wall. Then she would see the small school attached to the local synagogue, where the boys of the community learned to read the sacred scrolls. Then on to the outskirts of town, near the edge of a hill, where she could look out and see a valley full of fruit trees; there, she would see the last house in the village, the home of Zechariah the priest. It faced the road, so she could not miss it.

Halfway up the hill, Mary stopped to catch her breath. She was tired, more tired than usual. The changes that had been taking place in her body and the fact that she had been eating sparingly so her stomach would retain its food had left her with less strength than she normally had. After a few moments, she pushed on, not stopping again until she gained the crest of the hill and entered the village. She was surprised and relieved to see how small the place was. She could take in most of Carem in one glance. She could almost see the farthest house in the village before the road dropped off to descend into the next valley.

It was late afternoon. Many of the townspeople were crowded around a peddler. The bargaining was intense, so Mary walked by unnoticed. Water from the spring that Hadassah had told her about streamed down the slick side of the mountain into a man-made trough. Mary paused just long enough to scoop some of the cool water into her mouth with her hand; it was so refreshing. As she passed the synagogue school, she heard the familiar singsong memorization of scripture that was a part of her heritage. It brought back nostalgic memories of sitting on the floor beside her father while he taught her the scriptures. A tear made a dusty trail down her cheek. If only her father had total confidence in her story, it would be so much easier. If only her mother was not so worried. It pained her to think she had unintentionally shamed and disappointed her parents.

Once through the center of the village, it was a short walk to the last house facing the road. Outside the courtyard gate, Mary called, "Shalom, Zechariah and Elizabeth! I bring greetings from your relatives in Nazareth."

Almost immediately, a gray-haired woman appeared in the entrance. Her hand rested on her pregnant belly, and her face was filled with the glow of motherhood. "At the sound of your voice, my child dances in my womb!"

A bald man with a flowing white beard and a big toothy smile came up behind her. They both stood in the entrance to their home. "And whose child are you?" the old priest quickly wrote with a piece of charcoal on a tablet that hung from a string tied around his neck.

"I am the daughter of Heli, the scribe of Nazareth."

"Heli is the husband of my dear niece!" Elizabeth interrupted. "Come in, child. You must have walked at least six days to get here!" She opened the wooden door as far as it would go, and Mary walked through into their welcoming embraces.

At that moment in the spirit realm, the Holy Spirit transformed himself into golden oil and poured himself over Elizabeth. Immediately, the holy oil burst into heavenly flame.

Suddenly, Elizabeth announced, "*Blessed are you among women, and blessed is the child you will bear!*"[1]

Sensing the presence of holiness, Zechariah threw his hands into the air, and his lips moved in silent praise to his Maker.

"How do you know about the child in my womb?" Mary asked in amazement as her eyes moved from Elizabeth, to her husband, and then back to Elizabeth.

But Elizabeth did not answer. She just continued with her anointed words. "*But why am I so favored, that the mother of my Lord should come to me? As soon as the sound of your greeting reached my ears, the baby in my womb leaped for joy. Blessed is she who has believed that the Lord would fulfill his promises to her!*"[2]

Again the Spirit poured out his holy oil. This time, it covered Mary and burst into heavenly fire. Mary dropped her bundle to the ground and lifted her hands toward heaven.

My soul glorifies the Lord
and my spirit rejoices in God my Savior![3]

Tears of joy streamed down Mary's face as she continued under the anointing.

From now on all generations will call me blessed, for the Mighty One has done great things for me—holy is his name![4]

Zechariah began to clap his hands above his head, adding an eastern rhythm to Mary's song.
Mary continued in the delicious flow of the Spirit.

His mercy extends to those who fear him,
from generation to generation.
He has performed mighty deeds with his arm;
he has scattered those who are proud
in their inmost thoughts.[5]

Still filled with the Spirit, Elizabeth lifted her hands and danced in graceful circles while Mary continued,

He has helped his servant Israel,
remembering to be merciful to
Abraham and his descendants forever
just as he promised our ancestors.[6]

Elizabeth's feet moved, and her body swayed as she punctuated Mary's chorus with hallelujahs and amens. When the song ended, the women fell into each other's arms. Zechariah threw his manly arms around both women, hugging them to his chest. "Child," Elizabeth said, "I am so glad you have come. You are welcome in our home. We have so much to talk about."

Chapter 4

JOSEPH COMES TO CAREM

*When Joseph woke up, he did what the angel of the Lord had
commanded him and took Mary home as his wife. But he had
no union with her until she gave birth to a son.*

—Matthew 1:24–25

In Nazareth, Joseph furiously planed a long cedar beam. The muscles under his skin rippled, and beads of perspiration soaked through the rough fabric of his tunic. No matter how he threw himself into each job, he could not get Mary out of his mind. Her face was in his dreams. And their plans for the future were in his face every time he looked at the nearly finished bridal chamber and the cooking area attached to his shop.

With each steady stroke of his practiced arms, he asked, "Why, Mary? Why did you do it?" Heli had come by his carpenter's shop and related the most fantastic story, but Joseph just couldn't bring himself to put any faith in it. Much as he tried not to speculate, he could not help himself. "Who turned your heart away from me, Mary? Who is going to believe your wild story? Why couldn't you just come to me and tell me you wanted to marry someone else?" He straightened, ready to turn the beam over to plane the other side, but instead of getting back into the work at hand, he just sat down heavily on a nearby bench. Here it was, harvest time. The trumpets had been sounding for ten days. The fall feasts were being celebrated throughout the nation. But since midsummer, his heart had been breaking. It was a sorrow like none he had ever experienced.

Joseph looked outside. It was past noon. Slowly, he got up and began to close his shop. Before sundown, he needed to eat a meal and go to the community pool for ceremonial cleansing. There, he would completely immerse himself so he could enter the synagogue in a state of purity. Also, there was one more person in the town to whom Joseph had not yet gone—Heli. Before he could cover his head and enter the synagogue for the service that would mark the beginning of Yom Kippur, the solemn Day of Atonement, he must make sure things were right between himself and Mary's father.

Quickly, he swept up the curled wood shavings and laid his tools in their proper place on his workbench. Then, for the first time in two months, he walked to the home of Heli the scribe.

Heli was sitting in front of his house, copying a scroll in the bright afternoon sunlight.

"Shalom," Joseph forced the traditional greeting out of his mouth.

Heli looked up and gave the young man a welcoming smile. "Come sit beside me." He indicated the empty portion of the bench.

"I have very little time." Joseph remained standing and spoke directly, "Before this day of judgment begins, I want to be sure there are no resentments or hard feelings between the two of us."

Heli did not answer right away. Instead, he asked, "Have you divorced her?"

"Not yet, but I have determined to do so after the fall feasts," Joseph replied. Then he quickly added, "I am sorry. I can see no other way."

"I understand." Heli nodded his head sadly, his eyes downcast. "You are within the law, and you are even more generous than the law." He looked up at the man he had hoped would be his son-in-law. "My son, the writings of the prophets show us more fully how to live by the law. On this solemn day of fasting and soul-searching, consider the words of Micah, *'He has showed you, O man, what is good. And what does the* LORD *require of you? To act justly and to love mercy and to walk humbly with your God.'*¹ And when the shofar, that ancient trumpet made from a ram's horn, is blown to end this Day of Atonement, may your name be inscribed in heaven's Book of Life for another year." As he pronounced the traditional Yom Kippur blessing, Heli stood and walked over to Joseph. Throwing his arms around the carpenter, he said, "Joseph, you will always be like a son to me."

At sundown, Joseph covered his head with his prayer shawl and took his place with the other men of Nazareth in the synagogue. The scrolls were opened, and readings were given in Hebrew and then expounded upon in Aramaic. Corporate prayers were chanted.

Under his prayer shawl, Joseph struggled with the questions that had been tormenting him for two months. *Lord, how much mercy do I show Mary? Isn't my decision to divorce Mary just and merciful? What is preventing me from acting on my decision?*

"Are you motivated by mercy and justice or by pride in your own righteousness?" the Spirit of God posed the probing question.

Joseph squirmed as he considered the heavenly inquiry.

A spirit of Doubt countered the question the Holy Spirit had planted in Joseph's mind. "This problem does not require such deep thought."

"Mary never had feelings for you!" Like a whip laying open bear flesh, a spirit of Retaliation lashed out. Taking advantage of the emotions that Doubt had stirred up, the evil spirit struck again. "You need to divorce her. Stop postponing the inevitable. Get your two witnesses and go to the elders."

I have not seen her in more than eight weeks. What if she is not really with child? Joseph argued in his mind.

The spirit of Retaliation snapped back, "Whether she is with child or not is not the issue. Your betrothed has unlawfully known another man! It is the only explanation for the fact that she would even entertain the idea that she might be carrying a child. Joseph, you have been betrayed in the worst way and then lied to! You must take action!"

It is so hard to bring myself to actually go through with it. Joseph dropped his head into his hands; his thoughts pained him so. How can I stand before the Council of Nazareth and say that Mary no longer pleases me and that I do not want to take her to be my wife? Such a lie is an affront to the Almighty.

"Yes, it is," Retaliation agreed as he laid another stinging lash on Joseph's raw soul. "Two months ago, you should have brought her before the council, accused her of unfaithfulness, and then thrown the first stone!"

At the thought of hurting Mary or her parents, Joseph recoiled.

"Do you know why you cannot bring yourself to divorce her?" a spirit of Religion piously chimed in. "It is because her actions have made you unclean by association. You know that she should be exposed, subjected to the law. It is God's way. Only then can you be vindicated and continue your life as an upright man!"

Is there no other solution? Must I either divorce her on a false pretense or see her killed? God, help me! Under the cover of his prayer shawl, Joseph silently cried out to heaven.

An intense heavenly presence suddenly filled the room full of davening men.

The spirits of Doubt and Retaliation quickly slipped away. They could not maintain their functions in the presence of radiant holiness. The spirit of Religion quickly shrank back into a familiar corner of the synagogue. He would not leave this building where the laws of the Torah were elevated above the Spirit of the Most

Holy God. It was his territory. From behind a stack of scrolls, he eyed the Holy Spirit. "You're here again?" he hissed.

"Yes," the Spirit answered, "I am always present where there are men and women whose hearts yearn to please their Creator."

"I see no one in here who has more on his mind than completing his obligation to fast and pray," Religion smugly countered.

"The Eternal Ruler has a great interest in that man." The Holy Spirit pointed to Joseph.

"God is mistaken. The carpenter is worthless. He cannot make a decision. He wavers between righteousness and unrighteousness because he is consumed with lust for a woman."

"Three times a day, Joseph covers his head and faces my holy city. Under his prayer shawl, he pours out his heart and lays this problem before me. I have heard, and now I will answer." The emphatic words of the Spirit of God left no room for argument, and with a howl of rage, the spirit of Religion fled to cower on the roof until the Holy Spirit exited the building.

"It is only a few days until the Feast of Tabernacles," the Spirit spoke through Joseph's misery. "It is a requirement to attend, so go with the delegation from Nazareth. Make the traditional booth on a Jerusalem hillside in remembrance of your forefathers' wilderness experience, and I will meet you there."

Suddenly, there was hope. Nothing had really changed, but in his heart, there was more peace than Joseph had experienced for some time. With the rest of the congregation, he began chanting, "Praise be to you, most merciful Lord, who forgives the sins of your people Israel…"

Like the white robes in which most of the men wrapped themselves on this solemn day of repentance and fasting, the peace of the Spirit enveloped Joseph. Throughout the days of preparation for the Feast of Tabernacles and during the joyful journey to Jerusalem, the heavenly mantle of shalom shielded Joseph from the attacks of the demonic spirits that had been plaguing him.

"Joseph, give us a hand?"

Joseph dropped the bundle of long branches that he had gathered to build a booth that he would share with his two friends Moshe and Jethro. He hurried over to Heli and his wife who were struggling to keep the three sides of their booth from falling in before they could get a roof on it. Expertly, Joseph grabbed a coil of freshly cut vines and began tying the long boughs more securely to the supporting stakes. Then he bent them over at the top to make a support for the palm branches that would cover the roof. "You know? This is the fourth booth I have finished today," Joseph joked with Heli as he took the palm branches from the scribe and tossed them onto the roof.

"The people of Nazareth are indebted to you, and God will reward you," Heli responded, then he added, "You know, Mary is in Carem, only a day's journey from here."

Joseph did not respond. He just returned to his bundle of branches and moved on to build his own booth.

That night, the glow from four enormous candelabra in the Court of the Women lit up the Temple and the surrounding hills. From the shelter of his booth on the terraced side of the Mount of Olives, Joseph could hear three shofar blasts cutting through the crisp fall air. The Temple musicians began to play, and then the Levitical choir began the psalms for this season. Joseph knew the great and famous men of Jerusalem were dancing before the Lord with flaming torches in their hands, that the specially built stands were packed with Jews from all over the world, and that these festivities would go on all night. Everyone in the delegation from Nazareth had gone to spend the night in the Temple. Only Joseph stayed behind, lying on the brown grass in the booth he had erected under the trees on the Mount of Olives.

It was good to be alone with the Lord. Joseph began reciting the words penned by his ancestor, King David, "*Your word is a lamp for my feet, a light on my path. I have taken an oath and confirmed it, that I will follow your righteous laws. I have suffered much; preserve my life,* LORD, *according to your word."*[2]

He could not finish the psalm. He wished that Heli had not mentioned Mary to him. Once more, his mind was filled with uncertainty. How could he have life without Mary? On the other hand, how could he live if not by the law? *"O* LORD, *you have searched me and you know me. You know when I sit and when I rise; you perceive my thoughts from afar. You discern my going out and my lying down; you are familiar with all my ways,"*[3] Joseph continued his prayer.

"How can I speak the words that will dissolve my betrothal to Mary? It is lawful, yet I feel constrained. Are you, O God, moving me to another course of action?" He waited, straining to hear something other than silence, hoping to see something other than darkness.

Finally, with a resigned sigh, he adjusted his pallet and stretched out on his side. "I just need to get to sleep," he muttered as he dislodged and tossed aside a small stone that poked uncomfortably into his ribs. Heli said an angel had appeared to Mary and to Zechariah, the old priest from Carem. "Lord, I need an angel to appear to me. Unless I receive a messenger from heaven, I will have to go through with the divorce."

There was excitement in the throne room. Joseph's prayers had moved God to action, and Gabriel, the prince of heralds, had been summoned to the throne room. With intense interest, Ophaniel bent over, watching from his post above the sapphire throne.

"Hasten to Joseph," God directed. "Assure him that the child Mary carries has been conceived by the Holy Spirit, just as she has said."

"Holy, holy, holy!" Ophaniel began to sing. The other seraphs picked up the melody and then began a counterpoint of excited praise.

"Remind Joseph that I have spoken through the prophets, that a virgin shall conceive and bear a son." God instructed, "Then Advise my honorable Joseph to take Mary as his wife."

With all his heart, Ophaniel continued to sing his adoration of the Godhead.

Momentarily, God paused in his instructions to Gabriel. He looked up. "Ophaniel!"

The seraph heard the Eternal Ruler say his name, and he stopped singing. Without delay, Ophaniel swooped down to bow before God.

"Go with Gabriel. Escort him to the limits of Earth's galaxy and keep a watchful eye."

From the Mount of God, over the golden walls of the celestial city, through the vastness of space, the two angels traveled faster than light. Approaching the usual entrance to Earth's galaxy, they both paused in midflight. A wall of rebellious angels barricaded the starry portal that was still some distance away.

Without verbal consultation, a strategy was put into action. Ophaniel flew straight toward the heavily guarded entrance. "Make way for a messenger from the Eternal Ruler!" he announced.

Raziel, Satan's second in command, flew out to meet the seraph. "The Prince of this World has commanded that no messengers from God's throne room are to be admitted."

"There are other entrances to this galaxy," Ophaniel countered. "The words of Father God will be delivered!" Immediately, he flew off toward another entrance, and Satan's angel warriors immediately abandoned their post, some taking up the chase while others scrambled to block the next entrance.

Taking advantage of the diversion, Gabriel sped through the portal. Moments later, he stood beside Joseph's booth constructed on the Mount of Olives, facing the city of Jerusalem. The Spirit was already there.

Sleep eluded Joseph. He rolled over onto his back and stared up through the open spaces between the branches on the roof into the night sky. "I could try to count the stars," he muttered.

In his mind, the Spirit replied, "Only God knows the number of the stars. Remember, he challenged Abraham, *'Look up at the heavens and count the stars—if indeed you can count them.' Then he said to him, 'So shall your offspring be.'* And Abraham believed God, even though he was childless at that time. God spoke to Abraham about his offspring and his descendants. Could it be that God has spoken to Mary also and the child that she carries is the Messiah?"

If only I knew that to be true, Joseph replied in his heart. He rolled onto his side, letting his feet stick out of his booth. He stared at the brightly lit Temple until sleep finally overtook him.

"Joseph, son of David!" Gabriel imposed his image into Joseph's sleep-filled mind.

In Joseph's dream, a man taller than the nearby olive trees and brighter than a burning torch stood at his feet. It seemed to Joseph that he sat up immediately, his eyes riveted on the amazing stranger.

"Do not be afraid to take Mary home with you as your wife," Gabriel began delivering his message.

"How do you know about Mary?" Joseph challenged.

"I know because the child in her womb is from the Holy Spirit," the angel continued with kind reassurance.

"Are you saying that the child she carries is our promised Messiah?" Joseph anxiously asked.

"Yes, she will give birth to a son, and you are to give him the name Jesus, because he will save his people from their sins."

"But the law—" Joseph started to say.

"The prophet Isaiah wrote as the Spirit of God directed, *'The virgin will conceive and give birth to a son, and they will call him Immanuel.'*"

At the end of that pronouncement, the angel vanished, and Joseph was left in relative darkness, saying to himself, "Immanuel. That means God with us."

Suddenly, he woke up and jumped to his feet, hitting his head on the low roof of his booth. "I must speak with Heli." Hastily, he put on his festive clothing and hurried toward the Temple to find his future father-in-law.

"Mary?"

Mary looked up to see the silhouette of Elizabeth's very pregnant body against the early morning light.

"It's time." She paused and held her full belly while a contraction passed. "My labor started during the night, but I wanted to be sure so I—" She paused again.

Immediately, Mary was out of bed and on her feet. "What can I do?" She began pulling clothes over her head. This was her first experience with birth. The thought both thrilled and scared her.

"Go get my friend Hadassah and her daughter Rivkah." Another pause. "They are so good at birthing."

Mary deftly laced her sandals. "Zechariah?" she asked.

"He is getting wood for a fire," Elizabeth answered. "Praise God, he refused to leave me and would not go to Jerusalem for the Feast of Tabernacles!"

Mary picked up an empty water skin. "I'll bring water when I return," she stated as she hurried out the courtyard gate.

"There is time," Elizabeth called after her. "It is a long process." With her hand on her stomach, she leaned against the gatepost and waited for the pain to pass.

Satanic spirits hugged the shadowy corners of the room, waiting, hoping for an opportunity. "We cannot touch the infant or its mother," a spirit of Murder complained as he gestured toward the glowing presence of the Holy Spirit. "Normally, we could take advantage of the fact that this has been a long labor and the mother is beyond childbearing years, but they are protected. Even Mary is glowing with the presence of the Spirit."

"Still, we have been assigned to watch and wait for an opportunity," Fear admonished as he edged his worm-like body as close as he dared to the woman who had been in labor for most of a night and all of a day.

Through the open doorway to Zechariah and Elizabeth's sleeping quarters, Mary could see Zechariah pacing back and forth from one end of the courtyard to the other. Every so often, he would stop and raise his arms in silent petition to God, then he would stand in the doorway watching, waiting for the answer to his prayer.

Mary could see that he was approaching once more. His body filled the doorway, blocking out the last sunlight of the day. His silent questioning eyes tore at her heart. The pains had been unrelenting since sunup, and Elizabeth was suffering terribly.

"How much longer?" Mary anxiously asked Zechariah's question for him as she wiped the sweat from Elizabeth's forehead.

"Before sunrise," Hadassah answered with a matter-of-fact calmness that neither Zechariah nor Mary felt.

Again Elizabeth groaned and then cried out as a contraction reached its peak.

"All night?" Mary asked in dismay. "She has been in labor all day!"

Zechariah, standing in the doorway, was equally yet silently dismayed.

"I am all right, my husband," Elizabeth spoke to him in the brief moments between contractions. "You know I have always complained more loudly than I should."

Another contraction took over, and Elizabeth stopped speaking as the ever-increasing pain of the moment took her breath away. As it passed, she reached up and covered Mary's hand with her own. "I thought I would never have the joy of experiencing this pain. It is a blessing. Here"—she took Mary's hand and placed it on her abdomen—"feel how my body pushes the baby into this world." Mary's hand remained on Elizabeth's abdomen through the next three contractions. "I need to push!" Elizabeth suddenly cried as she strained through the peak of the contraction and then let out a soft moan as the pain subsided. "My tears are tears of thankfulness, and my moans are praise to my Maker. Mary, do not be afraid when your time comes. Remember all you have seen today. This is the way we bring children into this world. The Holy God of Israel will be with you as he is with me."

Immediately, both Hadassah and her daughter looked curiously at Mary. "I thought you were betrothed?" Rivkah questioned.

"I am," Mary replied, wondering whether or not she was still engaged to be married or if Joseph had gone through with the divorce.

"Are you with child?" Hadassah bluntly asked.

Mary knew what these women could do with the tiniest hint of a story. She hesitated to answer. "I—"

Mary's reply was cut short by an unusually loud gasping cry from Elizabeth. "The baby's coming!"

Hadassah placed a practiced hand on Elizabeth's taut belly and felt the strength of the contraction while she looked between her friend's legs. "It's time to get on the birthing stool," she announced with satisfaction.

All three women assisted Elizabeth into position, and a few contractions later, a ruddy, squalling infant lay on the clean cloths between Elizabeth's legs. The cord was tied off and then cut with a flint knife. Immediately, Rivkah went to work on the infant, clearing his mouth and nostrils by sucking with her own mouth and then rubbing him down with olive oil and salt before wrapping him in clean strips of linen. Elizabeth oversaw the whole procedure while her friend worked to complete the birth process.

"Mary, bring that wooden bowl over here," Hadassah ordered.

Obediently, Mary brought the bowl and held it out. Hadassah dropped the afterbirth into it. "Burn everything including the bowl in the fire Zechariah built near the garden," she said.

Mary took one look at the bloody mass and began to gag. She ran with the bowl into the garden, where she lost the contents of her stomach before continuing with her assigned task.

"That girl is with child," Hadassah put her lips near her daughter's ear so Elizabeth could not hear. "Remember, she lost her breakfast a few times while she was traveling with us. Take a good look at her when she returns. You will see that her breasts are too full for a girl her size and her hips seem a little too wide. Already she has the walk of one who is carrying, and her face— there is a certain look to the face. I have counseled many a young mother, and I know about these things. Mary has been unfaithful, and she is hiding out in the home of Elizabeth and Zechariah. I can sense these things."

As the satanic spirits moved to take advantage of Hadassah's observation, the glowing presence of the Spirit of God that covered Mary, Elizabeth, and the newborn suddenly flared. The spirits drew back, respecting the holy fire that could consume them. Taking an alternate approach, Murder cautiously reached out and embraced the thoughts that Hadassah had voiced. When he saw that the Spirit of God did not counter his approach to Hadassah, he quickly took possession of her thought processes. His bloody hand raked across her mind, stirring the soil of past resentments. Then the spirit of Murder planted his evil idea. "Mary should be brought before the town council, proven guilty, and then stoned."

Like rain on a freshly planted field, spirits of Religion swooped in, saturating both Hadassah and Rivkah with the laws that governed relationships between men and women in Jewish society. With the two women firmly in their grasp, Satan's agents watched as Mary returned to the room.

Rivkah and Hadassah exchanged knowing glances, and their lips curled into silent sneers. As if they had suddenly been elevated to the status of mistresses of the manor, they began piling Mary's arms with soiled linen and ordering her to complete the numerous chores of cleaning associated with childbirth.

For everyone in the room except Elizabeth, the atmosphere seemed to have changed. "Give me my son," Elizabeth held her arms out to receive her baby. Instinctively, the baby began nursing while Elizabeth kissed his forehead and feasted her eyes on the child she had thought she would never have.

Standing in the doorway, Zechariah waited for the women to complete their chores and leave. His eyes were on his son, and his lips mouthed a silent blessing. Glancing up at the old priest, Hadassah whispered to her daughter, "Zechariah and Elizabeth are so caught up in the miracle of their son's birth that they are completely unaware that Mary is using them."

Rivkah nodded her agreement but then said, "Zechariah and Elizabeth are both too kind. Even when they find out, they will not do what is lawful. They will continue to protect her. I will speak to Joram when he returns from the Feast of Tabernacles. He will know how to take this matter out of their hands."

Carrying the birthing stool, salt, and oil, the two women managed a little polite bow as they pushed past Zechariah and headed for their own home.

Spirits of Murder and Religion accompanied them.

Accusing spirits crowded into the largest room in the home of Zechariah and Elizabeth. Spirits of Murder and Religion made a place for themselves in the hearts and minds of many of the guests who had come to welcome the new baby, but they stayed away from those who were covered by the invisible-to-the-human-eye glow of the Holy Spirit.

Mary sensed their evil presence, but she could not put the feeling into thoughts that made sense to her mortal mind. She just knew that the eyes of the women in the village of Carem were on her. She could feel their sharp glances, like darts. The women huddled in little whispering groups that became suddenly silent or broke up when she came near. Even the men seemed to take a step backward when she passed by.

Only Zechariah and Elizabeth treated her normally. Today, the eighth day after the birth of their son, was the celebration of his birth and his entrance into his heritage. Mary could hardly expect them to notice how she was being treated. Wishing she could escape, she stopped trying to act as hostess and stepped behind Elizabeth to watch.

Zechariah gave Joram the privilege of holding his son while the village mohel, the man who performed all of the circumcisions in the vicinity of Carem, deftly removed the baby's foreskin with a flint knife and applied a dressing. While prayers were still being said, the infant was returned to his mother to be comforted by her milk.

"And now the scribe will record your son's name," said the mohel.

"Zechariah," Joram announced the child's name, and the town scribe began to write on the scroll that contained the record of all the births and deaths in the town of Carem.

"No!" Elizabeth spoke up from the back of the room. "We are naming him John."

"John?" the guests echoed in disbelief.

"There is no one named John in your family," Joram protested. "For a son to be named after his father is an honor. His name should be Zechariah!"

The mohel and all the men turned to Zechariah, who was holding his hands up for silence. When the old priest had everyone's attention, he signaled Mary.

She knew what he wanted and ran for his writing tablet and charcoal.

"*His name is John,*"[8] Zechariah wrote in large characters.

Immediately, the Spirit touched the lips of the old priest, and the seal that had been placed over his mouth dropped away.

Throughout the room, there was a low murmur of protest and speculation as the scribe carried out the wishes of the parents and inscribed the child's name in the town's records.

A little startled by the heavenly touch, the old priest looked around. Mary noticed his agitation and hurried to assist him. She took the writing materials from Zechariah and quickly turned to put them away. She kept her eyes on the ground so she would not see the piercing looks she had felt all afternoon. Suddenly, unexpectedly she bumped into a rock of a man who did not move to get out of her way.

"Oh, excuse me." She looked up. "Joseph!"

He bent down and whispered into her ear, "Your bridegroom has come for you. My friends and I are waiting to whisk you away." He nodded toward Jethro and Moshe, who grinned at them from the other side of the room. "I did not bring an entire wedding party. I talked it over with your father, and we decided it would be best just to make the journey with two witnesses. As soon as the Feast of Tabernacles ended, we came to Carem."

Above Zechariah, the Spirit emptied a golden cruise of anointing oil.

Suddenly, Zechariah was lifting his hands toward heaven and making his way toward the center of the room.

The Spirit of God intensified his presence. Unseen by mortals, holy fire filled the room. The spirits of Murder and Religion temporarily released the minds of their captives as they hastily exited the room.

"But I thought—" Mary started to say, but Joseph signaled her into silence.

Zechariah was saying, "*Praise be to the Lord, the God of Israel, because he has come to his people and redeemed them.*⁹ A deliverer is coming from the house of David."

"This is a miracle!" Mary whispered to Joseph. "Zechariah has been unable to speak since he saw the angel of the Lord." Both young people fixed their eyes on the old priest.

The Spirit wrapped Mary and Joseph in his presence, adding assurance to their own experiences. "Zechariah is speaking of your son, the child in Mary's womb," the Spirit whispered. "Jesus will be the Deliverer."

Without commenting, Mary and Joseph exchanged glances while Zechariah's voice continued, strong and clear, "*As he said through his holy prophets of long ago,* the 'seed of the woman' will bring *salvation from our enemies and from the hand of all who hate us*—God will send a Deliverer *to show mercy to our ancestors and to remember his holy covenant.*"¹⁰

Lingering just outside the closed door, the spirits of Murder and Religion trembled. The words of the third member of the Godhead flew from the mouth of the old priest like balls of fire. They lit up the sky as the Spirit translated them into the ancient prophecy. "*He will crush your head, and you will strike his heel.*"¹¹

Aware that the fulfillment of the promise given to Adam and Eve was at hand, the demonic spirits conspired. At any cost, they must prevent their lord, Satan, from receiving a crushing blow to the head.

"We will strike first," Murder announced.

Religion nodded his agreement as the evil spirits soared off to gather reinforcements.

"I saw the angel of the Lord also," Joseph bent down and whispered into Mary's ear. "He came to me in a dream. I'm sorry that I doubted your story."

Mary looked up into Joseph's face. There was such sincerity and peace. He looked happier than when she had first agreed to become his wife.

Zechariah was still talking, but Mary barely heard his words. Her eyes were on her husband-to-be—such a miracle!

Moved by the Spirit, Elizabeth stood up and came over to stand beside her husband as he prophesied. Looking down at the child in his wife's arms, Zechariah placed his wrinkled hand on baby John's forehead and blessed him, *"And you, my child, will be called a prophet of the Most High; for you will go on before the Lord to prepare the way for him, to give his people the knowledge of salvation through the forgiveness of sins, because of the tender mercy of our God."*[12]

Throughout the room, there was stunned silence. The people of Carem were awkwardly speechless as they groped to comprehend the prophetic words of the old priest. One by one and in family groups, they made their way to the new parents, saying their good-byes and quickly escaping the unfamiliar weighty presence of holiness that permeated the room.

Along the main road through Carem, spirits of murder and religion waited. They fell into step with the retreating guests. Attaching themselves to their conversations, the agents of Satan planted their lethal ideas. Entering the homes of these former guests, the demonic spirits fertilized and tended their hateful crop. Overnight, their evil ideas grew ripe and ready for harvest.

The next morning, shortly after dawn, Joseph heard footsteps on the path in front of Zechariah's house.

"Get up and prepare," the Holy Spirit warned.

Joseph obeyed. Getting up from his pallet, he pulled a sleeveless tunic over his head and then cinched it with a wide leather belt.

"Move back," the Holy Spirit issued orders to the angelic host that accompanied him.

Immediately, the Archangel Michael and his warrior angels withdrew to the tops of the hills that surrounded the town. Their hands rested on their swords, and their eyes never strayed from the scene that was playing out in front of the home of the old priest of Carem.

"Zechariah!" a man's voice broke the stillness of the morning.

Joseph moved to the window and looked out to see three men approaching, with a small crowd following at a distance. The men out front were obviously the elders of the town. He could tell by their dress that they were the authorities in charge of the local synagogue. A town this small would have only three governing elders, and all three were present.

Behind him, Joseph sensed that Moshe and Jethro had also been aroused and were moving about in the gloom of the sleeping chamber.

"I see you have been busy," the Holy Spirit, like a wall of fire, confronted the spirits of Religion and Murder as they approached the home of Zechariah.

"And successful," Murder gloated as he gestured toward all who had fallen under his spell.

"You will not succeed in eliminating Yeshua the Creator before he completes his mission," the Holy Spirit warned as his fire intensified.

"God cannot interfere. He is restricted by his own law. *If a man happens to meet in a town a virgin pledged to be married and he sleeps with her, you shall take both of them to the gate of that town and stone them to death—the girl because she was in a town and did not scream for help and the man because he violated another man's wife. You must purge the evil from among you!*"[13] God has sworn to uphold his laws." The spirit of Religion broke into sadistic laughter after quoting the scripture.

"That law does not apply here. Mary has not been unfaithful, and you know it," the Holy Spirit countered.

"Ha-ha!" Demonic laughter filled the space between good and evil as spirits of Religion peeled away and darted in and out among the crowd fanning the flames of misguided fervor.

Lying spirits suddenly emerged from the middle of the angry mob, shouting, "They don't know this law doesn't apply. They think they are defending their God and his Holy Scriptures, and ironically, we are only going to assist them."

To escape the righteous flames that confronted them, the spirits of Murder slid behind the spokesmen for the town, supporting their accusations while using their human bodies as shields.

"Zechariah! We have come for Mary, the relative of Elizabeth." Joram the priest, who served as one of the three elders, stood just outside the courtyard gate. His voice carried through the wood and into the sleeping rooms.

"She is with child," the women in the crowd, like crows in the trees, squawked their accusation.

"Mary is accused of unfaithfulness and of breaking the law that requires her to remain chaste until she enters the home of her husband. She must stand before the council," the ruling elder announced.

Rubbing his hand over his bald head and still shaking off sleep, Zechariah moved toward the gate of his home. Mary and Elizabeth fearfully followed behind him.

Before the trio could reach the gate in the wall that surrounded the house, Joseph filled the entrance to the courtyard with his massive carpenter's body. "Who is calling the name of my betrothed so early in the morning?" he bellowed.

The spirits of Murder could see that Joseph glowed with the presence of the Holy Spirit. It unnerved them, and they withdrew to the back of the mob, leaving the town elders unsupported.

Suddenly uncertain, the town elders froze in their tracks.

"Who are you?" Joram managed to ask.

"Joseph of Nazareth." Righteous anger coursed through Joseph's veins. He clenched his fists, and the muscles of his exposed biceps bulged, then he took several menacing steps forward. Jethro and Moshe also stepped through the open doorway, ready to back him up. Joseph glanced over his shoulder and saw Jethro move the folds of his cloak to reveal a sword. "My friends and I have come from Galilee to Carem to bring Mary back to Nazareth and into my home. Under the law, if there are any accusations to be made, it is my responsibility to make them after the wedding night before the elders of Nazareth."

Zechariah stepped through the courtyard gate. He pushed between Jethro and Moshe and then strode forward to stand beside Joseph. He looked over the crowd. These people were his neighbors and his close friends. "Why this?" His hand swept the area to take in the mob. "Any one of you could have come to me privately." His eyes rested on Joram. "My brother in the priesthood, you have been like a son to me. How could you be a part of this?"

The Holy Spirit reached out to the young priest and pricked his conscience.

Joram averted his eyes from the direct gaze of his mentor.

"Joram," Zechariah's voice commanded his attention, "I taught you mercy. I showed you how to calm the sacrificial lamb and how to take its life with one swift painless thrust. You have mercy for an animal but none for a Jewish girl? With no basis, you come to my home to accuse, humiliate, and lynch!"

A spirit named Lies propelled Joram's mother-in-law to the front of the mob.

"Mary said she was betrothed," Hadassah announced. "Her own relative, Elizabeth, told us that she was with child."

"I didn't," Elizabeth tried to push past the men and protest, but Moshe put out a restraining hand, and she stepped back.

"A woman in labor always speaks the truth," Hadassah shouted back.

The Lying spirit responded by giving her a reassuring pat on the back.

Then Rivkah joined her mother and added, "Even without being told, the situation was obvious to us."

Hidden within the mob, spirits named Religion moved from one person to the next, whispering ideas, manipulating them into action.

"She has broken the law," a voice from the crowd shouted. "We will not allow Carem to become a sewer of immorality. The evils from the court of Herod are spreading throughout our land. They have to be stopped."

"Mary has nothing to do with the court of Herod," Zechariah countered. "She is a chaste and God-fearing girl."

"Who is with child even though she has never been brought into the home of her husband," Rivkah snidely retorted.

"A child in the womb before the wedding—there can be only one explanation!" Hadassah added triumphantly.

"Make her an example!" a woman shouted.

Spirits who specialized in murder clamored to incite the mob to mindless action.

"Our daughters must see and understand that in Israel, there is no place for such behavior!" a man from the back of the crowd hollered over the general melee.

"Caution!" the Holy Spirit advised the chief elder of the synagogue of Carem.

The chief elder stepped forward and addressed Joseph, "Has she been unfaithful to you?"

"She has not been unfaithful," Joseph stated.

"Then are you the father of her child?" the elder asked.

"Do not give them information they will find too difficult to believe," the Spirit of God advised.

For a long moment, Joseph considered his answer before truthfully responding, "I am not the father of any child!" Then he quickly countered, "Do you think that I, an observant Jew, would behave improperly with my betrothed? I can assure you that both Mary and I have conducted ourselves in strict obedience to word of the Lord." He took a few more threatening steps forward. Moshe picked up a fist-sized rock, and Jethro brandished his sword while Zechariah raised his hands, signaling restraint to both sides.

Immediately, the representatives of the spiritual government in the town of Carem responded to Joseph's threatening demeanor and retreated into the crowd, which was abuzz with speculation and accusation.

"Joseph of Nazareth," the chief elder hid behind a stocky man as he made his parting declarations, "if you find anything amiss, as a son of the covenant, you are required to bring it before the elders of your own town."

"Do not lecture me on my duty to the law!" Joseph retorted. "I have been Torah observant since birth." He pointed a work-hardened finger at the man who accused his bride. "Those long fringes on the corners of your garments and a position of power do not make you Torah observant." Joseph pounded his chest with his massive fist. "It takes a heart that loves the law and the God who gave us that law."

"Trap him into making a rash vow," a spirit of Religion suggested. "Try to make him say if he finds that Mary is with child, he will bring her before the elders of Nazareth and he will throw the first stone!"

One voice in the crowd called out, "Take an oath!"

Others picked up the phrase. "Take an oath!"

It became a chant, then a chorus that could not be ignored. "Take an oath! Take an oath!"

Joseph cleared his throat, and the crowd became silent. Anticipation filled the air.

Zechariah stepped up beside Joseph and placed his hand on the young man's shoulder. "My son, be careful that you are not goaded into speaking rashly. *This is what the* LORD *commands; when a man makes a vow to the* LORD *or takes an oath to obligate himself by a pledge, he must not break his word but must do everything he said.*[14] An oath is a serious matter."

"The honor of my bride and my family is also a serious matter," Joseph responded.

In the doorway of the priest's home, Mary held her breath, as did Elizabeth.

Joseph's voice was firm and confident. "Before God Almighty and these witnesses, I pledge that should God Almighty reveal to me evidence of infidelity on the night that I bring my bride into my home, I will act according to the law and bring the matter to the attention of the authorities."

"I am satisfied," the chief elder of the synagogue of Carem stated as he turned his back on Joseph and his friends and walked through the crowd back toward the center of town.

Hadassah and Rivkah evidently were not satisfied, for Joseph could see them tugging at Joram's sleeves, urging him to say more, but the young priest ignored them, moving on with the other two elders. With considerable chatter, the rest of the people followed.

For a short distance, Jethro and Moshe shadowed the mob, ready to throw a stone or do battle with anyone who dared turn back.

Like a memorial stone, Joseph stood in front of the door to Zechariah's house, staring the townspeople down until they reached the ever-flowing spring and began to disperse into their own homes. Zechariah stood beside him. "You acted wisely, my son. You cannot tell anyone that Mary is with child from the Holy Spirit."

"You know?" Joseph asked in surprise.

"Yes. Mary has told us the whole story, and the birth of our son, John, was God's confirmation," the old priest answered. "But the people, they will not accept her story at this time. You do not want any harm to come to your family, and you do not want the child labeled a bastard, cut off from his people. He would never be allowed to enter the Temple."

Joseph nodded his head. He understood the customs and laws of Judaism.

The old priest stared thoughtfully down the road while he stroked his long white beard. "Even if we could tell the whole story"—he paused—"and they believed that the child Mary is carrying is the Anointed One, Herod has eyes. Rome has ears. They would never let the child survive. We must wait for the time when God himself reveals to Israel and to all the world that this is his son."

Joseph opened his heart and responded, "At times, it is still hard for me to believe."

"I know," Zechariah answered. "Our sinful flesh always questions the things of God. Take my advice. Go away for a time. Take Mary and live somewhere where people are not counting the months."

"I have my carpenter's shop," Joseph protested.

"It could be rented out," Zechariah pointed out. "Your first responsibility is to protect this special child."

"I will pray on the matter," Joseph answered.

"You filled him with your Spirit." From a spot in the middle of the town, near the spring, spirits named Murder and Religion raged at the Spirit of God. "You gave him courage and wisdom."

"Just like you filled that mob with your spirit," the Holy Spirit replied.

"He was outnumbered," Murder continued to rant.

"One or two righteous men empowered by the Spirit of God can undo the work of a thousand demons," the Holy Spirit replied. "Now I command you to leave!"

"We will be back!" the spirits of Murder and Religion screamed as they turned and fled toward Jerusalem.

"Pursue the enemy and maintain them at a distance from the Creator in the womb," the Holy Spirit issued a command for the angelic forces that lined the mountain ridges overlooking the town of Carem.

Michael and his warrior angels drew their ever-burning swords and swiftly pursued the agents of Satan.

Turning back toward the house, Joseph felt the adrenaline draining from his body. Zechariah walked beside him, shaking his head and muttering about the irrational behavior of his neighbors.

Pale, obviously shaken, Mary leaned against the gatepost. "Oh, Joseph, if you had not been here…" She could say no more.

"The angel of the Lord told me to take you into my home to be my wife," Joseph answered. "I had to come."

Coming up behind the couple, Zechariah put an arm around each of them. "Your lives are in the hands of the Almighty. Fear not!" he admonished.

"I'm so sorry." Elizabeth stepped forward and took Mary's hand. "I don't know what I said during the labor. I cannot imagine how Hadassah and Rivkah found out. I'm just not sure…" Her voice trailed off as she left Mary with Joseph and went to feed baby John.

"I'm sure of one thing," Joseph countered. "It's time for this bridal party to return to Nazareth." Over his shoulder, he called to Jethro, "Get the donkey ready to travel."

"First you will eat, and then I will bless you," Zechariah insisted as he escorted the couple back into the house.

Night chased after dusk and smothered it with darkness. It decreased visibility for the little band of travelers until their other senses worked harder than their sight. "Whatever we might feel about our Roman oppressors," Joseph commented as he felt his way along, "we have to bless them for good roads."

"Yes," Moshe agreed. "We couldn't continue otherwise."

Normally, the travelers would have made camp by now. They would have eaten their evening meal around a campfire and unloaded the bedding from the donkey cart, but they were so close to the end of their seven-day journey; this was the sixth day that they had been walking. One day, the Sabbath day, had been spent just resting in a wayside inn and rejoicing in the law that commanded them to indulge in such a luxurious use of time.

Now they were approaching the town of Nazareth. They expected to be at the home of Mary's parents before the crescent moon reached its zenith. Jethro stopped leading the little donkey and blindly dug around in the donkey cart until he produced two torches that Joseph lit from the little pot of coals from their morning fire.

Suddenly, they were able to see all the way to the edges of the raised-dirt highway and ten strides ahead. They all let out a collective sigh of relief. There was comfort and security in the light. It had chased the tension and uncertainty away.

"I told you we might need some torches," Jethro bragged a little about his foresight as he handed a lit torch to Moshe and picked up the donkey's reins. "Let's go, Lily," he spoke to the docile animal.

"Wait," Joseph called from behind the cart. "Mary's been walking all day." He looked at her tired face. "Why don't you ride in the cart?"

"I can keep up," she doggedly replied.

"You're the bride," Moshe announced as he came around and held up his torch so Joseph could see. "You need to come into town in style."

Immediately, Joseph began arranging their bedding into a little nest, and then he assisted Mary as she crawled up into the cart.

Throughout this entire journey, Joseph and his friends had treated her like a Roman princess, totally pampered. She had not lifted a jug of water or cooked a meal. At night, they had made up her bed close to the fire and arranged themselves in a protective semicircle a proper distance away. And now she reclined on cushions of bedding as she entered her hometown. A daughter of Caesar Augustus, emperor of Rome, could not have received better treatment.

In the cart, Mary settled into the rhythm of the ride: clop, clop, rock, rock, bump, rock, rock. Her eyes began to feel heavy. Her body sank into her humble cushions, and she relaxed.

"Mary? Mary!" They were in front of her home, and her mother was shaking her awake. "You can't sleep through your bridal procession!"

Her sister, Salome, came running with a large piece of blue linen. "Get up! Let me cover the bundles. This is not a sedan chair, but we can make it fancier than an old work cart."

Mary looked around. There were lamps everywhere. She sat up. Half the neighborhood must have come out to escort them from her parents' house to Joseph's home.

"The bridegroom has arrived!" someone shouted, making a jovial play on the traditional announcement "The bridegroom cometh."

"How?" Mary asked.

"Moshe ran ahead and let us know you were coming into town, then Father ran to the neighbors." Salome giggled in excitement. "We knew you would be surprised! Oh! I have to join the dancers!" Salome suddenly turned and ran to the front of the procession.

Mary began trying to straighten her hair and the disheveled mantle that had slipped to her shoulders. Neighbors milled about and congratulated Joseph. Someone struck up a song. The unmarried girls of the village began a few practice steps. Mary's mother ran back into the house and returned with a white linen veil. She took Mary's traveling mantle and arranged the fine linen over her head, a graceful traditional covering for her face. With a crown of blue cords, she secured the headpiece. "Have a blessed life with Joseph," she whispered as she lifted the veil and kissed her daughter on cheek. "I'll bring a meal in the morning," she added with motherly efficiency.

Salome led the maidens of the village as they began their dance on the road in front of the cart. Jethro urged Lily to take a few steps forward. The bridal procession began to move. "O God, thank you. I thought this day would never come," Mary breathed a prayer. She looked out over the sea of flickering lamps and blazing torches. It seemed that every person she had grown up with, every person that her family knew had come out to escort her to her new home. She could not have dreamed of a more beautiful bridal procession.

At Joseph's shop, the women of the village took over, going inside ahead of everyone, lighting all the lamps, clearing off his work benches, and setting out food and wine that they had brought from their own homes. The celebration lasted until the food was consumed and the wine jugs were empty.

Amid giggles and knowing looks, the females of the village escorted Mary to the bridal chamber that Joseph had built. The more mature women appreciated the sturdiness and craftsmanship of the room. They commented on the fact that Joseph had even built a sturdy wooden door to separate the living quarters from his carpentry shop. The younger romantics perfumed the bed covers and lighted the lamps that they placed in just the right places to give the room a soft glow.

"Out! Out!" The matrons began to shoo everyone out of the bedchamber, closing the door behind them, leaving Mary veiled and alone with her thoughts. She sat on a bench next to the wall and waited for her groom. At that moment, Mary felt the baby within her for the first time, just a tiny sweet flutter like a butterfly.

Reverently, she placed her hand over the spot where the feathery movements continued. In awe, she whispered to the child in her womb, "By the hand of God Almighty, you are being fashioned in my womb. His Spirit knits you together in my secret female places. I thank my heavenly Father because I am awesomely made, created so a child can thrive in the deep recesses of my body. You will save your people from their sins." She paused and tried to wrap her mind around the future of her child, but her thoughts were filled with prophecies, traditions, and the words of the angel. It was all so complicated. "For now, you are just a tiny gift of life from the hand of God, placed in my womb. I am blessed."

The laughter and general noise outside the door to the bedchamber had lessened to a few male voices. Abruptly, the door opened. By peeking around the side of the veil, she could see Joseph standing there, not taking that first step to enter the room. Moshe laughed at his reluctance, and then Jethro gave him a good-natured shove, which propelled his body awkwardly across the threshold. The door was then firmly closed behind him. Joseph looked back at the door and then at his bride.

Mary didn't know what to say. All the comfortableness they had felt as they walked along the road in the company of the others had vanished. She realized this was the first time they had ever been alone together, really alone. Awkwardness filled the room. Joseph continued to stand there just looking at her. Her fingertips played with the edges of her white linen veil. She felt a little nervous flutter in her chest.

Finally, he said, "It wasn't much of a wedding, just one night instead of seven days. The journey was longer than our wedding celebration." Joseph hadn't moved from his place just inside the door. There was another awkward silence, then he asked, "Are you tired?"

Mary let out a little sigh of relief. "No, I'm quite awake." Then she hastened to add, "It was a long trip, but the best trip I have ever taken."

He came over and sat beside her on the bench. "May I remove your veil?" he hesitantly asked.

"Yes," she shyly whispered her response.

With both hands, he carefully lifted the crown of blue cords, and the light linen fabric slid to the floor. Her dark hair was falling from the knot she had twisted it into earlier in the evening. His fingertips brushed back the falling strands that kissed her face. His head bent close to her head, and his lips were so close to her ear that his beard tickled her neck. "I've waited a long time for you to be my wife. So much has happened. I've spent a long time trying to figure it out." He paused and slipped his thickly muscled arm behind her back, pulling her into the crook of his shoulder. "Comfortable?" he asked.

Their eyes met, and she nodded. For a long time, they just sat together deep in their own thoughts.

The atmosphere in the room changed. Peace, gratitude, trust, love, and the Spirit of God—it was all there in the soft glow of lamplight, floating on the night air like the perfume from their marriage bed.

Joseph broke the silence. "Your father told me the story of the angel, but I would like to hear it from you."

Mary pulled back from him slightly so she could look into his eyes. "I've wanted to talk to you about it for so long." Her words began to tumble out. "I was just going through the dried lentils, looking for small rocks or twigs before I cooked them, when suddenly the courtyard became dazzlingly bright. I looked up, and right by the water jars, there was an angel." Mary paused and looked deeply into Joseph's eyes, trying to see if he believed her.

"Go on," he said with a little encouraging nudge. "What did he look like?"

"His head was higher than the roof, and his hair was snowy white. His skin looked like fiery bronze, and his voice, it was so compelling."

Joseph nodded his head as if he knew exactly what she was talking about. "Zechariah gave me a similar description," he inserted, "and in my dream, I saw a man very much like your description. Tell me what happened next."

"Well, the angel said, *'Greetings, you who are highly favored! The Lord is with you.'*[15] Such a greeting! I felt bewildered and frightened, but the angel seemed to know what I was feeling because he said, *'Do not be afraid, Mary; you have found favor with God.'*[16]

"In my dream, the angel knew my thoughts also," Joseph added. "He told me not to be afraid to take you for my wife because the child inside of you was from the Holy Spirit. I still do not understand. My mind thinks in human terms, and when I try to figure it out…" His voice trailed off.

"I did not understand either. The angel said to me, '*You will conceive and give birth to a son, and you are to call him Jesus. He will be great and will be called the Son of the Most High. The Lord God will give him the throne of his father David, and he will reign over Jacob's descendants forever; his kingdom will never end.* '[17] It must be the Messiah. The angel could only be telling me that I was to be the mother of the Messiah! But me? Why would an angel come to me?"

"Why wouldn't an angel come to you?" Joseph gently asked as he once again brushed the stray strands of hair from her face. "God could not have found a more beautiful or righteous girl to be the mother of the Anointed One." He kissed her softly on the forehead and then stood up. "There are prophecies…" Joseph paced the room a little as he tried to remember the scrolls he had studied. "In the writings of Samuel, there are words from God given through Nathan the prophet."

"I know that prophecy," Mary said. "Father used to read it to me and commented on it every time he copied it onto a new scroll. I remember Nathan told King David that when his days had come to an end and he was asleep with his ancestors, then God would establish one of his descendants, his own flesh and blood, as ruler of a kingdom that would last forever."

"We are both flesh-and-blood descendants of King David," Joseph commented.

"And there was more," Mary added. "The prophecy said that this ruler would be God's son."

"Yes." Joseph quoted, "*I will be his father and he will be my son.* "[18] He walked over to the bench and took his bride by the hand, gently pulling her to her feet. "It is almost exactly what the angel told you, but how?"

Mary understood his question. "It was not like anything you or I understand about procreation. I am still a virgin, physically untouched." Mary looked into Joseph's eyes as she continued, "The angel said that the Spirit of the Most High would come upon me and the power of God would cover me. Then it happened. The power of God was like wonderful fire all over my body. I could not stand. I fell to the floor and experienced waves of emotion. I knew God's love for his people. I was overcome with his glory. My spirit seemed to burst open." She shook her head and groped for a better explanation, finally giving up and saying, "My words don't really explain what happened."

Joseph's eyes were riveted on Mary's face.

"Believe, Joseph," the Spirit whispered. "Believe Mary. Believe Zechariah and believe your own vision."

As they stood together, Joseph whispered, "I believe you." Then he pulled Mary into his arms and held her for a long time.

"I felt the baby tonight," Mary whispered into Joseph's chest. "The Son of God is doing tiny leaps in my womb."

"Oh, Mary, this is a sacred trust we have been given—you to carry this child and me to protect and be a father to it." Joseph meditated on that thought a long time while he continued to hold his bride. "When Moses told the people that God was coming down to them on the mountain, they had to prepare. They washed, and they abstained from sexual relations." He took a step back from Mary, holding only her hands. "God is coming to us. We will abstain from sexual union until this Son of God is born."

Mary nodded in silent agreement.

"Go to sleep now." Joseph pulled back the covers of their marriage bed, and Mary lay down. Suddenly, she was tired, overwhelmingly tired. Almost immediately, she closed her eyes.

Her last memory was of whiskered lips brushing gently across her forehead.

For a moment, Joseph watched his sleeping bride, then he settled his bulky body on the bench and leaned against the wall to wait for dawn. He knew that Jethro and Moshe slept just outside the door that separated this sleeping chamber from his carpentry shop. He also knew this was not the night for him to return to the tiny room behind his shop where he had previously slept. It was important that Moshe and Jethro be as certain of Mary's purity as he was.

Dawn cast a rosy glow on the stone walls of the bedchamber. Joseph sat up and stretched the kinks out of his back. Without disturbing Mary, he opened the door to the bedchamber and stepped out into his shop. Jethro and Moshe were still stretched out on pallets by the door to the bedchamber, witnesses and guards for the wedding night.

"You're up early," Moshe said as he threw back his covers and got up. Jethro quickly got to his feet. For an uneasy moment, both men just stood there looking at Joseph while the unspoken question from their trip to Carem hung in the air.

"Mary is a righteous daughter of the covenant," Joseph said. "I am honored to have her for my wife."

Both men nodded, offered their friend congratulations, and then returned to their own homes.

Chapter 5

FROM NAZARETH TO BETHLEHEM

In those days Caesar Augustus issued a decree that a census should be taken of the entire Roman world. (This was the first census that took place while Quirinius was governor of Syria.) And everyone went to his own town to register.

—Luke 2:1–3

"Good morning, Lily." Mary scratched the short stiff hairs between the donkey's long ears. "You are such a faithful little animal." Every morning for nearly four months, she had cared for Joseph's donkey, such a gentle animal. She put a rope halter over her head. "And you're so pretty." She took another moment to scratch the petal-shaped white markings on the donkey's face before leading her out of the small stable and around to Joseph's carpentry shop.

Joseph was just putting the last few smoothly planed timbers on his work cart. Mary backed the docile work animal into place, and Joseph began to hitch Lily to the cart.

"I'm just in the way," Mary said as Joseph tried to work around her. She stepped back, but felt like there was not enough room in the little shop. She bumped into a saw that was leaning against the wall. It clattered to the floor. She bent over to pick it up and found herself struggling to accomplish that simple task. "I never imagined I could become so clumsy," she commented as she straightened up. Her body had expanded so much that she felt bigger than a mature camel. She even had a funny sway when she walked, not unlike the walk of a camel. She placed her hand on her protruding belly. The baby was kicking, such an exciting sensation—life within her womb.

"Mary."

She looked up to see Joseph watching her.

"I'm taking this load of wood to Ezra, son of Samuel. I'll help him place these timbers, and then I will meet you at the spring in the center of town when the women gather to bring water home for their evening meals. We'll water Lily and then bring water back to the house." He quickly checked Lily's hooves as he continued, "Wait for me. I don't want you carrying a full jar of water. It's too heavy."

"I'll be there." Mary's eyes met her husband's in a silent exchange of affection. For a long moment, she held his gaze.

"Ezra is expecting me," Joseph stated as he awkwardly pulled his eyes away.

Mary watched as her husband gave his donkey a little nudge. Joseph, donkey, and cart moved out of the shop and onto the dusty road that ran through the center of Nazareth.

This man puzzled her. He always seemed to know when to be helpful and protective, but when the moment called for affectionate words or gestures, he seemed awkward and lost, except for their wedding night; she treasured the memory. He is a good man, Mary reminded herself. He is thoughtful and practical, faithful to his personal vow of celibacy. Introspectively, she continued watching until her husband was nearly out of sight. Then she sat down to grind the grain she would need for the day's baking.

Hanging from a branch of the sycamore tree that shaded Joseph's carpenter shop, discontented demonic spirits eyed the angelic warriors that Michael had placed around the home of Joseph and Mary. Ever since their attempt to have Mary stoned, the Archangel Michael had kept them from approaching the couple.

Suddenly, Raziel arrived. The mighty angel, servant of Satan, still maintained an ethereal glow reminiscent of that heavenly kingdom they had all once inhabited. The spirits, draped over a branch like dusty old cloaks, perked up at the sight of the dazzling messenger from their evil ruler.

"Satan has a new plan." Raziel pointed to a dark spirit named Judgment and his even darker partner, Condemnation. "It is obvious we cannot touch the Creator's life at this time, but we can make his arrival ineffective by destroying his credibility."

"Gossip!" the spirit of Judgment suggested.

"Count the months since the wedding," Condemnation gleefully added. "Every person will come to the same logical assumption!"

"Then they will talk about it," Judgment continued the train of thought.

"They will talk until Mary and her child are convicted in the court of public opinion!" the spirit of Condemnation triumphantly announced.

"It is not necessary to physically harm Mary, Joseph, or the child," Raziel elaborated on the plan. "Any child born to a woman who by law could have been stoned because of the way the child was conceived is considered a bastard and is forbidden to enter the Temple or have any inheritance with the people of Israel." Then with a wave of his hand, Raziel released the dark spirits, like a plague on the town of Nazareth.

Insidiously, Judgment and Condemnation crept into carefully selected homes. "Have you seen Mary, wife of Joseph the carpenter? Her pregnancy is very advanced," they whispered. Over garden fences, through open windows, interrupting the domestic tasks of households, the evil spirits planted their seeds of gossip. "Count the months since her bridal procession. It doesn't add up."

In the home of Ezra, son of Samuel, Abigail sat at her loom. Her mind flew faster than her feet and fingers. Mary's bridal procession was after the fall feasts. It is now early spring. We're all watching the ripening barley. Passover will soon arrive, and Mary looks like her baby will be born before Passover. Abigail stopped working and counted the months on her fingers. "Two fall months. Three winter months. Spring is just around the corner. She will have that baby before the spring feasts, or her belly will burst!"

"Mary's family has always put on such righteous airs," the spirits of Judgment and Condemnation offered their thoughts. "Remember when you were girls how Mary bragged about how observant her family was! You felt like she was looking down her nose at you. Now who bears the shame and tries to keep it a secret?"

Abigail looked out the window. Mary's husband, Joseph, was working with her husband to set the timbers for a new shelter over their olive press. He was a strong, handsome man with a reputation for being honest and Torah observant. He could have done better than Mary. There were other maidens more noble than the daughter of Heli.

"Knowing how little men know about the process of birth and how easy it is for a woman to mislead them makes one wonder. Has Mary tricked Joseph into believing this child was conceived on their wedding night? Remember, Mary was away from Nazareth for three months!"

Abigail stopped working and filled a pitcher with water. Picking up two cups, she hurried out to where the men were working. "Ezra, Joseph, would you like a drink?"

Both men stopped working and walked over to meet her.

"Joseph, how has Mary been? I have not seen her in the women's section at synagogue for several weeks." Abigail tried to sound casual.

"On Sabbath, she rests," Joseph answered. "As pregnant as she is, she needs to rest and put her feet up."

"And when do you expect the birth of the baby?" Abigail inquired with forced nonchalance.

"In the Lord's time," Joseph answered.

"Men!" Abigail laughed. "They don't realize that God has set the time for all babies to be born. It is almost exactly forty weeks after the night of conception." She paused, watching closely to see if that statement elicited any reaction.

Joseph did not respond. He just held his cup out for a refill.

Abigail pushed a little harder. "Let's see, your bridal procession was a couple of weeks after the fall feasts. It's nearly spring, so your baby could not possibly be born before midsummer. You have another three, maybe four months to wait."

Joseph paused with his cup in midair.

Abigail continued, "Has Mary seen the midwife? It is unusual for someone to need rest so early in a pregnancy unless she is having twins or her pregnancy is more advanced than she thinks." Her voice ended on a speculative note.

"Mary's mother is watching her closely and sees no reason for concern," Joseph responded.

With a touch of snideness, Abigail commented, "Family is the best judge of these things." She picked up her empty pitcher and cups and then returned to the house.

"The righteous scribe and his wife are covering for their daughter!" Condemnation commented. "Do they think the people of Nazareth can't count?"

One by one, the women of Nazareth picked up their water jugs, and each made her late afternoon trip to the spring. Mary lifted her empty water jar to her shoulder and left her home. On the way, she met her neighbors, women she had known all her life. She smiled and nodded, but no one seemed to want to engage her in conversation. They walked in groups of twos and threes, but they did not invite her to join them.

A spirit called Fear met her on the road and tried to worm his way into her thoughts. "They know your secret."

In her head, Mary countered, They don't know that the angel of the Lord came to me and that the child I carry was conceived by the Holy Spirit.

"No, but they know your pregnancy is much farther along than it should be, and they suspect Joseph may not be the father of your child," Fear continued. "Now that you are married, you are probably safe enough, but do you know what they will say about your child? How they will kill him with their tongues? He will be labeled a bastard and not allowed a part in the synagogue or even to enter the Court of the Gentiles in the Temple. As a bastard, he can never be a son of the covenant, and his descendants down to the tenth generation will be outcasts."

Mary shivered at the awful prospect of her child not being allowed to take his place in the community—an outcast, like a leper. She wanted to argue with the voice in her head, but she could not deny the accuracy of its message. So many times, she had overheard her father conversing with the men of the town, going over the numerous interpretations of the law and its enforcement. The law that governed Jewish life was so exact, so unbending. Where was the mercy? She knew for sure there was no mercy in the speculation of the women in the town of Nazareth. Their small-town gossip could easily become an unquenchable and deadly fire. At the spring, she found a shady spot and set her water jar on the ground. Placing a protective hand over the baby in her belly, she waited for Joseph.

Leaving Ezra's house, Joseph urged Lily to move faster. He wanted to get to the well before Mary arrived.

"The women of the town are talking about Mary." The Spirit, now a recognizable voice in his head, warned, "They are looking at her and counting the months."

Suddenly, Joseph realized Ezra's wife had asked too many probing questions. "Lord, what do I do? How do I protect Mary and the child from a lifetime of scorn?" He considered the advice of Zechariah, the priest. Then he asked himself, If I take Mary away, where do I take her?

Before he could continue his prayer, a clatter of hoofs caused him to turn around.

Four Roman soldiers on horseback were galloping down the road. They rode side by side, laughing, competing with each other, arrogantly taking up the entire road.

Anxiously, Joseph looked around for a way to get out of their way without getting his cart stuck in the ditch at the side of the road. The soldiers bore down on him with no consideration.

Forcefully, Joseph pulled Lily's harness. The donkey balked and brayed before stumbling off the road into the ditch. The cart banged against her hind legs, leaving bloody gashes. Without a glance at the man and his donkey floundering in the ditch, the soldiers continued their race into the center of town.

After a backbreaking struggle to return both donkey and cart to the road, Joseph approached the spring. He could see that the Roman soldiers had taken over the town's water supply. Their horses drank at the trough while the people of the town hung back, waiting for them to leave. Joseph scanned the crowd until his eyes rested on Mary sitting by herself under a sycamore tree. He urged his limping donkey to move a little faster as he continued toward the spring.

"People of Nazareth," one of the soldiers announced.

Everyone stopped talking and looked up.

"By order of your Emperor Augustus…"

Most of the crowd chose that moment to spit into the dust at their feet. Coming up beside Mary, Joseph put a protective hand on her shoulder.

"Throughout the Roman Empire, there is to be a census. Every man who owns inherited property must return to his inheritance to be registered and pay taxes or forfeit that property to the emperor." After the announcement, the soldiers nailed a notice to the crossbeams that supported a bucket and pulley system for filling the trough. Then they took their horses and headed toward the outskirts of town where they would camp for the night.

"They knew better than to ask for a room in this town," Joseph commented as he helped Mary to her feet. Together, they led Lily to the trough. Mary bathed the gashes on the back of the donkey's legs while Joseph filled the trough and their water jar.

"Get in the cart, Mary." Joseph gave her a little lift onto the back of the cart and handed her the water jug. "Looks like we're going to Bethlehem."

"Bethlehem?" Mary responded.

"Yes." He pointed to the sign on the crossbeams above the spring. "I'm not losing the field I inherited from my father. We will stay with one of my cousins. They will make room for us. You will like them, and you will like Bethlehem."

At that moment, the Spirit filled Joseph, and he quoted, *"But you, Bethlehem… though you are small among the clans of Judah, out of you will come for me one who will be ruler over Israel, whose origins are from of old, from ancient times."*[1]

"Where is that scripture from?" Mary asked.

"I'm not sure, probably one of the prophets. It just leaped into my head," he answered as he prodded Lily to begin a slow amble toward his shop. In his mind, Joseph began making preparations for their journey to Bethlehem.

"Oh, Mary, are you sure this is a good time to travel? There will be at least five, maybe six days of walking or bumping along in this donkey cart before you reach Bethlehem," Mary's mother fretted as she put an extra roll of bedding into the cart. "And the road will be so crowded. The highways are being repaired. Herod will be moving troops. Merchants and pilgrims are already beginning to travel to Jerusalem for Passover. I don't know if you will find places to sleep."

"Mother, you worry too much." Mary was full of energy, excited about her trip. "We have almost two weeks before the first night of Passover. We'll go to Bethlehem and register and then return to Jerusalem to camp with the people from Nazareth. Father will be there. We'll share the Passover meal with him. Then we will stay for the seven days of Unleavened Bread."

For a long moment, Mary's mother studied her daughter's pregnant belly before wisely commenting, "Mary, you won't make it to all those events. Your baby is going to be born sooner than you realize, and I did want to be with you for the birth."

"Joseph will be with me," Mary confidently replied.

"Joseph? He's a man! Men are good for lifting, plowing, and building, but not for birthing," her mother scolded. "You need a midwife or an experienced woman who has had a lot of children. I told your father to talk to him." Her mother continued to load the cart. "Here's bread, oil, and salt. Don't use all the oil and salt for your meals. You will need some for the baby."

"Mother, you worry too much," Mary repeated.

"How can I not worry!" She gestured toward the packed cart. "It looks like you are moving away forever! I may never see my grandchild! When will I see you again?" She turned quickly and hurried back into the house so no one would see her tears.

"Joseph, my son, do you know the way?" Heli asked as he pulled his son-in-law aside.

"I've been to Jerusalem many times," Joseph answered, "and Bethlehem is just a half-day's journey beyond."

"Travel to Nain, then take the road to Beth Shan. There you will pick up the highway to Jerusalem." At this moment of parting, Heli seemed compelled to give instructions, so Joseph listened politely. "It is all right to go through Samaria. Just camp out or stay at the observant wayside inns. You have your own food and water, so you do not need to touch anything that may not be clean. I put an extra sack of roasted wheat in your cart, and there is grain for the donkey, and here"—Heli pressed a coin into Joseph's hand—"in case you need to pay a midwife."

"Thank you," Joseph responded. "I know you wish we would wait, but it is time to leave."

Heli nodded in resigned agreement.

"My tools are in the cart. We will stay for a while, either with my family in Bethlehem or in Jerusalem. I will find work. There is a lot of building going on throughout the country, especially in Jerusalem. You do not need to worry. I will take care of Mary and our new baby."

"You are a good man, Joseph," Heli responded. "Mary is a fortunate girl."

"When we return, no one will ask when the baby was born. No one will count the months," Joseph said.

"God go with you," Heli replied. Then both men turned to the task of hitching the donkey to the cart while Mary hugged her mother, and both women cried as they realized the uncertainty of the time when they would be together again.

Mary's mother had been right; the road to Jerusalem was crowded. Traders led camels loaded with merchandise to be sold in the city. Crews were making repairs on the roads. In preparation for the Passover crowds, Herod was moving an intimidating force of two thousand soldiers from Caesarea to Jerusalem.

The farther Mary and Joseph progressed toward the city of Jerusalem, the more crowded the road became. Whole delegations from various regions began filling the highway as they made an early pilgrimage to Jerusalem. At times, it seemed there wasn't room on the highway for the young couple with their little donkey cart.

Determined to make good time, Joseph pushed ahead of plodding pack animals, but when he came upon bands of pilgrims singing the songs of ascension from his ancestor, the psalmist, he would slow down and keep pace with them for a while. Then he would hear Mary's sweet voice as she sang the women's part, and he would sing and dance with the men. When the song ended, the men would exchange news from the areas of the country where they lived. It was a scene reenacted numerous times on all the roads leading to Jerusalem.

This was an early crowd, set on arriving and finding accommodations close to the Temple. Within a week, every room in every home in the city and beyond would be taken, then those arriving just before Passover would have to camp out, sometimes as far away as Bethany.

At the start of this Passover season, when Israel's roads were packed to capacity, an army of the heavenly hosts also marched along the Roman highway that ran north and south from Galilee to Jerusalem and beyond. Undetected by the crowd on the road, those angel warriors kept their stride even with the progress of the Jewish man in his midtwenties who led a donkey cart. Often resting in that cart, his wife, a fourteen-year-old girl, carried the commander in chief of all the heavenly hosts in her womb.

Those mighty warriors of heaven could not keep their eyes away from Mary. For them, it was mind-boggling to think that the Son of God, whom they had seen as Creator and Heavenly Ruler, was now a human-divine embryo. He had exchanged the golden structures and glorious rainbows of heaven for a dark human womb, a River of Life and a Sea of Glass for a fleshly umbilical cord filled with crimson blood, the majesty and adoration of all the beings of heaven for the parental love of this young Jewish couple. What love he had for mankind! What faith that his act of coming down to them and living among them would ultimately bring them back into face-to-face relationship with him!

Fallen angels fell into step beside their heavenly counterparts and whispered sedition. "The Creator is a fool!"

Following the orders of the Archangel Michael, the heavenly soldiers fixed their eyes forward on their angelic commander. Obediently, they refused to acknowledge their evil counterparts. Centuries before, they had debated with these angels in the heavenly courts. On the streets of gold, they had stood toe-to-toe, nose to nose, arguing the wisdom of Lucifer versus the Eternal Three-in-One. Then there had been that moment when, with drawn swords, they had sent Lucifer and his army tumbling over the walls of the celestial city into the void of space.

"A lot can happen on the road to Jerusalem." Satan, once called Lucifer, arrived to look over the situation in person. He fell into step beside Michael. "The road takes a sharp curve up ahead. My angels could spook the donkey and send the cart careening into the ditch. I'm sure the girl would be thrown out and seriously injured if not killed," the Evil One insidiously suggested.

"I would not try it!" the Archangel countered.

"You forget where you are!" Satan warned. "You are not walking on streets of gold. This is dirt!" He pointed to the dry dusty road. "My dirt! The Holy Spirit is not backing you up like a wall of fire. The Creator is now incapable of defending himself, and God Eternal sits in the throne room in heaven." With a triumphant laugh, the evil commander raised his hand and gave an offensive battle signal to his troops.

Two of his dark angels peeled off from their ranks and flew to the top of a boulder-strewn hill overlooking the road. Within seconds, a small avalanche of rocks and gravel cascaded down the hill.

Quickly, Michael raised a silver shofar to his lips. A series of staccato notes signaled his troops.

Angels flew to block the rockslide, to hold the reins of the donkey, and to shield Joseph and Mary.

In the middle of the road, Joseph stopped. Suddenly aware of a noise that was out of place, all his senses went on alert. He looked around and saw the rocks careening down the brown mountainside. It was too late to hurry past. The road was too crowded. He could not turn the cart around fast enough. All he could do was throw his sturdy body across the back of his little donkey, holding her in place with brute strength while he called, "Mary! Shield yourself!"

In an instant, the danger had passed. Miraculously, the rocks and boulders piled up at the edge of the road. Not even one piece of gravel skittered close to Joseph and Mary. The donkey remained calm, not kicking or braying. "You're a good girl, Lily," Joseph stood up and praised his faithful little animal.

Other animals had been on the road with their owners. Mary called to Joseph, "Did you see what just happened?"

"The rockslide stopped. Lily didn't bolt," Joseph replied.

"No, see that camel kneeling in the middle of the road?" Mary pointed behind them, where a drover was trying in vain to force his camel to get up and move on. "When the rockslide started, that camel got spooked and started running out of control toward us. Suddenly, it just stopped and knelt down."

Joseph stood pondering for a long moment. The other travelers on the road pushed past his stalled donkey cart. Finally, he said just one word, "Balaam!"

"The angel of the Lord stopped Balaam's donkey," Mary recounted a small part of the story.

Husband and wife looked at the rocks piled up beside the road and then exchanged meaningful glances. The hairs on the backs of their necks tickled, and little chills ran up and down their spines as they realized they were in the presence of spiritual beings. With a heightened sense of heavenly intervention in their lives, Joseph prodded their little donkey into motion, and once more, they became part of the endless stream of traffic moving toward the city of Jerusalem.

Afternoon shadows were lengthening as Joseph led their little donkey into the center of a U-shaped wayside inn. Fortunately, many of the travelers wanted to push on and reach Jerusalem, and so they bypassed the roadside hostel that was less than a day's journey from the city gates. After camping beside the road every night of the trip, Joseph and Mary were thankful to get a room, one of a number of bare cubicles that faced the court where animals munched their feed and men sat around the fire exchanging news from different areas of the Roman world.

There were many tasks to be accomplished before the Galilean couple could bring their day to a close. Together, Joseph and Mary launched into unloading their cart, caring for their animal, and cooking and eating their evening meal.

The stars had already scattered across the blanket of night when Joseph made up beds for Mary and himself. Mary lay down and fell asleep immediately, but Joseph felt restless, drawn to the fire and the male conversation in the courtyard. Without disturbing Mary, he left the cubicle that was their shelter. Casually, he moved toward the fire where he could see several men seated on the ground in deep conversation.

"Romans, Romans everywhere," one man complained. "The closer I get to Jerusalem, the more I see."

"And they always have their hands out for taxes!"

"Herod is the one who has his hand out for taxes. He uses our money to maintain his personal army. He's got over five thousand Syrian and Samaritan mercenaries wearing the scarlet tunic of Rome directly under his command. He has filled our streets with these soldiers!"

"He also uses our tax money to try to destroy our national identity and the sacred traditions of our fathers. He has desecrated our holy city with theaters and gymnasiums. In other cities, he has even constructed Temples to Roman gods! And he claims to be a Jew!" The man who was speaking punctuated his last sentence by tossing a heavy stick into the fire. A shower of sparks flew up. A few landed on the straw near Joseph, and he pounded them out with his hands while looking around to see who was speaking. The first man looked like a merchant and the second like a Pharisee.

"Herod is restoring the Temple.," the merchant attempted to insert a positive comment. "It's almost finished."

"And he has mounted the eagle of Rome above its gate! Herod has taken control of all its functions," the Pharisee resentfully countered. "People look at that grand structure, and they become as forgetful as old men. They forget that when Herod first became king over this region, he had the presiding high priest drowned in the swimming pool of the royal bathhouse. Then he brought in his own priests, Levites from the Jewish community in Babylon. He made them and their families powerful in the Temple. Every few years, the position of high priest goes to the man offering the largest bribe."

The merchant shrugged his shoulders and agreed, "Everyone knows there has been no legitimate heir to the position of high priest for more than a hundred and fifty years. The last direct descendant of the oldest son of Aaron fled to Egypt during the reign of terror before the revolt of the Maccabees. That priesthood has been serving the Jewish community in Egypt ever since. They even have their own Temple!"

"Herod brought in priests from the Jewish community in Babylon because they were more open to Hellenistic ideas," the Pharisee rejoined. "He could have just as easily brought in a priest from the line of Zadok, from the Temple in Egypt!" Then shaking his head in sad resignation, he asserted, "But a priest with a legitimate heritage would be quickly killed because he would pose a threat to the power of Herod. Never forget, Herod does not have a legitimate heritage! Our king is not really Jewish!"

The men in the circle murmured their agreement, and the Pharisee continued, "Even with his own handpicked man serving as high priest, Herod is so insecure that he has taken possession of the sacred garments of the priesthood. They are stored in the Fortress of Antonia. The high priest has to humbly request to use them on feast days."

From the shadows near the animal stalls, a man announced, "Herod's on his deathbed."

"That old goat has been on his deathbed for as long as I can remember," another traveler commented. "If he's going to die, I wish he would hurry up and do it!"

Joseph looked from man to man. In the firelight, their faces were grim, like the topic of Romans in the land God had given to Abraham. The only face Joseph could not see clearly was the face of the man in the shadows. He seemed to be deliberately staying back away from the firelight, and yet he was part of the conversation.

"Yes, before his body is cold, we will appeal to Caesar, then maybe we can appoint our own high priest, a descendant of Aaron through Zadok, anointed according to the directions of God Almighty," the Pharisee inserted.

"Careful," someone warned, "you never know who might be listening."

"I know a servant in Herod's household," the man in the shadows spoke again. "He said that Herod has spies everywhere. I know for a fact that when Herod was healthier, he used to disguise himself as a common person and visit inns and other public gathering places just to hear what the people were saying! Within a few days, people would disappear. They ended up in his torture chambers. He would torture them until they gave him names."

There was a rustling of straw, an uncomfortable stirring as everyone turned this way and that trying to get a good look at the faces of the men they were conversing with around the fire. No one offered introductions. Joseph looked hard at each face he could see. They were all good Jewish faces. He strained to see into the shadows, but all he could see was the silhouette of the man who seemed to know so much about the inner workings of Herod's court.

The merchant turned to Joseph. "You're from Galilee. What's the news from up north?"

"I haven't spoken. How did you know where I was from?" Joseph responded in surprise.

The merchant laughed. "I heard you speak to your wife earlier. You can always tell a Galilean by the way he speaks."

Joseph shrugged good-naturedly and began to relate the news that he would be most aquainted with. "Herod seems to have completed his building projects in Caesarea. He has even built a huge stone breakwater that goes out into the sea. Ships in the harbor are now protected from storms. I understand that the breakwater is so big that on it, he has built accommodations for seamen and paths for walking."

"Are you a craftsman?" It was the voice from the shadows.

"A carpenter," Joseph answered, not wanting to give any more information.

"There is always work for carpenters and stone masons these days," the merchant commented.

"I hear our pretend-to-be-Jewish king Herod also built a Temple to the emperor in Caesarea. It overlooks that fine harbor you are describing," the Pharisee added. The bitterness in his voice was undisguised.

Joseph continued to update the men on Herod's building projects along the Great Sea and in the region of Galilee. "He's built a palace for himself at Sepphoris. I expect he will begin to rebuild the city soon."

"He wouldn't need to rebuild the city if he had not destroyed it when he first came to the throne," the Pharisee asserted, and the men close to the fire murmured their assent.

"Herod's twin sons are dead, strangled by order of their father!" the voice from the shadows informed.

Joseph felt a chill run up his spine. When members of the royal family died, it seemed that Joseph's own people suffered the consequences.

"They were grown men with families, his heirs to the throne!" the merchant exclaimed.

The voice from the shadows replied, "Evidently, there were rumors that they wanted their inheritance before their father's death. Herod's torturers obtained witnesses against them. It was sufficient for their execution."

"I'm not surprised," the Pharisee cynically quipped. "He had already killed one of his wives, the daughter of a ruling high priest. It's all about legitimacy. Herod is paranoid about his ancestry, so he eliminates all competition."

"It's not healthy to be a member of Herod's family," the merchant commented.

"Now his oldest son, Antipater, is next in line for the throne." It was the voice from the shadows again supplying inside information.

"Antipater? I thought he had been passed over and was no longer favored by the king." The merchant seemed to be trying to get the story straight.

"He is back in favor now," the voice from the shadows responded. "At the moment, Herod cannot do enough for him."

"He won't take his father's place without the blessing of the emperor," the Pharisee added knowingly.

"I suspect this son can forget inheriting the throne. He'll probably be dead like the others before his father takes that final breath." It was the voice from the shadows predicting more violence in the royal residences.

"Do you see anyone tearing their clothes and pulling ashes from the fire like I tore my clothes when I mourned for my brothers? Three hundred Pharisees—Herod executed them less than a year ago!" the Pharisee spoke through gritted teeth.

In the firelight, Joseph could see emotion play across the man's face. It was obvious to him that this man had been close to the incident. Maybe he had barely escaped with his life.

"Those men spoke the truth," the Pharisee continued with a trembling voice. "Herod makes claims he has no right to make. He is no Jew and no friend of the Jews."

At this moment, Joseph expected a response from the man in the shadows, but nothing was said. Joseph turned his head and looked, but the man seemed to have disappeared. Around the fire, all eyes followed the direction of Joseph's gaze.

The merchant quickly stood and walked over to the place where the man had been. "He's gone!"

By the eerie light of the fire, each man looked into the eyes of the others and saw fear. Was this man a spy for the king? Without another word, each man returned to his cubicle. Joseph lay down across the open doorway, making his body an obstacle that someone would have to cross before entering. Every fiber of his being was on alert.

The Spirit hovered close and then flowed through Joseph's mind, pouring the words of the psalmist over his anxious thoughts. *"He who dwells in the shelter of the Most High will rest in the shadow of the Almighty. I will say of the LORD, 'He is my refuge and my fortress, my God in whom I trust."*[2] As he continued speaking, the Holy Spirit could see Joseph's body relax and his breathing settle into the steady rhythm of sleep.

That night, Joseph slept lightly, dreaming of angels with drawn swords guarding their sleeping place. He woke for a short time when he heard someone leave and then slept again until he heard another person move his animal out of the courtyard and onto the road. At first light, he and Mary were back on the road to Jerusalem.

Both good and evil angels continued to escort the couple. Once more, Satan positioned himself beside Michael. "You moved quickly to stop the rockslide, but everything in my kingdom is not so easily controlled." With a sweeping wave of his arm, he gestured toward the crowded highway. "People—they get to choose their actions, and usually they go along with what I suggest. To some, those most susceptible to my suggestions, I have given a portion of my power. My angels guard them, and my spirits assist them. Consider my subject, Herod the Great! What would he do if he learned that the Jewish Messiah was about to be born?" The Evil One broke into sadistic laughter, signaled his evil troops, and together, they soared away ahead of Mary and Joseph toward the city of Jerusalem.

Michael lifted his hand and signaled his troops into a song that the Holy Spirit had once placed in the mind of David.

A thousand may fall at your side,
ten thousand at your right hand,
but it will not come near you.
You will only observe with your eyes
and see the punishment of the wicked.
If you make the Most High your dwelling—
even the LORD who is my refuge—
then no harm will befall you,
no disaster will come near your tent,³
for God commands his angels to guard you.

Before noon, Joseph could see the Tower of David, the citadel that stood beside the gate to the upper city. Progress toward the city gradually slowed until Joseph and Mary found themselves stopped, waiting in line while tax collectors examined the merchandise of the caravans ahead of them.

Slowly, ever so slowly, they moved toward the city's northern entrance. It was the morning of the preparation day before the Sabbath, and Joseph kept an eye on the sun while he made plans. "Mary, we are almost at the gate. As soon as we get past the tax collectors, we can cross the city. I know a very direct route. Even though it is only a week before Passover, I think we will be able to find a place to stay over the Sabbath."

Mary smiled. Her husband was a man she could rely on. It made her feel so secure, and the thought of a real bed and a roof over her head—what luxury! "Tell me when to start looking for homes that are accepting guests. My father told me that nearly every home in Jerusalem and the surrounding towns is an inn. Each family has set aside a room or two for guests. You just have to look for a home that has a sheet hung out in front," she replied.

"It won't be for a while," Joseph answered. "First, we will pass Herod's palace." Then he joked, "I don't think he is entertaining guests of our social status."

Mary chuckled and replied, "I'm not sure his home is observant! We wouldn't want to stay there anyway! How about his neighbors?"

"The high priest? The leading members of the Sanhedrin or maybe a very wealthy Pharisee?" Joseph was caught up in their private bantering game.

"Now I'm not sure we would be observant enough for them," Mary responded, "even if we immersed ourselves seven times."

"When we get past the Upper City and the market, then we will start seeing homes that will welcome us for the Sabbath," Joseph answered. "I have stayed many times, and there is an unwritten law of hospitality. A Jew, especially one living in Jerusalem, must always be ready and willing to entertain strangers. Most homes do not even ask for payment."

As they approached the entrance, Mary got out of the cart to allow the tax collector to inspect their belongings. Then, wide-eyed, she walked beside her husband past the fortress-like palace of their tyrant king and the homes of the very wealthy. Most homes were concealed by high walls and shut off from public view by massive gates, but still, the impression of great wealth lingered and dazzled a small-town girl. "Joseph, I didn't know anyone lived in houses as large as these," she commented.

"Don't envy them," Joseph said. "Remember the commandment, *You shall not covet your neighbor's house. You shall not covet your neighbor's wife, or his manservant, or maidservant, his ox or donkey, or anything that belongs to your neighbor.*"[4]

"Oh, Joseph, I wasn't really wanting what is theirs," Mary answered. "It's just so amazing that anyone has so much."

"Things are not always as they seem," Joseph replied. "Did you notice that you are the only woman on this road?"

Mary looked around, and sure enough, there were very few people on the road, and all of them were men. "Why?" she asked.

"The women of the upper class are behind those walls," he answered. "They rarely come out, and when they do, their faces are completely covered." He reached over and rearranged Mary's mantle so it concealed more of her face.

"They never go to the well to get water or to the market to buy or sell?" Mary asked in disbelief.

"They have servants for that," Joseph replied.

"I feel sorry for them," Mary responded. As they left the homes of the wealthy and influential behind, she never looked back.

Feeling the push of the sun that was now beginning a descending path toward the western wall of the city, they hurried through the market. Ignoring the hawkers who were making their final sales before closing up their stalls, Mary and Joseph headed toward the working class homes near the southern wall.

"Now," Joseph said, "start looking."

Here and there, along the street, Mary saw sheets hung out, a sign that a guest room was available. "That one!" Mary announced, for no other reason than she liked the crispness of the sheet that hung over the courtyard wall.

Joseph went to the gate and called, "Greetings and peace to this household."

The woman of the house opened the gate, and Joseph, pointing to the sheet, asked, "Do you have a room for the night and the Sabbath hours? My wife and I will be staying until first light of the first day of the week."

"Are you ritually clean?" the woman asked.

"Yes," Joseph responded. "We have been traveling from Nazareth, but we have touched nothing that would make us unclean. Even so, it is my plan to go to the Pool of Siloam and purify myself before the sun sets. I am sure my wife would also like to bathe in the facilities of your home."

"You are welcome to stay and share our Sabbath meal," the woman said as she opened both sides of the gate to allow the donkey and cart to enter her courtyard.

The warrior angels under the command of the Archangel Michael surrounded the house while the Spirit hovered over the property, blessing this home with peace and prosperity.

On the first day of that week, the road running south from Jerusalem was clogged with travelers. As Mary and Joseph continued on toward Bethlehem, they were now moving against the overwhelming flow of traffic into the holy city. With the Passover beginning in five days, merchants and pilgrims packed the highway. It took constant vigilance not to run headlong into a string of pack animals accompanied by their drovers or to be overwhelmed by an eager band of singing pilgrims. It took equal vigilance to avoid the dung of the many animals that had already traveled this road.

Joseph's eyes were on the road, his mind on avoiding catastrophe. He gave little thought to his wife, who walked beside him, watching her step while doggedly keeping pace with his long-legged stride.

Short of breath, Mary grasped the side of the donkey cart and let it pull her along, taking some of the effort out of what seemed to be an endless journey. Since Nazareth, the road had been steadily climbing. Going up to Mount Zion literally meant going up, and now, after resting over the Sabbath, the last leg of the journey seemed to take more effort than all the previous days of walking. She moved a few steps closer to the edge of the road to allow a caravan of camels to pass them. It seemed to Mary that she was carrying more of a load than those pack animals. Her breath came in gasps.

"This is a long walk for a lady who could give birth at any time." Once more, Satan had swooped in on the heavenly escort and now took delight in trying to intimidate Michael, who led the heavenly band of warriors. "If I delay their progress, she will never make it to Bethlehem."

Michael ignored the enemy of heaven, keeping his eyes on the Spirit of God Most Holy, who hovered encouragingly over the couple as they made their way to the royal birthplace of King David. "It's not much farther," the Holy Spirit whispered into Mary's mind.

"I am Lord of this Earth!" Satan announced. As he spoke, his face changed from the mild human-like face into that of a snorting ox. "You cannot just ignore me!" He flew ahead, positioning his massive body so he blocked Michael's view of the Holy Spirit. "You are such a fool! Don't you know what I can do to you?" The evil commander placed his right hand menacingly on the hilt of the heavy sword that hung from his golden belt. "I could run you through with this weapon, and now that the Creator is in that girl's womb, there is no one to recreate the damaged parts of your body! You are as vulnerable as we are!"

Responding without hesitation, Michael drew his ever-burning sword, a weapon capable of destroying angelic bodies.

Satan drew his own glowing sword and advanced!

As their blazing blades clashed, sparks flew.

Then the Spirit flared. The fire of his being took the shape of an enormous fiery sword. *"I am God and there is no other!"* The Sword of the Spirit moved closer to the battling angels. *"By myself I have sworn, my mouth has uttered in all integrity a word that will not be revoked."*[5] and you, Bethlehem in the land of Judah have been designated by the Eternal Ruler. From you will come the Messiah who will redeem all the descendants of Adam." With one swift stroke, the Sword of the Spirit came down on the sword of Satan, the enemy of heaven.

Satan's weapon fell from his hand, losing its fire as it struck the ground. With a scream of frustrated rage, the evil commander changed faces once more, and like an eagle, he took flight toward the relative safety of the nearby hills.

From that distance, he countered, "That girl, Mary!" He pointed to the young Jewish girl holding onto the wagon to assist herself as she moved her very pregnant body along the road. "You'll see! She will have that baby before she reaches your prophetic destination." Satan then pointed once more, this time down the road toward Bethlehem. As he pointed, he threw scripture back in the face of the Spirit, *"The kings of the earth take their stand and the rulers gather together against the* LORD *and against his Anointed One!"*[6]

A detachment of soldiers from the Herodian, Herod's fortress south of Bethlehem, marched up the road toward Jerusalem. It was a force meant to bolster the troops already attached to the Fortress of Antonia that overlooked the Temple. and to remind the Jewish population that Rome expected order, especially when the city was packed to capacity for this spring feast.

Calmly, the Spirit raised his fiery hand, and Michael and his warrior angels broke into song. *"The One enthroned in heaven laughs; the* LORD *scoffs at them. Then he rebukes them in his anger and terrifies them in his wrath, saying, 'I have installed my King on Zion, my holy hill. I will proclaim the decree of the* LORD*!'"*[7]

There were eight hundred marching men. They were Syrian mercenaries, accompanied by Roman officers on horseback and wagons full of supplies. They filled the road. Joseph heard the troops before he saw them. He had no choice but to quickly find a spot to pull off the road. He urged his little donkey to the edge and over the soft shoulder into a rocky field. Mary followed, off balance, stumbling down the shallow embankment. Joseph caught her, and then they stood together watching the might of Rome acting on orders from their pseudo–Jewish king.

"I hope this festive season does not turn into another massacre," Mary whispered. Under Herod, the smallest disturbance, especially during the feasts, was often reason for a slaughter of prominent and pious Jews.

Joseph nodded in silent agreement before turning his attention to the cart and donkey.

It was while they waited for an opportunity to climb back up to the road that Mary first began to feel discomfort. Her back began to ache and her abdomen began to cramp. She reached behind, rubbing her lower back and shifting her weight to find a more comfortable way to stand.

Joseph didn't notice. He was busy checking the wagon's wheels and the donkey's hooves. As soon as the last soldier passed, he began urging Lily to climb back up onto the road, but the dirt on the shoulder was soft, and she couldn't get a firm foothold. It made the little animal skittish. Her ears went back; she brayed, sat on her haunches, and refused to try again.

"Oh, no!" Mary groaned to herself. She had so wanted to get back on the road and crawl into the wagon and ride. She remembered the prayer of the psalmist and whispered, "*O LORD, be not far off; O my Strength, come quickly to help me.*"[8]

"It will be all right," the Spirit assured.

Immediately, Mary sensed a new confidence and strength. She knew she could go on.

"We're going to have to travel carefully beside the road and try again farther down," Joseph said to Mary as he led the donkey along the edge of the field. The cart bumped over rocks, and both Mary and Joseph knew they were in danger of breaking a wheel.

Unselfishly putting aside her own discomfort, Mary followed behind the bumping cart. She didn't want to bother Joseph when he had problems to solve. They tried two more places before Lily cooperated and pulled the cart back onto the highway. Once on the road, Joseph paused to check the wheels and axle before continuing. Mary leaned heavily against the cart, feeling more discomfort than she was used to. Waiting for Joseph to finish so he could help her climb into the bundles of bedding, she rested her head on the rough-hewn side of the cart and closed her eyes.

"Mary?" She felt Joseph sweep her traveling mantle back so he could see her face. She opened her eyes to see worry etched on his handsome face. "The baby? Are you going to have the baby?"

"I don't know," she answered. "I just don't feel well."

Joseph looked around; not a house was in sight. As far as he could see, there were only rolling hills and flocks of sheep making their slow journey toward Jerusalem and the Temple. markets. "Get in the cart," he suggested as he helped her climb up and settle in. "I thought we had more time," he said almost to himself.

"We do." Mary tried to reassure him. "I think we have time. It took Elizabeth from before sunrise until well after sunset to have baby John, and I'm not sure that what I am feeling is even the beginning of birth. Let's just go on."

Joseph picked up the donkey's reins and began to lead her once more. The traffic moving in the direction of Jerusalem had thinned out, as most travelers were either camping or reaching their destination before sunset. Joseph walked briskly, feeling an urgency to arrive at the home of his cousin. Thank the Almighty the road was now mostly empty.

Mary turned this way and that, trying to find a comfortable position. Finally, she settled in, her body growing accustomed to the rocking rhythm of the cart. One verse of a psalm that she had sung as a child began running through her head. Like the rotation of the wooden wheels, it went round and round in her brain.

The Spirit of God sang to her, "*Wait for the LORD; be strong and take heart and wait for the LORD.*" As the words repeated, her body relaxed; she closed her eyes and slept.

The donkey cart stopped moving. Mary opened her eyes. Her back still ached a bit, but she definitely felt better. Sleep had helped. She wondered how long she had slept. It must have been awhile because the sun was now quite low on the horizon. She sat up. "Joseph, are we there?" She looked around. There were no houses, only a memorial monument standing on one side of the road and Joseph looking carefully at one of Lily's hooves.

"Lily's got a stone in her hoof," Joseph said as he came around the back of the cart to get a small file to remove the stone and smooth the hoof.

"I'll get out and stretch my legs," Mary offered, and Joseph lifted and eased her over the back of the cart. "Is that Rachel's Tomb?" she asked gazing over his shoulder at the one giant upright stone with flat stones laid around it.

"Yes," Joseph answered as he rearranged the contents of the cart to get to his tools. He looked at the sun, nearly touching the horizon. "I had expected to be at my cousin's home by now," he commented. "It has never taken so long to travel from Jerusalem to Bethlehem." He shook his head in disbelief.

Mary patted him consolingly on the shoulder before taking a few steps to the edge of the highway.

The ground was level. It was an easy walk from the road. Feeling the pull of her heritage, she strolled over to the gravesite, a monument to love and sorrow. Slowly, Mary made her way all the way around it, counting eleven flat white stones: one for each of the boys, excluding Benjamin who had just been born, she surmised. With all the grace of a camel carrying a lopsided load, she lowered her body to sit on one of the stones. It felt good to sit on a stationary object. She stretched out her sandaled feet and studied her swollen ankles. She could hardly believe that her usually thin, robust body had gone through so many changes, and now this over-sized body felt like a permanent condition. *If I keep growing,* she mused, *even a tent maker will not have enough fabric to cover me!*

A quick glance confirmed that Joseph was still working on Lily's hoof. Mary's eyes followed the shadowy contours of the grassy hills. A flock of sheep was entering a hillside fold for the night. Mindlessly, her fingers slipped from the coolness of the rock and played with the strands of wild grass that grew between the stones. She twisted the rough blades and tugged. They came out of the ground with soil clinging to their roots—the land of her heritage! Her fingers picked the soil from the roots. This soil had been promised to Abraham. Isaac and his bride, Rebecca, had made their home and pitched their tents in this dirt; so much history was in this soil.

The sun was now touching the western hilltops. In her imagination, Mary pictured a somber caravan on the horizon. It seemed that she could see it against the sunset: the patriarch, Jacob, walking ahead of a two-wheeled wagon carrying the body of his beloved Rachel. More wagons followed carrying massive flat stones, and beside each wagon walked a son of Israel. Leah, the mother of Judah and the ancestor of Mary, followed, weeping with each step. She had delivered baby Benjamin and heard her sister's last words: "This is the son of my grief."

"Mary, women die in childbirth!"

Startled, Mary looked around. There was no one except Joseph, who was taking a quick look at the donkey's other hooves.

Fear crawled up her spine. "Rachel prayed for a child, and God opened her womb." Fear paused, letting all the implications and possibilities run through Mary's mind.

The sun suddenly disappeared behind the tops of the trees along the western hills, and a thin cold wind seemed to whip around the upright stone. Mary shivered and then took comfort in the memory of the compelling words of Gabriel, "*Fear not. You have found favor with God!*"[10] In the gradually waning light, she saw Joseph coming toward her, reaching his hand out to help her to her feet. His grasp was firm and strong. It felt good and safe. She strained against his strength to pull her body into an upright position.

"Oh!" A look of surprise and mortification washed over her face.

"Mary?" Joseph asked in alarm.

"I'm wet." In spite of the fact that they had been living together for several months now, she felt embarrassed, thankful that the layers of robes that she wore concealed most of the wetness she felt. "As I got up, there was this sudden gush. There was nothing I could—"

The last word of her sentence caught in her throat, and both hands went to her belly as the first definite contraction cramped, peaked, and then diminished.

"Joseph!" That one word was filled with shock and the irrevocable fact that the process of birth had begun.

Ignoring Mary's protests and the wetness that seeped through her robes, Joseph swept her into his arms and carried her back to the cart. "We'll stop at the first house," he promised as he pulled out a small handheld lamp so it would be ready to light when complete darkness overtook them, then he hurried forward to lead Lily on toward Bethlehem.

"Their problems have just begun," Satan announced as he regrouped his dark horde of demonic spirits and fallen angels behind the monument to Rachel. Like bloodsucking bats swarming at sunset, they began positioning for another attack. "Spook the donkey," Satan ordered. "Make sure he runs off the road and that the cart is damaged beyond repair. That girl is going to have her baby in this field."

"Exposure," the spirit of Murder suggested.

"Oxygen deprivation and brain damage," the spirit of Confusion offered.

Receiving a command from the throne room in the sanctuary of heaven, the Archangel Michael blew one long note on his shofar.

Confusion broke out in the evil ranks. Demonic spirits howled in pain and disorientation. "No! No, not the trumpet of the Lord!" They covered their ears and screamed as the prophetic significance of that trumpet blast hit them—Yeshua the Creator was coming!

Above the darkening road to Bethlehem, the heralds repeated Michael's trumpet blast. The army of the Lord was on the move, preparing the way for their Creator to make his entrance.

Michael gave the command, "Attack!" A single unbroken blast emanated from a thousand heavenly trumpets, producing a sound wave that physically struck Satan's forces and sent them reeling backward.

"The trumpet of God and the Sword of his Spirit!" the angels on the right side of the road shouted. From silver sheaths, they drew their fiery swords, glowing beams of light that could slice through the paths of energy that made up the bodies of spiritual beings.

"Pursue!" Michael shouted, and one regiment of warriors flew, chasing the demonic horde.

At the approach of God's loyal angels, the evil spirits scattered amid terrified howls, each one seeking a hill to hide behind or a cave to enter. With sin-weakened shields, the fallen angels defended themselves long enough to resist the advancing forces, but they could not hold their positions. They too had to find cover or be captured.

Only Satan refused to flee. He hid behind the upright stone on Rachel's grave, and as the spirits of Doubt, Fear, and Dishonesty flew past him, he reached out an evil hand and drew them into his hiding place.

"Praise God in his heavenly sanctuary! Praise the Spirit, Mighty Sword of the Heavens!" The attacking regiment of angels returned, triumphant.

The demonic forces did not regroup. Another attack did not come. The angels on either side of the Roman road to Bethlehem began an antiphonal chorus.

"Praise the Creator, unsurpassed in generosity."

The column of angels on one side of the road sang, and the column of angels on the other side of the answered.

> *Praise him for his acts of power!*
> *Praise him for his surpassing greatness.*
> *Praise him with the sounding of the trumpet!*[11]

Back and forth, across the road, above the heads of the weary couple, the heavenly hosts sang to Father God on his throne, to the Spirit whose presence surrounded Mary and Joseph, and to Yeshua the Creator, now a soon-to-be-born infant son.

Chapter 6

A Baby in a Manger

While they were there, the time came for the baby to be born, and she gave birth to her firstborn, a son. She wrapped him in cloths and placed him in a manger because there was no room for them in the inn.

—Luke 2:6–7

Taking advantage of the faintly glowing twilight, Joseph paused and surveyed the road. The empty highway stretched ahead and behind. All the other travelers who had earlier clogged this main thoroughfare had found their destination for the night, and now they were alone on the road to Bethlehem. In the cart, Mary moaned softly, and Joseph anxiously scanned both sides of the road. No dwelling was in sight.

I should have known that I could not travel against so much traffic just before Passover! We should have stayed in Jerusalem, Joseph berated himself. He urged the little donkey into a trot, jogging alongside. Each time he heard a whimper or moan from the bumping cart, he pushed both the donkey and himself harder.

The last faint glow of twilight completely disappeared behind the western hills. A few gray fingers of moonlight slipped through the clouds. It was not enough light. The sky was overcast, and the road was dark. Joseph lit the hand-sized lamp that travelers carried in the darkness. It only illuminated the road for a short distance. "God of Israel and my ancestor David, help us!" It was the only prayer Joseph could think of, but he said it over and over as he pushed on toward Bethlehem.

He tried to plan but could only admit to himself that he did not know anything about bringing babies into the world. Why had it taken so long to travel from Jerusalem to Bethlehem? "Lord, we're in trouble!" He had planned to be with his relatives in Bethlehem, to hire a midwife, to have his aunts and cousins assist. But now there was no chance that he was going to push his donkey to make the steep climb up the hill to where the center of the town of Bethlehem sat, let alone make it to the other side of town where his family lived. Mary moaned again. "God of Israel, direct us to a house with a guest room. Provide an experienced woman." He sucked air into his lungs, and they burned with each breath. His body screamed for rest, but he kept up the pace. It could not be much farther.

He glanced at the lamp in his hand. The oil was nearly gone, and their extra oil was somewhere beneath the bundles in the cart. Soon they would be engulfed in total blackness. He did not want to ask Mary to get out of the cart so he could find the oil. Forward, forward, keep going, find a place for Mary, and get help. O God, help! Mary is crying. Joseph no longer paid attention to what his feet stepped on. He just kept moving. It couldn't be much farther.

With a tiny flicker and a whiff of smoke, the flame on the handheld lamp died. Joseph paused. He tossed the empty lamp into the cart and then bent double, trying to recover from his exertion. His breath came in great painful gasps, and between them, he heard Mary catching her breath and then crying softly for a few seconds.

"Look ahead, Joseph," a voice in his head spoke over the pounding of the blood in his brain.

With great effort, he lifted his head. A tiny point of light flickered in the blackness. A lamp! A lamp in a window! "Mary,

I see a light!" Without hesitation, he picked up the lead rope and once more urged Lily forward.

The house turned out to be very humble. As Joseph approached, he was struck by the smallness of the place, probably only two rooms, a small courtyard, and a stable. The wooden gate to the courtyard opened even before Joseph had an opportunity to call the traditional greeting.

"Who's there?" a shaky voice inquired.

"Travelers. Joseph of Nazareth and his wife," Joseph replied.

"Friend," an old man stepped through the gate, "you are traveling late tonight."

"We were delayed," Joseph responded, "and now we need a place to sleep, a room for the night. We can go no farther."

"I'm afraid I cannot help you," the man spoke with great politeness and sympathy. "I am just a poor man with a very small home. I have already given all of my extra sleeping space to another man on his way to Jerusalem for Passover. You are very late. I don't think you will find a room in any of the other homes of Bethlehem tonight either."

At that moment, Mary softly moaned through another contraction.

"Is someone injured?" The old man's voice quivered as if he was frightened, but he took a few curious steps toward the cart.

Joseph stepped in front of him. "My wife is with child, and it seems her time has come."

"Oh, I see." His voice returned to normal, and he stroked his white beard while he contemplated the situation. "When the ewes drop their lambs, there is no better place than a clean stable. My hay is fresh. There is only a cow and an old she-goat in there. It is all I have to offer, but I believe it is the best you can do tonight."

Under normal circumstances, Joseph would have never considered bringing Mary into a stable to have her baby, but tonight, the offer sounded like hospitality fit for a king. "Do you have a wife? Is there a woman who can assist us?" Joseph asked.

"My wife has delivered many a lamb and a few children." He put his head back inside the door to his house and called, "Zepporah! It's lambing time again."

Joseph felt his body flood with relief. "Thank you so much. The stable will be a blessing."

Mary let her breath out slowly in a long relieved sigh. That last contraction had been stronger than any before. The flickering light from a handheld lamp shined in her face. She opened her eyes to look into the wind-toughened, wrinkled smile of an old woman.

"I'm Zepporah," she said. Her voice was very soft and confident. "Your husband tells me you are having a baby, maybe tonight!"

"Yes," Mary responded, but she could not finish the thought until the contraction passed. She felt a capable hand on her abdomen. It rested there, measuring the length and strength of the contraction.

"You are on your way to becoming a mother, but it will be a while," Zepporah stated. "Shammah, make a bed of hay in the stable and tie the cow and the goat behind the house," she called instructions to her husband. "And now," she said to Mary, "call your husband. He needs to help you out of this cart."

"I'm here." Joseph didn't need to be called. He moved a few bundles out of the way and helped Mary over the back of the cart.

Before he could put an arm around Mary to lead her into the animal shed, Zepporah was there, supporting Mary and giving orders. "Get her some dry clothes. Bring the bedding." The two women walked slowly toward the stable. With each step, Zepporah issued more directions for the men. "Shammah, I need warm water from the pot near the cooking fire and clean rags."

"Your wife is in very capable hands," Shammah commented to Joseph in passing.

"Praise God," Joseph sincerely replied.

"I will accept whatever you think is proper payment," Shammah added.

Joseph stopped in his tracks, a little surprised, and then answered, "We will discuss it in the morning." For a Jewish householder to ask for payment for opening his home to a fellow Jew for the night was an unheard-of breach of the unwritten law of hospitality that pervaded the land, especially under these circumstances.

Around that humble house, the heavenly warriors closed ranks. Shoulder to shoulder, they formed an angelic hedge, and above them, the Holy Spirit hovered over the stable, every eye fixed on the scene below.

From a distance, Satan had followed the progress of the couple. In the company of several of his most effective spirits, he swooped down on the little house close to one of David's wells. Arrogantly, he soared by the Holy Spirit with his demonic spirits in tow. "This is the property of Shammah, the old shepherd," Satan announced. "He has left a door open for me."

Without comment, the Holy Spirit let Satan and his demons pass. He knew a spirit of Fear made his home in this place. Fear ran the old shepherd's life, making him wary of every nighttime noise. That was the reason the shepherd had opened the gate even before Joseph could call. A spirit of Doubt also lived in Shammah's home. The old shepherd doubted the promises of God, so he secretly hoarded untithed coins in stone jars on a stone shelf inside his well. His home had the appearance of poverty, but that was a staged lie. The lie allowed a spirit of Dishonesty to also reside in Shammah's home."

"You are limited!" the Holy Spirit announced as he drew an invisible-to-the-human-eye fiery circle on the hay-strewn floor of the stable. The circle included everything but the corners of the stable. "Stay outside the perimeter," he commanded.

"I only needed a small space in the garden," Satan tauntingly replied. "Just one fruit-bearing tree!"

Joseph stood in the gateless doorway to the stable. He saw that Zepporah had laid a large piece of cloth over a pile of fresh hay. Mary lay on that, wearing only a short thin undergarment but protected from the night air by a woolen blanket. Under her head, a rolled-up sheepskin made a comfortable pillow. "Mary, how are you doing?" Joseph came over and knelt down beside her.

"This is better than the cart," Mary answered, and then another contraction took over.

Joseph stroked her forehead, pushing her hair back from her face as she grimaced and whimpered through the peak of the pain.

"It's going to be a long night, sir." Zepporah brought a bowl of broth up to Mary's lips. "She has not even begun to push, and she is so small, like a very young virgin. I don't see how she ever came to be with child." Immediately, she blushed, as she realized that her comment had been improper. In an effort to whisk away her own embarrassment, she quickly waved her free hand in the air as if throwing away her words. "Never mind. It is none of my business."

Through the next contraction, Joseph continued to stroke Mary's head.

"You might want to catch some sleep in the courtyard," Zepporah suggested.

"No," Joseph replied. "Mary and I are doing this together." This, he wasn't sure what this entailed, but it had been important enough for angels to visit. It involved the Spirit of God Most Holy. It was an event he was not going to miss.

"You don't want to be involved in this process." From a dark corner, the spirit of Doubt tried to dissuade Joseph. "This is women's work. It is messy and unclean. You should wash and then remain clean."

"There is water near the cooking fire. At least go into the courtyard and clean your feet and hands, then you can rejoin us if you still wish to do so," Zepporah said.

Mary was whimpering again. He didn't like to see her in pain. The whole idea of the processes of birth made him uneasy, but as he stood up, he said to Mary, "I'll be back shortly."

There were, in the fields, shepherds keeping watch over the flocks designated for the Temple. services in Jerusalem. From the blowing of the trumpets that announced the first evening of Passover until the end of the Feast of Unleavened Bread, thousands of lambs would be sacrificed. Day after day, these flocks gradually made their way from the grazing areas around Bethlehem to the Sheep Gate in Jerusalem.

"Forty-eight, forty-nine, fifty, fifty-one—that's all of my year-old males." The last shepherd added his carefully selected lambs to the Passover lambs already in the large stone sheepfold on one of the hills just north of Bethlehem. He placed a temporary gate of briars over the entrance and then moved toward the small campfire that had been built only a body's-length away. A pot of lentil stew was simmering. A basket of fruit and another basket of flat bread sat nearby. One by one, the men pulled their bundled blankets close to the fire and found a comfortable place to sit or stretch out. They were old friends, regulars on the sheep route to Jerusalem. They shared the grass and water for their flocks, and now they shared the evening and a meal.

"Oved!" Nahum tossed his friend a plate-sized piece of flat bread.

"Do you think I'm not on my toes tonight?" Oved responded with jovial baiting as he easily caught the bread. He went to the fire to fill his wooden bowl with lentils.

"Just because you were able to name all the kings of both Israel and Judah in order last night, do not think you will remain superior as we discuss tonight's topic," Nahum challenged.

"Tonight's topic?" Oved bantered.

Everyone chuckled in response, knowing that they were in for an entertaining evening of matching memory and wit.

"Messianic prophecies!" Nahum announced. "Tonight we will see who can quote and name the source for the most Messianic prophecies."

"Do we have to expound on them also?" Toviah asked.

"If you can," Nahum answered. "It would certainly make the evening more interesting."

"And long," Ehud inserted. "The sages debate this topic endlessly. They never reach a unified conclusion."

"Actually, since Herod has been so obsessed with possible threats to his throne, no one reads a Messianic prophecy in the synagogues or even suggests the coming of a Messiah for fear of being thrown into one of his dungeons," Toviah stated.

"Or being strangled like his twin sons," Oved added while hanging his head to the side in imitation of a broken neck.

"Well, there are no spies in this company," Nahum asserted, "so we can debate freely the words of the prophets."

"Then I shall begin," Oved announced. He set his bowl of lentils on the ground to cool and began, "From the first Torah reading of the year, In the Beginning, *And I will put enmity between you and the woman, and between your offspring and hers; he will crush your head, and you will strike his heel.*"[1]

"Explain," Toviah challenged.

"This scripture tells the story of our first parents, Adam and Eve. They are being put out of the garden. God is speaking to them and to his adversary, Satan. God proclaims that a descendant of the woman and a descendant of the adversary of God will be enemies. They will fight. The woman's descendant will be injured, but Satan's descendant will be destroyed. It has always been assumed that the woman's descendant is the Messiah," Oved answered.

"The very next words spoken in that prophetic passage are to the woman. *I will make your pains in childbearing very severe; with painful labor you will give birth to children.*"[2] Nahum added. "Those prophetic words have certainly held true for generations, like a sign that the rest of the prophecy is just as reliable."

In a stable not far away, Mary tried groaning, not groaning, holding her breath, panting—nothing eased the pain. In all of her fourteen years, she had never known that a human body could feel such intense pain. So far she had endured with confidence, sure that all would be well, but now the pains were coming faster and harder. She felt her courage slipping.

"You will die from the pain," Fear shouted his lie from outside the fiery circle. "Remember Rachel the wife of Jacob. You sat by her grave today. She died in childbirth."

Over Mary's head, Joseph asked Zepporah, "How much longer?"

"This will take most of the night," the old woman answered, and Mary's heart quivered with fear.

Again from his dark corner, the disembodied voice of Fear shouted another twisted truth, "You are a daughter of Eve, and it is the will of God that you suffer! He did this to you."

Through the next three painful contractions, Mary grappled with Fear as much as with pain, finally crying out, "God, be near and help me!"

Understanding, Zepporah patted Mary's cheek with her wrinkled hand, and then with a crackling voice, she began to sing.

> *Surely God is my salvation;*
> *I will trust and not be afraid.*
> *The* LORD, *the* LORD,
> *is my strength and my song;*
> *he has become my salvation.*[3]

For a moment, the old shepherdess stopped singing and reassured, "The pain is temporary, dear. When your child is in your arms, you will sing." Once more, she broke into song.

With joy you will draw water
from the wells of salvation.
In that day you will say:
*'Give thanks to the L*ORD,
call on his name;
make known among the nations
what he has done.'[4]

Zepporah kept singing. Her crackling old voice bathed Mary in peace. Fear suddenly lost its grip, and even though the contractions were actually gaining in physical intensity, Mary relaxed and easily rode the waves of discomfort. Joseph never left her side.

The Holy Spirit gave a satisfied nod at Zepporah's willing response to his suggestion.

"Here is a prophecy. Our father Jacob spoke it to his son, Judah. It was his dying blessing for his children." Ehud stood up and paced a little as he tried to remember the exact wording. "It is from the Torah reading, He Lived. *'The scepter will not depart from the* family of *Judah, nor the ruler's staff until he to whom it belongs shall come and the obedience of the nations shall be his.'*"[5]

"So the Anointed One is to come from the seed of Judah?" Nahum commented.

"Actually, from the royal line of David," Toviah asserted. "The prophet Isaiah wrote, *'For to us a child is born, to us a son is given, and the government will be on his shoulders. And he will be called Wonderful Counselor, Mighty God, Everlasting Father, Prince of Peace. Of the greatness of his government and peace there will be no end. He will reign on David's throne and over his kingdom,*

*establishing and upholding it with justice and righteousness from that
time on and forever.*"[6]

"He will have to wrestle that throne from both Rome and
corrupt Judaism," Ehud cynically retorted.

"Maybe we are the ones who need to do the wrestling."
Nahum pondered his words as he spoke, "Like our father, Jacob,
who wrestled with the angel and would not let go until the angel
blessed him, we, God's chosen people, need to cry out to God for
this Messiah and not stop crying out until we see the Anointed
One with our own eyes!"

"Through sacrifices?" Oved asked.

"No," Nahum replied. "That is just a business, and we are a
part of it. God looks on the heart. When he hears the sincere
cries of enough hearts, he will act."

Mary had no strength to hold back her cries. They filled the little
stable and made the animals that were tethered outside nervous.
She trembled uncontrollably, and each contraction seemed to
take over her entire body. It seemed there was nothing she could
do to control or assist the process of birth.

"What can we do?" Joseph asked, his own concern evident.

"It is time for Mary to push," Zepporah announced. "Joseph,
get behind your wife. Help her sit up. Let her lean on you. When
each pain comes, use your hands. Use your voice to help her push.
She is tired, but you cannot let her quit. She must push until the
baby is born."

Joseph reached for his wife, pulling her into his arms. "Joseph,
this is too hard. I don't know if I can deliver this child," Mary
whimpered into his ear.

He eased his sturdy body behind hers, adding his strength
to hers. With his work-toughened hands, Joseph brushed her
sweat-soaked hair away from her ear and bent close. Then he

whispered, "This is the promised Messiah. God will see to it that this child is born."

"He has not promised that I will live," Mary cried out as her body instinctively bore down with the pain.

"No, Mary, hold on to the words of the angel, 'Fear not!' Say it with each pain," Joseph instructed. "Fear not," he repeated as his callused carpenter's hands gently pushed downward on her belly with each contraction. Over and over, Joseph said the words, "Fear not, Mary! Push, push harder. Fear not. Keep pushing."

"I feel like I'm splitting open, tearing apart!" Mary cried out as contraction after contraction gradually moved the baby through the birth canal.

"The child is almost here," Zepporah responded. "I think I can almost see a little bit of the top of its head." The experienced old woman began to apply rags dipped in hot water to ease the stretching and minimize the tearing. "Joseph, let your wife lie back and rest through the next few contractions."

Zepporah dipped her hands in warm olive oil and then began to massage and stretch the opening through which the baby would be delivered. "Don't push until I tell you." Zepporah worked to prevent Mary from tearing open as the baby emerged from her body. Suddenly, she stopped working, pulling her hands away from Mary in momentary amazement. "Your wife is still a virgin!" Zepporah's astonished eyes locked with Joseph's eyes.

"Yes, I know," was the only response that Joseph had time to give. Once more, Mary was crying out, straining to bring her baby into the world.

"There is no more time! Now, Joseph, get your wife up again. Hold her. Support her in a squatting position."

Joseph did as Zepporah directed, easing Mary into a position that would allow the baby to drop out easily. "I had no idea there was so much work involved," he whispered to Mary as he supported her with her head resting on his chest." He could feel her body beginning the next contraction. "Fear not," he whispered.

"Bear down," Zepporah directed.

Mary strained and cried out louder than ever with expulsive pain, then Joseph felt her body suddenly relax. Another wail filled the room, the wail of a newborn expelled onto a pile of rags on the hay-strewn floor of a stable.

"It's a boy," Zepporah announced, lifting the infant, which was covered with blood mixed with thick whitish mucus and still attached to his mother's pulsating umbilical cord.

Gently, Joseph lowered Mary down into the straw, and Zepporah handed the baby over for them to hold while she tied off and cut the umbilical cord.

"He's got curly black hair," Mary cooed, "and such tiny fingers and toes." She counted all of them.

"Joseph! Joseph!" Zepporah had to call him twice to get his attention. She held out a bundle of dirty rags. "Go burn these in the fire. Tell Shammah that I want the strips of linen that we were saving for our burial and bring back some more warm water." When he didn't respond fast enough, Zepporah added, "We're not finished here, you know! I need olive oil and salt also."

Reluctantly, Joseph left Mary's side to assist with the clean up. Zepporah turned her attention to completing the delivery. When Joseph returned with the things she had requested, he watched as she cleaned off the newborn and then rubbed him with oil and salt before wrapping him securely in strips of cloth. As long as Zepporah would allow, Joseph stood there, never taking his eyes off the infant. But there were piles of soiled hay and dirty rags to be burned. Zepporah gave him a stern look, and he began numerous trips back and forth to the fire. Finally, when he had completed all the tasks Zepporah could think of, Joseph returned to find Mary resting and the baby nursing. It was such a beautiful picture. He just leaned against a stall and took it in.

"I think we could all use a little sleep, now," Zepporah commented as she took the baby from his mother and placed him in the feeding trough that she had filled with fresh hay.

Straightening up, she spoke to Joseph, "You will need more covers." She pointed to the bedding he had brought in from the donkey cart. "I'm taking the lamp with me. I worry about fire around so much straw." She turned to leave, stopping short when she saw that the gateless entrance to the stable was filled with shepherds.

Indignantly, she put her hands on her hips. "Ehud? Nahum? What are you doing here? It's not even daylight! Toviah? Oved? Who is watching your sheep, and why are you gawking at this young woman and her husband? Can't you see they have just had a child?"

"Yes, and the babe is lying in a manger!" Toviah announced with undisguised excitement.

Oved added, "It is just as the angel of the Lord said, *'This will be a sign to you: You will find a baby wrapped in cloths and lying in a manger.'* Then they sang. It was too beautiful for words!" "Who are you? And what are you talking about?" Joseph asked.

Nahum stepped forward. "We are shepherds. We keep the flocks for the Temple. services. Tonight, while we were in the fields with our sheep, we prayed for the Deliverer of Israel, and while we were praying, an angel suddenly stood with us."

"What did he look like?" Mary asked from her reclining position on a pile of hay.

"He was tall," Ehud answered before Nahum could continue, "at least the height of two men. His hair was white, and his skin glowed like the coals in our campfire."

"His voice was both musical and commanding," Oved added.

"Our donkeys did not bray, and our sheep did not move. We fell on our faces, terrified," Nahum said. "Then the angel said—"

Before Nahum could get the words of the angel out of his mouth, Mary and Joseph said, "Fear not!"

"How did you know?" Nahum gasped.

"We have seen the angel also," Joseph responded. "Now tell us, what else did he say to you?"

Nahum continued, "*Do not be afraid. I bring you good news that will cause great joy for all the people. Today in the town of David a Savior has been born to you; he is the Messiah, the Lord. This will be a sign to you: You will find a baby wrapped in cloths and lying in a manger.*"[8] As Nahum spoke, the men moved reverently toward the manger, bending close to get a better look but not touching.

Oved picked up the story, "The angel that spoke to us was suddenly joined by a host of angels. They lined up along the hills like a wall of fire, and they sang,

> *'Glory to God in the highest heaven,*
> *and on earth peace to those on whom his favor rests.'*[9]

"As soon as they disappeared, it became very dark, and the only light we could see was the light coming from Shammah's stable," Ehud said. "So we came, and there was the babe," he whispered in a hushed voice.

"You can hold him if you want," Mary offered.

Joseph stepped over and lifted the baby out of the straw, placing him into Ehud's outstretched arms. For a moment, both men's eyes met.

"You are of the royal line of King David, aren't you?" Ehud asked.

"Yes, both Mary and I are direct descendants of our greatest king," Joseph answered.

"Enough of this!" Shammah stepped into the middle of the stable and pointed an accusing finger at each of the shepherds. "It is spring, the time of year when the ewes drop their lambs. You men should be out watching your flocks, helping the ewes safely deliver their lambs. And, Ehud!" Shammah pushed his face right into the younger shepherd's face. "Have you forgotten that tomorrow you must have a suitable Passover lamb for the High Priest? What are you thinking about? Are you going to be ready, or will you be sleeping under a tree?"

"We are ready for the High Priest," Ehud answered. "We have more than one hundred perfect one-year old male lambs in an enclosure near the watchtower. While he is selecting his lamb, we will tell him everything that has happened tonight!"

"He above all people would want to know that our Deliverer has been born," Oved interjected.

"We will tell him that angels directed us to your stable," Toviah added.

"You can't say that!" Shammah frantically screamed. "You can't tell anyone that you saw an angel or that this baby is the Deliverer!" Shaking with fright and frustration, the old shepherd made an exasperated exit.

Outside the stable, Shammah threw his hands up in horror. "Do you know what will happen in the morning?" Shammah looked up at the night sky as he answered his own question, "The high priest, with his entire entourage, will come to the sheepfolds and select his perfect lamb, and then these shepherds will lead the rest of their Passover lambs to the city. The roads will be lined with worshipers cheering and waving palm branches. Then these shepherds will tell every person they speak to their wild story about the baby and the angels. Ohhh, why did I let that couple use my stable? If one of Herod's spies gets word of this, they will torture and kill us all!"

"Shammah! I thought the baby was born, so now we can get some sleep?" It was Shammah's other houseguest, coming out into the little courtyard to see what else was disturbing his sleep.

"Visitors!" Shammah complained. "The new baby has visitors!"

"Ah, the child must be a little prince," the houseguest joked.

"Don't say that!" Shammah trembled again as he considered all the possible repercussions if word of this unusual night reached the authorities.

His houseguest ignored him and said, "Since all the others are paying their respects to the new baby and his parents, I might as well see for myself what has kept me awake all night." He joined the shepherds in the stable.

"Zepporah!" Shammah called his wife to come into the courtyard. "I cannot believe those dimwitted shepherds would come to my house with a story about angels and this baby!"

"This is a special child," Zepporah responded. "His mother was a pregnant virgin! How do you explain something like that?"

With a wave of his hand, Shammah dismissed his wife's words and continued, "At daylight, we have to send everyone away. It is too dangerous for them to stay here, and we must mention this to no one. Herod has spies everywhere!" Without allowing his wife to respond, the old shepherd turned and hurried to his bed.

The other traveler watched as Ehud passed the wide-eyed infant to Oved, who lifted him toward the rafters and announced, *"And he will be called Wonderful Counselor, Mighty God, Everlasting Father, Prince of Peace."*[10]

Oved then passed the child to Toviah, who quoted the prophet Jeremiah, *"'The days are coming,' declares the* Lord, *'when I will raise up for David a righteous Branch, a King who will reign wisely and do what is just and right in the land. In his days Judah will be saved and Israel will live in safety.'"*[11]

"What is so special about this newborn?" the houseguest asked.

At that moment, the baby began to whimper and was quickly passed to his mother, who put him to her breast while the shepherds told their story again. While the baby nursed, Mary memorized every word of the shepherds' story.

The blackness of early morning grayed to meet the rising sun. Ehud and his friends hurried back to their sheep. Joseph and Mary curled up on separate piles of hay, recovering from the night while baby Jesus lay tightly swaddled, silently looking around and taking in the rough rafters, the dark thatch of the roof, and the smell of hay.

Before the sun's rays had dried the dew on Bethlehem's hills, Shammah stood in the gateless doorway to his stable. "It's morning," he gruffly announced. "No one got much sleep last night, but the animals still need to be milked." He led the goat into a stall and went back out to get the cow.

"I think he wants us out of here," Joseph whispered to Mary as he nudged her awake. "Can you get up and travel? It's only a short distance to the home of my cousin. They will make us welcome."

"I'm sure I can," Mary answered as she pulled herself to a sitting position and then onto her feet. Immediately, she went to the manger, where little Jesus was already awake. She scooped him into her arms just as Shammah pushed past her with the cow in tow, leading the animal right to the manger where the baby had just been. Mary shivered a little as she wondered what would have happened if she had not happened to pick her newborn up before the old shepherd brought the cow into the stable.

"As soon as I load up the cart, we'll be on our way," Joseph said to Shammah.

"There is the cost of feed for your donkey, the services of a midwife—"

Joseph cut Shammah off. "And here is your payment." He pressed the coin that Mary's father had given him into the hand of the greedy homeowner. "Thank Zepporah for her services. She is a good and godly woman."

"I don't want to hear any talk around town that my wife delivered the Messiah," Shammah responded. He pushed past Joseph and sat on a low stool beside the cow. "I don't need Herod's soldiers knocking at my door." With gnarled old hands, Shammah began pulling and squeezing the teats that protruded from the cow's full udder. The old shepherd didn't turn his head to see if Joseph was still standing there; he just continued his fear-filled complaint, "Ehud and those foolish friends of his will probably tell everybody they meet. By tomorrow, the story will be all over the Temple. marketplace. From there, it could spread all over the land and then be traced back to me!" He hit his old chest with a milky fist and then wiped his hand on his cloak before checking to make sure that the coin Joseph had just given him was still securely tucked into a fold in his belt.

At that moment, he noticed Joseph had been standing there politely listening to him. Shammah looked him squarely in the face. "Take your wife and baby and begone. Don't tell anyone that Shammah gave you a place for the night."

"You did not give us a place for the night," Joseph pointedly quipped as he turned his back on the fearful old shepherd. He picked up the bedding that Mary had rolled into bundles. He comforted himself with thoughts of being reunited with his family. There he knew Mary would experience true hospitality.

Chapter 7

A Child of the Covenant

On the eighth day, when it was time to circumcise him, he was named Jesus, the name the angel had given him before he had been conceived. When the time of their purification according to the Law of Moses had been completed, Joseph and Mary took him to Jerusalem to present him to the Lord.

—Luke 2:21–22

The mohel nodded to Joseph, who raised his hands and recited the traditional blessing for the rite of circumcision, "Blessed be the name of him who has sanctified us with his commandments and has commanded us to lead our sons into the covenant of our father, Abraham."

Everyone in the room responded, "Even as this child enters the covenant, so may he enter into the Torah, the marriage canopy, and numerous good deeds."

From the back of the room, Mary anxiously peeked around the heads of Joseph's extended family. She could barely see the face of her sweet little son as he was held securely on the lap of Joseph's cousin, Toma. The baby was wide-eyed, looking around at all the faces. Then his expression changed. His lower lip trembled for a moment, and then he broke into a full-blown howl.

Everyone but Mary laughed one of those uncomfortable yet understanding laughs. In her heart, Mary felt her son's pain.

For a moment, the town mohel held up the little fleshy foreskin that he had just removed. It dangled between his index finger and thumb before he dropped it onto a little tray. As everyone got a good look at the significant piece of flesh, the man trained in the art of circumcision deftly sucked the blood from the tiny penile wound and then applied a dressing of ground cumin seed mixed with olive oil and wine.

Joseph's cousin Toma continued to hold the wailing infant securely on his lap while his wife handed a small strip of linen to the mohel for the final dressing.

Finished, the mohel stood up and loudly pronounced, "Bless the holy name of the one who has sanctified this child from the womb…"

"His name?" Joseph's uncle shouted over the wailing infant and the chanting mohel.

"In Hebrew, it is Yeshua. In Greek, it is Jesus," Joseph announced as the scribe wrote in Hebrew, "Yeshua, which means God saves, is the son of Joseph." When the ink had dried, the scribe held up the scroll for everyone to see. Everyone cheered, and then the men broke into an impromptu dance around the scroll, around Toma holding the baby, around the room. Joseph, proud papa, danced with all his might. Wine flowed. Food covered the tables. It was a celebration fit for an eight-day-old prince.

Mary came to Toma, arms outstretched for her son. Quickly, she slipped into a quiet corner to comfort Jesus, who was still insisting that circumcision was a painful ritual. She gave him her breast and then relaxed, taking in all the activity in the room. She felt so much a part of this large family of Joseph's cousins, aunts, and uncles. She wanted to stay forever.

"He'll be cranky for a few days." Sarah, who was married to Joseph's cousin Toma, had come to stand beside her. Avrahm, her eight-month-old, was at her breast.

"How do I care for it?" Mary asked, grateful for someone close to her own age who was experienced.

Sarah sat beside her. "Wash it several times a day and dress it with olive oil and wine," she responded. "It will heal in no time."

Both young mothers sat together, watching the gaiety around them. Mary's eyes followed Joseph as he renewed old acquaintances and picked up the news, both old and current. "He certainly seems happy here," Mary commented to Sarah.

"Joseph?" Sarah inquired.

Mary nodded.

"Every childhood story my husband tells has Joseph in it. See all those men?" She pointed to the group that Joseph was laughing with. "They grew up together, went to the synagogue school together, and ran from one end of Bethlehem to the other together. They are as close as brothers."

"How did Joseph end up in Nazareth?" Mary asked.

"Joseph's father died before he could learn a trade from him. His mother had to find someone to teach her son a trade. A master carpenter in Nazareth took Joseph to be his apprentice, and he never returned except to visit."

For a long time, Mary just sat and watched her husband interact with his family and friends. Their marriage was so new; there was much to learn about this man who had taken a son who wasn't his own. Jesus finally fell asleep, and Mary gently stroked his cheek until he let her nipple slide out of his mouth. Joseph's Aunt Elisheva walked by and held out her arms. Mary gratefully turned the baby over to her. Yes, it was nice to be part of this family, where everyone loved and wanted to help everyone else.

It was early afternoon. Four and a half weeks had passed since the infant Jesus had become a son of the covenant. Mary and Sarah sat in the courtyard, working amiably on the household chores while keeping an eye on their babies. How much fun it is to have another female my own age to talk to, Mary thought. It seems we always have something to share. It's like having my sister, Salome, with me.

Sarah suddenly started giggling, and Mary looked up to see what was so funny. Her eyes followed Sarah's gaze to see baby Avrahm crawling on the sun-drenched stones of the courtyard. He had come to a small puddle, and the difference between the warm smooth stones and the cool wetness of the water puzzled him. He would move forward until his hand touched the water, then he would stop, back up, and then go forward again. Over and over, he went through those same motions until Mary asked, "Shall I show him the way around?"

"Don't get up," Sarah's mother-in-law, Leah, said as she walked through the courtyard and scooped up the baby, kissing him until he squealed so loudly that Mary was afraid Jesus would wake up.

"Take him out to see the chickens," Sarah suggested, and Leah took the laughing baby behind the house to visit the animals.

"Thank you," Mary said, and Sarah nodded in response. We are so close, Mary thought. I didn't even have to tell her I didn't want Jesus to wake up.

For a little while, their conversation fell into comfortable silence. The only sound was the thump of the beater and the swish of the shuttle on the loom as Sarah worked with both hands to turn coarse thread into fabric. The afternoon sun warmed Mary's back and bathed her peacefully sleeping son. She looked at his sweet face. He had found his fist and was sucking on it as he slept. This was a good time in her life. Picking up another water-soaked willow branch, she deftly added it to the basket she was working on. As her fingers worked the supple branches in and out, her mind wandered back over the past year, over all that had happened to her, and her heart seemed ready to burst with blessing: a miracle child, a husband, an extended family.

She looked up to see Joseph entering the courtyard, returning from repairing the roof on a neighbor's house. Whenever he entered the room, her eyes and her heart were drawn to him.

She longed to be alone with him, like they had been alone on their wedding night—just the two of them sharing their deepest feelings. Mary let out a little sigh. They had not been alone since the baby had been born, and even before that when they had been alone, Joseph didn't usually have much to say. He talked, but he didn't talk about feelings. He talked about carpentry and weather, about the Torah and family. It had just been that one night, their wedding night, when his words had touched the deep places in her heart. She wanted to be touched like that again. Her eyes never left his face.

Not even pausing for a cup of water, he came directly over to her, and her heart started beating like a maiden meeting her betrothed for the first time. "Come take a walk with me," Joseph took Mary's hand and gently but insistently pulled her away from her task. Immediately, Mary's eyes went to the sleeping baby. "Sarah will watch him," he urged.

Sarah nodded her agreement as Mary responded and went willingly, relishing the time she was going to have alone with her husband.

"Where are we going?" Mary asked as they stepped onto the hard dirt road that ran through the town and past the well.

"To my field, to the land I inherited from my father," Joseph answered as they turned off the main road and onto a well-used footpath.

"The taxes on the land were quite high, weren't they?" Mary asked. She wondered if they were going to have to sell the land. So many people lost their inheritance because they could not keep up with the taxes.

"One-third of the value of the harvest," Joseph replied.

"Were you able to pay that amount?" Mary asked.

"Since Toma actually farms the land, we met the tax collector's demand together." They stepped off the path into a freshly harvested barley field. For a long moment, they both just gazed at the land. On two sides, the field touched the property of other farmers. Low stone walls delineated the boundaries. At the far end, Joseph's property stopped just beyond a small stand of olive trees. "There is a spring by the olive trees," Joseph commented as he gave Mary's hand a gentle tug, and together, they crossed the brown-stubbled field.

Under the olive trees, there was grass, evidence of water. Joseph began poking around in a tangle of vines and shrubs. He found the spring, just a small puddle of muddy water choked with dead leaves and grass. Excited, he knelt down and with his massive hands began to muck out the worst of it. In just a few minutes, the spring cleared a little and took on a more definite shape.

Satisfied, Joseph got up, wiping his hands on his work clothes as he looked around. Mary watched his every move, wondering what he had in mind. "There is a foundation near here." Again he began walking through the trees, looking at the ground, poking here and there with a stick. "Here!" Joseph stopped at an area where scattered patches of grass found a little nourishment between carefully laid embedded stones. "This was the home of Boaz and Ruth, also their son, Obed," he stated.

"Obed," Mary repeated, "the father of Jessie, the father of King David."

"Yes," Joseph answered. "Somewhere near here, maybe on this very spot, the prophet Samuel anointed David to become the next king of Israel."

Mary looked at the land she stood on, and little chills ran up and down her spine. This was sacred land.

"We could build on this foundation," Joseph suggested, his eyes searching hers for a response. "It would mean not returning to Nazareth, except for visits."

Mary knelt and ran her hand over the old gray stones. Time, footsteps, and the elements had erased most bumps and crevices. "I would love to have a home here," she answered. "Jesus, our special son, should walk where his ancestors walked." She smiled to herself as she imaged his little feet taking their first wobbly steps in a new home on this foundation. "How long would it take to build here?" She looked up.

Joseph was already pushing back overgrowth, finding the perimeter of the ancient home, determining where the foundation needed repair and where support beams should be placed. "It depends on how many paying jobs I can find, but maybe we could be in it before the winter rains" he answered.

"And the field?" Mary asked.

"Toma will still work the field. We have come to an agreement about crops and taxes. I will still be a carpenter. Bethlehem is growing. I think there is enough work." Joseph looked at Mary. "What do you think?"

Mary looked at Joseph. "I think you look very happy." She put both of her arms around his waist. "This is more than I ever dreamed of." She squeezed him tight, and he responded by engulfing her in his massive arms. For a long moment, they stood together, both lost in their own thoughts. Mary pulled away first. "We had better get back. Jesus will wake up, and there will be no peace until he is fed."

In silent agreement, Joseph took his wife's hand, and together, they crossed the field, rough with barley stubble and dirt clods. "I told Toma I would help him plant and bring in his next crop. He's also lined up a few jobs for me, friends who need the services of a carpenter."

Mary nodded absently. Her mind was full of plans for a new home: the furniture she would ask Joseph to build, the draperies she would weave, the layout of the cooking area.

The Spirit moved close and whispered, "Enjoy, enjoy this time together."

Joseph's voice broke into Mary's thoughts, "Let's sleep on the roof tonight."

"It would be good to get out of that stuffy little room," she agreed. They were entering the courtyard of the crowded home they were sharing with Joseph's cousin. Mary could hear that their son was awake and calling for his next meal. Without saying more to Joseph, she hurried to her baby, scooping him into her arms, cooing comfort while she arranged her garments so he could nurse.

On the roof of Toma's home, Joseph laid out their pallets, placing Mary's close to his own. This was the first time they had had any privacy since Mary had completed her purification by totally immersing herself in a pool of water on the seventh day after the birth. At that time, according to the law, her time of being separated from her husband had come to an end. On this evening as the sun set, marking the beginning of a new day, her additional thirty-three days of remaining separated from all the sacred rituals of her people would also come to an end. Before dawn, they would take the road to Jerusalem, and barring any problems, they would arrive at the Temple. for Mary's purification and Jesus's dedication before the priests began the morning prayers.

Joseph heard footsteps on the stairs at the side of the house that led to the roof. His heart beat faster just anticipating Mary with baby Jesus joining him. First the top of her mantle and next her head appeared, then the rest of her body. She was beautiful, glowing with motherhood. Joseph rushed over, taking Jesus from her arms so she could step onto the roof unencumbered.

For a moment, Mary paused and looked around. "You did so much: the beds, lamps, a waterskin. You even brought the cradle up. It's like the Feast of Tabernacles! All we need is a little booth made from branches."

"You missed the fall feasts because of the birth of John and the spring feasts with the birth of this little one." Joseph stroked the soft cheek of his son with his work-roughened finger. "I had no idea that babies could cause so much disruption in the normal course of life." He put his free arm around Mary until the moment became awkward for him.

"Well, this makes up for it," Mary replied as she made herself comfortable on her sleeping pallet and held out her arms for the baby. Joseph returned the baby and then settled on his own pallet, sitting cross-legged, staring out across the town, waiting for her to nurse the baby and put him down to sleep.

The sun was setting over the Judean hills, streaking the sky with red, purple, and gold. It reflected on the stone houses, so close together that a person could travel from one end of Bethlehem to the other by traversing the flat roofs of the homes. Both Joseph and Mary were silent, lost in their own thoughts until the sky grayed and the first few stars hung just above the horizon. Joseph pointed to one of the lights in the sky. "That is the biggest star I have ever seen."

Mary looked up from tending to the baby. "It is unusually bright," she agreed. "I'm not sure that I ever noticed it before."

"I saw it for the first time on the night Jesus was born, but I did not have time to give it more than a fleeting glance," Joseph stated.

Feeling the romance of the moment, Mary replied, "That's our star. It shines brighter than any other star because it reflects our total happiness." She laid her sleeping infant down in the little cradle Joseph had made for him.

Joseph chuckled self-consciously. He didn't know how to respond to such sweet words. "God help me. What do I say?" he whispered to the heavens. He looked at his hands, then back at the stars. I'm a man who works with my hands. I don't have the words for what is in my heart.

Mary returned to her pallet, lowering herself gracefully to a sitting position. For a long moment, husband and wife stared at each other. Joseph could see the lamplight, like stars, reflected in Mary's dark brown eyes. Those were the stars he wanted to look at for the rest of his life. "Come share my pallet tonight," he finally said.

With her eyes never leaving the face of her husband, Mary rose from her own bed, blew out the lamp, then for the first time, lay down beside her husband.

Between the couple and the starry night, the Spirit of God made of himself a covering for their union. Into the heart of Joseph, he whispered the words he had given Israel's most romantic king, "*Your eyes are doves.*"[1]

Joseph whispered those same words into the ear of his sweet wife.

The Spirit had a response for Mary.

She repeated his words as she touched the sun-kissed cheek of her husband and played with his curly beard, "*How handsome you are, my beloved! Oh, how charming!*[2] Our bed is soft, like greenery." She stroked from his firm biceps down to his work-hardened hands. "Your arms, they are like beams of cedar for our house and rafters of cypress for our roof."

Eagerly, the Spirit continued to pour out on Joseph his gift of passionate words. "*How delightful is your love, my sister, my bride! How much more pleasing is your love than wine, and the fragrance of your perfume more than any spice! Your lips drop sweetness as the honeycomb, my bride; milk and honey are under your tongue. The fragrance of your garments…*"[3]

Joseph sighed and buried his face between her breasts.

The Spirit moved close, tenderly directing and encouraging their first union.

The sun had not yet risen and the birds were still silent when Joseph moved away from Mary to light the oil lamp beside their pallet. "Mary, we need to get started so we are at the Temple before the morning prayers. I can hear Toma and Sarah downstairs. They are already up and preparing to go with us."

"It's cold." Mary felt a little chill as the covers fell off and the predawn air washed over her.

Their voices called their son to a new day, and he began to wail. Immediately, Mary felt her milk drip, ready to be taken by her infant. "Bring Jesus to me," she asked Joseph as she pulled the covers over her head, making a little tent where she could nurse and keep both Jesus and herself warm.

Handing her the baby, Joseph said, "I'll go down and help Toma with the animals, then I'll return to help you down the steps." Mary nodded and then tried to get on with the business of feeding her son, but he only nursed for a few minutes before falling back asleep. Repeatedly, she had to let the crisp morning air tickle his little toes so he would wake up and finish nursing. Finally, after Joseph had made several trips up and down the steps, she was able to go with him down to the living area of Toma's home.

In the cooking area, Sarah was filling a basket with figs, olives, and flat barley bread, things that would be easy to nibble on as they walked to the holy city. On the table, Mary could see bundles of clean rags for diapering their sons. Toma's cloak and walking stick were nearby.

You've done so much this morning!" Mary exclaimed. "You're so organized. All I have managed is to get dressed and nurse Jesus."

Sarah laughed. "I'm just excited to be going to the Temple. with you to dedicate Jesus." She closed the basket full of food and reached for a length of blue fabric. "I used this to carry Avrahm to the Temple. for his dedication." She held it out, and Mary could see that it would fit around her body so she could carry her baby and still have her hands free. "Let me help you put it on," Sarah offered. She slipped it over Mary's head and adjusted the length before placing Jesus in the loose pouch. "Now when you want to nurse, you just position the baby like this," Sarah demonstrated.

Mary exuberantly responded, "This is wonderful! I thought I was going to have to carry Jesus in my arms all the way to Jerusalem."

"Enjoy it while you can," Sarah advised. "When your little one gets bigger and becomes as active as Avrahm, he will never stay in a sling. Today, Toma is going to have to carry his son to Jerusalem on his shoulders."

"Ladies, there will soon be light on the eastern hills," Joseph announced as he picked up the handheld lamp. Toma hoisted his son high in his arms while Sarah grabbed the basket of food and rags. Two young families, grown close after weeks of sharing a home, were off to spend the day in the Temple. at Jerusalem.

"Anna, daughter of Phanuel," the Spirit of God called the old woman of the Temple. to wake up and talk with him.

Slowly, Anna moved to a sitting position on her pallet, which was spread on the hard white stones of an unheated room just off the Court of the Women. "Speak, my Comforter, my Friend," she whispered into the predawn darkness.

"Sixty-three years ago, you came to this place," answered her Friend.

"Yes, Elias and I had been married for seven years and had no children." In her memory, she could still see the strong lines of her husband's face and the little wrinkles at the corners of his eyes. He was always laughing. How she had loved his laugh. "My dear Elias brought me to the Temple. to pray for a son," she reminded the Holy Spirit of the event she had discussed with him so many times.

She could not help but smile to herself as she remembered the way Elias had held her hand as they walked toward the Temple and the way he seemed to understand her need to bear him children. He could have berated her or condemned, even divorced her. Instead, he loved her. There was still a little place in her heart where the flame of their love glowed like the last coal on the altar of incense.

She spoke to the Holy Spirit again, "How I have missed my Elias. On that day, we had no warning. Pompey had Jerusalem under siege, but we did not expect that the gates of the city would be opened for him, neither did we expect to be caught on the Temple. grounds when the resistance closed and barred the Temple. gates to the advances of the Roman army. I'll never forget the relentless beat of the Roman battering ram or the moment when the northern gate gave way and the soldiers poured in. Elias pushed me into the room where the wood was stored. He piled logs over me and then picked up a piece of wood to use as a club. He went out to defend the Holy Place. I never saw him again." Anna covered her eyes with thin, wrinkled hands, but she could not block out the scene that lay before her when she had finally emerged from her hiding place. It was a mural on her mind: blood and bodies covered every square cubit of the old second Temple. Roman soldiers on horseback and on foot ranged from one court to another, up the steps, and into the sanctuaries of the Temple. Ruthlessly, they had slaughtered priests and worshipers. Then in a final act of desecration, Pompey himself had strolled into the Most Holy Place. "Oh Lord, if only your people had been more diligent to follow your Torah, then we could have had your blessing instead of your curse."

"My blessing is on you, Anna," the Spirit responded.

"I know. You hid me in the woodpile, and you did not allow the soldiers to find my hiding place," Anna answered.

"I have not forgotten your prayer for a son. *'Sing, barren woman, you who never bore a child; burst into song, shout for joy, you who were never in labor; because more are the children of the desolate woman than of her who has a husband.'"*[4]

"Do you see the reality of my situation?" Anna responded with a disbelieving shake of her head. "I am too old, and without a husband."

"Do not be afraid; you will not be put to shame. Do not fear disgrace; you will not be humiliated. You will forget the shame of your youth and remember no more the reproach of your widowhood.[5] Today, I will place in your arms my Son, the Deliverer of your people, the promised Messiah,"* the Spirit assured.

"At what hour, Lord? Where in this vast Temple. do I find this child?" Anna asked with eagerness. She was surprised to find that her arms ached to hold this infant, just like her arms had ached so many years ago to hold her own newborn.

"Before the time of prayer, go to the place of purchasing offerings for the purification of women and wait for me to speak."

Torchlight danced on the stone walls of the bare room where Anna lived. She knew it was the early morning procession of priests making their daily inspection of the Temple. grounds. Soon the first lot would be cast to determine which priests would clean and prepare the altar for the morning sacrifice. As was her custom, Anna stood and faced the Holy Place, where the Spirit of God was said to dwell. She crossed her hands over her breast and bent her head in reverent submission. "God, hear the prayers of your people this day. Accept the sacrifices we bring. Turn the hearts of your people to your Holy Law, and bring to this place your promised Deliverer..." Her prayer continued until she heard the creaking of the great gates to the Temple. as they were pushed open, then three blasts on the silver trumpets signaled that the lamb for the morning sacrifice was at that moment being slain. Its blood was being caught up in a golden bowl and would be taken to the altar, where some would be sprinkled and then the rest poured out at the base of the altar.

Every morning, she remembered that Elias, her own husband, had been slaughtered in this place, not unlike the many lambs that gave their blood for the sins of the people. "Lord, what does it mean, all this shedding of blood in your Temple.?" She had asked this question every day for sixty-three years.

"I was there. I saw it," the Spirit responded. "In my Book of Remembrance. I have placed the names of every person and every deed. The righteous will be rewarded, and the wicked will face my fury. *Rejoice, you nations, with his people, for he will avenge the blood of his servants; he will take vengeance on his enemies and make atonement for his land and people.*"[6]

For a long time, Anna contemplated the words of the Holy Spirit. She did not understand all of what God's Spirit spoke to her, but she tucked it away in the back of her mind for a day when he would explain it more fully. After folding up her pallet, she walked barefooted to the Pool of the Israelites, where she completely immersed herself. Then hurrying to the Court of the Women, she stood near the third treasury box, the box designated for the payment of women's sin offerings.

"In the spring and summer months, the walk from Bethlehem to Jerusalem is unbelievably beautiful," Sarah commented. "There are olive trees, and then as you get close to the city, there are vineyards, and gardens cover the hillsides." She pointed to a hillside covered with rosebushes. "We have the most beautiful roses in the world because they are fertilized with the blood from the sacrifices."

Mary looked around. On that difficult journey from Jerusalem to Bethlehem just forty days earlier, she had not noticed the beauty of the countryside. Now the terraced hills covered with early summer vegetation were pleasant to the eye. As they neared the city, she noticed the country estates of the wealthy scattered along the hills like gemstones tossed on a green floor covering.

"There's the city," Toma announced as he lifted baby Avrahm high above his head and held him there for a good look at the place that was so important to every descendant of Abraham.

"I can't believe how quickly we made the journey!" Mary remarked.

"Never in my life have I run into as many obstacles as we ran into the day before Jesus was born," Joseph added.

"Forget the problems of that day. Today will be great," Sarah admonished as they all quickened their paces.

"Where, Lord? How will I recognize your promised Salvation?" Simeon walked slowly between the columns that lined the wide covered walkway that bordered the Court of the Gentiles. His knees ached, and he heard very little of what people said, but God had given him a keen spiritual ear. When the Spirit of God spoke, Simeon heard. This very morning, before dawn, the Holy Spirit had roused him and called him to the Temple grounds to bless the Deliverer of Israel.

Under the covered walks that bordered the Court of the Gentiles, devoted young men drifted into small groups to study both Torah and tradition with the famous rabbis of Jerusalem. Simeon paused and observed each cluster of devout men. It seemed to him that some of them had regal bearing. Simeon could imagine one or two of the men leading the Israelite armies into battle against Rome and then wearing the crown of David and reestablishing the monarchy. As unobtrusively as possible, he moved from group to group, pausing only long enough to give the Spirit time to speak, but the Spirit of God remained silent.

Simeon had made a complete circuit of the Court of the Gentiles and now moved past the Temple. guard and into the Court of the Women. Would he recognize the Deliverer by the size of the offering he brought to the Temple? Simeon surveyed the thirteen cubicles containing trumpet-shaped chests designated for the various offerings that were received from the population. He could see nothing unusual. He could only sense that the Holy Spirit was not speaking. Wanting to draw closer to the Spirit, Simeon moved toward the dwelling place of God on Earth. Slowly, he walked up the fifteen circular steps to the gate that separated the Court of the Women from the Court of the Israelites. Only Jewish men could move past this point, and only for the purpose of making a sacrifice. Here, the Temple. guard stopped him because he brought no sacrifice, but he was allowed to remain at the gate, peering in. Through the open gate, he could see the white-robed priests flaying the lamb they had slain for the morning sacrifice; he watched them skinning, cutting, and cleaning it according to precise rules, carrying each piece to a spot near the altar where it was salted and stacked, waiting to be put on the altar.

From the Hall of Polished Stones, a faint chant drifted over the open courts. The priests who had not yet been assigned a duty were singing their morning prayers. "With great love you have loved us, O Lord our God…"

Simeon could not hear them. His eyes scanned the people entering the Court of the Women. He saw Anna, his old friend, hurry through one of the entrances and walk directly over to the treasury boxes.

"I called Anna to bless the Deliverer also."

Delicious chills ran up and down Simeon's spine, and all the achiness left his knees. The Holy Spirit had spoken.

"Over here," Toma directed as he led the little group to the money changer's tables at one end of Solomon's Porch.

Joseph pulled out the small bag of coins, the second tithe that he had been saving since his last visit to the Temple.

"I don't know which is worse," Joseph commented to Toma, "paying Roman taxes or paying these money changers."

"The family of Annas needs more than the portion God allotted to the priesthood," Toma cynically responded as he laid down twelve ordinary shekels and received five Temple. shekels in return. Joseph also turned away from the money exchange pocketing less than half of the coinage he had exchanged.

"I've never been in a place so large," Mary commented to Sarah as she kept turning her head from side to side, trying to take it all in. "So many people! Such high walls and beautiful columns! It takes my breath away!"

"We're going over there," Sarah pointed, "through the Gate of the Firstborn."

Mary nodded, still trying to take everything in.

"We will stop at the third treasury box. That's where you will pay for two doves," Sarah informed her.

"How will I carry the doves and the baby," Mary asked.

"You won't have to carry the birds. You just tell the priest that your offering is two doves. They keep them in a basket near the altar. They will take out two and sacrifice them for you."

"We're ready," Joseph announced as he and Toma returned and led their wives away from the lines of people waiting their turn to exchange their coins for Temple. currency.

The two families hurried past one of many Temple. guard checkpoints and into the Court of the Women. "Over there," Toma directed as he led the little group toward the treasury.

Still standing on top of the circular steps, Simeon surveyed the court below and all the people who were either passing through or milling around.

"There!" The Spirit directed Simeon's eyes to a group of four adults with two babies who were making their way directly across the vast expanse of pavement, moving toward the treasury.

The old man needed only one word of direction. He too began to move, setting a course to intercept the people that the Spirit had pointed out to him.

"As soon as you pay for your sacrifice, then you and Joseph will need to go to the steps." Sarah nodded toward the steps leading up to the entrance to the Court of the Israelites. "One of the Levites there will line you up with other couples who have brought their firstborn. Then after the offering of incense, each couple will be brought to the gate. You can look through and see—" Sarah stopped midsentence. An old man had stepped in front of them, blocking their way to the treasury boxes.

"Excuse us." Toma was trying to lead them around, but the man kept moving in front of them, waving his arms as if signaling them to stop.

"I don't think he heard you," Joseph said. And then he bellowed, "We would like to go around you to the treasury."

"Wait please." Simeon responded very loudly. A few people nearby stopped, anticipating a confrontation.

"Wait?" Joseph repeated in an attempt to understand.

"We don't have time," Toma asserted. We have to pay for a sacrifice and be on the steps before the offering of incense."

Simeon held out his hands, imploring their patience.

A Temple guard immediately stepped into the little crowd that was gathering. "Old man, there is no begging in the Temple courts. You may beg at the entrances."

"I am not begging for money, just for a moment of their time," Simeon responded in a voice much too loud for normal conversation. "The Spirit of God has promised me that before I die, I will see the Deliverer of our people." He paused, his eyes resting first on Toma, a sturdy Jewish man.

"No," the Spirit said.

His eyes then moved to Joseph, a man of great physical strength who had the bearing of a warrior.

Again the Holy Spirit responded to his silent question, "Not this man."

Simeon looked at baby Avrahm and then at baby Jesus. His eyes rested on the infant.

At that moment, in the spirit realm, the Holy Spirit poured out his invisible-to-mortals prophetic anointing oil. It soaked Simeon's hair and dripped from his beard in shimmering golden droplets.

Responding to the Spirit of God, Simeon raised his hands and, in a loud voice, proclaimed, "Sovereign Lord, you have kept your promise!" Ever so gently, he reached out and placed one arthritic hand on the forehead of the baby in Mary's arms. With his other hand still reaching toward heaven, he continued his prayer, "Now, God, allow your servant to sleep with his ancestors in the place where your righteous servants wait to be called out. My eyes have now seen your Yeshua, your salvation!"

At that moment, Anna pushed her way through the curious crowd that encircled Simeon and the two young families. She stepped up beside Mary, who was wide-eyed and silent. "May I?" she asked, holding her arms out toward the baby.

Mary placed Jesus in her arms, and responding to the prompting of the Spirit, Anna turned and placed the infant in Simeon's arms. Her old friend carefully supported the infant's head as he lifted the child toward heaven. "Salvation is now being revealed in the sight of all you people!" he announced.

A soft murmur of amazement rolled through the small crowd that had gathered.

"Here you see an infant who will become a light of revelation to the Gentiles and glory to our people, Israel!" Above Simeon's head, Jesus started to squirm and kick, his little arms flailing in the air. Carefully, the old man lowered the infant and brought him into the security of his chest. He planted a kiss on the child's forehead. As his whiskers brushed the baby's face, Jesus responded with a little grimace.

Both Anna and Mary reached for the baby. Anna's arms got there first. Mary nodded her silent consent as the old woman of the Temple took the infant, cradling him in her childless arms. "I delight in the goodness of the Lord! He has placed in these empty arms, his own son!" Anna turned away and began moving from person to person, showing them the infant, speaking the words that the Spirit of God put in her mouth.

She came to Sarah, who held her own baby while Toma stood beside her. "You know this child, don't you?" Anna asked.

"He's just an ordinary baby," Sarah responded with a touch of annoyance. "He cries. He nurses. He needs to be cleaned."

"The Spirit of God cautions you," Anna spoke gently. "Do not question and do not covet." She reached out her free hand and stroked Avrahm's little head. "This one is also a gift from God. He is a gift just for you to enjoy." Her gentle smile took in both Toma and Sarah. For a long moment, she looked at Avrahm. Suddenly, a look of horror crossed her face, then tears began to run down her wrinkled cheeks. "Enjoy every moment you have with your son," she choked on her words as she slowly turned away.

"Wait!" Alarmed, Toma reached out an arm to pull her back.

"You're crying?" Sarah's statement pleaded for an explanation.

"What did you see when you looked at our child?" Toma anxiously inquired.

"It was Rachel. I saw the wife of our patriarch, Jacob. She was weeping for her children, and she could not be comforted," Anna answered. Her voice quivered as she continued, "I felt her loss. It was tragic, so sad, so tragic." She shook her head and then comforted the parents with these words, "I am an old lady. In my lifetime, I have seen much tragedy and shed many tears. I cannot tell you exactly what the vision of Rachel's weeping means or explain my own reaction. So do not concern yourself with my tears. Just enjoy this precious little one." She reached out and caressed Avrahm's chubby cheek with one wrinkled hand. "What a dear child he is."

Toma and Sarah huddled together, clinging to each other and to their child, wondering why the strange words from the old woman struck such a chord of fear in their hearts.

Anna moved on to show the infant Jesus to anyone nearby who would pause long enough to see the promised Messiah.

"Come near to me," Simeon said as he beckoned to Joseph and Mary.

As they stepped toward him, he placed a gnarled hand on each of their shoulders and looked directly into their eyes. "The Spirit of God Most Holy has caused me to speak today. You must know that this child is destined to cause the downfall and the rising of many in Israel. He will be a sign that many will speak against because he will reveal the secrets of many hearts." His face turned directly to Mary, and tears filled his eyes. "You, dear mother, will experience such sorrow over this child that it will be like a sword piercing your soul."

"I don't know what to say," Mary responded.

"Only say what you said to the angel, 'I am the servant of the God of Israel. Let it be to me as you have said,'" Simeon answered.

"Only a man of God could know the words you have spoken," Joseph said. Putting his arm around Mary, they both sensed the presence of the Spirit and bowed their heads in reverent response.

A gong sounded, reverberating throughout the Temple courts.

"You must hurry. It is almost time for the morning prayers." Toma and Sarah had stepped up beside Joseph and Mary. The small crowd began to disperse. Everyone in the Court of the Women seemed to be moving toward the entrance to the inner courts.

"Mary, you and Joseph go to the steps," Sarah suggested. "Toma and I will put your money in the treasury boxes."

"Yes," Anna concurred as she placed baby Jesus back in his mother's arms. Taking Mary by the elbow, she led the couple through the milling people, across the vast expanse of pavement, to the base of the fifteen semicircular steps that led up to the inner courts. There, she signaled to one of the Levites who were lining up those who had come for purification or to offer a sacrifice. Recognition flashed across the man's face, and he came down the steps. "Place this couple at the head of the line," Anna requested. "Let them be first at the gate."

With a respectful nod of his head, the Levite led Joseph and Mary to the top of the steps to stand beside the open gate, where they could see beyond the altar of burnt offering into the Court of the Priests.

Tentatively, Mary peeked through the open gate. The spectacle was even grander than she could have imagined. Five priests carrying gold and silver vessels ascended the steps to the entrance of the Holy Place with ritual precision. Behind her, she sensed Joseph covering his head with his prayer shawl. The priests disappeared into the building that was meant to be a dwelling place for God on Earth. While Jesus sucked on his little fist, Mary kept watching. A short time later, four of the priests returned, leaving one priest to pour the incense over the coals that had been spread on the altar of incense.

Deep silence filled the Temple grounds. The solemnity of the moment seemed to touch even the infant in Mary's arms. The child stopped sucking and just looked around quizzically, taking in everything around him.

Barefooted priests quickly withdrew to a respectful distance from the sanctuary and then prostrated themselves on the pavement with their hands spread toward the dwelling place of God. A whiff of fragrant white smoke and then a cloud of white smoke rolled out of the sanctuary and drifted heavenward.

It was then that the priests and the people began to pray in unison. Behind her, Mary could hear her husband's deep voice. "True it is that you are Jehovah our God, our Help and our Deliverer. Appoint for us seasons of peace, goodness, and blessing. Pour out your grace, mercy, and compassion for all Israel. Look upon us with the light of your holy countenance…"

Light of your holy countenance—Mary pondered those words as she looked into the sweet face of her son. The old man said you were going to be a light. Mary tucked that thought away in her heart.

The corporate prayers ended, and once again, the priests began moving on the steps to the sanctuary. Activity was also beginning at the altar of burnt offering. Piece after piece of the morning sacrifice was being thrown onto the fire. Mary was fascinated with all she saw. The pieces were thrown in a reckless manner, so that the blood of the offering splattered the area, then the officiating priest began to arrange the pieces of the animal. With long tongs, he placed each piece so that, when he finished, the pieces lay on the altar like the whole animal.

"*The LORD bless you and keep you.*" Mary's eyes were drawn away from the altar to the steps, where several priests raised their hands in blessing while the priest who had burnt incense before the veil intoned, "*The LORD make his face shine upon you, and be gracious to you; the LORD turn his face toward you and give you peace.*"[7]

Mary and all the people responded, "Blessed be the Lord from everlasting to everlasting!"

At this point, the music began: two blasts on the silver trumpets and then the psalm of the day. The Levite choir, men and boys, sang,

God stands in the assembly of his people…

The melody soared, the fragrance of burning incense and roasting meat filled the air. Mary looked around; on all sides, the magnificence of the Temple. nearly took her breath away. It was an awesome experience.

When the last note of the hymn of praise had died away, a young priest stepped through the open gate and inquired, "What brings you to the gate of the house of the Lord?"

Bowing her head, Mary responded modestly, "It is now the fortieth day since the birth of my son. I have come to fulfill the requirements of the law."

"What is your offering?" the priest asked.

"Two turtledoves," Mary answered.

She watched as the priest walked back to the altar where he wrung the necks of two birds, catching their blood in a silver vessel. Their bodies he placed in a basket where they would wait to have their wings ripped from their bodies and the feathers removed before being burned on the altar.

Returning to Mary, he dipped his fingers in the blood, flicking it, so it splattered over both her and the child she was holding. "By this blood, atonement has been made for you. You are clean!"

At that moment, Joseph stepped forward and placed five shekels in the hand of the priest. "For the redemption of my firstborn," he said. *"For the Lord said to Moses, 'Consecrate to me every firstborn male.'"*[8]

Very briefly, the priest touched the forehead of the infant, chanting a short blessing over the family before he moved on to the next couple. Joseph took hold of the fringes of his prayer shawl and stretched out the mantle so it covered both him and his family, a symbol of his protection over his wife and child and also a symbol of God's covering. In this way, he led Mary, with the baby in her arms, down the steps.

Resentment and Jealousy had attached themselves to Sarah and Toma. The evil spirits were at work inflicting their own specialized emotional torment as they clung to the unusually silent group of four adults and two babies. The spirits of Lies and Accusation moved from person to person, finding Toma and Sarah most receptive.

"The Lord certainly has blessed us with good weather today," Mary tried to start a cheerful conversation.

No one picked up on her comment. The hard-packed dirt road from Jerusalem back to their home in Bethlehem seemed to be blocked by a mountain of silent resentment. Concerned, Mary's eyes roamed from person to person, looking for some hint that they would be able to break free of this oppression. Just a few paces ahead, Joseph and Toma led the way. Toma's back was as stiff, as unbending as the columns in the Temple. Mary watched as Joseph reached out with both arms in a wordless gesture that offered to carry baby Avrahm for a while. Toma responded with a long level stare, then a slight negative shake of his head.

Even the men are feeling this tension, Mary realized as she shook her head sadly and wondered how long the cold silence could last. She sighed under the weight of it. How she longed to return to the carefree camaraderie of their morning walk. If only someone would say something that would break down the silent wall that shouted an end to their relationship.

"What is so special about baby Jesus?" Resentment whispered the question.

"What is so special about baby Jesus?" Resentment's words jumped out of Sarah's mouth before she could stuff them back down her throat.

Instantly, everyone paused. No one could take another step until the question was answered. Mary looked at Sarah, then at Joseph. She waited, giving her husband the opportunity to answer.

"Before Jesus was born, both Mary and I were visited by angels," Joseph said.

Mary could tell that he was picking his words carefully, and she loved him for it.

"We know that God has a special purpose for this child, but we do not know the details." Joseph gave Mary an almost imperceptible nod of his head, indicating that she should add something to the explanation.

"Unusual things have happened," Mary added, "things that we never expected. On the night that Jesus was born, shepherds showed up telling us that they had seen angels who told them about the birth."

"Then today," Joseph picked up the story, "Anna and the old man, Simeon, totally surprised us."

"They scared me," Sarah said. "When Anna looked at our child, I felt such fear! I think she saw something, something terrible!"

"Now, Sarah, don't get carried away by the strange actions of an old lady," Toma advised.

"I also received frightening words," Mary said. "Simeon said that a sword would pierce my heart."

"Did he mean you would be killed?" Sarah asked.

"I don't know, and there is nothing I can do but wait and see what all of this actually means," Mary said. "Each time something happens, I tuck it away in my mind, hoping that one day it will all become clear."

"If Herod got wind of these strange events, he would kill all of us," Toma stated.

"Herod has killed every man who has attempted to lead the people in righteousness," Joseph stated. "It only takes a hint of authority from heaven, and Herod knows it is a threat to his wicked reign."

"But this little baby couldn't be a threat to anyone." Mary looked lovingly at the infant who slept cradled in the sling that hung from her shoulders.

"He threatened our friendship," Sarah said contritely.

"Not really," Mary responded.

"Forgive us," Toma requested. "I don't know what got into us."

"Parenthood!" Joseph responded, "That's what got into you. Ever since I became a father, my thought patterns have changed."

Suddenly, the cloud of oppression lifted, and all four burst into laughter. Joseph relieved Toma of baby Avrahm, lifting him onto his sturdy shoulders, while Sarah slipped her arm through Mary's. Toma began a psalm as he led the little group toward home.

> *I will extol the LORD at all times;*
> *his praise will always be on my lips.*
> *My soul will boast in the LORD.*

Joseph and the ladies joined in.

> *Let the afflicted hear and rejoice.*
> *Glorify the LORD with me;*
> *let us exalt his name together.*
> *I sought the LORD, and he answered me;*
> *he delivered me from all my fears.*[9]

Like a glowing shield, the Spirit moved with the two families as they continued toward Bethlehem.

Resentment and Jealousy howled in impotent rage as they fled from the song of praise.

The quick clippety-clop of horses' hooves bearing down on them caused Joseph and Toma to turn and study the road behind them. "Roman soldiers," Toma stated.

"Only three," Joseph commented as he guided the women to the side of the road. The little group continued walking, but their feet hugged the edge of the hard-packed earth. They had not traveled very far before the horses and riders passed, leaving only clouds of dust in their wake.

"One of the men on horseback is a Jewish man," Joseph commented.

"I know that man," Toma responded. "Malachi! He is the senior tax collector for this region. Someone in Bethlehem is in serious trouble."

"You know him?" Joseph asked in surprise.

"What I mean to say is that I know who he is because I have paid taxes to him on a few occasions," Toma explained. "Only rarely do we see him in Bethlehem. He usually sends a servant. For Malachi to make a personal appearance escorted by a couple of Roman soldiers"—Toma sighed—"it can only mean he intends to make an example out of someone."

"How can a man turn on his own people?" Joseph asked.

"Money. It corrupts," Toma responded, "and he has plenty. Malachi lives on an estate closer to Jerusalem than to Bethlehem. He is really not welcome in our town. We've made sure he knows that!"

Joseph raised a quizzical eyebrow. "How?"

"One Sabbath, he tried to attend the synagogue." Toma threw up his hands in a mock-hopeless gesture. "Well, the entrance became blocked. It seems we were so crowded that day that no one else could get into the building. He had to turn around and leave. Another time, his horse became untethered. The animal wandered so far away that it took him two days to get it back. Then there was the time—"

"Toma!" Sarah interrupted. "Look, the soldiers' horses!"

"That's the home where Jesus was born!" Mary exclaimed.

"I should have known old Shammah would be the one to try to cheat Rome out of its taxes and Malachi out of his unfair portion," Toma stated. "Do you know that old shepherd owns enough land to have his own estate?"

"He seemed so poor!" Joseph exclaimed.

Toma chuckled. "That's what he wants everyone to think. He leases his land to the Temple shepherds, and no one ever seems to know exactly where the boundaries are."

"Have pity on the man and his wife," the Holy Spirit whispered. "He is your neighbor, and this is his time of need."

Looking ahead, Joseph could see the soldiers bringing Shammah out of his house. The old shepherd had his hands tied in front of him, and Zepporah followed, sobbing and begging for mercy. "We've got to help them." Joseph took a couple of quick steps in the direction of Shammah's house. "He is too old to be put in Herod's dungeon."

At that moment, a spirit of Fear seized Toma, binding him, preventing him from responding to the Spirit of God.

Quickly, Toma caught up with Joseph, bringing him to a halt with a restraining hand. "There is nothing we can do," Toma insisted. "If you interfere, you will only make yourself an enemy of Rome. Then what will you do? Live as a bandit? Hide in the hills and steal for a living?"

Joseph clenched and unclenched his massive fists. "I know Shammah is a greedy man, but what right do foreigners have to tax the land God gave to his family?"

"They have the right," Toma said, shaking his head sadly, "because God has allowed them to govern the land. God sets rulers on thrones and then sweeps them away. Blessed be his holy name. We must wait for the Anointed One, the promised Deliverer."

Mary looked down at the infant sleeping in the sling that hung from her shoulders. Would this tiny babe take on the armies of Rome? She shivered at the fearful thought.

Malachi and the soldiers wasted no time at Shammah's peasant home. Before Joseph, Toma, and their wives had come within shouting distance, the soldiers were mounted and pulling Shammah behind their horses at a clip that was too brisk for the man to keep up.

"He's going to fall!" Sarah gasped.

"Then they will drag him," Mary added. She was too horrified to say more.

"He will never make it to Jerusalem," Toma stated the obvious.

"Joseph, speak to the tax collector," the Holy Spirit urged.

Watching and supervising the capture of this man, Satan laughed to himself. "Today, the Spirit is assisting me!"

The tax collector and his entourage were nearly abreast of the little group. Everyone could see that old Shammah was struggling to keep up with the horses and the horses were fretting at the slow pace. Joseph stepped forward. "Malachi!"

The tax collector reined his horse to a quick halt. "Do I know you?"

Mary held her breath. This was a man of power and authority. He could take her husband just like he had taken Shammah!

"No, I am from the region of Galilee."

Malachi snorted in disgust before asking, "What do you want with me?"

"Horses," the Spirit prompted.

"I noticed that your horses are walking with an abnormal gait. It's because they are going too slow for their normal canter. If you would let the prisoner ride behind one of the soldiers, then your horses could move at a normal pace. You would also reach your destination sooner." Joseph gave a little respectful bow as he finished his suggestion.

"So you are concerned about my horses?" From his elevated seat, Malachi looked down his nose at the common laborer who had the audacity to offer a suggestion.

"The God of our fathers commands us to treat our animals humanely," Joseph responded.

"Humph!" Malachi snorted his contempt for the man who spoke to him.

"Take good advice when it is given to you," Satan pushed the thought into the tax collector's mind.

"Let the prisoner ride," Malachi ordered.

One of the soldiers dismounted and roughly assisted the old man onto the back of the other soldier's horse. Joseph watched until Toma gave him a hard nudge, propelling him away from the authorities and down the road before Malachi could think of any other orders to give.

The Roman guards, with their prisoner sitting behind one of them, were well on their way toward Herod's dungeon when the two couples walked into Shammah's courtyard. Zepporah lay in a crumpled heap on the packed dirt floor.

Mary was the first to reach her. "Zepporah?" She stooped down and brushed her young hand across the old woman's tearstained cheek.

Sarah gently lifted the old shepherdess by her shoulders and helped her to a bench by the wall.

"Why did they take him?" Toma asked.

"They said he owed taxes on the land," Zepporah choked on her words.

"How much? How much do they want?" Toma pressed.

"I don't know. He has to go before the judge." Zepporah began to sob again. "They are going to put him in Herod's dungeon. I don't know what they will do to him!"

"Zepporah!" an alarmed voice came from the entrance to the courtyard.

Joseph turned to see the shepherds who had come the night Jesus was born.

"We saw the soldiers," Ehud said, "and came as fast was we could." Following Ehud, Nahum, Toviah, and Oved piled into the small courtyard, looking as if they were ready for a fight.

"The soldiers have taken Shammah to Jerusalem, to Herod's dungeon," Joseph informed them. "He will remain there until a judge decides what he must pay."

"Zepporah can come home with us," Sarah offered.

"That won't be necessary," Ehud responded. "Shepherds take care of each other. She can come to my home. My wife will make her welcome, and Oved will care for her animals. Old woman," he addressed Zepporah with the respect that a young man should have for the generations that precede him. "We are getting ready to take another flock to the Temple tomorrow. When we arrive, we will go to the dungeon and see what we can find out. You do not have to fear for yourself. We will take care of you, and we will do our best for your husband."

"Greedy old man," Nahum muttered. "If Herod takes his land, then where will our flocks graze?"

"We may need a little money to bribe the guards," Ehud looked directly at Zepporah. Her initial fear seemed to have subsided. "Do you know where he keeps his coins?"

"He has never told me, but I am not stupid!" There was a tinge of anger in her voice. "He makes more trips to the well each day than I do. His money has to be in the well."

"I'll look." Oved ran to the back of the house.

"If only Shammah would just do what he is supposed to do and trust in the Lord to take care of him!" Zepporah threw her hands up in exasperation.

The babies were starting to cry. Mary and Sarah looked at their husbands, who understood their unspoken messages.

"You're in good hands," Toma said to Zepporah. "We will leave you with these men of the covenant."

Looking back as they left the courtyard, Mary called to Zepporah, "May God smile on you."

The old shepherdess nodded, accepting the gentle blessing from the young mother.

Chapter 8

ROYAL VISITORS IN JERUSALEM

*After Jesus was born in Bethlehem in Judea, during the time
of King Herod, Magi from the east came to Jerusalem and
asked, "Where is the one who has been born King of the Jews?
We saw his star in the east and have come to worship him."*

—Matthew 2:1–2

Satan and his demonic horde escorted Malachi and his prisoner to the gates of Herod's dungeon.

"Old man! Shammah!" Satan called the old shepherd's name as the guard pushed him off the horse to land roughly on the stone pavement of the courtyard.

Crouching fearfully on his hands and knees, Shammah hesitantly looked up and around. The great wood-and-bronze gate to the prison loomed in front of him. Slowly, it opened like the jaws of an evil monster. "No! No! This is all a mistake!" Shammah cowered as he pleaded, but the soldiers paid no attention to the groveling Jew. Roughly, they pulled him to his feet and dragged him into the tomb-like maze of cells and torture chambers.

"Think, old man," the master demon spoke again. "You must bargain your way out of here."

"Money!" Shammah whined. "Do you want money?"

One of the guards laughed. "Look around, old man. Do you think Herod needs your money?"

"Then why am I here?" Shammah cried in confused panic.

"You are here because Herod needs to make an example out of you," one of the soldiers offered.

"He also may want your land," another soldier added. "There are rumors that he wants to build a magnificent tomb for the sons he recently executed!"

Realizing he was in the hands of a man who had no qualms about killing his own children, Shammah began to tremble and babble incoherently.

"Get ahold on yourself!" Satan commanded. "You have valuable information, Shammah." Confidently, the Prince of Darkness burned an encouraging thought into the old man's brain as he whispered, "You can tell Herod the Jewish Messiah has been born. You can tell him where to find this threat to his throne. That is worth more than money and more than land!"

The prison guard shoved Shammah into a tiny cell, slamming the wooden door shut and locking it with a key. Shammah ran to the small barred window in the center of the door. "I have information!" he yelled at the backs of the guards as they walked down the torch-lit corridor toward the guardroom. "Tell Herod I know where he can find the Anointed One. He has been born! Angels announced his birth!"

One of the guards glanced over his shoulder before turning to his companion. "This one is really desperate!"

"He has not even felt the whip, and he is willing to say anything!" the other guard responded.

"I liked it better when he was offering money!" the first guard quipped.

"Keep trying," Satan encouraged the trembling old man as he sank onto a moldy pile of hay in the corner of his cell. "Keep trying. They will believe you eventually. When the guards believe you and carry your information to Herod, then you will be freed."

The winter sunshine warmed Mary's back as she bent to pick up another bundle of thatch to hand up to Joseph. Once they got this thatch roof on their new home, they would be able to move in. After the next Passover, Joseph would add a sturdy flat roof and another room.

Bundle after bundle, she handed them up to her husband, pausing only occasionally to stretch her back and look at Jesus, who was holding onto Zepporah's fingers while taking wobbly tiptoeing steps.

Joseph came down the ladder and picked up the waterskin. Mary watched him take a long drink before she shared her thoughts. "Joseph, it is so sad to see Zepporah all alone. Shammah has been in Herod's dungeon for nine months. How much longer do you think he is going to be in that awful place?" Mary asked.

"It's hard to say. I think Ehud made a mistake the first time he bribed the guards. I know it bought Shammah better food and a blanket, but it also made those Roman soldiers greedy," Joseph replied.

"I don't understand," Mary responded. Her eyes remained on the old woman who was watching her son.

"When the soldiers learned that Shammah had money, most likely they decided to delay his appearance before the judge. They know the longer he stays in prison, the more bribes they will receive."

"Is there no authority in the land that will do what is lawful?" Mary exclaimed.

Joseph shook his head as he responded, "There will only be justice in the land when God reigns supreme." He turned to climb back up the ladder.

"How much longer do you intend to keep Shammah in Herod's dungeon?" The Holy Spirit met his adversary, Satan, near the northern guard tower next to the entrance to the palace.

"Why should you care what I do with this man?" Satan responded. "He is mine."

"The Creator has not given any of his creatures to you," the Spirit of God replied.

"Shammah has chosen," Satan countered.

"From his cell, he has repented of that choice and desires to be brought back under the covering of God," the Spirit announced.

"He has a mission to complete first." Satan argued. "He must be brought before Herod with the news of the birth of the Messiah."

The Spirit mocked, "Was this old man the best you could do to marshal the forces of Herod under your banner? He has shouted his story so many times that no one listens anymore!"

"I'll make Herod listen," Satan growled.

"Shammah can go," the Holy Spirit announced as he tapped the commander of the guard on the shoulder.

The Roman soldier in charge of Herod's prison responded by picking up the jailer's key ring and walking directly to Shammah's cell. "You are free," he announced as he swung the door open, allowing the old man to stumble out.

"What do you think you're doing?" Satan shouted. "You have no right!"

"You don't need him." The Spirit of God pointed down the road toward a caravan of camels flanked by guards and led by three nobles from the former Medo-Persian Empire now known as Parthia. "You know these men, rulers from the city-state of Edessa, between the Tigris and Euphrates Rivers."

Frustrated but not yet ready to turn away in defeat, Satan clenched his jaw and studied the three men mounted on Arabian steeds. They were dressed like noble warriors, with bows and arrows strapped to the sides of their mounts.

Confidently, the Spirit of God introduced the magi from Edessa, "The first rider is Prince Abgar, destined to inherit the throne. With him is his close friend, Zarbin, who will become his military commander. The third man is Abdu—"

"A Zoroastrian priest!" Satan interrupted. "These men are not descendants of Abraham, neither are they worshipers of God. They look to the stars, believing each man's destiny is fixed and mirrored in the movements of the heavenly bodies."

"I have moved on their minds."

"Were you invited? You can't just force yourself on men!" Satan insisted.

"They prayed for enlightenment," the Holy Spirit responded, "and I laid out before them ancient scrolls, the books of Moses, and the notes from Daniel of the Persian Empire."

"Moses! Daniel!" Satan repeated the names with undisguised contempt.

Spirited steeds with their royal warrior-mounts, along with heavily laden camels escorted by shouting drovers, clattered up to the entrance of Herod's palace in the elite Upper City of Jerusalem.

"You want Herod to know about the birth of the Anointed One?" the Spirit challenged his adversary. "These men, royal magi, schooled in the sciences of the East have been chosen by God to announce to the usurper of Judea's throne that one greater than he has been born!"

"So here is the battleground!" Satan scoffed. "God has chosen the palace of Herod the Great, a piece of Jerusalem that definitely belongs to me!"

Guards from Herod's personal regiment scurried to find someone in authority.

Abgar dismounted. Handing the reigns of his stallion over to an attendant, he began the impatient pacing of a prince who was not used to waiting. Zarbin and Abdu joined him, making an impressive trio.

Volumnius, the military commander on duty, was the first to arrive at the gate, conferring briefly with the sentry before approaching their unexpected visitors. "May I inquire as to the nature of your business at the palace?" he asked.

"A new king of the Jews has been born. We have seen his star and have come to honor him," Abgar made a slight respectful bow as he completed his statement and placed in the hand of the military commander a parchment containing their credentials and a message from Manu III, the reigning king of Edessa. Volumnius handed the small scroll over to an aid, who immediately carried it into the palace.

"A new king?" Volumnius nearly choked on the words. "I'm afraid you are mistaken. Herod is king of the Jews and has been for at least thirty years. No infant has been born in the palace, and—"The military commander lowered his voice to a whisper as if he were about to reveal more information than he should, but before he could tell these men how inflammatory and dangerous it was to mention a possible threat to Herod's throne, Corinthus, Herod's chief chamberlain, came rushing out of the palace to greet the visitors.

"King Herod welcomes you to his court. He has read your parchment of introduction from the king of Edessa and is most interested in your mission and your astrological sightings. He will call you into his chambers shortly," Corinthus announced. Then he commenced giving orders for the camels and horses to be taken to the royal stables, for the three visiting dignitaries to be escorted to guest apartments in the palace, for their valuables to be taken to the treasury, and for their military escort to be housed in the barracks. The royal courtyard immediately broke into a frenzy of activity.

In the royal residence of the palace, Herod pulled himself out of bed and beckoned one of his eunuchs to assist him in dressing for this unexpected audience. His hands trembled, and his legs barely supported his frail body. Carefully, his attendant slipped a linen toga over his head. For a moment, Herod paled and leaned heavily against one of the supporting columns in the room.

"You had better see to your king," the Holy Spirit goaded his adversary, Satan. "He may not live long enough to hear the good news."

"He'll live," Satan responded with grim indifference.

"Physician! Physician!" Herod clutched his abdomen, nearly bending double with pain. "I need my physician!" he screamed. Servants scurried down the maze of corridors to the apartments of the royal physician while Herod's attendant assisted him to a couch in the adjoining room.

Corinthus and Volumnius entered the royal bedchamber just as the court physician arrived with a pain-killing draught of wine mixed with medicinal herbs. Herod swallowed the bitter drink in one gulp, registering his opinion of the vile-tasting but necessary potion using several crude phrases that had become part of his vocabulary during the military campaigns of his youth. Then for a short time, he rested, leaning back into the cushions and saying nothing. Servants and attendants took their unobtrusive leave, disappearing behind massive walls of hanging drapes. Herod's chamberlain and military commander remained in the room, silent and respectful, waiting uneasily for their violent and unpredictable ruler to speak.

"Parthians," Herod muttered to himself. "When I first became king, I drove them out of this land. I chased them all the way to the Euphrates, but Rome would not allow me to cross that boundary and finish the job.

Both men leaned forward to catch his words.

"Rome does not want any trouble with Parthia," Herod bitterly complained. "Volumnius?" he suddenly commanded.

"Sir!" The military commander snapped to attention.

"Do you know why Rome does not want any problems with Parthia?" Herod queried, as if testing the knowledge of his commander.

"Fifty years ago, Rome sent her armies across the Euphrates. We found out that the Parthians were excellent archers. They defeated Rome and beheaded the Roman General Crassus. We have not crossed the Euphrates since that time."

"If I may, sir?" Corinthus, the chamberlain, stepped forward. "This is not a military expedition. These men are ambassadors whose visit is based on some astrological sighting. I understand that the study of astrology is forbidden to the Jews, so you may not see any significance—"

Herod interrupted his chamberlain's placating speech. "Do you think I am an ignorant man? A Galilean fisherman, perhaps?"

"No, Your Majesty." Corinthus bowed and took a few discreet steps backward.

With great effort, Herod pulled himself up to a sitting position on the couch. "I have been to Rome! The same astrologers who explain the significance of celestial movements to Caesar have explained it to me. Caesar plans each day by the stars! He does not move his armies unless the stars are in correct alignment! Now the stars have brought to my court men with knowledge of a threat to my throne. I will hear these men now!"

Before Herod's last word slipped away to be replaced by the labored breathing of their ailing king, Volumnius and Corinthus both scurried to do his bidding.

"Satan, do you remember when the Creator filled the heavens with balls of fire and reflective bodies?" the Spirit asked.

The former covering cherub just turned his back on the Spirit of God and refused to acknowledge the creative power of his Maker.

"He gave each one an orbit and set their intersections. The interpretation of those movements belongs to their Maker. He has given this knowledge to his chosen messengers."

"When their message is received by King Herod, I'm going to turn the universe upside down!" Satan muttered. "It will be more spectacular than all six days of creation!"

As Abgar, Zarbin, and Abdu, now changed from their traveling clothes into the silk robes of the Court of Edessa, followed the Roman commander Volumnius into the royal chambers of the king of Judea, all heads turned. The attendants of Herod's court had seen foreign dignitaries before, but never had they seen such an ostentatious display of their wealth! In open-mouthed amazement, Herod's servants and courtiers gawked at the shimmering robes embroidered with threads of gold that the three nobles wore. They stared at their feet, encased in silk slippers, a fabric unknown in Palestine, and they wondered what techniques were used to style and oil their thick braided beards. Every person the magi passed was dazzled as lamplight sparkled on the polished bronze-and-silk turbans that sat on the regal heads of the three royal visitors. But the cause of the greatest amazement was the number and size of the many-faceted jewels that hung from golden chains around their necks.

At the entrance to Herod's private rooms, Corinthus met them. He paused a moment, surveying the three magi from head to toe and obviously groping for the correct words. Taking a deep breath, he finally said, "Our Majesty will be honored to see that you have dressed so lavishly for a few moments of his time. I want you to be aware that our king is not feeling well. Therefore, he prefers to meet with you in his private chambers. This will most likely be a very brief audience, so address the purpose of your visit quickly."

Unobtrusively, a servant drew back the draperies, and the nobles of Edessa followed Herod's chamberlain into the room adjacent to the king's sleeping chamber.

With unheard of self-confidence, the three young men approached the aging monarch, greeting him with polite sweeping bows. From his half-reclining position on a couch, Herod eyed the royal emissaries from Edessa. He pressed his mouth into a thin hard line, then finally, he forced it into a half smile. "Welcome to Judea. I hope your accommodations in the palace are comfortable." As he spoke, Herod gestured toward three seats that had been brought into the room for his guests.

"I believe Herod is feeling a little jealousy," the Holy Spirit pointed out. "He's considering throwing these nobles from Edessa into his dungeon and taking everything they have."

"He will keep himself under control," Satan snapped. "Herod is a man with priorities!"

The three emissaries from the Court of Edessa bowed once more before taking the seats they were offered.

Herod spoke again. Fighting back waves of pain and nausea, he fell into the dishonestly polite rhetoric that was the backbone of court intrigue. "I have never had the privilege of visiting your kingdom, but I am honored that you have visited mine." In the back of his devious mind, he calculated the number of troops he would need to march northeast, cross the Euphrates, and decimate the population of Edessa. If only he was younger and healthier! He eyed their jewels and wondered how many wagons it would take to carry their wealth back to Jerusalem—and how much of it he would have to turn over to Rome!

"We have come to honor the new king of the Jews who has recently been born," Abdu stated their mission.

"A new king of the Jews?" Herod pondered their mission before responding.

"Play along," Satan urged. "Gain their confidence."

"As you can see, my health is failing. It may be that my reign is coming to an end, but before that happens, I would like to see my successor." Herod paused and leaned weakly back into the cushions. He allowed his face to show all the fatigue and pain he had been living with.

"Good, good," Satan encouraged. "You have stirred their sympathy—such a weak, useless emotion. They want to help you."

Gloating, Satan turned to his adversary, the Spirit of God, "The old fox is playing his role well!"

"Yes, he has learned from the master deceiver," the Spirit responded.

"I have many children," Herod continued. "There has been much squabbling and some plotting over who will inherit my throne, but now the stars have solved the problem!" He sighed and then gave a slight groan.

"King Herod," Abdu spoke up, "we also have some knowledge of the healing arts. We would be most willing to speak with your physician."

"You are too kind," Herod responded with grandfather-like gentleness, "but first tell me about this new King of the Jews. If I could go to him and lay my crown at his feet, then his throne would be secured without bloodshed and I could die a contented man."

"We thought you would know where to find him!" Abgar exclaimed.

"No. my court does not have an astrologer," Herod responded, but I am familiar with the science. So please, explain your sightings to me."

"Our calculation of time and our traditions are not the same as yours, so we cannot pinpoint the exact date or even the exact event. It could be the conception of a ruler, the birth of a ruler, or some ceremony like the coronation of a ruler. All we know is that there is a new ruler for Judea. We have seen the regal star in Aries, the ram," Abgar began the explanation. "We have seen it several times over the past two years."

"Aries is the sign of the Jews," Zarbin interjected.

"Yes, I know that," Herod responded.

Abgar continued to explain, "At the same time, the star that confers kingships emerged in the east and traveled through Aries."

"The sun was also in Aries, and the moon was in close conjunction," Abdu inserted. "The stars are telling us that a powerful ruler, one who is blessed by both the sun and the moon, is now in the land of Judea."

Herod stroked his close-cropped beard and tried to take in the significance of these events. "The stars say a king has been born," he muttered. "Do you have any other clues as to time or place?" he questioned.

"In one of the books of Moses, it says, '*I see him, but not now; I behold him, but not near. A star will come out of Jacob; a scepter will rise out of Israel. He will crush the foreheads of Moab, the sculls of all the sons of Sheth. Edom will be conquered; Seir, his enemy, will be conquered, but Israel will grow strong,*'[1] Abdu quoted.

"You're not a descendant of Jacob," Satan whispered into Herod's ear. "As a matter of fact, your ancestors come from the land of Edom. If this so-called King of the Jews is not destroyed, he will crush you and your dynasty! You have to move and move quickly! You know what will happen if the people get word that a legitimate heir to David's throne has been born. They will rise up, amass against you! Rome will not tolerate such an insurrection!

Whether the people are successful or not, Caesar will take your throne and your head!"

Herod ground his teeth and clenched his fists in an effort to control the rage that billowed up inside.

"Your Majesty," Abgar spoke with concern, "are you in pain? Should we come back at another time?"

Abdu suggested, "Maybe we should call your physician?"

"No, no, I'll be fine." Herod reined in his rage and then nodded to Corinthus. "Bring us all a little wine." Leaning forward, he then looked intently into the eyes of the three men. "Where?" he asked. "Where is this ruler to be born?"

"We don't know," Zarbin stated. "Jerusalem was our best guess. It is your holy city…" His voice trailed off in thoughtfulness.

"Could we have access to more of your scriptures?" Abdu asked.

"Herod, listen to me! These men do not need to waste time reading through the law and the prophets," Satan pushed. "Call the experts, the Pharisees, the scribes who know every jot and title."

Nearby the Holy Spirit watched. A little amused smile played across his face. Satan was working so hard to accomplish the will of God.

Immediately, Herod came to his feet, nearly knocking over the tray of wine that a servant was offering. "Corinthus! Send for Hillel and Shammai! Bring them to the palace immediately. Don't let them give you any excuses about vows, fasting and prayer, clean and unclean, new moons, or special sacrifices. Tell those two stuffy Pharisees it is a matter of life and death—their life or possibly their death." The burst of energy that had accompanied his orders seemed to have drained the king. He sank back down into the cushions of his couch looking pale and weak.

Immediately, Corinthus dispatched two servants, then he turned his attention to the king. "Your Majesty, it might be wise for you to retire to your sleeping chamber until the esteemed rabbis arrive."

"Yes," Herod responded in a thin, almost lifeless voice. Reaching for the arm of his chamberlain, he pulled himself up from the couch and allowed himself to be supported as he moved into the adjoining chamber.

The three ambassadors from Edessa watched with concern. "Your king seems to be suffering greatly," Abdu observed.

Volumnius, the Roman commander who had remained in the room, replied, "He has been ill for some time, but he is still the undisputed ruler of this land."

"Commander," Zarbin inquired, "it appears these scholars that the king has sent for might be unwilling to assist us?"

"Does your king usually have to threaten his subjects to get them to appear at the palace?" Prince Abgar asked.

"No. Herod is a powerful and respected ruler. It is just that these two men are the most learned and most important scholars in the city. Each one has his own school of followers. If Hillel says you should wash your hands three times a day, half of the city starts washing their hands three times a day. If Shammai says you should fast every fourth day of the week, the king himself is obliged, for the sake of appearances, to fast. They are powerful men in their own way."

"And critical of the king?" Abdu observed.

Volumnius nodded. "They have had their differences. Shammai is the most conservative of Jews. Hillel is a little more open-minded, but neither man is as broad-minded as our king."

"These are things to consider," Abdu remarked.

"The servants will bring you refreshment, and I will take my leave," Volumnius excused himself from the room.

"All things may not be as they seem," the Spirit of God whispered to the magi. "Be cautious and see with a spiritual eye."

All three emissaries exchanged knowing glances and then waited in meditating silence until the sound of footsteps on stone corridors announced the arrival of Hillel and Shammai, the most eminent Jewish scholars of the day. Corinthus accompanied them. He gave a courteous little bow to the dignitaries from the city-state of Edessa in Parthia before making introductions.

"At this time, gentlemen, I suggest we proceed to the palace library, where there are copies of the law and the prophets," Corinthus said as he moved to lead the way.

Prince Abgar paused to inquire, "Will the king be joining us?"

"No," Corinthus replied. "His majesty, King Herod, has retired for the night, but he is most interested to know what you find in the scriptures. He has requested a full report in the morning."

"Who is expected to give this report?" Hillel asked in a challenging tone as the group moved along the corridor toward the library.

Authoritatively, Corinthus responded, "You will dictate it to a scribe before you leave the palace."

"Herod does not desire to see us any more than we desire to see him," Shammai commented under his breath as they entered a massive room filled with scrolls.

To accommodate the Pharisees who he knew did not make it a practice to associate with non-Jews, Herod's chamberlain sat the men at separate tables, close enough to converse but far enough to prevent accidental touching that would cause these men of the law to consider themselves unclean. Before Corinthus could begin with some formalities that might bridge the cultural gap, Shammai spoke up, "Why have we been summoned to speak of the law and the prophets with Gentiles?" He asked his question in Hebrew, expecting that the emissaries, who had been using Greek, the language of the court, would not understand.

Before Corinthus could draw upon his limited Hebrew vocabulary to answer the question, Abdu spoke up, "This large number of scrolls that contain the writings of your prophets is not available to us in Edessa."

The conversation continued in Hebrew. "You have read from the law and the prophets?" Hillel asked.

"Only small portions from Moses," Abdu answered, then he added, "If we could speak in Aramaic or Greek, then my friends would also understand."

"What is your interest in our writings?" Shammai asked in Greek.

Prince Abgar answered, "We are men who study the stars with the same intensity that you devote to these scrolls. In Aries, the sign of the zodiac that rules the Judean world, we have seen the royal star rise and be blessed by both the sun and the moon. This can only mean that a ruler sent from the heavens has arrived in Judea."

Both scholars exchanged glances, then Hillel repeated, "A ruler sent from the heavens?"

"Yes," Abdu clarified, "like a god-king."

"We do not study the zodiac or have anything to do with it. It is forbidden to us, and any Jew practicing or seeking information from someone who practices this craft is to be stoned." Shammai stood and turned as if to make a righteous exit and remove himself from this compromising situation.

"But"—Hillel stood to offer the counterpoint—"our ancestor, Joseph the beloved son of Jacob, was given a vision of the sun, moon, and stars, not unlike what these men are talking about."

Shammai paused and turned to face Hillel. "The Creator's purpose for the stars is stated in the first book of Moses. He set them in the expanse of the sky to give light on the earth, to govern the day and night, and to separate light from darkness!" His voice rose as he added, "That is all!"

"No!" Hillel matched the volume of his counterpart.

Corinthus stood and stepped between the two men, begging them with hand gestures to lower their voices. He was ignored. The debate was on.

Hillel continued his argument, "There is more! The Holy One has used the stars to speak to his people. He spoke to our father, Abraham. Look at the stars, can you count them? You, Abraham, shall be the father of a great nation, and your descendants shall be numbered like the stars!"

Prince Abgar, Zarbin, and Abdu turned their attention from Hillel to Shammai, anticipating a heated response.

"*When you look up to the sky and see the sun, the moon and the stars—all the heavenly array—do not be enticed into bowing down to them and worshipping things the LORD your God has apportioned to all the nations under heaven.*"[2] Shammai gestured toward the Parthians. "These things, the Lord your God has given to the other nations! They may study the stars. We can have nothing to do with it!"

"We have not allowed these men to explain sufficiently to make a determination as to whether or not they are asking us to do something that is contrary to the Torah!" Hillel countered.

"Have you not read the prophet Amos?" Shammai challenged. He then reverted to quoting in Hebrew. "The Almighty said, '*You have lifted up the shrine of your king, the pedestal of your idols, the star of your god… Therefore I will send you into exile!*'[3] It is bad enough to be ruled by Rome and have these foreigners in the land"—he gestured toward Corinthus—"but at least our people remain in the land, and we have the hope of deliverance. But if the Almighty, blessed be his name, sends us into exile, what then?"

Abdu suddenly jumped to his feet. "'*I see him, but not now; I behold him, but not near. A star will come out of Jacob; a scepter will rise out of Israel. He will crush the foreheads of*'[4] your enemies! It is from one of your books of Moses." He bowed and then seated himself again.

The debate ceased immediately. Both scholars turned to face the foreigner who had quoted their scripture in perfect Hebrew.

"Please," Abdu implored. "We have seen this star. What do your scriptures say about the time and place for this ruler?"

"This star?" Shammai repeated, as if trying to realign his thinking.

"A star out of Jacob, a scepter out of Israel, crush the heads of our enemies." Hillel pondered the phrases.

Always near, the Spirit whispered to Hillel, "The Anointed One! The Promised Deliverer!"

Hillel began to get excited. He did a little dance as he moved closer to Shammai. "The Messiah!" he whispered.

Shammai's face lit up. Both Pharisees glanced at Corinthus and then nodded to each other in satisfaction. Herod's chamberlain seemed to be having difficulty following their Hebrew dialogue.

"Translate for your friends," Shammai said to Abdu. "We know about this star. It is the hope our people have clung to through all their trials."

Immediately, there was a flurry of languages: Hebrew, Aramaic, Greek, and the local dialect of Edessa. Corinthus looked back and forth from one group to the other, unable to follow the conversation.

Slowly, Shammai walked around the room, looking at the scrolls, then he pulled one from its cubicle and carried it to the table. Together, he and Hillel rolled and unrolled the spindles until they reached the passage both men were searching for. They gestured for Abdu to come and read for himself the words of the prophet Micah.

Both men stepped back, allowing room for Abdu to approach the table. He read it out loud, first in Hebrew and then translating it into the local dialect of the city of Edessa.

"Marshal your troops, O city of troops, for a siege is laid against us. They will strike Israel's ruler on the cheek with a rod. But you, Bethlehem…though you are small among the clans of Judah, out of you will come for me one who will be ruler over Israel, whose origins are from of old, from ancient times…He will stand and shepherd the flock in the strength of the LORD, *in the majesty of the name of the* LORD *his God. And they will live securely, for then his greatness will reach to the ends of the earth. And he will be their peace."*[5]

While the significance of those words hung in the air like the spirits of good and evil that surrounded them, all of the men in the room paused in contemplation. Only Corinthus seemed flustered and confused by the words that had just been read.

"Corinthus!" Satan filled the man's mind with directions. "Don't be a fool! Those Pharisees are not going to give you accurate information. Call a scribe in here immediately. Have him copy and translate the passage into both Greek and Aramaic. The length and quality of the rest of your life may depend on getting this report!"

Corinthus moved, breaking the Spirit-filled silence with a barrage of orders. Scribes entered the room. The three emissaries were escorted back to their chambers. Hillel and Shammai stood to take their leave, but Corinthus blocked their way. "Dictate your report," he ordered.

Shammai responded by calling over his shoulder to the scribes who were busy copying the passage from the prophet Micah, "Bethlehem!"

Hillel added, "But we cannot be sure how accurate the prophecy is!"

Both men pushed past Herod's chamberlain, ignoring his demands that they report in more detail.

Shortly after the sun reached its zenith, Volumnius entered the stable area, where the escort and attendants for the emissaries from Edessa were preparing their caravan for departure. Parthian military men groomed their mounts and checked their weapons. Drovers loaded camels. Volumnius sniffed the air. The Middle Eastern sun had warmed the straw-caked dung and the oiled leather. It drew the body odors out of man and beast. The whole operation smelled like a military campaign. It stirred his blood and made him wish he was moving on to conquer distant lands for Rome. A fine Arabian mare snorted impatiently. Absentmindedly, the Roman commander paused to stroke her glossy flanks. Court life is making me soft, he mused. Then pushing past the kneeling camels, he scanned the activity in the stable yard, looking for Prince Abgar.

He spotted the prince talking with Zarbin. Both men were wearing their military-style traveling clothes. It was obvious they planned to depart soon. Without wasting any more time, he strode directly toward them.

"Good day to you!" Volumnius greeted the Parthian dignitaries. "King Herod regrets that he is unable to meet with you this afternoon, but he has asked me to escort you to the outskirts of Bethlehem. I will leave you there to conduct your search for this ruler as the stars direct, but Herod begs you to return to him after this child-ruler has been found, to tell him every detail so he can also go and honor him."

"King Herod has been most generous," Prince Abgar replied. "We will certainly honor his request. In appreciation for his hospitality, we would like to leave a small gift." The prince pointed to a basket. An attendant lifted the lid and brought to Volumnius a bolt of soft shimmering fabric.

"This is a rare and valuable gift," Volumnius responded, awed at the incredible, light texture of the material in his hands. "King Herod thanks you."

"It comes from a land far to the east of Parthia," Zarbin informed. "The threads are magically spun by caterpillars."

"I will relay this information to the king," Volumnius promised as he passed the gift over to a servant who transported it into the palace.

"As soon as Abdu completes his prayers and incantations, we will be ready," Zarbin informed Volumnius, who distractedly nodded his response. His eye had fixed on the brass-tipped bow with its matching quiver of arrows that was securely lashed to the side of Zarbin's steed.

"You are appreciating a fine Parthian weapon," Zarbin stated as he pulled the bow from its casing and placed it in Volumnius's hand.

Volumnius tested the tension and balance of the bow. "This is a well-made weapon."

"Do you shoot?" Zarbin asked.

"I have trained troops in archery," Volumnius responded in an overly casual tone.

"I have also trained troops," Zarbin stated. "I have trained and been in command of this escort for several years."

A knowing look passed between the two military men. Orders were issued, and before the drovers could finish stringing the camels into a line, Roman and Parthian archers had lined up facing a series of improvised targets. Volley after volley of arrows flew, with servants running to check the results. Volumnius had to acknowledge that the Parthians were certainly accurate at every distance.

The camels were standing in a line, ready to begin the short journey to Bethlehem. Zarbin eyed his Roman counterpart. "How about you and me?"

The competitive spirit in Volumnius soared. "Your dagger for mine?" he challenged.

"Done!" Zarbin placed his jewel-encrusted dagger on the ground, and Volumnius removed the short squarish Roman sword from his own belt. He set it beside the elaborate Parthian weapon. "Winner keeps both!"

"Three arrows in the center of the leather shield hanging above the arch." Volumnius offered.

"Agreed!" Zarbin let the first arrow fly unerringly to the mark. Volumnius matched his shot.

Zarbin's next two shots landed a bit wide while those of the commander of Herod's personal regiments were exactly on the mark.

"My weapon is yours," Zarbin bowed and graciously removed his dagger from the dust, placing it in the hand of his Roman counterpart.

"Mount up!" Prince Abgar ordered as he cantered from one end of the stable yard to the other. Zarbin and Volumnius both hurried to their mounts. With a clatter of hooves and the squeaky straining of leather, the Parthian caravan moved out of the royal compound. Volumnius pushed his horse to move on to the head of the line, from there directing the procession onto the road to Bethlehem.

"They are on their way," Satan gloated. "Escort!" he commanded, and a dark cloud of demonic spirits emerged from Herod's royal residence and encased Volumnius, moving with him to the front of the column.

"Shield!" the Holy Spirit issued a counterorder. In response, an invisible-to-the-human-eye cloud of glory enveloped the three Parthian emissaries, with trails extending out to their troops and all that God had placed under their authority.

By the time the gates of Jerusalem were no longer in sight, the sun had disappeared from the late afternoon sky. As they continued toward the ancestral home of Judean kings, dusk gradually deepened. Prince Abgar left the road to gallop to a nearby hill for an unobstructed view of the sky. From their positions at the head of their caravan, Abdu and Zarbin also kept their eyes on the darkening sky. Earnestly, the three men, serious students of astrology, scanned the horizon, searching for familiar points of light.

"Look!" Abdu shouted. "The star!"

"It leads the way!" Zarbin confirmed.

Prince Abgar galloped from the rear of the caravan to join his companions. "Do you see the star?" As he pointed, the three men broke into cheers that could be heard from one end of the caravan to the other.

Volumnius, who led the caravan, turned and looked quizzically at the three men who were so deliriously excited that they appeared ready to fall off their horses. "Disgusting," he spoke to the soldier who rode on his right. "No dignity, definitely inferior men!" His hand touched the hilt of the jeweled dagger he had won. Zarbin deserved to be bested by a commander in the legions of Rome. Volumnius turned and looked at the three emissaries again. They were pointing at the sky, babbling in some strange language. With a demonic-inspired air of self-importance, he muttered to himself, "Foreigners! Who can figure them out?"

Chapter 9

Gifts for a Child

When Herod realized that he had been outwitted by the Magi, he was furious, and he gave orders to kill all the boys in Bethlehem and its vicinity who were two years old and under, in accordance with the time he had learned from the Magi.

—Matthew 2:16

"Yes! I am raising the cost of grazing your flocks on my land." Shammah rose from the bench he had been sitting on and stubbornly planted his feet on the hard-packed dirt of his courtyard.

Ehud took an imploring step toward the old shepherd while behind him, Oved and Nahum muttered about the ungrateful old man. "We cared for your wife, your home, and your animals for nearly ten months, and this is how you repay us?"

"You depleted my funds!" Shammah pointed an accusing finger at the men who had stood by him during his incarceration. "Who gave you permission to go into my well and take my money?"

"Your wife sent us to the well to take what was needed," Ehud replied. "Be reasonable!"

"You listened to a woman!" Shammah threw his arms in the air and gestured contemptuously toward his wife, who cowered in the cooking area. "God did not make women capable of making financial decisions."

"Old man"—Oved stepped forward—"with that money, we kept you alive! You had enough food and an extra blanket."

"And you never felt the whip," Ehud added. "We paid for that too!"

A clatter of hooves and riders, like a small army moving along the road to Bethlehem, brought the shepherd's squabble to a sudden halt. Shammah stepped around the men and peered out the gate that faced the road to see three wealthy foreigners dismount from magnificent horses and approach. Cautiously, he stepped out to meet them, the other shepherds close behind.

"Peace to this home," Prince Abgar addressed Shammah in Aramaic, the local tongue.

"May the Holy One smile on your journey," Shammah responded with eastern politeness. A little fearfully, he asked, "Why do you stop at the home of a humble shepherd?"

"Yours is the first house in the vicinity of Bethlehem." Prince Abgar paused to scan the countryside, then he looked up at the evening sky. "A star, that one"—he pointed to a bright dot in the sky, one that seemed to hang over the town—"has brought us here to find a baby who was probably born within the last year."

Shammah began to fidget. He felt his hands begin to sweat. "I don't think I can help you. My wife and I are old. We have no children."

"Keep pressing for information," the Spirit whispered to all three Parthian emissaries.

"But you may have heard something." Abdu stepped up. "It is a special child, and we expect that unusual phenomena surrounded the conception and birth of this child."

Zarbin approached. "We have come from Herod's court."

Shammah began shaking all over. He wanted nothing to do with Herod's court or his dungeon, but before he could vehemently deny any knowledge of any unusual birth, Ehud, Nahum, and Oved came rushing forward, pressing themselves into the conversation.

"We saw the child! Angels told us where to find him!" Oved announced.

"He was born in this stable," Ehud pointed to the animal shed attached to Shammah's house.

"It was a normal birth," Shammah protested. "A couple traveling on the road could not make it to their destination before the baby was born. It was nothing!" He waved his hands in the air as if to indicate that the incident flew away.

"The angels lined the hills, and they sang to us," Nahum explained. "The melody was so beautiful, and the words were 'Peace on earth, good will to all mankind.' I will never forget the experience!"

Ehud added, "The angel spoke to us and said, 'Today in Bethlehem, the city of David, a Savior has been born. He is the Anointed One you have waited for.'"

"Where is this child?" Abdu asked.

"Is he still in Bethlehem?" Zarbin chimed in.

Ehud began to direct, "The parents of this child live beside the ancient field of Boaz, their ancestor. Go to the well in the center of town, then take the path that leads to the fields south of town—" He paused and studied their faces. They looked so intent, following every word and puzzling as though they were not sure. "Never mind, I will show you the way."

"Joseph! Joseph!"

In the distance, through a fog of sleep, Joseph heard his name. He rolled over and snuggled comfortably next to his wife. He would sink back into whatever dream this was.

"Joseph!"

Again he heard his name. Who could be calling him after he had retired for the night? Didn't they know he had worked all day and had to begin again at dawn?

Mary stirred beside him. Jesus started to cry. Mary moved to bring the child into their bed to nurse. Suddenly, she stiffened, alert. "Joseph! Someone's coming! I hear horses, lots of them!"

Bang! Bang! "Joseph!" *Bang, bang!* A fist was pounding on the wooden gate to their small courtyard. Quickly, Joseph pulled his tunic over his head and hurried to the gate.

"Ehud?" Joseph stared first at his friend and then past the excited shepherd to see men with torches, wealthy foreigners on horseback, foreign troops, even a camel caravan! "What?" He could not find the words to utter all the questions that tumbled through his mind.

Mary, with baby Jesus in her arms, came to the door and cautiously peered at the breathtaking scene. Men and animals covered the field in front of their home. Three of them were dismounting and coming toward the house. What was this? Where could they hide? How could they get away?

"Be at peace, Mary," the Holy Spirit whispered. "Look at Ehud. He is not alarmed. He is joyful."

Before Joseph could make sense out of Ehud's excited babbling, Prince Abgar, Zarbin, and Abdu came forward. They knelt in the dust at his feet.

"Oh no!" Joseph exclaimed. "You should not kneel before me. I am just a peasant carpenter." For a moment, he stood there in bewildered shock, groping to make sense out of the moment. "Do you need a wagon repaired?" He looked around to see if he could see something broken, something he could relate to. "I can repair most anything made of wood." He could not think of another reason for these men to be in his field.

"We are not here for repairs," Prince Abgar spoke. "We have come to honor a child from heaven who is destined to be a mighty ruler."

Abdu looked up into the work-roughened face of the man in the doorway. "We also honor the parents of that child."

"This night will be a sign to you, Joseph." The Spirit pressed himself into Joseph's thoughts. "After tonight, you will never doubt that Jesus is my son. Present my son to these men."

Without a word, Joseph stepped aside, and slipping his arm around Mary and the child, he brought them forward to the men who were still kneeling in their doorway. Both Mary and Joseph exchanged glances that said, "What other unusual events are going to accompany this child?"

For a moment, Mary clung to the toddler in her arms.

"It's all right, Mary," the Holy Spirit encouraged. "Share your son."

Gracefully, Mary bent down and set Jesus on his wobbly feet. She supported him as his bare toes touched the dust and his chubby arms reached for the bronze-and-silk turbans on the heads of the men who were still kneeling at his eye level. The baby's face broke into a big drooling grin. He took a wobbly assisted step toward the visitors and laughed.

Prince Abgar, Zarbin, and Abdu looked into his sweet baby face and laughed with him. The smiles and the joy of this child were infectious. Prince Abgar held both hands out, and Mary released Jesus, allowing him to topple into the arms of the wealthy stranger. The prince of the city-state of Edessa in Parthia gently brought the child to his chest, laughing as little Jesus found the end of his silk turban and began to chew on it. "I sense the wisdom of the ages in this little one," he pronounced.

"The stars never lie," Abdu stated as he held out his hands for an opportunity to touch this toddler from heaven.

Graciously, the prince passed Jesus over to his companion. Jesus found Abdu's styled beard fascinating. His chubby fingers separated the braided strands, and he laughed when Abdu wiggled his bushy black eyebrows up and down.

The Spirit of God bent close and blew on the Zoroastrian priest.

Abdu opened his mouth and prophesied, "This child is a gift from the heavens. He is life to all people who have ever lived and who will live in the future. There will be joy and sorrow. For a time, he will be called back to his heavenly home, but he will not stay there, for he is an eternal gift to the nations of the world."

The anointing of the Spirit of God was heavy on the Parthian rulers. Both Zarbin and Prince Abgar pressed their faces to the ground. Mary and Joseph recognized the presence of holiness and silently marveled that God would share his presence with non-Jews. Even the baby seemed to sense the solemnity of the moment. He quietly laid his head against the soft leather of Abdu's vest, his dark baby-curls brushing the man's cheek.

Out of the corner of his eye, Jesus spotted the reflection of torchlight on the polished bronze fittings of Zarbin's turban. Tentatively, he reached for the sparkle. Zarbin caught his little hand and kissed the tiny fingers.

The Spirit of God then spoke through the Parthian warrior.

"These are the hands of a healer and a cosmic warrior. His mortal enemy is the dark god of the universe. This little one will triumph, but the battle will be fierce. He will lose his mortal life only to gain an immortal life."

For some time, there was silence, broken only by the occasional gurgling of the baby. No one understood the words that had been spoken. They pondered various phrases, trying to make them fit into the world they understood. It was too much.

Ehud, who had watched this whole event, finally broke the silence. "Joseph, we must be hospitable to our guests."

Shaking himself back into his responsibilities, Joseph offered, "Your men may camp in my field, and my humble home is at your disposal."

"We know that it is not lawful for an observant man of the Jewish faith to bring non-Jews into his home. Your willingness to accommodate us is deeply appreciated, but we will camp with our men," Prince Abgar responded.

"But please, father of this heavenly child, come sit by our fire," Abdu requested. "We have many questions. I feel certain there is much you can tell us."

"I will come out once your camp is set up," Joseph answered. As he spoke, he could see servants setting up tents and troops tending to their mounts. The whole scene was a little overwhelming.

Mary reached for Jesus, who was falling asleep on Abdu's shoulder. Carefully, he placed the child in her arms. Properly, she offered a soft and shy, "Good night and peace to you," to the three foreign dignitaries who had come to see her son. She would spend the night inside, secluded from the men in the yard.

Joseph walked out of his house. He had taken time to dress in his best robes. What is the proper way for a modest workingman to approach nobility? he wondered.

As he entered the camp, Zarbin ran up to meet him. "Come." The noble warrior from Parthia led him to a brightly burning fire in front of a large tent. Woven mats and heavy rugs had been spread on the ground. Prince Abgar and his priest, Abdu, were already seated on the rugs. Joseph gave a little bow and sat where Zarbin indicated.

"Tell us everything that makes this child different from other children," Prince Abgar requested.

"Yes, everything," Abdu repeated.

For a moment, Joseph hesitated. Both he and Mary had guarded the secrets of the conception and birth of this child. No Jew would ever believe their story. It would only cause problems. Now foreigners were asking!

"Speak, Joseph," the Spirit urged, "it is safe to tell the whole story."

"I am not the natural father of this child," Joseph stated. "Before we came together as man and wife, while Mary was still a virgin, an angel visited her, and the Spirit of the one true God came upon her."

"The Great Spirit of the heavens is the father?" Abdu asked.

"Yes," Joseph answered, "the Spirit of God, the God of the Jews."

"I was also visited by an angel. He came to me in a dream and told me to take Mary for my wife and to care for the child as if he were my own son." Joseph studied the faces of the men that he was speaking to. Would they believe such a story?

"Signs?" Prince Abgar asked. "Were there signs or prophecies?"

"Well, an angel visited the husband of Mary's relative while he was ministering in the Temple…" Through the night, Joseph talked, telling every detail. For the first time, the whole story came out of his mouth.

Always present, the Spirit of God Most Holy pulled each detail into alignment with the mystical understandings of the nobles from Edessa.

Orion, the hunter of the night sky, moved closer to the dark outline of the Judean hills as Joseph told his story. When Joseph finished speaking, all four men sat for a time in contemplative silence. Finally, Prince Abgar spoke, "We need to sleep on all that you have said."

Zarbin stood, preparing to escort Joseph to the door of his home. "There is not much time before daybreak, but we will see you and the child again in the morning."

The other men stood, and servants appeared as if from nowhere, tending the fire and rolling up the rugs and mats. Joseph bowed and, with Zarbin at his side, returned to his home. This night seemed so unreal. Would he wake in the morning only to find that he had been dreaming?

Shortly after daybreak, the three Parthian emissaries sat together to take their morning refreshment. At first they ate in silence, not speaking until the servants removed the food. Abdu spoke first, "I had a visitation last night."

Prince Abgar and Zarbin leaned intently toward the Zoroastrian priest.

"I saw a heavenly being like the one Joseph, father of the child, described," Abdu answered their unspoken question.

"Tell us," Zarbin urged.

"He brought a warning from the Great Spirit of the universe! The being said, 'Do not return to Herod. He will harm you and the child!'" Abdu stated.

"Herod does have a reputation for deceit and cruelty," Zarbin remarked.

"It has even reached the ears of my father, King Manu III, that Caesar was heard to say he would rather be the piglet of a sow than a son of Herod," Prince Abgar recalled.

"He kills his children," Zarbin added. "Commander Volumnius told me that not long ago, Herod had two of his sons strangled to death because in his mind, they were a threat to his throne."

"He will kill any potential threat to his throne," Abdu reasoned. "He has lied to us! He does not plan to lay his crown at the feet of this child. He plans to kill this child!"

"Herod must never know that we have found the one announced by the stars," Prince Abgar ordered.

Zarbin suggested, "We could return by another route. If we travel south and then take the road to the Great Sea, from there we can take a ship to Antioch and then follow the trade route eastward to Edessa."

"What about the camels and horses?" Prince Abgar asked.

"The caravan can go up the coast. Without us, they will look like any other trading caravan with an escort," Zarbin replied.

"Why not have them function like a trading caravan?" Abdu asked. "Our head drover could purchase balsam, almonds, and dates and then transport them back to Edessa."

All three men agreed.

A servant appeared in the doorway of the tent. "Bring the treasures," the prince ordered, "and then prepare to travel."

When the tent flap opened again, several servants entered carrying two large pack baskets designed to be strapped to the sides of the camels. One by one, treasures from the Eastern world were laid out on the rugs that covered the floor of the tent: gold coins, cut jewels, silk from the Far East, pearls from the Red Sea, rare spices, and fragrances.

"We will each choose one gift for the child," Prince Abgar ordered. Immediately, he bent over and scooped up the gold coins. "Every ruler must have gold in his treasury."

Abdu meditated for a moment before he picked up a silk bag containing the dried resin from the frankincense tree. "When this is burned, it makes a sweet aroma that is pleasing to the gods."

Studying what was left, Zarbin placed his hand on a stone flask containing oil of myrrh. "I sense a terrible wound in the future of this child." He lifted the vial. "For the healing of that wound."

As the three emissaries from Edessa in Parthia left their tent, servants scurried to repack the treasures and prepare for departure.

"Joseph! Joseph! They're coming!" Mary had been sitting by the window all morning. She hastily threw a modest veil over her face and picked baby Jesus up from a rug-covered area of the floor before the three strangers reached the door to their courtyard. Feeling a little unsure, she hung back, watching as Joseph opened the door, inviting the foreigners into their home. Beneath the veil, she sucked in her breath. This was unheard of—Gentiles in the home of an observant Jew, nobility in the home of a peasant!

She felt her eyes grow big like they were going to pop out of her head. The men were moving past Joseph! She didn't know what to do. All three men were walking toward her and the baby.

"Relax, Mary," the Holy Spirit soothed. "These are my men. You are safe."

Mary looked at Joseph, who nodded, signaling that everything was all right. Before the men actually came close enough to touch her, they stopped and knelt down on the ancient stones of her courtyard. Each man held out a gift. Mary did not know what to do. As she looked to Joseph for help, he stepped to her side.

"Gold," Prince Abgar said as he poured two heaping handfuls of gold coins in a pile at Mary's feet.

"Myrrh," Zarbin offered as he placed his stone container next to the pile of gold.

"Frankincense," Abdu announced as he added the silk bag filled with fragrant powder to the pile of gifts.

"I-I-I don't know what to say," Joseph stammered. "We are peasants, and these are gifts for a king."

"These are gifts for a king!" Prince Abgar insisted as he held up his arms to hold the baby one more time.

"Do not kneel," Joseph said as he took Jesus from his mother's arms and placed him in the arms of the prince from Edessa.

"We are departing, heading south and then west to the Great Sea. We will not return to Jerusalem," Zarbin informed Joseph. "Last night, in a dream, Abdu saw a heavenly being who warned him that Herod intends to harm the child, so be careful."

"Do not tell your story again," Prince Abgar advised.

"Thank you for the advice," Joseph replied. "I have taken it to heart."

Mary was not listening to the men; she was looking at the fabulous wealth at her feet. "These gifts?" she said in a small voice. "What do we do with them?"

"You keep them for the child, or sell them for any need you have," Abdu answered. For a moment, both Joseph and Mary were speechless.

Finally, Joseph responded, "Thank you. May God bless you with peace and safety as you journey to your home." He reached for his son.

The ancient field where Boaz had met Ruth was empty, the dry wheat stubble trampled by the hooves of camels and horses and the ground gouged by tent pegs. As he walked along the path to Joseph's home, Toma studied the evidence that Ehud had not been spinning an exaggerated tale. He would have to hear the story from Joseph's lips. "Joseph!" he called his cousin's name as he approached the home Joseph had just completed for his family. "Joseph!"

The door to the courtyard opened, and Joseph stepped out.

"You were not working on Jabek's barn today." It was both a question and a statement.

"No," Joseph responded. "You can tell him I will be there at dawn tomorrow."

Toma looked at his cousin, who was not bubbling over with information like Ehud had been. "What happened to this field?" he subtly probed.

"Some foreigners camped here last night," Joseph responded without even an inflection in his voice. "The crop has been harvested, so no harm was done."

"Ehud had more to say about last night's events than you are saying," Toma challenged.

"Ehud always has a lot to say. I don't know what to say about last night." Joseph studied the horizon.

"Joseph! Wealthy Parthians visited your son! The entire town is talking about it." He stepped into Joseph's line of vision. "I want to know, what is so special about your son?"

Joseph had taken Prince Abgar's warning to heart—too much said could put the whole town in danger. If only Ehud had not been so free with his information! Joseph weighed his words carefully before he spoke. "Whatever unusual events have occurred, they have not been of my making. Ehud saw the angels. I did not, so you will have to talk to him about that. Yes, foreigners did visit here last night, but no one could have been more surprised than I. We had gone to bed early. They woke us up. They talked about the stars and the baby. Tell me Toma, what do I know about the stars? I hardly understood a word they said. All afternoon, Mary has been silent. I can see she is puzzling over their visit."

"What about when we went to the Temple with you for Jesus's dedication?" Toma challenged. "That was certainly an eventful trip!"

"We did not ask for special attention," Joseph protested. "It just happened." Joseph sighed. "What does it all mean? I have spent the afternoon trying to figure it out, and all I can say is, one day at a time. I will be obedient to the God of our fathers and trust that he has a plan. Now, Toma, I'm going to continue my humble life by making a new wheel for my donkey cart. I suggest the whole town stop discussing this event. It is not a safe topic." He turned and walked toward the small building where he kept his tools.

"Herod! Herod!" Satan roused his subject from quiet repose in the royal bath. "Have you heard from the Parthians?" he needled the cantankerous King of Judea. "It has been several days, and they have not returned or sent a messenger."

Herod sat up, pulling a white linen sheet over his disease-ravaged body. In the steamy room, a eunuch took a step forward, offering a massage. Herod waved him away with an abrupt hand gesture. "Corinthus!" he called. "Corinthus!" Impatiently, he threw the sheet on the floor and reached for his toga. Immediately, his eunuch was there, picking up the knee-length white garment, helping him pull it over his head.

"Corinthus!" Herod was still calling the name of his chamberlain when the little man from Arabia came rushing into the royal bath.

"Have you heard from the Parthian emissaries?" Herod asked.

"No, your majesty. They have not returned to Jerusalem," Corinthus answered. "Would you like a search party sent out?"

"Yes, I want to know if those men have found the child ruler they were looking for."

Corinthus raced off to do the king's bidding.

"They found him," Satan whispered to Herod. "You know they found the child-ruler predicted by the stars. You can feel it in your bones, can't you?"

Herod rubbed his knees. The bones in his legs ached like they used to ache after a long horse ride as he led his men to a battlefield. The more they ached, the closer he came to his enemy. When the pain became almost unbearable, then it was time to dismount, draw his sword, and fight. "This ache makes me long for the days when I was young and healthy, when I could leap from my horse and thrust my sword over and over until the ground was heaped with bodies and running with blood," Herod muttered to himself.

"You will see that day again," Satan lied.

The king of Judea gave a satisfied little sigh, then he moved shakily to a nearby couch where he reclined. Fantasizing battles and victory parades, he slept.

"Volumnius!"

The commander of Herod's personal military troops looked up from his third cup of wine into the face of Corinthus, the king's chamberlain.

"Can't you see I am relaxing," he said.

"I can see you are hiding," Corinthus responded. "I have looked all over the palace complex for you."

"I am with my men." Volumnius defended himself with an arm gesture that swept the great hall of the barracks where dozens of Roman soldiers lounged.

"You have royal quarters and an officer's lounge."

Volumnius cut in, "I don't need to explain myself to you. Why are you looking for me?"

"Herod wants you to find those Parthian emissaries. If you don't find them, you will be the one to explain to him!"

"I left them on the road to Bethlehem. They were heading for the first house in the vicinity," Volumnius stated.

"Don't tell me where you left them!" Corinthus retorted. "Just bring them back to the palace."

Shoving his half-empty wine cup away, Volumnius rose to his feet. He picked up his decorated helmet and shoved it hard on his head. "You!" He pointed to a group of six soldiers engaged in a little gambling. "Come with me!"

There was a distinct cadence to their march, a steady dirge of hobnails hitting the firm surface of the ancient highway from Jerusalem to Bethlehem. Roman soldiers! Shammah knew they were coming before he peeked through the knothole in the wooden gate to his courtyard. One officer on horseback accompanied by six foot soldiers entered his yard.

"Zepporah!" The old shepherd could not hide the panic in his voice.

From the cooking area, his wife came running.

"You go to the gate and see what they want." Shammah was trembling from his covered head to his sandaled feet. Before Zepporah could protest, her husband was running, slipping out the rear entrance, heading for the fields and the caves that surrounded Bethlehem.

Insistent banging on the gate to their courtyard covered the sound of Shammah's retreat. "Open! Open this gate!"

"I'm coming," Zepporah fearfully called. The old gate was shaking like it might fall of its hinges. Timidly, she opened it just far enough for the soldiers to see her face.

"Woman!" Volumnius called to her from his mount. "Several days ago, Parthian nobles stopped at this home." His horse pranced, and the Roman commander reined the animal in. "What were they looking for?"

"They were asking about a baby or a young child," Zepporah responded, "but there are no children here. My husband and I are too old."

"Where is your husband?" Volumnius asked.

"In the fields," Zepporah truthfully answered.

"Sir!" one of the soldiers interrupted. "I see someone in the field behind the house. He is running away."

Immediately, Volumnius guided his horse around the house.

"Go after him!" Satan commanded. "He has your information!"

Volumnius obeyed. Digging his knees into his mount, he broke into a gallop.

"Halt!" the Roman commander ordered.

Shammah glanced over his shoulder. Panicked, he continued running. The steady beat of horse's hooves pounded in his ears. The old shepherd kept running, running until he couldn't breathe. Pain filled his chest, then his legs would no longer support him. He sank to the ground.

When Herod's military commander dismounted, he found an old man, recently fallen and not breathing. A hand signal brought his detachment of soldiers to the body. They carried Shammah's body back to the house, dropping it unceremoniously onto the bare ground of the yard.

"Shammah!" Zepporah fell on her husband's body, wailing and tearing her clothes.

"Why was he running away, old woman?" Volumnius questioned, but he got no understandable response.

"I know that man," one of the soldiers offered. "He was in the dungeon for a long time. He kept talking about the birth of a new king of the Jews. We didn't believe him."

"The Parthians found the child!" Satan whispered.

"Where are the Parthians?" Volumnius picked Zepporah up by her shoulders and shook her, hard. "Where have they gone?"

"Away." It was all Zepporah could say between sobs and wails.

In disgust, Volumnius threw her back into the dust. "Go into the town," he ordered his troops. "Knock at every door and ask every person where the Parthians have gone."

Sarah took her time walking along the path beside the ancient field of Boaz and Ruth. She took slow steps so Avrahm, who was nearly two years old, could toddle beside her. She and Mary were going to spend the day making flat bread. It was a tedious task— patting out numerous lumps of dough and slapping them one by one on the walls of a hot clay oven. It was a job better done with company. Today, she would make bread at Mary's house, and next week, Mary would come and make bread at her home.

She could see a thin column of smoke drifting from the oven behind Joseph's house. "Come here, Avrahm." Sarah scooped her child up so she could hurry the rest of the way. She had kept her cousin by marriage waiting long enough.

Mary met her in the yard. "I expected you earlier."

"Oh, Mary," Sarah answered. "There were Roman soldiers all over town this morning. Toma would not let us leave until they were gone."

"What were they doing?" Mary asked.

"They stopped at every house asking about those Parthians who were here a few days ago."

Mary gasped and turned pale.

"Don't worry. No one is talking. The people of Bethlehem know nothing about anything that a Roman soldier or a member of Herod's personal armed forces wants to know."

Both women walked together to the oven behind the house. They put their boys in a little enclosure that Joseph had built so the babies could play together without coming to harm while their mothers worked at the hot oven.

Volumnius rode slowly up to the gate of Herod's palace. With a distracted nod of his head, he dismissed the detachment of soldiers that had accompanied him. All the way from Bethlehem, his mind had been preoccupied. What was he going to tell the king? A carefully worded report—that was what he needed. He could not stand before Herod and admit failure. Herod didn't accept failure. The military commander handed his mount off to a royal groom and began slowly walking across the open courtyard.

"Herod will accept a plan of action," Satan suggested.

Volumnius was a little taken aback and looked around to see who had spoken to him. No one was close enough to be heard without shouting. A plan, he pondered the possibilities— Perhaps they could place checkpoints on every major road leading out of Judea? But that would mean mobilizing a lot of manpower, and there was no guarantee of success.

"Herod is not really interested in the Parthians. He wants to destroy any threat to his throne. You need to get rid of the child-ruler that has been born in Bethlehem. He is probably still living there," Satan drove the idea into his brain like a living spear.

I'm brilliant! Volumnius lightly knocked on the bronze helmet that covered his head. "I'll go back to Bethlehem and find the child!"

"Volumnius! You just left Bethlehem!" Satan continued to manipulate the commander's thought processes. "Those people wouldn't give you any information about a caravan of foreigners. Do you think they are going to betray one of their own?"

That thought ignited a smoldering rage. It started in the commander's chest and spread through his body until his mind was on fire. Who do those country people think they are, withholding information from a representative of the greatest power on earth! "I'll kill every boy in Bethlehem that is under two years of age!" he announced.

"Now that is a brilliant idea!" Satan rubbed his hands together in glee.

Certain that his suggested course of action would be applauded by the king, Volumnius strode directly to the royal chambers. After receiving permission to enter, the military commander stood in the arched doorway, waiting for Herod to look up from his evening meal and beckon him to come closer.

The king was picking through his food, taking bites of this and that, spitting some out, swallowing others, choking now and again. "Nothing has any taste!" He impatiently shoved the food away, and a servant jumped to catch the dishes before they fell on the floor. "I'm going to starve to death if I don't get some food that doesn't make me want to vomit! Take this away and bring me a bowl of dates from Jericho!"

Servants scurried, and Herod fell back into the cushions of his couch before he noticed Volumnius waiting at the entrance to his private chambers. He beckoned him with a weak nod of his head.

"What is your report?" Herod asked.

"The people of Bethlehem are most uncooperative!"

Herod stirred and then pulled himself into a sitting position.

"Three foreign dignitaries, a military escort, and a camel caravan entered the little town of Bethlehem, yet no one remembers what they did or where they went!" Volumnius paused and let the absurdity of that statement sink into Herod's brain. "It's an insult to your authority and the authority of Rome!"

"What you are telling me"—Herod leaned forward in an intimidating manner—"is that you could not find three foreign dignitaries, their military escort, or their camel caravan! Can something that big just disappear into the Judean hills or the desert?" His normally sickly voice rose to a roar.

"Possibly." Volumnius kept his tone humble as he continued, "But we do not need the Parthians to locate this threat to your throne. I have been considering a different plan of action."

"Go on." Herod gestured to signal his impatience with both the military commander and the situation.

"We know the child was born in the village of Bethlehem and most likely still lives there," the commander suggested.

"And we know he could be any age from infant to two years," Herod mused.

"I could launch an effective attack on the village of Bethlehem," Volumnius offered, "and kill all the boys that are under two years of age."

"Kill every boy two years of age and younger," Satan issued his orders to the king.

"Kill every boy two years of age and younger," Herod repeated the command as if it was his original idea.

"I will carry out your orders, not only in the village but also in the surrounding countryside," Volumnius replied as he gave the Roman salute, fist to heart.

"Attack in the middle of the day!" Herod spoke thoughtfully. How he loved to plan a military campaign! The evil old king felt new life flowing through his veins as he thought out loud. "The men will be in the shops and the fields. Women and children will be at home. You will face very little resistance." His face was animated now as he continued, "Take a cohort, about six hundred men. It will look like I am just moving some of my troops from this palace to the Herodian, my fortress that is just past Bethlehem on the road to Hebron." Herod chuckled sadistically. "They will not know what is happening until it is over! Spread your troops out in a column that stretches almost the length of the town. Make it look like you are marching through, then suddenly stop and give the command to attack!" Herod closed his eyes and leaned back into his cushions.

"Picture it, Roman soldiers peeling off from the ranks in pairs, daggers drawn, rushing into peasant homes, snatching babies out of the arms of mothers, and then, one thrust!" Satan rolled the moving picture through Herod's brain.

The monarch smiled.

Volumnius bowed and made his exit. As he walked down the corridor toward his own quarters, his hand rested on the jeweled hilt of the dagger he had won from Zarbin. The irony of using this weapon to kill the child they had come to honor did not escape him. How could the gods be so good! This would be more satisfying than winning an archery match against the Parthians!

"Mary, how many lamps are you going to light?" Joseph asked as Mary put the tenth lit lamp in one of the five narrow windows that lined the stone walls of their home.

"It's the Feast of Dedication! I'm going to light every lamp I have. After all, it is the first time I have celebrated in a house of my own!" Mary smiled and looked around at the wonderful house that her precious Joseph had constructed with his own hands. "I love this home, and soon there will be more children to fill it."

Joseph's face broke into a wide grin.

"I think I am expecting again." Mary rubbed her hand over her flat stomach.

"Should I start building an addition tomorrow?" Joseph teased.

"Maybe." Mary thought about the valuables hidden in a niche in the stone walls. "Tonight, instead of building stone walls, take this stone"—she placed a fist-sized rock in Joseph's hand—"and crack open these almonds." She poured a heap of almonds on the sturdy table her husband had built. "I'm making a sweet almond paste to spread on the cakes that I'm taking to the holiday banquet at Toma's." Mary prattled on as she heaped some shelled almonds into a stone bowl and began to pound them into a paste, "Remember when our house was completed, I made this same paste and baby Avrahm got into it? He smeared it from one side of his face to the other. Oh, Joseph, you should see how well Jesus and Avrahm play together. It is so sweet to watch those two little boys toddle around. Jesus follows Avrahm everywhere he goes. They are going to grow up together just like you and Toma did."

Joseph didn't say much; he just smiled and continued to crack nuts. God had surely blessed him with a wonderful wife and a strong, healthy son. They were building a good life here in Bethlehem. "It's getting late." Joseph pushed the last of the shelled almonds over to his wife. She quickly mashed them with her stone pestle and mortar and then added a generous measure of honey. Joseph began blowing out all the lamps but one. "We will light them again tomorrow night and every night of the eight-day celebration," he assured his wife as he left the house in darkness except for the one lit lamp that he carried into their sleeping chamber.

"Our enemy is on the move!" God suddenly announced as he rose to stand in front of his royal throne. "We must move quickly to protect Yeshua and his parents!"

"Send me!" From above the throne, Ophaniel volunteered.

"Go!" God ordered. "The entrances to Earth's galaxy are not guarded because Satan has gathered all his forces into one place and is preparing to try to break through the heavenly forces that are protecting Yeshua. My enemy's plan is to destroy Yeshua along with all the other baby boys in the region of Bethlehem. Make haste. Warn Joseph! Save Yeshua! He is the one who will one day release these little ones from the Place of the Dead.

The presence of the Spirit filled the room where Joseph and Mary slept. It hovered over them, brushing away the fatigue of their peasant labor.

"Joseph!" Ophaniel, the seraph of the Lord, spoke his name.

The vision of a heavenly being penetrated Joseph's sleeping mind.

"Take Mary and the child and flee! Leave immediately! Go to Egypt, for Herod is searching for the child to kill him! Remain in Egypt until I come to you again and tell you that it is safe to return to the land I gave Abraham."

Instantly, Joseph's eyes popped open. He sat up in the bed. "Mary! Mary! Wake up!" He shook her a little.

"What?" A little confused, Mary propped her head on her elbow and looked quizzically up at her husband.

"The angel of the Lord spoke to me."

"Gabriel! Was it the angel Gabriel?" Suddenly, Mary was very awake. She sat up, intent to hear the message.

"I don't know the name of the angel, but he said we have to leave immediately! Herod is coming to kill Jesus!"

Before Joseph could relate all the details, Mary was on her feet, finding her sandals, pulling her warmest robe over her head. Joseph dashed to the stable. Lily, their faithful donkey, had to be fed and watered, then hitched to the cart.

In the cooking area of their home, Mary began piling flat bread in a basket.

"Remember the gifts from the Parthians," the Spirit of God reminded. "Abdu said to use them for any need."

Mary went to the wall and wiggled a loose stone from its place. Then she reached far inside to withdraw the silk bag full of frankincense, the stone flask containing oil of myrrh, and lastly a clay pot full of irregularly shaped gold coins. Without hesitating, she placed the silk bag between the loaves of bread.

"In the Temple, frankincense is placed between the loaves on the table of showbread. It gives off a pleasing aroma to the Lord," the Spirit informed Mary.

How unusual, she mused, the things that leap into a person's head at a time like this! Another thought, like a voice in her mind, seemed to come from somewhere far from the danger of the moment.

"Your obedience and your sacrifice are also pleasing to the Lord, like a sweet fragrance," the Spirit commended her.

For a moment, Mary paused and looked around her home. Realization swept over her; she was leaving this home that she loved, possibly never to see it again.

The Holy Spirit placed a comforting hand on her heart, and the moment of sadness and loss passed.

She wrapped the stone flask in a piece of wool. The pot of gold, she also wrapped, placing both of them in the bottom of another basket, which she continued to fill with food and cooking utensils.

Joseph returned. The donkey and cart were just outside the door. Wordlessly, he picked up both baskets and took them to the cart. Mary began gathering up their bedding, rolling it into bundles, then their clothing. She piled it all by the door before hurrying to pick up her baby. Praise God, little Jesus was sleeping through all the activity of this night. By the light of a full moon, she carried her son out the door and placed him in the cart, in a nest of cloth bundles. She and Joseph exchanged looks that asked, "Are we ready?"

Mary nodded, and Joseph prodded their little donkey into motion. At that moment, Mary looked back. One tiny lamp sputtered in a window. She felt the emotional tug of parting with a loved one before she turned her face to walk the path that was before her.

Down the path that skirted the ancient field of Boaz, through the sleeping village of Bethlehem, and onto the main road leading south, away from Jerusalem, toward Hebron, neither Mary nor Joseph said a word. On and on they moved along the moonlit road.

Unseen, the Spirit led the way while Michael and his warrior angels marched in battle-ready ranks. High above the heavenly procession, Ophaniel flew. His eyes scanned the sky above the

Judean landscape. Michael had commissioned him to signal the first sighting of the enemy of Righteousness.

Black and menacing, the Herodian, Herod's fortress south of Bethlehem, loomed against the night sky. Joseph and Mary held their breath, knowing a Roman guard could step out of the shadows and challenge them at any moment.

"There is a strong demonic presence in Herod's southern fortress!" Ophaniel announced.

In response, the Spirit moved out farther ahead of the holy family. Silently, the Holy Spirit drifted through the halls of the Herodian, into the barracks, and out to the guard posts. His fiery presence sent demonic spirits into hiding and caused an irresistible sleepiness to envelope every man stationed at the auxiliary palace of the wicked Judean king.

In the silence of the night, it seemed to Joseph and Mary that Lily's hooves beat on the hard-packed dirt like the marching feet of a legion. Briefly, Joseph considered wrapping the donkey's feet in cloth, but if they were challenged, it would be too hard to explain. Instead he worked on their explanation.

Suddenly, Jesus let out a wail. Both Joseph and Mary jumped. Joseph rushed to the back of the cart, quickly lifting his son over the side. "It's all right," he whispered into the baby's ear. Safe in his father's arms, Jesus began looking around, curious about his new surroundings, pointing and babbling his questions. "Shh," Joseph tried to quiet the inquisitive child.

"I need to stop and nurse him," Mary said. She held out her arms for her son. "Then he will go back to sleep."

Joseph looked at the huge irregularly shaped mass of rock silhouetted against the moonlit sky. Herod's dark rocky fortress and winter palace was uncomfortably close. "Here?" Joseph asked incredulously. "There could be soldiers around the next bend."

"It's the only way to distract the baby and get him back to sleep," Mary answered as she settled herself on a flat boulder at the side of the road.

At that moment, a horde of demonic spirits came out of their hiding places and rose above the Herodian. They hovered briefly, anticipating the arrival of their dark commander, then they flew straight toward Jerusalem.

Ophaniel saw them fly into a dark thundercloud that was moving swiftly south from Jerusalem. "Our enemy comes!" the angel shouted. "He rides the violent black clouds!"

Immediately, the Spirit rose up like a billowing white thundercloud that became an impenetrable wall in the sky. Behind him, Michael stood ready to order the holy angels to defend their Creator, who was in a toddler's body, and his earthly parents. Every heavenly being knew an attack was imminent.

While Mary nursed the child, Joseph waited impatiently. He scratched the donkey's head. He watched the sky. By the white light of a full moon, a huge silver thundercloud grew from nothing. It billowed to a massive height and then stood like a shimmering pillar reflecting the moonlight. Then from the north, black wispy clouds began ominously moving in, passing over the face of the full moon but never passing by the shimmering pillar of cloud. Joseph could not tear his eyes away. He had never seen a sky like this. A cold wind suddenly sprang up, rattling the branches of the shrubs by the side of the road. A solid mass of churning black clouds then rushed across the sky, hiding the moon, extinguishing its reflected light. Joseph felt an involuntary shiver run through his sturdy body. "It looks like it might rain," he commented as he continued to scan the turbulent sky. Impatiently, he glanced at his wife, hoping she would finish soon.

"This battle is on my ground!" Satan exclaimed as he rode the fast-moving black clouds like a warrior on his battle-tried steed. Every fallen angel and evil spirit that inhabited the city of Jerusalem had risen up and fallen into ranks behind their leader. Sword in hand, he soared directly down the road toward Hebron, following the path of the fleeing family. "There!" He spotted Mary nursing the child and swooped down, only to come to a sudden confusing halt as a wall of celestial fire rose up before him. "What?" Satan roared as he nearly collided with the billowing white fire.

With a short blast of the shofar, Michael signaled the attack. Burning bolts of lightning flew from the bows of heavenly warriors and threw the demonic ranks into temporary confusion. Immediately, Ophaniel flew down to stand unseen beside the holy family.

On a distant hill, lightning flashed. Its long white fingers hung in the sky before striking a lone tree that became a shower of sparks. Thunder rolled across the land, followed by more lightning. "Mary, are you ready? We might need to find shelter from the storm that is moving toward us," Joseph urged.

Rallying from the barrage of fiery arrows, Satan's troops, led by the evil angel Raziel, drew their swords and charged. Michael and his warriors met them. Swords, like bolts of lightning, clashed while in the center of this melee, Satan and the Spirit faced each other.

"Whoever attacks this child before he is of age will surrender to me!" The voice of God sliced through the blackness of space, piercing the towering black clouds that enveloped Satan like a shield.

"No!" the enemy of Rightness protested.

Sharon Lindsay

The Spirit of God, like a wall of fire, continued to block Satan's path, preventing him from moving closer to Joseph and Mary and the child.

"I was present when you were created," God continued to assert his authority. "I saw that you were made to be an angel of light, but you chose to cast that aside. Now you are like a blacksmith who forges weapons against the beloved of the Heavenly Father. No weapon forged against this child or his family shall be effective. I have spoken!"

"A time will come!" Satan raged. "A time will come when I will face this clone of Adam and the Creator! You will not be able to interfere! He has come to face me! We will have that battle, and I will show every being that Yeshua has created. I am worthy of their praise and allegiance." Contemptuously, he pointed to the child in Mary's arms. "God in a baby? You cannot defeat me with such a ridiculous strategy!" With a wave of his hand, he signaled his evil troops to break away from Michael's warriors and return to the safety of Herod's palace.

"Joseph," Mary softly called her husband's name.

Joseph tore his eyes from the retreating black clouds.

"My little Yeshua is asleep." Mary had used his Hebrew name. It was the name she used when she felt most tender toward her son. "Come take him from me."

"I think the storm is moving on," Joseph said as he lifted the sleeping baby from Mary's arms. Carefully, he placed his son in the middle of the bundles in the cart. Moonlight flooded the road, and without more conversation, the little family continued to travel away from their home and the evil king who would harm their special child.

Glancing over his shoulder at the little family on the road, Satan hurled his parting threat, "A time will come!"

Chapter 10

THE SLAUGHTER

Then what was said through the prophet, Jeremiah was fulfilled: "A voice is heard in Ramah, weeping and great mourning, Rachel weeping for her children and refusing to be comforted, because they are no more."

—Matthew 2:17–18

Toma stood on the top rung of a crude wooden ladder lashing together the supports for the roof of Jabek's barn. He tried hard to control the resentfulness that he felt. Joseph should be on the roof with him. Together, they had bargained with Jabek: a new barn in exchange for timber from his land and wine from his grape press.

From his lofty perch, Toma's eyes scanned the countryside. It was too much to hope that he would see Joseph coming. He could see the well-traveled road leading from Bethlehem to Jerusalem. He could see Old Shammah's house. A funeral procession slowly made its way over the grassy hills where sheep often grazed. It was going to the cave on a distant hillside where the shepherds buried their dead. Maybe Joseph knew the shepherd who had passed. Maybe he was walking with the shepherds, following the bier.

Toma thought about Shammah, who had been placed in a burial cave a few days ago. What a desecration! Toma tugged hard on the twine as he lashed long thin boughs perpendicular to each other. How could it be, as the eight days of celebrating the Feast of Dedication came to an end, that an old man could be run down, chased to his death by the officer of a foreign occupational force? Where was the Lord of Hosts? Where was the God of Israel whose Spirit had filled Mattathias, the old priest of Modin?

As he worked, Toma mentally rehearsed the story he was supposed to tell that evening. About one hundred and fifty years ago, Syrian soldiers under Antiochus Epiphanes had entered the little town of Modin. They brought a pig into the town square and ordered all the people to attend the sacrifice of this unclean animal. The priest, Mattathias, was ordered to kill the animal. Resolutely, the old priest planted his feet, not making a move to comply with the order to sacrifice a pig. But another Jewish man stepped forward and volunteered to perform the heathen rite.

At that moment, the Spirit of God fell on Mattathias. He grabbed the sword of the Syrian captain and thrust it through the Jewish man who had offered to slay the pig. His five sons also managed to wrestle weapons from the Syrian soldiers. The pig survived that day, but the Syrians were slaughtered.

Toma paused in his silent recitation of the familiar story. He stood up straight, balancing near the top rung of the ladder, stretching his back, resting his fingers from their cramping work. The sun was high, past its zenith. Looking out over the Judean hills, he could see people gathering near the burial cave, like ants on a distant hill. He turned northward, his eyes following the road to Jerusalem. It was filled with Roman soldiers. The early afternoon rays magnified the red cloaks and white tunics of a cohort moving south with military precision. Toma put his hand to his forehead, shading his eyes so he could better see this national disgrace. They marched four abreast. Six hundred brass helmets reflected the golden rays while the polished metal of armor and weapons glinted with each step.

Looking heavenward, Toma asked, "How can I look my little son in the eye and say God is our Deliverer? How can I tell him that long ago, God's Spirit filled men like Mattathias and later the anointing passed to his son, Judah Maccabee?"

The sun continued to shine, the Roman troops continued to move toward Bethlehem, and there appeared to be no answer. Toma went back to work, continuing to mentally recount his story in preparation for the celebration planned for that evening. "Whoever is for God, let him come join me!" Mattathias had sent a call throughout the land, and an army had gradually formed. It was a ragtag group of warriors. They hid in the Judean hills and came out to destroy one Syrian unit at a time. The courageous priest, Mattathias, fulfilled his years and died, but the Lord was still with the renegade army. Leadership fell to one of the sons of Mattathias. Judah Maccabee, God's Hammer, defeated the Syrians at Emmaus and negotiated a peace that included restoration of the Temple and its functions.

Toma paused and thought about celebrating this event in his home. Tonight, in honor of the cleansing and dedication of the Temple after that victory over the Syrians, Toma's home would be filled with burning oil lamps. Mary and Joseph were coming. Little Avrahm would be so excited, toddling around and laughing. Toma's mother Leah and his wife, Sarah, would serve wonderful food, but why were they celebrating? Romans were in the land—not as bad as Syrians, but not independence! He sighed. What could one man do but live for his family and his God? Toma kept working, hurrying to finish for the day so he could go home and be with his family.

"They are coming!" Ophaniel shouted to Michael and the heavenly warriors as he pointed toward Volumnius at the head of Herod's troops and the spirit named Murder who rode with him.

"One spirit! That is all we have to go up against!" another angel exclaimed.

"That one spirit has infected every man in those ranks," Michael pointed out. "They are so possessed by Murder that nothing other than blood will satisfy them."

In the Temple in Jerusalem, a priest sharpened a short thin knife. Time after time, he ran the blade over a smooth gray stone. An apprentice to the priesthood placed a clean gold basin on the table and then stood ready to learn. Nearby, the lamb for the evening sacrifice was being inspected for blemishes. As he continued to stroke the blade over the sharpening stone, the priest instructed, "The life is in the blood." Back and forth his blade moved over the sharpening stone. "One thrust to the neck, then a quick slit, and the life of this animal will gush out. It will be caught in this gold basin and poured into the openings at the base of the altar. From there, it will flow into a holding basin which is flushed with water every night." The priest paused in his task to give his apprentice the added emphasis of eye contact. "Tonight you will assist in purifying the basin of the altar. You will pour sufficient water into the openings at the base of the altar to flush the blood into the drainage system under the Temple. From there, it will flow through a series of tunnels until it empties into the Kidron Valley where the most beautiful roses grow." The apprentice priest nodded his head in understanding.

Volumnius and his troops were now abreast of Shammah's house, beginning the climb up the steep hill to the level summit where the town of Bethlehem and its people were going about their ordinary lives.

"When do we stop him?" the Archangel Michael looked to the Spirit for direction.

"We will not stop him," the Spirit of God replied. His words, like a spirit of sorrow, drifted through the heavenly ranks, touching each angel warrior.

In the highest heaven, a portal opened, and three angels bearing stacks of gold basins from the heavenly Temple rapidly descended, passing them out to the heavenly host in Bethlehem. The warriors of the Lord of Hosts needed no instructions. So many times since the death of Abel, those faithful to God had been attacked, their physical bodies destroyed only because they bore his name.

"Every life is precious to me," the voice of God proclaimed from the throne room. "These innocent ones will rest within the Gates of Sheol, in the labyrinth of tunnels on the side of the chasm where the righteous wait for their Deliverer. I swear by my holiness that they are mine and that they will be restored to eternal life with us."

Only a few more boughs needed to be bound together. On top of the ladder, Toma paused to watch the Roman troops enter the village of Bethlehem. The commander gave an order and a hand signal. The column divided, and the soldiers continued to march, now two abreast, moving north to south. The ranks of red and gold seemed to stretch endlessly down the road, past the center of town. The might of Rome—it was an awesome sight! Toma could not take his eyes off of it.

The head of the column had reached the farthest point before leaving Bethlehem while the rear guard had not yet entered the town. Suddenly, there was a trumpet blast! The Roman soldiers began leaving their ranks, unsheathing their swords, entering houses! Toma could not believe his eyes!

A scream pulled Toma's attention to Jabek's house. Two Roman soldiers ran out through the open door. One of them dangled the lifeless bleeding body of Jabek's one-year-old son from his left hand while the other fended off Jabek's screaming wife. With one swipe of his sword, the soldier sliced off her arm, never looking back as she crumpled into a puddle of blood beside her dead baby.

Horrified yet reacting to the situation, Toma nearly leaped from the roof, running to the woman's side. He stopped the flow of blood by tightly binding the stump. As he worked, he could not tear his eyes from the lifeless child. Why? Had the soldiers entered his home? "I must go to Sarah!" The words flew out of his mouth as he left Jabek's wife to survive as best she could. He took off, running toward the center of town.

Terrified screams and horrified wails filled the air. Roman soldiers with drawn swords filled the main road. For a moment, Toma stopped, his eyes wildly scanning for a way to get through to his own family. He ran toward the house on his right, only to come to a horrifying halt. The decapitated body of an infant lay in the dirt at his feet. "My God!" Vomit rose in his throat, but he pushed on, climbing the stairs at the rear of the home, crouching and running across the roof. It was only a short leap to the next flat roof. Crouching, running, leaping, he made his way to his own home on the south side of town. The only thought that filled his mind was his family: Sarah, Avrahm. He could see their faces, but beyond that he could not, would not allow himself to think.

On his own rooftop, he crouched and paused to listen. He could hear the voices of the soldiers in the road in front of his home, but there were no screams. His eye caught sight of a good-sized branch that had fallen from a nearby shade tree. He picked it up, breaking off the small branches. It wasn't much of a weapon. Holding it like a club, he crept down the staircase at the side of his home and slipped around to the rear entrance.

Cautiously, he lifted the latch and opened the door. At first glance, everything looked normal. Only the silence screamed a warning that all was not well. After a moment, Toma noticed the front gate to his courtyard hung precariously by one leather hinge. A slight breeze made the damaged gate move as it dangled, ready to fall.

An invisible hand seemed to grip Toma's stomach. Swallowing his fear, he stepped through the rear door and began to enter the rooms of his home, one by one. His mother's neat sleeping chamber still smelled like the scented oil she dressed her hair with. He took a firmer grip on the branch in his hand and moved on to his own sleeping chamber, the room he shared with his wife and child. Stepping over the threshold, his breath caught in his throat. The branch fell from his hand to the floor. The limestone walls were splattered with blood. Puddles of dark sticky fluid covered the floor stones around the lifeless bodies of his wife and mother. Gaping wounds penetrated the chests of the two women in his life.

For a long moment, Toma stood like the living dead. Reality fought for a place in his mind. He could not believe. He did not know how to respond.

"Toma! Where is your son? You must find Avrahm!"

The voice in his head was like cold water reviving his mind. Frantically, Toma tore through the room, throwing the bedding aside, looking in the basket where they kept their clothing. He had to find his son! Nothing! The child was nowhere to be seen! He stood in the center of the room and screamed, "God!"

"Look at the bodies," a voice in his head directed.

Toma turned his eyes to the part of the room he had been avoiding, the mutilated bodies of his wife and mother. He looked closely. A little arm was protruding from underneath Sarah's body. With hope and horror in his heart, he pulled his wife's body from its resting place. Avrahm lay on the stones, so still, covered with blood but breathing.

Toma scooped the child up into his arms, running his hands over his little body, searching for a wound. There was none. But why didn't the child wake up? Why didn't he cry?

"Avrahm!" he called his name as he carried his son to the water jars in the courtyard. He splashed water over the child's limp body, washing off clumps of dried blood. "Avrahm!" Still the child did not respond. The only mark on his body was an ugly purple bruise that covered the entire right side of his head. Toma pressed his ear to the child's chest. He could hear the little heart beating, air moving in and out of the lungs.

There were physicians in Jerusalem. He grabbed a clean blanket from his mother's room and bundled his son. With Avrahm in his arms, he cautiously crept to the broken front gate. He peered out. The last of the Roman soldiers was falling into the ranks and continuing to march toward the Herodian. Toma turned back and exited through the rear entrance. Darting from house to house, he ran the length of the town behind the houses. By the time he reached the edge of town where the hill descended to the road, there were no soldiers in sight. Near Shammah's house, he came out on the deserted road to Jerusalem.

Silence and sorrow filled the heavens. In the court closest to the throne room of God, four cherubim attended the heavenly altar, raking its glowing coals, fanning its embers into living flames. One by one, the warrior angels arrived and took their places in a semicircle around the ever-burning altar. Each angel carried a gold basin containing a life from the village of Bethlehem.

From the throne room of God flowed a sorrow-filled voice, "My children. My children." At the four corners of the altar, seraphs covered their faces and wept. God, like a brokenhearted father, continued, "This is the work of my enemy. It will not continue forever. Wait for my son. Sleep in safety in the place that is reserved for the righteous in Sheol until all things are done that must be done."

From inside the golden basins, a cry went up, "How long? How long will you allow the Evil One to hold the descendants of Adam in death within his kingdom?"

With power and authority, God replied, "It will be just a little longer until the sacrifice of the Perfect Lamb. Then my enemy, Satan, will have reached the limit of my tolerance. The children of Adam will increase in number. Then they will cry out for my kingdom to come. I will hear them and send Yeshua. He will judge the earth, its inhabitants, my enemy, and his legions. Be assured vengeance is mine, and I will repay!"

Another cry went up from the recently departed souls in the golden basins, "Hallelujah! You are faithful and true, righteous and just!"

From his place beside the throne, the angel Gabriel flew quickly to a platform beside the altar. In his hand, he held a scroll, The Book of Remembrance. From it, he read the first name, "Kefa, son of Jabek."

A warrior angel flew up to the altar. He dipped his thumb and forefinger into the basin. They came out covered with blood, which he flicked onto the side of the altar, adding the blood of the infant to the perpetual visual reminder of all the lives that had been sacrificed beginning with Abel, the son of Adam.

The basin was then swiftly carried from heaven down to the Gates of Sheol, past the gloating principality of Death. There, it was placed in one of the many comfortable chambers where the righteous waited for the fulfillment of all things promised. The soul of Kefa, son of Jabek, had joined the martyred of the ages.

"Leah, wife of Zaccur, mother of Toma," Gabriel continued to call the names of those who had given their mortal lives in spiritual battle. Angel after angel approached the golden altar and sprinkled the blood, then carried each soul to the place where Satan held all the deceased of Earth. "Sarah, beloved wife of Toma, and mother of Avrahm…"

Alternately running then walking, Toma quickly left Bethlehem behind him as he hurried toward Jerusalem. They had physicians in Jerusalem. He would find the best one. He would pay whatever it cost. "Oh, God, help!" He pushed his body beyond endurance, never pausing, only slowing then speeding up again.

Beside the road, Toma could see the upright stone of Rachel's tomb standing starkly against the dusky sky. His strength was failing. Just for a moment, he had to stop and catch his breath. The bundle in his arms was so still. Fearfully, he pulled back the flap of fabric that lightly covered Avrahm's face. Oh, he was a beautiful child, with dark curls and olive skin. The love he had for his son filled his chest until it felt like a searing pain. "Avrahm," Toma whispered his name. "Wake up, my son. Open your eyes and look at me." There was no response.

Evening was coming, and the light was fading. Toma stared hard, trying to see the rise and fall of the little chest; it was not moving. He put his cheek next to the mouth and nostrils of the child—no breath. Frantically, he threw off the blanket and pressed his ear to his son's chest; there was no heartbeat. "My son! My son! Avrahm, my son," Toma's anguished cry cut through the stillness of the empty road. He clutched the limp body of his baby boy to his chest.

Suddenly, Toma's muscles lost all strength, and he collapsed into the dust of the road.

Swiftly flying through the portal to the Holy City of the Eternal Ruler, one last angel arrived with a golden basin. "Avrahm, son of Toma and Sarah," Gabriel announced. Tiny drops of blood, representative of his life, stained the side of the altar. Avrahm's short life became an indelible memory in the mind of his Heavenly Father. His life was then carried into Sheol, the domain of the Evil One.

The stars were out when Toma regained consciousness. It took him a few moments to orient himself, to remember how he came to be lying in the middle of the road clutching the lifeless body of his son. "Ohhhh," a groan like the cry of a mortally wounded animal escaped his lips. Then for the rest of the night, he sat in the dust with little Avrahm in his arms. His tears flowed.

As the sun rose from behind the eastern hills, Toma pulled himself to his feet and staggered over to the giant slabs of stone that made Rachel's tomb. His eyes searched the ground until he found a pointed rock. Between two of the eleven slabs of stone that surrounded the upright memorial to Jacob's wife, Toma found a space big enough for his boy.

Using the pointed rock, he began to dig, loosening the dirt with the stone and then scooping it out with his bare hands. He worked like a man without a mind.

The Spirit of God wept with Toma. He hovered over the grieving father who dug a grave for his little boy with his bare hands.

The usual number of Jewish travelers made their way toward or away from Jerusalem.

"Look, look at the man digging beside Rachel's grave," the Spirit called to each person on the road. "Go over to him. Assist him."

No one stopped.

"Can't you see? This man is your brother, a fellow Jew! A terrible calamity has befallen him!" The Spirit kept speaking to every man who passed by. "Stop! Stop and help!

No Jewish man stepped off the road to inquire after the wailing man who dug between the slabs of Rachel's tomb with a pointed rock and his bare hands. Only Kheti, an Egyptian merchant, responded to the Holy Spirit.

"My brother, what is your trouble?"

Toma looked up into the face of a very dark-skinned man who spoke in faltering Aramaic. "My son, my wife, my mother…"

Toma could not put his words into complete thoughts. "Killed... grave..."

"Is this your son?" The Egyptian bent down and cautiously moved the fabric that covered little Avrahm. He moved it just enough so he could see the child's face.

At that moment, the Spirit filled him with compassion for the father who had lost such a beautiful child.

"I have a trowel that I use to bury garbage and waste. Let me get it." The Egyptian walked back to the road to a string of salt-laden camels held by several drovers. Getting his trowel and a wineskin, he returned to Toma. "You rest. I will dig." He pushed the wineskin into Toma's hands and then bent to the task of making the hole deep enough for a grave that would remain undisturbed by wild animals.

The sun was high when Kheti picked up Avrahm's little body. He held it out to Toma, who sat on one of the stone slabs like he was part of this monument to sorrow. "Say farewell to your little boy."

Toma moved the fabric from Avrahm's face and kissed his forehead. The Egyptian merchant then turned and placed the body in the grave, quickly covering it with dirt and packing it down.

Kheti turned back to Toma. "Where is your home?"

"Home?" Toma repeated the word like it had no meaning.

"Where do you live?" the merchant tried again.

"Gone," Toma said, "my home is gone."

"Then, for now, make your home on the road with me." The Egyptian merchant put his arm around Toma's shoulders and led him back toward the road. "I convey Egyptian linen and salt from the Dead Sea to your Temple in Jerusalem, then I carry wine to the desert regions, then I take salt to your countrymen who have built a Temple to the God of Israel in my land, then I transport more wine to the desert regions near the Dead Sea. Men in the desert are always thirsty, and the Temple uses a lot of salt and linen, so I make the journey often. Maybe after you have made a journey with me, you will forget the evil that has been done to you and remember the good times. Then you will want to return to your home."

Chapter 11

Desert Journey

The people who survive the sword
will find favor in the desert.

—Jeremiah 31:2

Joseph led his donkey by her halter rope. Without meaning to, he tugged a little impatiently, pulling her away from the scrub bushes that grew along the dry creek bed. He had hoped there would be at least a trickle of water in the brook. A little anxiously, he scanned the sky—no sign of rain. The thunder and lightning he had seen several nights ago had not produced a drop of moisture in the semiarid hills west of Hebron.

"Is Lily through grazing?" Mary asked, looking up from her toddler, who was clinging to her breast and sucking with all his might. She glanced down at Jesus with worried eyes and then looked back at her husband. "Jesus just keeps nursing and nursing, but I don't think he is getting enough."

Joseph looked down at his son, who was persistently trying to draw the last drops of milk from his dehydrated mother. "Let's give him some water," Joseph suggested as he lifted his last skin full of water from the back of the cart.

"Do we have enough?" Mary's tone was anxious.

"This is a caravan route," Joseph answered. "I'm sure we will come to a watering hole soon." He paused and looked both east and west along the road that led from Hebron to the coastal city of Ashkelon. Shading his eyes, he stared hard toward the rising sun. "There is a caravan approaching from the east. We can go slowly and let them catch up with us. I should be able to buy some water from them."

Mary withdrew her breast from Jesus. Her toddler sat up on her lap, knowing he was not satisfied but not complaining.

"Let's have a little water," Joseph said to Jesus, putting the opening of the waterskin up to the baby's lips and trying to pour just a little into the child's mouth. Jesus choked and spluttered. Precious water trickled down his chin. Patiently Joseph tried again and again until he was satisfied that Jesus had managed to swallow enough water to replace the milk he was not getting.

"And now, you drink." He handed the waterskin to his wife, who took a few swallows. "More," he urged.

"But you need to drink," Mary protested, "and the donkey hasn't had water in two days."

"Lily gets enough moisture from the plants. I am not thirsty, but you need to drink in order to produce enough milk for Jesus."

Obediently, Mary drank until she felt satisfied, but she still worried. There was so little water left, and they had two more days to travel before they reached a coastal town that was not under the authority of King Herod.

Joseph hitched the donkey up to their cart. Then before starting, he dug deep into one of the baskets and pulled out one of the gold coins. Securely tucking it into the folds of his belt, he looked behind them to the east one more time. Yes, he reassured himself, the trading caravan was coming. It would probably overtake them by midday. Satisfied, Joseph grasped his staff in one hand and pulled on the rope halter with the other. Lily started moving, pulling the cart that held Jesus and all their worldly belongings. Mary walked beside the cart, making sure her little one did not climb over the sides or get into the baskets.

By noon, Joseph could smell the camels. It was a smell that was even stronger than the smell of his own perspiration. He led his donkey and cart to the side of the road so there would be room for the caravan to continue beside them. Unexpectedly, Lily suddenly balked, rising up on her hind legs between the hitching poles of the cart!

Mary screamed and caught Jesus just as he started to tumble out of the cart along with the rest of their belongings.

A snake slithered through the dust of the road between the bucking hooves of their work animal. While trying to avoid the snake, Lily was effectively shedding the cart. Reacting instantly, Joseph caught the serpent with the end of his staff and flung it far up onto the rocky hillside.

Still responding to the situation, Joseph calmed the donkey while Mary soothed her frightened son. After a few deep breaths, they started rehitching the donkey and repacking the cart.

"You're here again, I see," the Spirit confronted Satan.

"Are you referring to the serpent on the road?" Satan replied. "That snake was not my doing, just one of those things that happens to ordinary people. The Creator has taken on the physical limitations of an ordinary human. He must deal with the problems of life on Earth. As the Creator, he could have forbidden the serpent to cross the road or turned it into a harmless fly. As an ordinary human, he does not have the power to speak things into existence or to command and have nature obey."

"You forget that God is his Father and I carried the genetic material that made his conception possible. Through me, he has power to speak things into existence and to bring heaven and Earth into submission," the Holy Spirit responded.

"If he has come to prove something by living like a human, he will have to live like a human, or he proves nothing!" Satan asserted.

"Elijah was a man who submitted himself to me. When he prayed earnestly that it would not rain, the heavens were sealed for three years, and when he prayed again, rain fell upon the earth.

My power flows through those who hear and obey my voice. The more they submit to my control, the more I can work through them. It will be so with Jesus," the Spirit of God informed.

"So far, all of your precious humans have at some point in their lives turned their backs on your authority. What makes you think Jesus will be any different?" Satan taunted.

"The Creator's love is so strong!" the Spirit replied.

"Love?" Satan sneered. "You mean his desire to control and manipulate is overwhelming! His need for adoration is all-consuming!"

"I will hear no more!" The Spirit of God turned away and refused to be drawn into the age-old argument.

Joseph fell into step beside the lead drover of the Nabataean trading caravan. In the tradition of all eastern conversations, he did not get right to the point. "Sir, what goods do you carry, and what is your destination?"

"Who wants to know?" the drover replied in broken Aramaic. His eyes were shifty. They kept looking back at Mary, who was walking behind the donkey cart with Jesus in her arms.

Joseph glanced back at his wife, and he was thankful she was so modestly covered that only her eyes could be seen. "I'm Joseph, a carpenter from Nazareth," he answered.

The drover did not respond right away; instead he studied the hills on either side of the road as if he were looking for something. Finally he said, "It is unusual to see a man and his family alone on this road."

"A family emergency has come upon us, and we had to travel hastily." Joseph could feel the suspicious and lustful nature of the man. It made him uneasy.

"Bandits frequent this road," the drover stated while staring Joseph in the eye as if accusing him of being one.

"We are just a peasant family," Joseph assured. "Bandits would find us too poor to bother with." Joseph wanted to end his conversation with this distasteful man, so he tried to get to the point uppermost in his mind. "You must be familiar with this road."

The drover grunted an affirmative response.

"Where is the next watering hole?" Joseph asked.

"About a day from here," the man responded.

"A day," Joseph repeated in dismay. "Do you have some water you could spare? I will purchase it," he added.

A spirit named Greed wrapped itself around the drover and whispered, "How much is this man willing to pay for water?"

"Water is very valuable when it is scarce," the man responded, licking his lips in anticipation.

"How valuable would two full waterskins be?" Joseph asked.

"More than a peasant could pay," the Nabataean trader scornfully responded.

The spirit of Greed intensified his presence. "Your people did not become the builders of Petra and the great traders of the desert by giving things away. Hold out. Make this Jew desperate. Desperate men will sell their valuables or even their wives for water."

Joseph could see the man's eyes kept going back to Mary. He wanted to finish his business with this uncircumcised foreigner as quickly as possible. Pulling the gold coin from his belt, he asked, "How much water can I purchase with this coin?"

The lead Nabataean drover stopped walking and sucked in his breath. The entire caravan came to a halt. "Gold!" His eyes became large, and his nostrils flared like a predator picking up a scent. "Where would you get a coin like that?" he asked without taking his eyes off the glittering irregularly shaped coin that lay in Joseph's open palm.

"It was a parting gift," Joseph responded before adding, "My question is how much water will you give me in exchange for this coin?" It did not escape Joseph's notice that the man could not pull his eyes from the coin. "How much water?" Joseph pressed.

"Two waterskins," the drover replied.

"Five," Joseph responded.

"Three," the drover countered.

"Four," Joseph said with finality as his fist closed over the coin, hiding it from the man's greedy eyes.

"Bring four waterskins," the drover shouted to one of the other drovers on the line. When the skins full of water were tossed into the cart, Joseph handed the man the gold coin.

The Nabataean grinned, as if congratulating himself on a successful bargain. With a few words in a language that Joseph did not understand, the drover set his caravan in motion.

By the side of the road, Joseph and Mary waited for the caravan to pass. Safe in his mother's arms, Jesus stared and pointed as each shaggy beast passed. "Camel," Mary repeated the name of the animal several times. When the dust of the caravan had settled, Joseph picked up Lily's halter rope. Mary placed her son in the cart, and their journey continued toward Ashkelon on the shores of the Great Sea.

Ashkelon—Mary had never seen such a pagan city! As they emerged from the arched gate in the city wall, her head turned from side to side. Everywhere she looked, there were majestic columned Temples and statues of a half-woman, half-fish goddess that was the patron deity of the city. Moving toward the center of the city, they passed an amphitheater, a gymnasium, and Roman baths. "Where is the Jewish section of town?" Mary whispered to her husband.

"There is no Jewish section in this Greek city," Joseph replied. "As a matter of fact, we may be the only Jews in the city!"

Mary gasped! In her entire life, she had never ventured away from the physical confines of traditional Judaism. She took a closer look at the people on the street. Sure enough, no one else was wearing the layers of long flowing robes typical of Jewish society. "Where are we going to stay? How will we keep Sabbath? I mean—" She stammered as she tried to get her mind to accept the fact that in this location, there was no little enclave of Torah-observant Jews. "We cannot stay in the home or the inn of a Gentile! Why, we would become unclean!"

"We'll camp on the shore of the Great Sea well before the sun sets and Sabbath begins," Joseph reassured her as he continued to lead his little family through the city, toward the gentle waves and the warm sands of the Mediterranean. In the center of town, he stopped to water the donkey and fill all six waterskins. "On the first day of the week, we will go into the market near the harbor," Joseph informed Mary. "That's where I plan to sell the myrrh and purchase what we need to make the desert crossing into Egypt."

Mary nodded, ever thankful that her husband could be counted on to provide.

A vast expanse of water filled the western horizon. Wave after wave rolled and then broke on the sand. "It's beautiful!" Mary paused on the road that ran parallel to the seashore. She could hardly believe her eyes. Standing under a shade tree, she looked out at the Great Sea for the first time in her life. "I never imagined there was any place like this in all of the world," she exclaimed. Then she started walking again, carrying Jesus, following her husband and their donkey cart as they made their way along the shore.

"Here. Stop here. This is the place I have chosen for you to spend the Sabbath hours." The Spirit hovered over the family, directing Joseph now as he had through the entire journey.

Joseph paused and then cautiously led the donkey and cart off the road, through the foliage, and on to the sandy beach. He looked around. It was a secluded spot, away from the busy harbor, away from the seaside market, away from the residential areas of Ashkelon.

Deliberately, Joseph planted his staff in the sand, then in a sudden carefree gesture, he threw off his heavy cloak and the long robe underneath. He stretched his arms wide and felt the sea breeze. "Mary, it feels good to be out of Herod's territory! We're not in Egypt yet, but I feel safe here." He unhitched the donkey and led her knee-deep into the gentle surf, washing her down, cooling her off. "Come on in!" he called to his wife. "Bring the baby and wash off in the waves."

Quickly, Mary undressed Jesus and threw off her own outer clothing. Wading into the waves, she was surprised at how they pulled at her to go deeper, but with the baby in her arms, she stayed near her husband, bobbing up and down in the water, washing off the grime of their journey.

Joseph took the donkey back up on the beach and then rejoined his family in the water. He held his hands out to Jesus, and the toddler, laughing and kicking at the waves that were tickling his toes, reached for his earthly father. Together, they ducked all the way under the water, coming back up spluttering and laughing. In Joseph's strong arms, Jesus knew no fear. Over and over, they played that game. Mary let her hair down and began to wash it in the waves. When she felt satisfied, she walked out to sit contentedly on the beach while the waves broke over the water-soaked sand and foamed around her ankles. She watched as Joseph and Jesus played tirelessly in the water.

Above them and around them, the Spirit of God, partner in the conception of Jesus, smiled and anointed the moment. To the babe, he whispered, "Jesus, you can trust your Father. You are always safe in his arms, even when the water is over your head."

Dawn broke on the first day of the week, sending fingers of light through a few date palms and onto the sandy shore of the Great Sea. Mary was up first, checking to see if the clothing she had washed before sunset on Friday had dried over the Sabbath. Then she tended to the baby: cleaning him, feeding him. Joseph rose, built a fire, put some water on to boil, fed a measure of barley to the donkey, and then brought another measure back to Mary for morning porridge. While their simple breakfast cooked, Joseph checked the wheels and axle. Mary could hear him hammering a little every now and then.

At last he sat down ready to eat. First, Mary handed their last piece of flat bread to her husband. He broke it in half. Holding a piece in each hand, he lifted it heavenward. "Blessed are you, O Lord our God, ruler of the universe, who brings forth bread from the earth." He took a bite and then handed one piece to Mary.

She placed a bowl of cooked barley in his hand. He used the bread to scoop the hot cereal into his mouth. Before taking her first bite, Mary asked, "How will we get to Egypt, and where in Egypt are we going?"

"In the Nile Delta, there is a community of Jews who have a Temple and a high priest from the family of Zadok, a true descendant of the firstborn of Aaron. I thought that would be a good place to live," Joseph answered.

"Do you know how to get there?" Mary asked.

"I have never been there," Joseph replied, "but I do know the way to Egypt. We will follow the Way of the Sea across the desert into the delta. We will need to carry a lot of water, feed for the donkey, and food for ourselves. There are a few towns and trading posts along the way, so we should be able to replenish our water every few days. As we travel, I will talk to people on the road. Someone will tell me how to get to the Jewish Temple in Egypt."

"And if they don't?" Mary asked.

"Then I expect the angel who told me to take you to Egypt will give me directions," Joseph answered with confidence. "Are you worried?" He stopped eating and looked across the dying fire at his wife.

"I'm just anxious to have a home again," Mary replied. "I want to be in my own home in a Jewish community.

"We will have a home," Joseph promised as he stood to break camp before returning to the city to sell the myrrh and purchase enough supplies for the next leg of their journey.

Rocks and bare earth—since leaving Ashkelon, the terrain had become increasingly dry and desolate until, as they approached Gaza, there was not a green leaf in sight to refresh the eye. Only occasional glimpses of the Great Sea offered any relief. The Way of Sea, the ancient highway of the pharaohs, seemed to stretch into barren eternity.

On and on Lily plodded, pulling their cart piled high with waterskins, food, and all their possessions. Step after step, Mary and Joseph carried Jesus toward Egypt. It had been two weeks since they left Bethlehem. The journey seemed as endless as the wasteland they were traveling through.

Just to assure herself that they really were making progress, Mary had taken to counting the Roman mile markers on the side of the road. She knew how many steps she took between each of the markers and how many mile markers they could pass in a day. Joseph broke the monotony of the journey by striking up conversations with caravan drovers. It seemed they were always either passing a caravan or being passed by one.

"Mary." Joseph shortened his steps so Mary could walk beside him. "Let me take Jesus for a while." He lifted his son from her arms and placed him on his shoulders. Jesus wrapped his little arms around Joseph's forehead and held on while he surveyed the flat bleak landscape and the sun-baked wall of the ancient Philistine city in the distance.

"Are we spending the night in Gaza?" Mary asked.

"We'll find a place to camp," Joseph answered. "I'll make inquiries when we get into town. I think it may be best for us to join a trading caravan for the rest of the desert crossing. I have been told that between here and the River of Egypt, the sand drifts across the road and sometimes the road is completely hidden. I would not want to inadvertently begin wandering over sand dunes."

Mary's eyes, the only part of her that could be seen, grew big. Join a caravan full of uncircumcised men who smelled worse than their camels? The thought was shocking! Like a proper eastern woman, she did not associate with men other than those who belonged to her family and her close-knit Jewish community. Joseph expected her to travel with those desert wayfarers? She had seen them and smelled them as they walked by! She couldn't help but remember that disgusting trader who had sold them water. She shuddered at the thought of traveling with such men.

As if he could read her thoughts, Joseph added, "We may stay more than one night. I want to find a caravan where you will feel safe and I will have confidence in the men with whom we are traveling. There are some good men among the traders."

The only response that came from Mary's lips was, My mother would be aghast!

Joseph chuckled. "Your mother is a practical woman. She would understand that we are no longer in our land and we do not have the luxury of confining ourselves to dealing exclusively with our people. Remember, our ancestor David went to Ziklag, not far from here, to live among the Philistines when he was fleeing from Saul."

"Yes, and I remember all the times our ancestors got themselves into serious trouble dealing with the Gentiles in this same region," Mary countered, beginning to recount a list of names, "Samson, Abraham, Isaac—"

"Do not fear, Mary," Joseph answered. "The messenger of the Lord who came to me said we were to go into Egypt and that he would tell me when we were to come out of Egypt. You can be sure we will return safely to our land and our people."

Ever present but unseen, the Spirit heard and smiled. "Joseph, my obedient man of faith, how you please me!"

Also present, lurking in the wastelands on the desert side of the road, Satan heard and sneered. "The man has placed too much confidence in a dream," he bitterly announced to the retinue of demonic spirits who attended him. Then from his evil mouth, he blew a long hot blast of wind. It picked up the dust of the desert. Spirits named Discouragement, Fatigue, Doubt, and Resentment rose up with the dust and began to fly round and round, swirling the fine particles of dirt until they had created a cloud of extreme discomfort and misery.

On the horizon, Mary and Joseph could see a cloud of dust approaching as a dry wind from the desert bore down on them. Immediately, they both stopped talking. Joseph took Jesus down from his shoulders and handed him to Mary who rearranged his tiny head covering so his little face was completely protected from the flying particles of dirt. As the cloud of dirt enveloped them, Joseph threw an old piece of linen over Lily's eyes. Taking a firmer grip on her rope, he led her forward through the swirling dust.

Kheti, the Egyptian wine, linen, and salt merchant, walked the length of his caravan, checking the ropes that attached camel to camel and the short strings attaching the camels to the donkeys. Beside each donkey stood a hired drover, and at the very end of the caravan, beside his own donkey loaded with his personal supplies, stood Toma. "You are looking well this morning," Kheti commented. "Life on the road is good for you."

"I do not know about that," Toma replied. "I have no life. It is gone, taken by those Roman dogs!"

"There was much mourning when I came through Bethlehem. People were in the streets wailing and tearing their clothes. I heard about a massacre of young children and mothers. Are you from Bethlehem?" the merchant asked.

"It was my home," Toma answered. His face remained stony.

"We will go through there again," Kheti offered. "Until then, would you like to be one of my drovers? I pay my men each time I sell my goods. You will be paid three times before we pass through Bethlehem again."

Toma clenched his fist like he was grasping the hilt of a sword. "I want to take to the hills and join the resistance. Give me a sword, and I will run it through every Roman I meet!

"That is your grief speaking," the Egyptian counseled. "Rome is too big, too strong. Stay with us. We will be in Gaza in a few days. Lead my pack animals. Help me sell the wine and purchase more salt."

Toma turned and started to walk away.

"Don't let him leave without one more try," the Spirit urged.

"It takes money to buy a sword," Kheti called after Toma. "I will pay you in Gaza, in Leontopolis and Engedi."

Toma hesitated and then turned to face the Egyptian merchant. "To buy a sword and to be outfitted as a warrior, I will continue with your caravan."

The dust storm passed as quickly as it had come, leaving Joseph's little family covered with fine dirt. Even the insides of their mouths seemed to be coated with dust. "The gates to the city are just ahead," Joseph tried to encourage his wife, but talking was difficult.

As they walked through the heavy wooden gates, Mary looked around. Gaza was not the beautiful city that Ashkelon had been. It was a mud-brick fortress in a sun-parched desert, a town that lived by and for the desert caravans. It offered little in the way of refreshment, only a market with high-priced imported food, a few wells with slightly brackish water, and a dusty large open campground for caravans and travelers. Mary set her teeth together to endure, but the grit between them just seemed to put her nerves on edge.

"Where are we going to stay?" The question flew from her lips like the fire-tipped arrow of a Roman archer.

"I'm going to find a place!" Joseph responded with equal impatience.

"They are tired, dirty, and miserable!" Satan laughed. "This is my moment!" He moved close to Mary and whispered, "Mary, your husband is a stupid man who is just making this journey more difficult than it has to be."

"Couldn't we have taken another route to Egypt?" Mary resentfully asked. "How much would it have cost to take a ship from Ashkelon to Alexandria?"

"Do you think they just let you lead a donkey and a cart full of possessions onto the ship's deck? In order to go by ship, I would have had to sell the donkey, the cart, my carpentry tools!" Joseph's voice rose. "We need those things to live! How do you expect me to provide for you and the child without the tools of my trade?"

"That's right," Satan spoke to Joseph. "Mary is just a simple country girl. She doesn't know anything! Look at the child in her arms. That child is not your child. What right does God have to ask you to provide for that child? And what right does Mary have to question you about anything? If it were not for your sacrifice, she would be an immoral woman with a bastard child! Speak up for yourself, man!"

"Woman, don't speak to me about things you don't understand," Joseph added with unnecessary harshness.

"Have it your way!" Mary retorted. "I won't speak!" She pulled her dusty mantle even further over her face and positioned her body so she walked beside her husband with her back to him. Her posture screamed for her, "I'll make you regret your insulting words!"

"That's right, Mary! Think about yourself! You cannot be spoken to as if you are not important!" The spirits of Resentment and Pride worked their way under her mantle. They sat on either shoulder. Their voices filled her mind. "Joseph is not the considerate man you thought he was. You are expecting your second child, and not once on this long journey has he asked how you feel!"

At the edge of the campground, in the shadow of the city walls, Joseph stopped. "We'll camp here." He began to unhitch the donkey.

"Look around," the spirit of Resentment suggested. "Dirt! He expects you to sleep in the dirt!"

"Here?" Mary broke her silence with a shrill accusatory question. She set Jesus down. Her toddler stood in the dust, hanging onto her robe, looking back and forth from parent to parent.

Joseph stopped caring for the donkey. He folded his arms across his chest and leveled an exasperated gaze at his wife. "Have you got another suggestion?"

"You have not asked if there is a Jewish home anywhere in this city." Mary gestured toward the residential area.

"No," Joseph replied with undisguised impatience. "It is almost dark. I plan to be camped before the sun sets, not walking up and down the streets of a foreign city searching for something that is probably not here!"

"Tell her again," Satan suggested. "Tell her what a stupid woman she is!"

"Hold your tongue," the Holy Spirit countered. "Look at your little son."

Joseph dropped his gaze. Little Jesus stood between them. His thumb was in his mouth, and tears were making muddy trails through the dust that covered his face.

"Pity your son," the Spirit of God counseled. "He understands your words and Mary's words. He feels the tension between you two. Your words have wounded him. Your words are wounding each other."

"Forget the boy!" Satan countered. "Let Mary know that she cannot question your judgment! Put her in her place!"

"Speak with compassion," the Spirit offered. "Ask for forgiveness. With your words, break the curse that now clings to your family! *A gentle answer turns away wrath, but a harsh word stirs up anger.*"[1]

Joseph squatted to the level of his little boy. His eyes looked deeply into the big tear-filled eyes of his son. "I'm sorry, Jesus." He pulled him into his strong arms and stood while holding him high on his chest. "I'm sorry this has been such a difficult trip. I'm sorry I have spoken so impatiently." He turned to his wife. "I'm sorry, Mary. I have spoken far too harshly."

"He has not repented sufficiently!" Resentment shouted!

"You did no wrong! Do not accept responsibility for any of your words," Pride admonished.

"Humble yourself," the Holy Spirit urged. "Submit to the compassion of your husband. Bow your head and crawl under the prayer shawl of his kindness."

Mary took a deep breath. The struggle within felt like a battle.

"Your son is brokenhearted," the Holy Spirit pointed out. "Look at his tears. His eyes are begging you to make things right again."

Mary pulled a relatively clean piece of cloth from the folds of her belt. She took a step toward Joseph who was still holding Jesus. With the cloth, she reached up and wiped her son's face. The dry cloth did little more than smear the dirt, but the gesture was important. "It's all right, Jesus. I love your daddy." Her eyes met her husband's, and then she bowed her head. "I'm sorry. I was out of place to question your judgment. This will be a fine camping place." She looked at the spot her husband had chosen. "I'm glad we are near the wall. It makes me feel less exposed, more sheltered." She felt Joseph put his free arm out and pull her in under the shelter of his mantle.

"I'll put up a makeshift tent for you. I'll make this a comfortable spot for as long as we have to stay," Joseph assured.

She looked up into the face of her husband. His beard and face were caked with sweat and dust, but he smiled, and his eyes were only for her. In her heart, gratitude and love welled up like a fountain in the desert. She drank from it and felt refreshed.

"The words of the man and woman have given me authority to carry out their wishes. I order you to leave!" The Spirit of God flew in the face of Satan.

Michael shouted, "Swords!" and his warrior angels, with blazing swords, routed the demonic spirits who quickly fell from Mary and Joseph and fled into the wastelands.

Satan, his power broken by humility and submission, moved beyond the walls of Gaza to watch from a distance and wait for another opportunity.

In the predawn darkness, Mary stirred on her pallet under the makeshift tent that Joseph had constructed using the hitching rails of the cart as a frame. From all over the campgrounds, she heard camels bawling and grunting as they rose to their feet, hoisting the loads they would carry through the Northern Sinai Desert. In the darkness, she reached for her husband. His sleeping place was empty. Concerned, she crawled out from under the shelter and surveyed the area. Campfires were burning. Camels and donkeys were being loaded. Drovers were berating their animals for stubbornness and stupidity. Everywhere Mary looked, caravans were preparing to depart.

"Joseph?" Mary called her husband's name as she walked around their small camp. Where could he be? She wondered. Jesus woke up. He crawled out of his sleeping place and over to his mother's side. With one hand, he took hold of her robe and pulled himself up to a standing position. By holding tightly, he could walk as she moved about their campsite.

Finally, through the smoke of a nearby campfire, she saw her husband coming. Half running, half walking, he carried two buckets of water. "Mary!" he called out to her. "I wanted to get water before the camels drained the well." He placed one bucket at her feet. "All the caravans are moving out this morning, and we're going with them!" He rushed off, carrying water to Lily. "Hurry," he called over his shoulder. "Get ready to go!"

Mary did not have to be told twice. Three days they had camped within the walls of Gaza. The constant dust, the stench of camel dung, the smell of men who never washed—she could not wait to get back on the open road. At least there she could hope for a steady breeze to carry those unpleasant odors away. Immediately, she started to wash Jesus and prepare him for the trip.

"We did well, my friend!" By the light of the early-morning campfire, Kheti counted out Toma's wages into his hand. "Here in Gaza, the wine trade was very profitable. And the salt, I purchased for practically nothing!" He patted Toma on the back. "Did you know it is good luck to have a Jew in the caravan?"

Toma looked at the Egyptian merchant skeptically.

"I know a little of your scriptures. We have them in my country translated into Greek. I have been told that your God spoke to Abraham, the father of all Jews, and said, *'I will bless those who bless you, and whoever curses you I will curse; and all peoples on earth will be blessed through you.'* [2] You have been my blessing!" He held up a bulging bag of coins and grinned at Toma.

"How can one who has been cursed be a blessing?" Toma bitterly retorted before turning his back and lifting a basket full of sea salt to load onto a kneeling camel. "It would have been better if I had never been born," he muttered to himself as he prepared for the caravan to depart.

Kheti stood silently, watching the back of the man he had taken into his caravan.

"Don't give up on him." The same voice that had called the Egyptian merchant to assist this Jewish man still spoke to him.

"Keep reaching out to Toma like he was your own brother. Continue to care for him. The man has suffered a terrible loss, but through you, he can heal."

"When we camp tonight, break bread with me," Kheti called after Toma, then he turned away to supervise the stringing of his camels and donkeys.

"Why do they call this a river?" Mary asked as they followed the first of three caravans through the flat, dry bed of the Wadi Gaza. "Because occasionally it is a raging torrent," Joseph replied. "The drovers tell me that sometimes in the winter, it rains in the high desert and then the runoff from those rains gathers in these dry riverbeds and rushes to the sea. Everything in the path of that rushing water is washed into the Great Sea."

"It is winter now!" Mary responded with some alarm.

"They tell me it is a rare occurrence," Joseph offered reassurance, "but we will not be camping in the wadi. See how we keep moving? We will not stop until we are out of this riverbed. I understand that in a few days, we will traverse one more dry riverbed, the River of Egypt."

Mary looked around, noting how large boulders and piles of bare earth formed the sides of the sandy riverbed. "I have never seen land like this before," she stated. "If this riverbed suddenly filled with water, how would we get out?"

"By the hand of the Lord," Joseph replied in a tone that indicated only the miraculous would be able to save them.

At the very end of all the caravans traveling from Gaza to the delta of Egypt, Toma prodded Kheti's string of donkeys to keep up. His eyes roamed over the bleak landscape, and he knew the terrain was only a reflection of his own life. "Why, God, do you seem far off? Where are you hiding in my time of despair?"

The Spirit of God whispered into his mind words from his harassed and persecuted ancestor, David, *"In his arrogance a wicked man hunts down the weak, who are caught in the schemes he devises. He boasts of the cravings of his heart; he blesses the greedy and reviles the LORD."*³

"Why, Lord?" Toma groaned.

The Spirit answered, "That evil man has allowed my enemy, Satan, to fill his mouth with curses and lies and threats. *He lies in wait near the villages; from ambush he murders the innocent, watching in secret for his victims... He lies in wait to catch the helpless... His victims are crushed, they collapse; they fall under his strength.'* My enemy, Satan, says to this evil man, *'God has forgotten; he covers his face and never sees,'* ⁴ and the evil you have done will go unpunished."

Toma felt his stonelike heart cracking and crumbling. Tears began streaming down his face. *"Arise, LORD! Lift up your hand, O God. Do not forget the helpless!"*⁵ He sobbed as he walked.

"It is an ancient ploy of my enemy to use men whose hearts are as evil as his own. I have seen your trouble and your grief," the Spirit responded. "I am the helper of the fatherless and the oppressed, the Righteous Judge. I will break the arm of your oppressor and call into account those who bear responsibility in order that these men will never again terrify the innocent. I am the Lord. I have spoken it!"

In the palace courtyard, sitting proudly on his mount, Volumnius surveyed the royal caravan. His hand rested on the hilt of the jeweled Parthian dagger in his belt. The visor of his brass helmet shaded his eyes, and the red plumes on top of the helmet advertised his rank. Prodding his horse into a slow canter, he rode the length of the column. At the head of the caravan, Herod's curtained litter rested on the ground, four bearers positioned at the corners. The physician's wagon, loaded with herbs and treatments for the ailing king, was next, followed by a wagon with relief bearers, a string of loaded camels interspersed with donkeys, more wagons, and a military escort: four hundred marching men with mounted officers and supplies. Herod's military commander nodded in satisfaction. They were ready to head for Jericho and the warm mineral springs that were expected to bring their monarch back to health. With a few words, he dispatched a servant to tell Corinthus, the king's chamberlain, that all was ready. The king could be escorted to his litter.

There was a little commotion at the palace gate as Herod emerged, not walking but carried in a chair. It had been a couple of weeks since the military commander had seen his monarch and mentor. He had not been called into the royal chambers since the day he had reported on the raid of Bethlehem. It shocked him to see the king so physically wasted that he could not walk. Moved and dismayed by the king's condition, Volumnius rode out into the center of the courtyard, where he could pay his respects by saluting Herod as he passed by.

Positioning himself in the open, almost directly in front of the king and his entourage, Volumnius removed his helmet and placed his right fist over his heart. Honor was due this great warrior, architect, and king.

"God, '*The* LORD *examines the righteous, but the wicked and those who love violence his soul hates!*'"[6] the Holy Spirit proclaimed.

From within his sanctuary, God responded, "I have promised to break the arm of this wicked and evil man, to call him into account for his wickedness!"

Instantly obeying orders from the throne room, Michael, with drawn sword, flew directly toward the mounted Roman commander who was honoring his king.

Suddenly and without obvious cause, the military mount under Volumnius reared, front hooves flailing the air. In front of the king, his courtiers, and all the troops under his command,

Herod's commander fell to the ground, the hooves of his fear-crazed horse pummeling his right shoulder and arm.

Uncontrollably, the Roman commander writhed on the ground. Pain filled his body, and screams filled his ears. It took a moment for his thinking processes to return, but when they did, Volumnius realized the screams he heard were his own and that the blood he saw came from broken bones protruding through his own flesh.

In that moment of awareness, he looked up into the face of his king.

Herod, gaunt from his long bout with illness, still had the mind of a ruthless warrior. Like the general he had been, he assessed the situation. "You will never lift a sword again," he stated. Without another word to the man who had faithfully served him, he waved his bearers on as he called to Corinthus, his chamberlain, "Fetch the second in command to take charge of my caravan and dispatch a servant to find a physician in the city."

Groaning in the dust, unable to even pull himself into a sitting position, Volumnius watched the royal caravan pull out of the courtyard. A short while later, a Jewish physician came through the palace gates. Only then was the military commander placed on a litter and carried to his quarters. His jeweled Parthian dagger and plumed helmet were forgotten, left in the bloodstained dust of the courtyard.

Toma tossed a few pieces of dried camel dung on the fire before sitting down next to Kheti to share his evening meal. The Egyptian merchant handed him a basket of flat bread and gestured toward a bowl of olive oil with herbs for dipping. "I've never eaten a meal with a Jew," Kheti commented. "I understand usually they only eat with their own people."

Toma shrugged and then replied, "We usually wash our hands with water before each meal also. I just gave mine a good rubbing with sand like the rest of the drovers." He looked at his hands and then added, "Some things just don't seem as important as they used to."

"You'll find yourself again," Kheti remarked while he dipped his bread into the savory oil. "After time heals your wound, you will reunite with your former life."

Toma chewed thoughtfully for a few moments and then responded, "I cannot imagine a time when my soul will no longer be like a raging sea of pain and loss and anger. I am so consumed by my anguish it no longer matters to me that I am Jewish and that I have always observed the laws of my people. Those laws offer me no comfort."

For a while, the men ate in silence: mashed chickpeas, some almonds and dates, followed by a little wine. The sun set, and a warm wind picked up. It came from the desert and gradually increased in intensity.

"This is unusual," Kheti remarked. "While a wind like this can be expected anytime in the spring, I have never known a desert windstorm to bear down on us during the winter months." Suddenly, the fire went out, smothered by the sand and dirt that was flying through the air.

"Should I see to the animals?" Toma asked.

"No. The donkeys will turn their tails to the wind, and the camels will kneel down and close their eyes. We are the ones who need to find shelter." Kheti pulled a large heavy piece of tent fabric from his pile of belongings. He threw it over his head and gestured for Toma to come sit under it with him. With their backs to the desert's blast, they waited out the sandstorm.

"Joseph! What shall we do?" Mary crouched down beside the cart with Jesus sheltered beneath her robes. "The sand and dirt are flying through my clothing! I can hardly breathe!"

Joseph wrestled with their large piece of heavy tent fabric, trying to make a shelter, but the wind would not allow him to attach it to the cart. Finally, he gave up. Tossing a waterskin on the ground beside Mary, he squatted next to his wife and child and then wrapped himself and his family in the tarp.

Unaffected by the howling wind and flying sand, angels of the Most High moved through the camp, taking positions of protection near Mary and Joseph and near Toma and Kheti while the Spirit extended his protection over the entire caravan.

The entire caravan waited a night and most of a day. The wind howled, and the sand blasted their backs. "I have never known such misery," Mary sighed as Jesus crawled up under her robes and began to nurse.

"It is enough," the Spirit called the wind back into its desert home. The flying dust gradually settled to the ground.

"It is passing," Joseph offered hope. "I can feel it. The wind is letting up." He lifted up the tarp and put his head out. "It is much better. I can see some of the camels. Most of them are kneeling. Some are almost buried in the drifting sand. There are a few men walking through the flying dust, checking their animals." He crawled out from under the shelter of their tent fabric to better assess the situation. "There are a couple of camels out here behind the cart," Joseph called to Mary who was still huddled under the heavy fabric. "They have their lines so tangled they cannot move! I'll take care of Lily, then I'll see what I can do for those poor animals."

"The worst is over," Kheti announced as he threw the heavy tent fabric that had been their shelter to the ground. "We had better see to the animals."

The air was still thick with flying particles of sand, but the fury of the storm had abated. Toma immediately began to feed and water the camels. A few had to be dug out of drifting sand.

Only two had wandered off. He began to walk the length of the caravan to find them.

While feeding his own donkey, Joseph heard a man's voice nearby, "You stupid, stupid beasts!" Leaving the bucket of barley under Lily's nose, Joseph came around his donkey cart to see a man unsuccessfully trying to get one camel to lift a leg and begin the process of untangling. In exasperation, he shook his fist at the shaggy beasts. "Only camels are so stupid! How did you manage to get yourselves so tangled that you cannot even take a step?"

The camels had no response. They just stood looking off toward the horizon, batting their long eyelashes.

"I have a knife," Joseph offered as he walked toward the entangled animals.

"I am annoyed enough to slit their throats with your knife, but these beasts of burden do not belong to me," the man replied. His voice was muffled by the folds of cloth that still covered most of his face.

"If we cut their lines, then they should be able to walk away," Joseph suggested as he pulled a flat-bladed multipurpose knife from a sheath on his belt. "I'll hold one animal, and you hold the other," he suggested as he handed his knife over to the drover.

At that moment, their eyes met. For an instant, they were frozen while their minds tried to process the impossible. "Joseph?" Toma ripped his own mantle from his face.

"Toma!" Joseph could not think of another thing to say.

The camels were forgotten; both men fell into each other's arms. Toma spoke first, "Mary? Jesus? Were they killed?"

"Why no, they're here with me," Joseph gestured toward the tarp that still covered his wife and child. "What are you doing here? Where is your family? Why aren't you in Bethlehem?" The questions tumbled.

Toma looked deeply into Joseph's eyes. "You don't know? How did you escape?"

"What should I know other than the fact that the angel of the Lord came to me in a dream? He told me to take Jesus and go to Egypt because Herod was trying to kill him," Joseph answered. "There was no time to tell you, and I thought it might even be dangerous for you to know, so we just left in the middle of the night."

"I wish the angel had come to me also." Toma's voice caught, and his face began to contort as he tried to hold back the tears that were welling up. "Herod sent his troops into the town. They entered every home, and everywhere there was a young male child, they killed that child."

"O my God, my God, how could this happen?" Joseph dropped to the ground and began to beat his chest and groan under the weight of such tragedy.

Immediately, Mary, with Jesus holding onto her robe, came out from under the tarp to see what was happening. She ran to her husband, bending down to see what was wrong just in time to hear a familiar voice say, "Avrahm is dead. Sarah my wife and Leah, my mother, were also killed. I saw the soldiers slay Jabek's son. They maimed his wife when she chased after them trying to save her child." Then Toma fell on the ground beside Joseph and Mary. Jesus sat in the dirt beside them, pressing his face into the folds of his mother's robe. Their wails were heard throughout the camp, and no one could understand the cause of their grief until Kheti came and told the story of the massacre of young children in the town of Bethlehem in the land of Judea.

The next morning, the caravans moved on, pushing through the sand that had drifted across the highway and buried most of the mile markers. At the trading town of Raphia, they camped under palm trees, replenished their water, and washed away some of the grit that seemed to have become a permanent part of their skin.

Two more days they walked. Toma and Joseph often walked side by side, but neither man had much to say. In the evenings, Toma would sit by their campfire and share their evening meal. Sometimes Kheti would join them.

It was Kheti who finally asked the question that had been gnawing at both men. "Why did an angel come to warn you, Joseph? Why didn't the angel also warn Toma?"

For a long moment, Joseph hung his head and stared silently into the embers of their dying fire. Finally, he spoke, "I have been struggling with that question for days. I have prayed. I have even asked for the angel to return to me and give me an answer, but I have not been visited." He sighed a heavy sigh and continued, "I'll tell you what I do know." He looked at Toma. "Several times since we arrived in Bethlehem, you have asked what is so special about Jesus."

Toma nodded. "Some unusual things had happened. Ehud told me about the angels coming on the night of your son's birth and about the visit of the Parthian nobles." He paused before continuing, "And when we went to the Temple for your son's dedication, that old man and that old woman prophesied over him. Sarah and I were jealous because Jesus got so much attention."

"I know," Joseph replied. "There is something special about Jesus." He took a deep breath before beginning, and in his mind, he prayed, Lord, help Toma to believe. "I am not the father of Jesus."

Toma's eyes got big, and Kheti's mouth dropped open.

Joseph could sense that he had their complete attention. "Before Mary and I came together as man and wife, an angel visited Mary. He told her she had been chosen by God to have a son and the father of that son would not be a man. The father of that son would be the Spirit of God Most Holy."

"The Holy Spirit?" Toma inquired.

"Yes." Joseph nodded his head. "The only way I can understand why Jesus was spared is to understand that God is his Father and his Father was taking care of him." Joseph looked at Toma and Kheti, waiting for their reactions.

"Then Jesus is the Anointed One?" Toma asked. "The promised Deliverer?"

"Yes, Toma. That little boy sitting on Mary's lap is my adopted son, and he is also the Anointed One,"

the Spirit of God urged Toma and Kheti to believe.

"We think that is so, but our understanding is very limited," Joseph said. "This much I do know, Mary is expecting a second child. I am the father. We have not been visited by angels, and nothing out of the ordinary has happened regarding this child."

"It is a lot to think about," Toma responded.

"Isn't the Jewish Messiah supposed to free your people from Rome?" Kheti asked. "To set up a sovereign Hebrew nation?"

"That has always been my understanding," Joseph replied.

Simultaneously, all three men turned and looked at Jesus. He was asleep on his mother's lap. His dark curls fell across his little suntanned face. From time to time, his lips moved ever so slightly. For a long time Joseph, Toma and Kheti could not tear their eyes away from the sleeping child as they tried to see the man he would become.

Chapter 12

ENTERING EGYPT

In that day there will be an altar to the LORD in the heart
of Egypt, and a monument to the LORD at its border. It will
be a sign and a witness to the LORD Almighty in the land
of Egypt. When they cry out to the LORD because of their
oppressors, he will send them a savior and defender, and he
will rescue them. So the LORD will make himself known to
the Egyptians, and in that day they will acknowledge the
LORD. They will worship with sacrifices and grain offerings;
they will make vows to the LORD and keep them.

—Isaiah 19:19–22

High over the Red Sea, moisture gathered in the atmosphere.
A few winter rain clouds began to form.

Satan noticed the gathering droplets and, with his demonic
entourage, hurried to the scene.

"Hold back those clouds," he ordered, and Raziel led the evil
angels as they fanned the clouds with their wings, keeping them
in place over the sea until they were massive and black, bloated
with water. Then Satan began to blow, and his angels began
to push the rain-laden clouds toward the high central plateau
of Sinai.

As the clouds were demonically forced into the cooler air of
the higher elevation, the moisture that they carried became too
heavy, and it fell in a downpour like that high desert had never

seen before. The ground, too hard and dry to absorb the water, became a massive shallow lake. Water ran everywhere, looking for and being drawn to lower elevations. It poured into the wadis. Those dry riverbeds became channels filled with turbulent, silty water that rushed with an unstoppable force through canyons and ravines toward the Great Sea.

With his dark entourage, Satan eagerly followed the course of a massive wall of water as it rushed through the Wadi Al-'Arish, also known as the River of Egypt.

"Your wife looks tired," Kheti commented to Joseph as they continued their long dusty trek toward Egypt.

"I know." Joseph looked at his wife with concern. She was walking beside the cart, keeping an eye on Jesus, who rode on top of the waterskins. "We have had to haul so much food and water that there has not been room for her ride in the cart."

"The journey will soon become easier after we cross the River of Egypt," Kheti said. "Water will gradually become more plentiful, and you will not have to carry so much."

"I have heard the other drovers speak of that wadi," Joseph responded.

"It is quite a large dry riverbed, and it runs from the interior of the Sinai Desert to the Great Sea. Many smaller wadis feed into it. Once we have crossed it, then we will be in Egypt. I expect we will be crossing very soon," Kheti informed.

"More water and an easier journey is something to look forward to," Toma commented.

"Mary is looking forward to actually arriving in Egypt, to making a home again in a Jewish settlement," Joseph said. "Every evening, all she talks about is new neighbors, a garden, the furniture she wants me to build. I know she wants to return to the life she is familiar with."

"The caravan seems to be slowing," Toma mentioned.

"Probably the first string of camels is making its way down into the River of Egypt," Kheti said. "It is a rather steep descent to the floor of the wadi."

Soon the caravans were completely stopped as each string of camels waited for its turn to wind down the boulder-lined embankment before reaching the smooth floor of the Wadi Al-'Arish. Joseph took advantage of the delay to check the wheels of his cart and the hooves of his donkey. Mary threw their tarp under the cart and crawled into that little space of shade with Jesus to take a short nap.

To descend, cross, and ascend on the other side seemed a tedious, time-consuming process. Joseph, Toma, and Kheti stood around beside the road, waiting for their turn.

"Joseph!" Satan spoke into his thoughts. "You have wasted most of the day waiting for your turn to cross. When you finally get to go, move your donkey and cart down the trail quickly. Make sure Mary and Jesus keep up with you. Don't waste another moment on this side of the River of Egypt."

By noon, most of the caravans had made their descent into the wadi. Only Mary and Joseph, with their cart, and Kheti, with his camels, donkeys, and drovers, waited their turn.

"You go first," Kheti suggested as Joseph led Lily to the point where the road narrowed and began a curvy descent into the dry riverbed.

Hovering above the caravans, Satan could see a surging wall of muddy water rushing between canyon walls, an unstoppable force of nature. He measured its speed and calculated the moment of impact. Immediately, he dispatched the spirits named Impatience and Poor Judgment.

"That's right, Joseph. Take your turn. Get moving!" the demonic spirits urged.

In anticipation, Satan could not tear his eyes from the scene. The timing was right. Very soon, the wall of water would roar into sight, but by then it would be too late for anyone on the floor of the wadi.

"Tell Mary to pick up Jesus. Don't let him try to walk. He is much too slow," the spirit called Impatience counseled. "Kheti's caravan is waiting. You cannot delay them any longer!"

"Mary!" Joseph called. "Follow close behind the wagon and carry Jesus. We don't want to prevent Kheti from getting through before dark." Taking a firm hold on Lily's bridle rope, Joseph began to guide her over the edge down between the boulders.

"Pull harder!" Poor Judgment advised.

"Hurry! Hurry!" Impatience screamed.

"Stay!" the Spirit of God whispered into the little donkey's heart. "Listen!"

Suddenly, Joseph's faithful animal planted all four hooves on the path. Her long gray ears perked up, as if listening.

Joseph tugged on her bridle. "Come on, Lily! We have to go!"

The donkey would not move.

"Lily!" he yelled in frustration.

Moments later, the donkey's ears went back flat against her head, a sign of stubborn refusal. Between the hitching poles of the cart, she sat on her hunches and began to bray.

"Make her move! Make your donkey move!" the spirit of Impatience ranted.

"No! Lily!" Joseph exclaimed in dismay. "Not now! You can't sit down and be stubborn here! Come on!" He pulled hard on her rope. Mary, with Jesus in one arm, came up beside the donkey and began to talk to her, to urge her to get up and move forward. Toma ran down to help, pushing on the animal from behind. Still, the donkey refused to budge.

"What a good and faithful animal you are," the Holy Spirit whispered into the heart of Joseph's donkey. "You can hear the danger. You know a wall of water is coming. Sit firmly. Save yourself, your master, and your Creator."

Animal and cart completely blocked the path. Joseph threw up his arms in disgust as he called up to Kheti, "Have you got any suggestions?"

"There is time. You do not have to hurry," the Spirit advised Kheti.

"Let your donkey calm down," Kheti called, "then coax her with some grain."

Mary and Jesus kept stroking the donkey, Mary talking calmly to her while Joseph and Toma paced the path down toward the floor of the wadi and back again.

The Spirit spoke to Kheti again, "Listen! What do you hear?"

Kheti paused and listened. He could hear Joseph and Toma still ranting about the stubborn donkey. He could hear Mary's soft voice. He could hear the other drovers and their animals as they made their way across the floor of the wadi and up the far side. But there was another sound, a faint distant roar. Kheti stepped forward close to the edge of the wadi and looked inland toward the high desert.

"Flood! Flood! Flash flood!" Kheti screamed at the top of his lungs.

"Go back up!" Joseph yelled to Mary as he and Toma began running back up the path from the floor of the wadi.

Kheti and a couple of his drovers ran down and began pulling the cart from behind. Lily instantly stood up and cooperated, backing up the hill.

The water was in sight now, a rolling brown torrent. It filled the channel. High on both sides of the bank, men hollered a warning to those still on the floor of the riverbed. The drovers on the floor of the wadi abandoned their animals and ran for their lives, scrambling up the loose dirt and rocks of the far embankment.

Horrified, Joseph watched two donkeys and a string of camels as the wall of water slammed into them. It turned them head over heels and then swept them away.

"Bless your little donkey," the Holy Spirit whispered. "Ask her forgiveness for your impatience. She heard the flood coming, and she obeyed my voice. She saved your lives."

Joseph went over to his faithful little work animal and put both his arms around her neck. Into her long gray ears, he whispered, "Thank you."

Two days later, they completed the crossing of the River of Egypt without incident and made their way to Rhinoculura, a small town at the mouth of the wadi. Mary's eyes feasted on the tall date palms and the white sand of the beaches, where gentle waves from the Great Sea rolled toward shore. There they renewed their water supplies, purchased dates, and had a meal of fresh baked fish.

Kheti sold a little wine and purchased a few more waterskins. He tossed one more on top of the six Joseph had on his cart. "From here to Pelusium, there is some water, but it is foul. A man could die from drinking it."

"I will pay you," Joseph replied as he reached into the bag on his belt for the price of the waterskin.

"No," Kheti responded. "I owe you far more than a skin full of water. If your animal had not refused to enter the wadi, I would have been right behind you. We would have all been swept away."

"Kheti thinks Jews bring him good fortune." Toma stepped up to help Joseph hitch his donkey.

"I sell them salt, I buy their wine, and they pay a good price for my Egyptian linen," Kheti responded. "They have certainly done more for my trading business than the Romans." As he spoke,

Kheti gestured toward a regiment of Roman soldiers marching along the coastal highway toward Palestine.

"Even in this desert there are Roman soldiers!" Toma angrily exclaimed. "Isn't there any place where a man can make his home and not have to deal with them?"

Kheti pointed in the direction they were traveling as he spoke, "Rome always has its soldiers on the move. They have an outpost not far from here." His remarks were directed at Toma.

The men watched as the soldiers came closer, hundreds of them marching in step. Kheti commented, "Fourteen miles a day, from outpost to outpost, they march until they reach their assignment. Rome never seems to run out of soldiers." He looked directly at Toma. "You cannot defeat all of them."

"Then the Lord of Hosts will have to defeat them for me," Toma stated with fist raised toward the heavens.

"Good," Kheti responded. "Now you won't have to waste my good wages on a sword!"

"Mary? Jesus?" the Spirit whispered.

All three men looked around to see where Mary and the child were. Joseph saw them first. They were coming out of the market area carrying several fresh cucumbers. "I'll take them down to the beach until the soldiers pass," he said as he hurried away toward his family.

Toma finished hitching the donkey while Kheti made a final inspection of his caravan. When the soldiers had passed by, their journey continued.

Desert gave way to foul-smelling swamps and salt marshes. As they neared Pelusium, they were once more walking near the shores of the Great Sea. They could see ships on the horizon making their way to and from the busy seaport.

"Now this is a trading city," Kheti commented. "They don't need my salt, but I saved some wine to sell here."

Customs officials were waiting at the entrance to the city. They levied a tax on each person, every animal, and the goods that Kheti carried.

This was the first major city they had entered since leaving Ashkelon, and once again, Mary, the simple young girl from Nazareth, could not tear her eyes from the sights. They passed a Roman fortress and then stopped at a busy market where caravans traded their goods. While the men negotiated the sale of Kheti's wine, Mary took Jesus and climbed a nearby hill. From that vantage point, she could see that the city boasted an amphitheater, a racetrack, and several Temples. The busy harbor was especially fascinating for Jesus. He kept pointing to the ships, with their large square sails, and Mary talked to him about the wind and water, about fishing, and about people traveling on boats.

For a few days, while Kheti purchased more salt and rested his animals, they camped on the beach. Joseph found a piece of driftwood and made a little boat for his son. "Follow me," Joseph called as he jogged toward the wave-washed sand.

Mary watched while Jesus took a few unsteady steps, then dropped to his hands and knees and quickly crawled after his father. At the water's edge, Joseph squatted down and, using his work-hardened hands, began to scoop a large hollow in the sand. For a moment, Jesus watched. Then he put his little hands in the wet sand and began imitating, scooping and throwing aside the sand just like his father. When the hole was large enough for a little boy to sit in the middle and splash, Joseph carved a narrow channel in the sand from the hole to edge of the waves.

When the next wave foamed onto the shore, part of it ran through the little channel and washed into his small pool. Jesus laughed and tried to catch the water with his little hands. When the hole had filled with water, Joseph placed the little toy boat on the water, and it floated. Then he lifted Jesus over the packed-sand edge of the pool and placed him in the water. As Jesus kicked and splashed, the little boat skittered across the waves that his feet made. All afternoon, Joseph laughed and played with his son.

Always nearby, the Spirit of God smiled and approved. "This is the best time, the time you spend with both your earthly father and your heavenly Father," he whispered. "Your fathers have much to show you, and everything they have to show you is so amazingly wonderful!"

Resting in the shade of the date palms, Mary remembered her second child, the one still in her womb. She had been so caught up in all that had happened—the visit from the Parthian dignitaries, fleeing from Herod, the journey to Egypt—that she had hardly given this second pregnancy a thought. It was startling to think that she was going to have her second child in Egypt and that her mother had not yet seen her first child! Her parents did not even know that she had left Bethlehem. When they found out about the massacre, they would be so worried. She got up and walked down the beach to where Joseph and Jesus were splashing in the water.

"Joseph?"

Her husband looked up at her and smiled.

"Can we send a message to my parents? If they hear about the massacre, they will be so worried."

"There are many caravans in this city. I'll talk to Kheti. He'll help me find a caravan that is going to Jerusalem and then north to Nazareth," Joseph responded. "We'll write the message tonight."

Mary sighed as a weight lifted from her heart. She knelt down and began to build up the sides of the pool by firmly packing the wet sand.

At that moment, the Holy Spirit breathed a blessing over the family, "To you I give peace, along with strong bonds of love and trust. For the rest of your married life, I give you joy in each other and satisfaction in the work of your hands." Then the Spirit added a special blessing for Mary. "I have listened to your heart, and I promise to return you to your family in Nazareth."

Traveling with Kheti and his trading caravan, Joseph walked every day with Toma and the other men. Most of each day, Mary occupied herself with Jesus— meeting his needs, talking to him about the sights.

As they approached the Nile Delta, vegetation increased. Water became readily available, and there was now room in the little cart for Mary to ride part of each day. She welcomed the opportunity to get off her feet. From her perch on top of the empty waterskins and bundles of clothing, she took in all the new and fascinating sights of Egypt: peasant farmers working the fields, papyrus boats on a branch of the Nile, the production of mud-and-straw bricks.

"This is the land of your ancestors, freed from slavery by the hand of God through his servant Moses," the Holy Spirit reminded. "As slaves, your ancestors worked these fields and made bricks from mud and straw."

Mary turned to Jesus, who sat beside her on a bundle of bedding. "Jesus, see those people? They are making bricks. That man"—she pointed—"is bringing straw from the field. A long time ago..." For the first time, she told her son the story of deliverance.

The day ended. It seemed to be an especially long day, and their journey seemed endless. Mary could hardly recall the last time she had had a conversation with another woman, and her conversations with the men, except for giving and receiving basic information, were limited to her husband and Toma. While the men tended to the animals, Mary made a small fire and cooked a meal. Following the directions of her husband, she made enough for Toma and Kheti to join them.

Feeling a little worn-out, Mary bent over the fire and stirred the lentils. The pot was full and boiling rapidly. As she quickly moved it to a cooler part of the fire, the lentils in the iron kettle sloshed, and a few drops of the scalding liquid landed on the exposed skin between the laces of her sandal. "Oh! Why does my husband do this to me?" she angrily exclaimed. "Every night!" she muttered to herself. "I have to give up my time with Joseph and play hostess to a foreigner!" Dissatisfaction stirred in her soul.

"Kheti is not one of the chosen people of God," the spirit of Resentment urged. "Joseph has no right to ask you to wait on him night after night!"

Joseph should know that he is not setting a good example for his son, Mary grumbled to herself as she cut up the fresh vegetables she had purchased that morning.

"Your parents never broke bread with non-Jews or tax collectors! They only dealt with them in the market place and then purified themselves," Resentment pushed. "You should have a word with your husband! He should not be sharing his evening meal with this Gentile. He is preferring this foreigner over you!"

Mary spread their tarp on the ground, making places for the men to sit. Because Kheti would be at the meal, she would have to place the food in front of them and then withdraw a discreet distance. Propriety dictated that she could not share the meal or contribute to their conversation. She would have to be content to eat with Jesus and overhear what she could.

She could see the men coming. Joseph rushed ahead. Taking a waterskin from the back of the cart, he poured water over Kheti's hands and then over Toma's hands.

At least they are washing, Mary thought as she recalled all those days in the desert when they dared not waste any water to wash hands.

Jesus came toddling to greet his father, holding up his little hands. Joseph poured water over them, and the little boy rubbed his hands together, imitating the washing motions of the men. Mary stepped forward, and taking the waterskin from her husband, she poured water over his hands. Something in her posture and her silence must have spoken because Joseph looked at her quizzically before she turned to resume the duties that, at this moment, seemed like an unfair burden.

"Mary," the Holy Spirit spoke, "remember I have said, '*The alien living with you must be treated as one of your native-born. Love him as yourself, for your ancestors were aliens in Egypt!*' Understand that your husband honors the man who helped his cousin. Submit to your role as a helper and supporter of the man who took you to be his wife. In this way, you honor your husband. In this way, you honor me."

As Mary dished out small portions of the food for herself and Jesus, she struggled to lay down the resentment that seemed to have attached itself to her. Deep inside, she knew those feelings were wrong. Finally, she prayed, "Lord, fill me with the hospitality that I do not feel."

Immediately, the spirit of Resentment released its grasp on her thoughts, and in the face of her submission to the voice of the Holy Spirit, it fled to a desolate place.

Kheti handed Joseph a wineskin and some drinking cups made from the dried fruit of the papyrus that grew so abundantly along the many tributaries of the Nile. "We will be in the Land of Onias tomorrow, and then you will see your Temple in Egypt," the Egyptian merchant announced as he and Toma made themselves comfortable for the evening meal.

"It's hard to believe that there is another Temple and a large community of Jewish people so far from Jerusalem," Toma commented.

"There are many large communities of Jews outside of Israel," Kheti responded. "In Babylon and throughout the entire ancient Persian Kingdom live all the descendants of the Jews who did not return to Jerusalem. In Alexandria, two out of the five sections of the city are Jewish!"

"But only in this place is there a copy of the Temple in Jerusalem," Toma stated. "I'm surprised the Sanhedrin allows it."

"It is tolerated because everyone knows that the high priest in Jerusalem does not have the correct ancestry to hold that position," Joseph informed. "He cannot challenge the Jewish Temple in Egypt without exposing himself to being replaced by a legitimate priest from the line of Zadok. The priests from the line of Zadok are only to be found at the Temple in Egypt."

"The line of Zadok?" Kheti queried.

Mary placed several dishes of food in front of the men. Her eyes met her husband's.

Silently, Joseph seemed to ask, Is everything all right?

She gave him a slight nod and a genuine smile and then withdrew to eat with Jesus. The men continued their conversation, and from her place next to their cart, Mary listened.

"When Solomon built the first Temple, it was determined that the families of Zadok were the direct descendants of Aaron, the first high priest, and that they held the hereditary right to the position of high priest," Joseph answered.

Kheti nodded his head in understanding. "So what national calamity brought your priests to Egypt?"

"Antiochus Epiphanes," Toma and Joseph said almost simultaneously.

"I've heard of him," Kheti replied. "A ruthless Syrian tyrant!"

"About one hundred and fifty years ago, the Syrians conquered our land, desecrated our Temple, and tried to wipe our faith from the face of the earth," Toma said. "It was our finest hour when another brave family of priests led the revolt against them."

"The Maccabees," Joseph said their name with reverence.

"I pray that God will raise up another to give the land back to his people," Toma added.

Joseph continued the story. "Judah Maccabee was able to reestablish Temple worship, but he was not able to completely free the people from the domination of the Syrians, so the priesthood became corrupt. When the high priest Onias III was murdered, his son, Onias IV, fled to Egypt and lived under the protection of the government there. Onias IV was the last of the Zadok line. His descendants now serve in the Temple in Egypt."

"I can't wait to see this Temple," Toma said. "Is it as beautiful as the one in Jerusalem?"

Kheti shook his head. "I'm afraid you will be disappointed. Mud bricks and ancient stone pillars cannot rival the beauty of the white limestone Herod has used to construct the Temple in Jerusalem."

"I have heard the services are the same," Joseph said with a hopeful inflection.

"You will have to be the judge of that," Kheti responded. "I just sell them salt. I do not witness what goes on at their altar."

As Kheti and Toma returned to their camping place, Mary followed her husband as he made a last check on their donkey. "Joseph," she called to him, "I heard Kheti say we are going to arrive tomorrow?"

He stopped walking and waited for her to catch up to him. As she drew close, he reached out and drew her close to his side. "It's been a long journey, but you heard correctly. We will arrive tomorrow."

"A home?"

Knowing her heart, Joseph interrupted, "While Kheti is selling his salt at the Temple, I will make inquiries. I will try to find a house for us to rent."

Mary let out a long satisfied sigh and laid her head against her husband's firm chest.

The Spirit of God fanned the flames of their commitment to each other.

It was a moment rich in the contentment of just being together.

In that tender interlude, the Spirit spoke to Joseph. "Look at your wife, the helpmate I have given you. She is worth far more than all the treasures on all the caravans in the Roman Empire. Have you noticed that every day, she rises before dawn to provide food for her family, and at the end of the day, she provides food for your guests? The men of the caravan and the villages see your wife. They see her modest and faithful demeanor, and then you are respected as head of your household. Look at her and see that I have clothed her with strength and dignity. I have placed laughter, wisdom, and faithful instruction on her tongue. Her children will honor her, and her husband should speak praise and blessing over her."

"Mary," Joseph whispered into her ear. "Many wives are good and dutiful, but you surpass them all." He pulled her close, and when her body pressed against his, he remembered that his child was in her womb. "Truly the Lord has blessed me!" he exclaimed. "It is enough. I cannot ask for more."

The weariness that Mary had carried for many days fell away to be replaced by renewed love for her husband and eager anticipation of their new life together.

In the Land of Onais, shade trees abounded. Narrow straight streets were lined with nearly identical mud-brick homes. Walking behind the cart, Mary took in every detail of her new community. There were Jewish men and women on the street going about their daily lives. Everything about the town of Leontopolis in the province of Heliopolite reminded her of Nazareth, except the cats. The little furry animals were everywhere, and some of them seemed quite aggressive. They followed the cart, and one dared to nip at the bottom of her robe.

"Joseph! These cats are everywhere, and they keep following us," Mary called to her husband, who walked beside Toma and Kheti as he led their donkey. "Give me your staff. I'll shoo them away."

"You cannot harm the cats!" Kheti quickly responded before Joseph could hand his staff to Mary. "They are sacred animals in Egypt, especially in this town that was dedicated to them before your people made it their home and their place of worship."

"But they are following me and getting under my robe!" Mary protested.

"They want you to feed them," Kheti responded. From a basket on the side of his own donkey, he pulled out a handful of dried fish. He tossed it onto the side of the road, and all the cats immediately left Mary and ran to feast on the fish.

"I cannot believe this Jewish community would allow these unclean animals to take over their streets in this way!" Mary continued to protest while she made sure Jesus was not going to tumble out of the cart as he eagerly pointed at the animals.

"Your Temple"—Kheti pointed ahead to a massive wall of mud bricks with a high stone tower behind it—"was once a Temple to the Egyptian cat goddess, Bubastis-of-the-Fields."

Mary sucked in her breath in astonishment!

Joseph exclaimed, "You mean they turned a heathen house of worship into a Temple to God?"

"This is not Jerusalem." Kheti chuckled. "Your people have adapted to the country they live in. They have accepted some of the Egyptian culture and some of the Greek culture, but they still are distinctively Jewish."

"Mary, do not pass judgment on your new neighbors before you even meet them," the Holy Spirit cautioned. "Think of all the adaptations you and Joseph have made while on this journey."

Mary closed her mouth and focused on the Temple complex ahead.

Walking in front of the cart, the men were still talking. Their voices drifted back to her. "Toma, Mary and I are going to make our home here. You are welcome to live with us," Joseph offered.

There was a long silence. Mary strained to hear Toma's next words.

"Kheti has offered me employment with his caravan," Toma finally responded. "The highway is all the home I want right now."

"Toma, we are your family," Joseph protested.

"Yes, and every time I look at Jesus, I remember Avrahm. Every time Mary serves me, I think of Sarah." Toma's voice caught. "The routine of small-town life would bring back too many memories, cause too much pain. I will stay with the caravan."

"I did not know," Joseph replied with sadness in his voice. "I do not want to add to your sorrow."

"I did not want you to know," Toma answered. "It is my burden and my sorrow. There is nothing you can do. Only God can comfort me." He put his arm around Joseph's shoulder. "You have been a brother and a comfort. God will reward you."

"My caravan travels through here regularly," Kheti asserted. "You will see each other again and again, and on one of those trips, the joy of meeting will not be marred by memories."

Joseph nodded, and Mary silently blessed the Lord for the wisdom of the Egyptian

Mary smiled and, in her spirit, affirmed the heavenly message. She looked up to see Toma approaching. He lifted Jesus out of the cart and hugged him. "Good-bye little man. I'm glad that you are safe," he whispered. merchant.

Kheti led them around the Temple complex to the rear entrance. "This is where I do business," he said as he approached the gate. "I will not be here any longer than it takes to unload the camels. My linen supplier is not far from here, and I will go there to spend the night."

"Then this is good-bye." Mary watched as Joseph threw his arms around the Egyptian merchant like he was a family member.

The spirit of Criticism took advantage of the moment. "He touched a Gentile!"

Immediately, Mary dismissed the thought. Kheti had become like a member of the family.

The Spirit repeated the ancient command he had given to Moses, this time specifically including Kheti. "And you shall love your neighbor, even your dark-skinned Egyptian neighbor, as you love yourself."

Mary could see that tears were rolling down Toma's cheeks. She felt her own eyes begin to sting as she remembered how he had loved his son. Through the tears, she saw her own son reach out with his little hand and begin to wipe at the tears on Toma's cheeks. It was as if he understood and offered comfort to the man who held him.

A little smile broke out on Toma's face. He placed his bearded cheek next to the smooth cheek of Joseph and Mary's son. "You are a dear and precious boy," Toma said as he walked over and placed Jesus in his mother's arms. "Good-bye, Mary. You have been a kind sister. Sarah loved you." Again his voice cracked.

"You know our home is always your home," Mary repeated Joseph's offer.

"On my next journey, I will come to your home," Toma promised before he turned away to help Kheti unload the camels.

Continuing around the outer wall of the Jewish Temple, Joseph found the pool of fresh water for cleansing. Leaving Mary, Jesus, and the cart under a large shade tree, he prepared to enter the Temple. He left his staff in the cart, removed his outer robes, and entered the enclosed area designated for the men. Performing the traditional Jewish rite of purification, he walked down the stone steps and ducked under the water, completely immersing himself three times. Coming up out of the water, he was now refreshed and ceremonially clean, ready to walk through the Temple gates and inquire of the various worshipers and Temple staff where he might find a home for his family.

Chapter 13

LIFE IN EGYPT

*"For I know the plans I have for you," declares the LORD,
"plans to prosper you and not to harm you, plans to give you
hope and a future."*

—Jeremiah 29:11

Flinging her arms out wide, Mary spun around in the main living area of the home Joseph had rented. Since they had no furniture, the room seemed so spacious. It made her feel deliciously free and light. She had a home to make her own once more! Laughing, enjoying the moment, Mary twirled round and round until her head began to spin, then she sat on the floor, and Jesus crawled up in her lap. She tickled him, and he laughed and drooled.

"Shalom?" a woman's voice interrupted Mary's hilarious celebration.

Getting to her feet and lifting Jesus into her arms, she somewhat cautiously opened the door to her new home. A young woman who was obviously expecting a child stood in her doorway.

"I'm your neighbor, Arsinoe." The young Jewish woman smiled and held out a small pottery container. "Honeycomb. My husband found a beehive." She looked a little uncertain about how to continue. "It is a gift for you."

"Come in." Mary opened the door of her home and stepped aside. "We have no furniture yet, so if you don't mind, we will sit on the floor." Mary took the gift, and for a moment, both women stood looking at each other.

"I can see you have a son," Arsinoe commented.

"Yes," Mary answered, "and another child on the way, but my child will not be born before yours!"

Both women laughed and instantly bonded as Arsinoe put both hands on her enormous belly. "My mother-in-law says I should have delivered this baby yesterday."

"Mothers have a lot to say about first babies," Mary responded as she remembered all her mother had told her.

"I don't have a mother. She died when my younger brother was born."

"Then I'll tell you everything my mother told me," Mary offered. "I'm assuming this is your first?" she added.

"How can everyone tell?" Arsinoe laughingly protested. "I must look too young!"

"Your first child is the most special child," Mary said, and her eyes followed Jesus as he looked up and gave them a grin that showed off his baby teeth.

"Such a sweet boy. I can hardly wait for my own!"

That was all the encouragement Mary needed. She began talking about her son: his sweet disposition, his curly hair, the way he imitated his father. When she mentioned that he was born in a stable with the assistance of an aging shepherdess, Arsinoe gasped. "My mother-in-law would never allow it! She has hired a midwife who was trained in Alexandria."

"Is she Jewish?" Mary asked. The idea of a specially educated midwife was an absolute novelty. In Nazareth and in Bethlehem, the midwives were just women who were very experienced in childbirth.

"Yes, but she knows all the methods used by the Greeks and the Romans. She is very educated and has assistants who will come with her. My mother-in-law wants this baby very much." Arsinoe patted her stomach. "It will be her first grandchild."

"I cannot imagine making such a production out of having a baby," Mary said. "If I were back in Bethlehem, I would ask that same shepherdess to be with me for the birth of this baby."

"What are you going to do when your time comes?"

"Well…" Mary hesitated as she considered the question. "I have not met many of the women here, so I cannot think of anyone I would ask to be with me. Maybe Joseph and I will just do this alone."

"Your husband, Joseph!" Arsinoe exclaimed. "Men don't assist in childbirth! It's just not done!"

"He was a great assistance when Jesus was born," Mary protested.

With a note of sadness in her voice, Arsinoe responded, "My mother-in-law would never allow such a thing." Then she smiled at Mary. "I think you are more courageous than I am."

"No, I have just learned to trust God and the husband he gave me for the good things in life," Mary answered. "You will see. Call on our God, and he will give you strength and courage when you need it most. You will be blessed with a beautiful baby."

In the early afternoon, Joseph returned to find the two young mothers still talking. Pushing aside his disappointing day, he forced a smile and a neighborly greeting. He was happy for Mary. He knew she had missed the companionship of other women on their long tedious journey to Egypt.

Arsinoe stood quickly. "Phabeis, my husband, transports goods on the river. I will tell him that I met you." She made a polite bow and quickly returned to her own home.

After her new friend left, Mary turned her attention to her husband, studying his face. "Did you find any work today?" she asked.

"There does not seem to be very much building going on in this community," Joseph responded, "at least not the kind of building I am used to." He lifted his hands imploringly. "Mary, I do not want to make mud bricks. I am a carpenter. I work with wood and tools."

"There are plenty of trees here," Mary stated the obvious.

"There are plenty of trees because they don't cut them down," Joseph responded with annoyance. "You have to get permission from the government to cut a tree, to plant a crop, or to practice your craft. Everything is regulated." He sighed as he sat on the floor.

"You have been looking for two weeks, and you can't find work anywhere?" Mary asked in dismay.

"There is a stonemason who needs a helper. The wages are minimal," Joseph replied, "but at least I will be working with tools."

"Will it be enough?" Mary questioned. "I mean will we be able to live?"

"We have enough gold, and we still have the frankincense." He pulled her down next to him and tried to put a little levity into the situation. "I will not send you to beg at the entrance to the Temple."

"Joseph! How can you make light of such a serious situation?"

"Because it is only a temporary situation. We are not going to live here forever, just until the angel of the Lord returns." He reached out and pulled her into his arms, and for a long time, they sat together in silence.

One by one, Joseph placed wedges in the crack he had chiseled into the wall of the stone quarry. Then he began to hit each wedge with a weighted mallet. Over and over, he pounded each wedge until the crack became a fissure and the rock finally split. It was backbreaking work.

"There is no craft to this labor," the voice of Resentment needled. "In this job, you are nothing more than a common laborer."

Joseph straightened up and wiped the sweat from his forehead. It was only early spring, but the humidity in the Nile Delta made the heat seem worse than any he had experienced in his own land.

"I need that piece of granite today." The chief stonemason pointed at Joseph as he walked by.

Joseph picked up the heavy mallet and went back to work.

"You are a skilled craftsman. You should not be treated like a slave. If it were not for Mary and Jesus who is not really your own child, you would be your own boss, working in your own carpentry shop," the spirit of Resentment persisted.

Joseph put a determined effort into forcing those thoughts from his mind. He could not imagine life without Mary and Jesus! How could such a thought even enter his head? He started working on a second seam. Blow after blow, he brought the mallet down on the wedges. When the crack had widened sufficiently, he pulled the wedges out and started a third seam in the face of the rock wall. The muscles in his shoulders and across his back rippled and glistened with sweat as he wrestled to remove a block of granite from a wall of stone.

"Haven't you finished cutting that block of stone?" The chief stonemason was looking over his shoulder again. "I have to make a grave monument. The family is pressuring me to get started."

"By evening," Joseph answered between the crashing blows he was laying on the wedges. "I'll have this block of stone cut before I go home."

"You will be too exhausted tonight to work on the table that you have promised to make for Mary. You haven't made much of a home for your family," Dissatisfaction added his voice to the voice of Resentment.

Together, they kept up a constant commentary. "Because of this job, you have not built any of the furniture you promised your wife. You know, you could have stayed in Bethlehem. Your home was not actually in the town. The soldiers would have never found Mary and Jesus. God did this to you. He pulled you away from the comfortable home you had built and brought you to this mosquito-infested land!"

Joseph stopped pounding long enough to slap an insect that was trying to suck the blood from his sweaty neck. "Lord, why am I tormented in this place?" The words slipped out in the discomfort of the moment. Immediately, he repented.

"I am not tormenting you," the Holy Spirit spoke into Joseph's thoughts. "It is my enemy, Satan. He is persistent, but you can resist him. Do not allow him to fill your mind with thoughts that are contrary to the messages I have sent you. I promise you, he will give up and leave."

Joseph picked up a flat metal bar and began to pry the block of granite away from the wall.

"In this unlivable land, God has deserted you." The spirit of Dissatisfaction pushed this lie into Joseph's mind.

The LORD is my rock, my fortress and my deliverer.

As Joseph worked, he began to sing one of the psalms of his ancestor David. The weariness seemed to slip from his muscles.

My God is my rock, in whom I take refuge.
He is my shield and the horn of my salvation, my stronghold.

He gave a final push and a tug. The block of granite separated from the wall of rock.

I call to the LORD, who is worthy of praise.[1]

Joseph was through working for the day. After gathering up his tools, he collected his wages and hurried home.

Joseph strode through the door and straight to the water jar. After stripping to his loincloth, he began dipping out water, pouring it over his head, letting it run down his back. The house seemed too quiet. Looking around, he wondered why Mary had not come to him, offering to wash his back like she usually did.

"Mary?" he called, realizing that his home was empty even as the words left his lips.

"Mary is so inconsiderate! She does not appreciate how hard you work just so she and Jesus can live in Egypt." Resentment had been lurking nearby, waiting for another opportunity to speak.

Forcefully, Joseph dismissed the idea that Mary was neglecting him. A few minutes later, she came in.

"I'm so glad you're home." She set Jesus down on the floor and hurried to hand her husband a fresh tunic. "Arsinoe is having her baby. She wants me with her, but I have only been able to stay a brief time here and there. Could you watch Jesus while I stay with her? Her husband is on the river, though her mother-in-law is there. She also has a midwife with three assistants."

"With all that help, why does she need you?" Joseph asked.

"It's just that she's fearful. The midwife is so professional. The mother-in-law has so much advice. She needs someone to just sit with her and hold her hand."

Joseph glanced at his active son; already he had his hands in the water jar.

"Mary just doesn't appreciate—"

Joseph didn't allow the spirit of Resentment to finish its thought.

"Yes, Mary. Go be with your friend. Has our son eaten?"

"Not yet." Mary finished giving instructions as she prepared to go to her neighbor, "You will find dried fish, bread, and fresh vegetables in the cooking area."

Joseph looked a little wistfully at the door to his home as it closed behind his wife. Then he turned his attention to his son, who was already quite wet from splashing in the water jar. Joseph bent down and removed his wet clothing.

"After the day you have had, Mary should not expect you to take care of her son," the Resentment made one more attempt.

"You are my son, and I love you," Joseph stated. He began to pour water over the little boy, who laughed at the delicious coolness. "I bless the day an angel visited your mother and the day you were given to me."

"Begone!" The Spirit of God flew in the face of the demonic spirits. "With his statement of praise and agreement with the plans of God Most Holy, Joseph has defeated you. You must leave." Before the Spirit of God finished speaking, the demonic spirits had fled to other homes in the community.

In the blackness just before dawn, Joseph felt Mary crawl onto their sleeping pallet and move close to him. Very sleepily, he reached for her, mumbling, "Was it a boy or a girl?"

Mary didn't answer. Instead, she started to weep uncontrollably.

"Mary?" Through the fog of sleep, Joseph tried to make sense out of her reaction. "What's wrong?" He sat up on one elbow and tried to see his wife in the dark.

"Arsinoe died," Mary sobbed.

"How?" Joseph remembered Mary's friend. She seemed so young and healthy. He could not imagine what could have gone wrong.

"The baby was too big, and she could not get it out. Arsinoe was so courageous. She pushed and pushed. Even though she was very weak, she tried every position the midwife suggested. We held her while the midwife tried repositioning the baby. She injected oil so the baby would slide out. Nothing worked."

Joseph could hardly believe the tragic story his wife was telling.

"She was in great pain, but toward the end, she became too weak to cry out. Then we knew she was dying." Mary's voice caught before she continued, "She was breathing only very shallow breaths. That was when her mother-in-law screamed, 'Save the baby!' and the midwife cut open Arsinoe's womb and removed the baby that way. But the baby was already dead. They could not get him to breathe. Poor Arsinoe took her last breath with her womb gaping open and the dead baby on her mother-in-law's lap."

Sleepiness fled from Joseph's mind. He could not imagine the horror Mary had witnessed. "Lord, how do I comfort her?" Joseph prayed as he scooped his wife into his arms. "I'm sorry. I'm so, so sorry." He said it over and over again as he rocked her back and forth.

Joseph read the poetic epitaph that the master stonemason was carving into a large stone marker.

> *This is the grave of Arsinoe,*
> *Stand here and weep for her,*
> *a most unfortunate woman whose life was tragic.*
> *She was bereaved of her mother when only a little girl.*
> *In the bloom of young womanhood,*
> *her father joined her in marriage with Phabeis.*
> *Her life, a short span of years,*
> *ended in the travail of bearing her firstborn child.*
> *This grave holds in its bosom a young woman of great grace*
> *and beautiful in spirit.*
> *Her soul has now flown to be with the holy ones.*
> *This is a lament for Arsinoe.*

"Joseph, should you be here?" the Holy Spirit asked. The question, one that had entered Joseph's mind more than once, was louder and more persistent than ever.

It had been two months since Mary had witnessed the travail and death of her friend. The question that had been running through his head for weeks would not die.

"Consider the unfortunate circumstances of your wife's life. She has moved away from her parents, been forced to flee from her home in Bethlehem, learned of the death of her dear friend Sarah and Sarah's child, and now she has witnessed the death of her new friend Arsinoe. All this has happened in two years, a very short span of time."

Joseph picked up some of the stonemason's tools and turned away to begin grinding them back into sharpness.

"Do not work here another day!" The Spirit was very insistent. "Stay home with your wife. Be a comfort to her in her sorrow. Do not allow the spirit of Fear to enter your home and shout lies that will make the birth of this next child difficult."

Joseph considered the minimal wages that he earned and the resources he still had.

"I have provided for you. You have gold and frankincense. My arm is not short. I saved your family and brought you into Egypt. I will sustain you while you are in this foreign land, and I will bring you back into your own country."

> *He who dwells in the shelter of the Most High*
> *will rest in the shadow of the Almighty.*
> *I will say of the LORD,*
> *'He is my refuge and my fortress,*
> *my God, in whom I trust.'*

Joseph sang the psalm as he worked.

> *He will cover you with his feathers,*
> *and under his wings you will find refuge;*
> *his faithfulness will be your shield and.*[2]

Before the psalm had ended, Joseph had made a decision. At the end of this workday, he would go home to stay with his wife and son, at least until this next baby was born.

"Shalom, greetings to the house of Joseph!"

Mary recognized the voice and hurried to the door as fast as her very pregnant body would allow. "Toma!" she exclaimed while throwing the door wide open. "Joseph will be so happy to see you! Come in. Have you come to stay or are you just passing through?"

"We will be here a night and a day, and then we will move on." Toma pulled off his sandals as Mary brought water to wash his feet and hands.

Always attracted to water, Jesus came running to put his hands in the basin.

"My little man, how you have grown!" Toma patted him on the head.

"And you," Joseph asserted as he came from the back of the house, "have become almost as dark as Kheti." He came over and gave his cousin a warm hug. "Life on the road seems to agree with you."

"It is a good life," Toma agreed. "I enjoy working with the camels and donkeys. We are carrying more goods now. Kheti and I went to Alexandria and purchased imports to carry to the markets in Jerusalem."

Mary brought wine to the men and then went to prepare food. Her back ached, but she pushed her discomfort to the back of her mind and listened to the men while she worked.

"Have you been to Bethlehem?" Joseph asked.

"Yes." Toma's face became somber. "At first, I felt too ashamed to face my uncle and cousins. They had been left to deal with the carnage in my home. But Kheti brought us together. They thought I had been carried off to one of Herod's dungeons or killed."

"Your house?" Joseph asked.

"Torn down, not one stone left on another. There was no other way to cleanse the property."

"My home?" Joseph asked.

Mary had to stop working for a moment so as not miss Toma's response.

"Uncle Shaul has leased both the field and the house. Here, I have brought you the money from this transaction."

"No," Mary heard Joseph protest. "You keep it. Your loss has been so much greater than mine."

"I don't need money," Toma objected. "I am paid well and take care of no one but myself. Keep it for your family."

"Let's split it evenly," Joseph suggested. "It will help to pay for the services of the midwife I have retained for the delivery of our next child." With exaggerated amazement, he added, "Toma, you would not believe the price for the services of this midwife. I could purchase a field!"

Mary placed several kinds of fruit, some almonds, and flat bread in front of the men.

Toma looked at Mary as she served him and asked, "What is so special about this midwife?"

"She has been trained in Alexandria, and she has assistants." Mary did not seem very enthusiastic.

Joseph attested, "She is the only trained midwife in this area."

"Joseph knows I would rather have a good Jewish woman like Zepporah. She was so wonderful when Jesus was born," Mary said.

"Zepporah has died," Toma stated as kindly as possible. "When she heard about the carnage, all the mothers and babies that died, she collapsed and never got up again."

"Oh no!" Mary was dismayed. "So much tragedy! I can hardly make my mind believe that so many people have died."

"Here, this is good news." Toma pulled a small rolled piece of parchment from the folds of his robe. "It's from your parents. When they got your message, they sent a message to Uncle Shaul to hold for you in case you returned."

Mary could not unroll it fast enough. "Here, you read it." She handed it to Joseph.

Joseph read, "My dear child, we thank God that you and your son are safe and that you are with Joseph. Come to us in Nazareth as soon as you are able. Your sister, Salome, has been betrothed to Zebedee, the fisherman. She longs for your return. Much love, your parents."

"Oh, Joseph, my heart longs to be with my family again." Mary's voice sounded strangled. Unable to say more, she just turned away and returned to the cooking area.

"Mary, come eat with us," Joseph called after her.

"I think I will rest," Mary responded. "Jesus will eat with you." She gave her son a little nudge, and he ran to his father, crawling into Joseph's lap to share the meal.

"God, be near me." Mary whispered into the shadows of her windowless sleeping room. "Once you sent an angel to me, and that angel said I had found favor with God. Please, may your favor continue as I bring another child into the world?"

Mary heard Joseph enter the room where she was resting. She could feel his eyes on her, but she did not move. Instead she counted to herself as her next contraction peaked and then waned. She had been feeling them off and on for several days. They would start. They would stop. Then they would start again, just to stop. But today, she felt like it was the real thing.

"Mary? Are you awake?" She sensed that her husband was moving closer to the bed.

"Yes, Joseph."

"I thought I would take Jesus and go with Toma back to his camp. I want to see Kheti, and Toma is promising Jesus he can ride on a camel."

For a moment, Mary considered just sending them off without mentioning the contractions. Then she thought better of it. She did not want to attempt delivering this baby alone. Hard as she tried, she just could not get the picture of Arsinoe's fruitless struggle out of her mind. What if she could not deliver this baby?

"You should not be gone long," she responded. "Our next child may be born tonight." She tried to sound light and positive.

"Tonight?" Joseph sat down beside her and placed his strong hands on her belly. Through the layers of thin linen robes that Mary was wearing, he felt the slight tensing of her abdomen as the next contraction started. "Why didn't you tell me sooner?" he asked.

"It's just the beginning." Mary tried to sound casual. "You remember how long it took when Jesus was born."

"It may not take so long this time," the Spirit stated with some insistence.

"I will ask Toma to take Jesus to spend the night at the camp with him." Joseph got up and hurried toward the door.

"Joseph," she called after him, "I am not sure."

"I am sure you could use a night without a child to care for," Joseph replied as he left their sleeping room.

Through her open door, she could hear muffled voices and the squeal of delight that came from Jesus when he learned he was going to ride a camel and spend the night in a tent.

"Watch him, Toma." She heard Joseph's parting instructions to his cousin.

"Like he is my own, Joseph," Toma assured.

Those words reminded Mary how well Toma had cared for his son. She could still see them together as they walked to Jerusalem. Toma had always seemed truly happy with Avrahm on his shoulders. A wave of sadness rolled over her as she realized how much Toma had lost.

For a little while, Mary slept. When she awoke, the windowless room was almost completely dark. Getting up, she felt her way out to the cooking area, where a small fire always burned. The waning light of late afternoon entered through two small windows, making rectangular patterns on the floor. From the coals of her cooking fire, she lit an oil lamp, then she moved awkwardly around, putting a few things back in order. She knew Joseph was behind the house; she could hear him hammering.

Mary felt really uncomfortable, but she continued to push herself to put away the remains of the meal she had prepared earlier. It must be this little bit of exercise, she mused as suddenly, a hard contraction took over her body. She held onto the table, waiting for it to pass. When it had subsided, she began to walk again, moving only a few steps before another contraction, longer than the first, captured her. Before the third contraction, she had managed to walk to the rear door of their home. "Joseph!" She got her husband's name out before she had to stop speaking while the next contraction rolled through her body.

Instantly, he was at her side, supporting her shaking body. "You're having the baby?"

Mary could only nod in the affirmative.

"Kheti! Look who I have brought to spend the night with us!" Toma called to the Egyptian merchant who was walking from camel to camel collecting the big clumps of fur the animals were molting.

"Joseph's boy! It's only been about six months and look how he has grown!" Kheti grinned, and his white teeth filled his very dark face.

On Toma's shoulders, Jesus was bouncing up and down, pointing at the shaggy one-humped beasts and saying repeatedly, "Camel! Let me ride the camel!"

"I promised him a ride," Toma said, and Kheti pointed to one of the more docile females.

"Where is Joseph?" Kheti asked as he pulled on the leather strap attached to the peg in the camel's nose.

"Waiting for the birth of his second child," Toma answered.

"It is a blessing to have many sons and daughters," Kheti responded.

The camel's head came down, and she turned her twitching nostrils to get the scent of the little boy Toma had placed on the ground. Toma put his left foot on the camel's neck just behind its head and then brought his right knee to a point further down on the neck. Kheti released his hold on the leather strap, and the camel lifted his head as Toma slid down into position in front of the single hump that characterized the Arabian camel. As soon as Toma was well situated, with the leather straps firmly in hand, Kheti lifted Jesus up to sit in front of Toma. With just a little prodding, the camel lumbered to a standing position.

Jesus dug his little fingers into the shaggy fur and held on as Toma coaxed the animal into a slow shifting walk.

Mary dug her fingers into the covers of her bed. She had forgotten how painful the contractions were. She did not remember them coming so hard and close together. She groaned a little and then prayed, "God, remember your maidservant."

A commotion at the entrance to her home briefly caught her attention. Joseph was returning with the midwife and her attendants. My husband means well, she said to herself, but I really do not want this midwife.

The room was suddenly full of people. Mary saw the midwife's face for the first time since the tragic death of her friend, Arsinoe. Memories flooded her mind. Panic started to rise.

The spirit of Fear began taking advantage of the recent events in Mary's life, reaching out, binding her heart with strong cords.

"God," Mary whispered as the next contraction nearly took her breath away.

"I will keep in perfect peace my daughter whose heart is anchored to me." The Holy Spirit placed his calming hand firmly on Mary's heart, and the cords fell off.

Unable to face the burning touch of the Spirit, Fear had to remove itself from the room.

Joseph stood just inside the doorway, watching Mary's lips form the name of God Most Holy. He sensed the spiritual and physical struggle that his wife was going through.

"You may leave the room now. We will care for your wife." The midwife made shooing motions with her hands. Her three attendants stood by, ready to proceed with their duties, but waiting for the man to make his exit. "Birthing is women's work." The midwife persisted in her efforts to convince Joseph to leave the room. "You have been a good husband. You arranged and paid for my services. That is your complete duty."

"Stay, Joseph. Your wife needs your strength," the Holy Spirit countered the directions of the professional midwife.

"I will stay," Joseph responded as he took a step toward his wife.

The eyes of the attendants grew large, and the midwife took two steps to block Joseph's way. "You will have to leave!"

"Stay!" the Holy Spirit insisted.

"This is my home. I will stay," Joseph spoke firmly as he took another step toward his wife and was again blocked by the midwife.

"It is not good for the woman to have her husband present. She might hesitate to participate like she should, and that could prolong her labor."

Mary groaned and felt the overwhelming desire to push. Her body naturally bore down. Neither the midwife nor her attendants noticed. They were focused on expelling Joseph from the room.

"I believe it was I who employed you," Joseph pointed at the offending woman.

"And I am the one who is trained in the art of birthing!" Her voice rose and took on an authoritative tone that would have sent most men out of the room.

"The baby!" Mary hollered between contractions. No one noticed that she was straining and bearing down.

Joseph and the midwife had locked eyes. They stared at each other, each one waiting for the other to blink.

"Now!" Mary screamed. "The baby is coming now!" She gave a mighty grunt, and the midwife abruptly turned. Grabbing a piece of linen, she squatted down in front of Mary just in time to catch the baby as it came out.

Joseph, looking over the midwife's shoulder, announced to Mary, "We have another son!"

"Well, I never!" Indignity was written all over the woman's face as she looked up to see Joseph standing behind her. The midwife shook her head in disgust and disbelief. The man was staring at his newborn son, oblivious to the immodesty of his wife's position.

"Peasants! Uneducated country peasants! That's what these people are!" the midwife mumbled to herself between directing her attendants to place a pillow under the baby and fetch a basin for the afterbirth.

"Would you step out while we clean your wife and son?" the midwife asked in a tone that indicated her extreme frustration.

Joseph glanced at Mary, who gave him a slight affirmative nod. Only then did he respond, "I'll be sitting in the courtyard. Call me when you are finished."

Alone with her new son, Mary relaxed. The scent of citron left in the room by the midwife's attendants lingered pleasantly. There was a little movement in the doorway. Mary looked to see Jesus standing in the doorway, curiously trying to see what his father had been telling him about.

"Jesus, come in and see your new brother," Mary beckoned to her son.

Eagerly, he ran to Mary's bed, then he suddenly stopped, a little unsure how he should approach the infant in his mother's arms.

"We are going to name this baby James." Mary held him so Jesus could see. "You can touch him."

Jesus reached out one small hand and rubbed it across his brother's cheek. "Do you remember how you used to play with your cousin Avrahm?" Mary asked. "When James gets bigger, he will play with you just like you used to play with Avrahm."

Suddenly, Jesus giggled and then turned and ran out of the room to tell his father what he had seen.

Through the open doorway, Mary could hear Toma and Joseph. "Joseph, there is work for carpenters in Alexandria," Toma insisted. "Every ship that comes into port needs repairs of some kind. All you have to do is go down to the docks with your tools, speak to the captain or an officer of the ship, and you will be working."

"Ships?" Joseph questioned. "I have never worked on ships."

"Ships are made of wood, and I don't know anyone who understands wood better than you," Toma persisted.

"I don't know." Mary could hear the uncertainty in her husband's voice.

Toma continued to promote the journey. "The Nile is in flood stage now, so this is not a good time to travel, but by the time Mary has completed her days of purification and you have taken little James to the Temple for dedication, it will have receded. It is not hot and sticky in that city. There is always a sea breeze."

"What about places to live?" Joseph asked. "I mean Jewish communities."

"There are more Jews in Alexandria than in Jerusalem," Toma stated. "They have synagogues and schools."

"I've heard they also attend the gymnasiums and the bathhouses," Joseph pointed out.

"It's true that some of the Jews, especially the wealthy families, are as decadent as King Herod," Toma agreed. "There are no Pharisees in the city to point condemning fingers. In spite of that, the majority of working class families are just like us."

Mary heard her husband say, "I will talk it over with Mary," but the tone of his voice indicated to her that he had already made up his mind.

"I expect we will be moving to Alexandria," she whispered to her new son. It would be good to make a new start in a new place. The Land of Onais had been filled with too many problems and too much sadness.

Forty days after the birth of their second son, Joseph and Mary, with both Jesus and baby James, approached the entrance to the Temple of the Most High God in the land of Onais, Egypt. It was not the grand structure that dominated Jerusalem. There was no marketplace where animals were purchased, no money changers, and no court for the women. An ordinary mud-brick wall separated the Temple complex from the rest of the Jewish community.

As a family, they approached the gate: Mary carried the infant in a reed basket. Joseph carried two pigeons that he had purchased in the town market, and Jesus walked between them, taking two steps for each step his parents took.

Approaching the Temple in Egypt, Jesus could not take his eyes from the entrance. The gate opened, and something inside seemed to beckon to him. He felt a strong sweet presence flow out and meet him.

"My son, in your heart is the desire to dwell in the presence of God your Father all the days of your life."

Jesus looked at his father and then his mother; neither had spoken to him, yet he was certain someone had spoken, someone who loved him very much.

"Gaze upon the beauty of your Heavenly Father and learn of him through the rituals of the Temple," the Holy Spirit instructed.

At the gate, a white-robed priest met them, receiving from Joseph the two birds and going directly to the altar. Through the open gate, the whole family watched as the officiating priest wrung their necks and collected the blood that he brought back and sprinkled on Mary. He paused to pronounce a blessing on the newest addition to the family before returning to the altar, where he quickly plucked the feathers from the dead birds, tore off the wings, and placed their bodies on the ever-burning altar. Throughout the entire ritual, Jesus stood transfixed, fascinated by every movement that the priest made. As they turned to leave,

Jesus hesitated. He kept turning back, looking over his shoulder as if he were leaving someone behind.

Leaving the city of Leontopolis in the Nile Delta, Mary did not look back. She could only hope the streets of Alexandria would not be overrun with begging cats. Once again, the little family traveled with only the barest of necessities. The furniture Joseph had constructed for their first home in Egypt had been sold. They would start anew in another Egyptian city.

From her resting place in the cart with baby James, Mary watched her husband lift Jesus up onto his shoulders. Another trading caravan approached, and Jesus pointed excitedly. She could hear him saying, "Toma? Is Toma coming to see me? I want to ride on a camel with Toma."

With each passing caravan, Joseph patiently responded, "No, that is not Toma's caravan."

"Toma? Kheti?" Jesus kept repeating the names of his friends while he studied the face of each man who walked past as the caravan moved on. It was the same with every caravan they met.

"Toma and Kheti are not in this caravan," Joseph patiently repeated. "By now, they are most likely in Jerusalem."

Chapter 14

PROTECTED IN EGYPT

*Surely he will save you from the fowler's snare and from the
deadly pestilence. He will cover you with his feathers, and
under his wings you will find refuge; his faithfulness will be
your shield and rampart.*

—Psalm 91:3–4

At the northwest gate to the Court of the Gentiles in the
Temple in Jerusalem, Toma unlashed the last basket of sea
salt from a kneeling camel. Staggering under the weight of a tall
basket filled with salt, he carried it through the massive double
doors, depositing it near the bolts of fine Egyptian linen that had
already been unloaded.

He looked around. It had been a long time since he had
come to the Temple as a worshiper. He glanced at Kheti, who
was negotiating payment. He knew the shrewd Egyptian did not
need his assistance!

Nearby, apprentice priests were moving the four baskets of
salt to one of the many Temple storerooms. He crossed his arms
and waited for them to return with the empty baskets. It wasn't
even a feast day, yet the Temple seemed full of worshipers. Toma
strained to see across the court to the Eastern Gate, but it was
hard to see past the crowds.

The baskets were returned. Toma took the first two by their
handles and then stopped. Over by the Eastern Gate, there

was a commotion: angry shouts, challenging voices. He heard a thundering crash, like a large block of stone hitting the pavement. A shout of triumph went up from the crowd. Before Toma even thought, he was running toward the mass of humanity that surged just inside the gate.

A man's voice rose above the frenzied mob. *"You shall have no other gods before me! You shall not make for yourself an idol in the form of anything in heaven above or on the earth beneath or in the waters below!"*[1]

Seeing that it was futile to push through the crowd, Toma took the stairs up to the roof of the portico. From there, he looked down and saw the golden eagle of Rome that Herod had mounted over the entrance to the Temple had been pulled down and was now being chopped into pieces by young men, zealots for the Lord.

From his perch, Toma had a commanding view of the Temple Mount. He was the first to see the Roman soldiers streaming out from the Fortress of Antonia, and he shouted a warning before fleeing back down the stairs and across the Court of the Gentiles to the Northwestern Gate, where Kheti was preparing to depart.

Behind him, hysteria swept through the worshipers and the zealots. People began stampeding all the gates. Roman soldiers in the Temple courts could only mean one thing—bloodshed! Departure was out of the question. Kheti and Toma could only press themselves against the wall and wait for the fleeing people to clear the entrance.

When most of the people had made their escape, Toma saw the Roman soldiers coming their way. At the same time, he noticed several of the young men who had been involved in the incident trying to blend in with the last of the worshipers and slip out the gate. Their chances of getting away seemed very slim.

At that moment, Kheti stepped away from the wall and ran up to the closest Roman soldier. He was waving his arms and babbling excitedly about his camels. Responding to the distraction, Toma ran to the empty baskets and signaled the men. One man jumped into each basket, and Toma secured the lids.

Moments later, Toma and Kheti found themselves standing beside their baskets while the Roman soldiers streamed by, pursuing anyone who appeared to have been part of the desecration of the golden symbol of Rome.

Kheti directed his drovers to pick up the unusually heavy baskets and mount them on the camels, but before he could move his caravan away from the Temple gate, the officer in charge approached. "We are looking for Judas the son of Saripheus and Matthais, the son of Margalothus, the leaders of this rebellion. The roads leading away from the Temple are closed. No one can depart."

"Sir, can't you see I am a foreigner," Kheti protested, "a trader? This incident has nothing to do with me. I am not involved in the rebellions of these Jews. My camels are loaded and ready to depart for Jericho."

Toma felt all the resentment and anger he had against the men who wore the scarlet uniform of Rome rising in his chest. He looked around for a weapon, a stone—anything. If they were going to be found out and taken into custody, he would not go without doing some damage. Toma picked up one of the sticks they used to prod the animals into motion.

"Maybe you would like to inspect my goods," Kheti offered.

Toma's throat suddenly went dry, and he tried to catch the eye of the Egyptian. Could it be he did not know several of the young men who had torn down the eagle of Rome were hidden in the baskets where they normally carried salt from the Great Sea and the Dead Sea!

Gripping the stick, Toma followed as Kheti led the officer up to the first camel in the caravan. From the basket on the side of that camel, he pulled out a full wineskin. "You must be very thirsty." He pushed the wineskin into the officer's hands. "This is the finest wine from vineyards near Bethlehem." He moved on to the next string of camels and pulled out a bolt of very fine Egyptian linen. "Have you ever seen fabric so sheer and light? In this climate, sometimes a man just wants to be comfortable." Toma noticed how the soldier reached out and felt the fabric. "Let me give this bolt to you." Then Kheti reached deeper into the basket and pulled out a bag full of gold and silver coins. "I could use a Roman escort. How much would it cost for four soldiers to take us out of the city gates and see us on our way to Jericho?"

An amount was agreed upon, and almost immediately, two mounted soldiers took their places at the front of the caravan and two at the rear. Kheti gave the order, and the drovers prodded their animals into motion.

Soldiers were everywhere. As they passed the main gate to the Fortress of Antonia, Toma could see about forty young men, bound and under guard. He shivered for them as he considered the ruthlessness of Herod, vassal king to the Roman emperor.

About forty paces outside the city gates, their Roman escort departed and returned to the city. Kheti's trading caravan moved on, not stopping until they could no longer see the walls of Jerusalem. Only then did they bring their animals to a halt and let the men out of the baskets. Without revealing their identity, the young men slipped into the hilly countryside, and the caravan moved on.

In Jericho beside the mineral baths, Herod's personal attendants prepared to lower him into an oversized vat of warm oil and balsam. As the aging warrior slowly and painfully removed his clothing, even his Roman physician had to turn away. He had never seen a living body so ravaged by disease. Maggot-infested ulcers covered the lower half of the monarch's body. Even the physician's pagan heart had to believe in the rumored curse of the Jewish God.

In this place, there was no heavenly presence. Near the monarch who had given himself over to the forces of evil, Satan hovered, working to keep his most effective tool alive. He did not care that Herod suffered under the judgment of God His only concern was the usefulness of the man. As long as this man breathed, he could be manipulated into destroying the faithful people of God.

A small commotion behind the heavy curtains that shielded the king from the eyes of his staff caught the physician's attention. Motioning for the attendants to continue assisting the king into the oil, he stepped through the curtains.

"I have a message for the king." A Syrian mercenary from Herod's personal guard waited for permission to enter the king's presence.

"The king cannot receive anyone at this time," his physician stated. "Give me the message, and I will relay it to him."

"There has been an uprising at the Temple. A riotous crowd, incited by the well-known Jewish scribes Judas and Matthais, has pulled down the golden eagle from over the entrance to the Temple. The captain of the guard at the Fortress of Antonia has forty young men, along with their leaders, in custody. He desires to know how the king would have him dispose of this matter?"

The physician nodded his understanding. "Wait here. I will return with a response."

The soldier waited as he had been instructed.

"Do not show those ungrateful peasants any mercy," Satan whispered. "You restored their Temple and made it one of the architectural wonders of the Roman world, and this is their way of showing their appreciation! You have been insulted! The emperor has been insulted! If you do not grind those rebels into the dust, they will take your throne before this illness defeats your body."

Through the heavy curtains, the messenger heard Herod roar, "Bring the rebels to me! Bring them here, to Jericho! I know the rumors that are circulating. My spies have informed me. The people think I am dying. They think I am too weak to maintain order. I will show them the strength of their king!"

Within the safety of the Jewish community in Alexandria, Egypt, Jesus stood beside his father and watched as Joseph placed a mezuzah firmly against the wooden beam at the entrance to their new home. He nailed it in place.

The Holy Spirit moved close and spoke, "I have placed in your heart the desire to teach your children to follow me."

As he worked, Joseph glanced down at his son. "Tell me, Jesus, why am I placing this little box containing the words of God on our doorframe?"

To answer, Jesus began to repeat the latest verse of scripture Joseph had been teaching him. "*Love the* LORD *your God...*" He hesitated, trying to remember the next phrase.

Joseph prompted, "*With all your heart and with all your...*"

"*Soul!*" Jesus shouted with a little hop for punctuation.

"*And with all your strength!*"² Joseph said as he showed Jesus his amazingly big bicep.

Jesus touched it, felt its firmness, and then tried to make his own little muscle stand out from his upper arm.

Joseph bent down and picked up his son, bringing him within arm's reach of the mezuzah. "God said, '*These commandments*'"— he took his little son's hand and reverently pressed it against the box that contained the words of God—"*that I give you today are to be upon your hearts.*³ You are to '*talk about them when you sit at home and when you walk along the road, when you lie down and when you get up.*⁴ You are to '*tie them as symbols on your hands and bind them on your foreheads*⁵ so that you will never forget." As Joseph spoke, Jesus looked intently into his face, seeming to hang on every word that his father said. "Today we have written them on the doorframe of our house. We will put another one on our gate. Every time we enter or exit, we will touch the mezuzah and remember that the word of God orders our lives." Joseph lowered his son to the ground, and together they walked to the courtyard gate. "Do you remember the scripture we learned last week?" Joseph asked.

"*O God, I have hidden your word in my heart, that I might not sin against you.*"[6]

Joseph smiled proudly at his son. He was such a bright boy! Joseph had been amazed how his language skills had suddenly blossomed. Leaving Bethlehem, Jesus had only a word or two in his vocabulary. While they journeyed, his words had become phrases, and then while living in the Delta, he had learned to construct sentences and had begun memorizing simple scriptures.

"That's right. Hear my voice and hide my word in your heart," the Spirit of God confirmed the rightness of Joseph's teaching in the heart of Jesus. "It is the guide for your life and your only defense against our enemy."

The Spirit paused and omnipotently scanned the operations Satan had in progress. "Even now, our enemy is at work."

The Holy Spirit knew that the spirits of Sickness and Death had been following this family from the delta region to the coast. They had attached themselves to the bloodsucking insects that had plagued the family as they had journeyed to their new home.

Walking or riding in the cart, each person had held a palm branch to wave the biting bugs away. Only little James had not had the ability to shoo those annoying pests away. For all the attempts of his loving parents to keep the irritating insects away, without their knowledge, the satanically engineered microorganisms the insects carried had entered the baby's bloodstream and multiplied.

Mary had not had an opportunity to enjoy her new home with its view of the Pharos Lighthouse and the Great Sea. Ever since they had arrived, baby James had been sickly. Filled with foreboding, Mary put another pot of water on to boil and looked through her supply of medicinal herbs. She had no experience with childhood illnesses. What had her mother used to bring down a fever?

Hearing her newest son whimper, she left the cooking area to pick him up. Anxiously, she pressed her cheek to his, and it burned her skin. For the tenth time that morning, she tried to put him to her breast, but he was listless and had no interest in nursing. With a prayer on her lips, she laid him down again and returned to select the herbs she hoped would bring his temperature down to normal.

"Yeshua?"

Jesus clearly heard his Hebrew name. The little boy looked up from the scraps of wood he was stacking. There was no one in the room except his baby brother, asleep in the cradle.

"Yeshua?" The voice filled his head and could not be ignored.

Full of curiosity, little Jesus stood up and began to walk slowly around the room, looking in each corner.

"Go pick up your baby brother," the Spirit of God impressed the thought in his mind.

Immediately, Jesus went to the wooden cradle. There was something right about the voice in his head. It was as if his father, Joseph, were speaking to him. He stood on his tiptoes and peered inside. James was very still.

"Your brother is very ill. When you pick him up, the fever and the illness will leave his body."

Obediently, Jesus reached over the side of the wooden cradle, straining to get his little hands under the baby and lift him out. He put every bit of his strength into the effort, staggering backward when he finally brought the infant to his chest. Holding his little brother close, he sat on the floor.

"Your obedience has restored your brother to health." The power of God flowed from the Spirit through Jesus.

At first, Jesus was a little startled as he felt a warm tingling sensation flow through his body.

Immediately, Death and Sickness jerked their hands away as if they had suddenly been burned. Without their nourishing touch, the deadly microorganisms died.

Then James began to cry, a lusty demanding cry that insisted upon food and brought Mary running. She stopped short when she saw her young son holding her infant. How could Jesus have gotten the baby over the side of the cradle, and what if he had dropped his little brother? Condemning words were about to fly from her lips.

"Mary, your son is well," the Holy Spirit directed her attention to the baby. "See how carefully Jesus holds his brother. Speak no rebuke! Just feed James and remember this incident."

The Jericho market was an exciting place. Here at the crossroads of several caravan routes, trading was brisk, profitable, and multilingual.

"Toma, you have a good head for business," Kheti complimented his friend. "I have never received a better price for Egyptian linen. You are right. We do need to expand our trade route and the commodities that we deal in. From here, we can carry almonds and balsam to the coast and sell to ships that will carry our merchandise to distant harbors."

"I will start looking for suppliers." Toma turned to stroll through the market and make casual inquiries. Instead, he stopped short. A mass of red-clad soldiers entered the market area. They filled the road as far as he could see.

Conscious of the role they had played in the incident at the Temple, both Toma and Kheti stepped back into the shadows of one of the market stalls to watch as one of Herod's personal legions passed.

"Barbarians!" Kheti muttered.

"Mercenaries," Toma added, noting that most of the men were obviously Syrian. "This is Herod's own legion. He is not content with the men he receives from Rome. He must have more troops, so he arms at least three thousand additional men from neighboring countries to carry out his evil orders."

"Look!" Kheti pointed and Toma's eyes followed his line of vision. In the middle of the legion, bound and obviously suffering from the beatings they had already received, were the forty men who had been captured at the Temple. In addition, under special guard, the two ringleaders were being dragged to their destiny.

"Why would these men be brought to Jericho?" Toma questioned.

"So their punishment would not cause unrest in Jerusalem," Kheti responded.

"God, have mercy," Toma whispered. But in the face of such overwhelming numbers, he had little faith in the ability or the will of God to save. As the last unit of soldiers passed through the marketplace, they suddenly broke ranks and began impressing people into the procession.

"Herod is going to make sure he has an audience," Kheti commented, but he did not get to say more. The butt of a Roman spear pressed hard against his back. It was obvious that he and Toma were going to be part of that audience.

It was a short forced march to the hippodrome, the site of races and sporting events attended by those with a Roman lifestyle. As they entered the arena, the guards pushed them into the spectators' stands.

Toma ground his teeth in frustration and resentment.

"Hold your tongue and keep a cool head," Kheti advised. "A rash warrior dies on the battlefield, but a wise warrior lives to fight another day under more favorable circumstances."

"Are those the rash warriors?" Toma asked as he nodded toward the forty young Jewish men under guard in the middle of the arena. Their two leaders, the well-known scribes Judas and Matthais, were tied to posts nearby.

"I'm afraid we are here to witness the execution of men who could have walked under that golden eagle a few more times without pulling it down. If only they could have waited until their king was actually in the grave." Kheti pointed to the royal seating area. Herod was there, lying on a stretcher.

"How long, O Lord?" Toma asked with bitterness.

"The finger of death is on him. See?" Kheti pointed. "He can hardly raise himself to speak."

"People of Jericho and representatives of the Jewish people, I have been a good king and a faithful worshiper of God." Herod spoke these words with all the strength he could muster, but still, they had to be repeated by a herald standing at his bedside. "Because of my devotion to my people and my God, I restored your Temple and made it a magnificent house of worship! I spared no expense, filling it with gold and silver!" He paused, waiting for affirmation from those he had assembled.

There was an uncomfortable silence that broke when a few strategically placed soldiers nudged those closest to them with the butts of their spears. Ragged cheers broke out here and there and then swelled into an insincere chorus of agreement. Toma bit his lip and refused to make a sound that would encourage the self-centered despot who was responsible for the deaths of his mother, wife, and son.

"Now I have brought before you men who have defaced the Temple of our God. They have insulted me, but more than that, by their actions they have blasphemed God. Don't you agree that the punishment for desecrating what has been dedicated to God is death?"

As Herod's question echoed through the hippodrome, Kheti exclaimed, "The old fox is trying to make the people pass his sentence on these men!"

A few frightened men voiced their agreement.

"They are too intimidated!" Toma felt as though he would burst with frustration and anger. "Look! There are soldiers all around, forcing the people to respond!"

"Do not be rash, and you will live to see that old man in his grave," Kheti advised again.

"How can I sit here and watch these men die?" Toma asked.

"Remember, some men live because you helped them escape," Kheti said. "You have done something."

Firewood was being piled around Judas and Matthais.

"They are going to burn them!" Toma was horrified. He saw soldiers approach with torches. He watched the wood ignite, and then he turned away. Tears streamed down his weathered cheeks. "My God, my God, why have you turned your face from us?"

The stench of burning flesh filled the arena. A dreadful silence gripped the captive audience. It was broken only by an occasional prayer or a deep sob. Toma did not look up, but after a while, he sensed that the soldiers were moving in on the forty men who had been forced to watch their leaders burn. He heard the metallic swish of Roman swords and then the cries of the dying. With his eyes closed, he could see Jabek's wife and the bleeding stump that had been her arm. He saw his own wife and mother with gaping wounds in their chests. He knew if he opened his eyes, he would see much worse. Beside him, Kheti muttered a pagan prayer to an Egyptian deity for the men who were being slaughtered before his eyes. Then he began calling the curses of the Egyptian gods down on the head of Herod. Toma uttered a heartfelt, "Amen!"

When the soldiers allowed them to leave, they routed the men past the bloody and burned corpses of the rebels. Somehow, Toma managed to avert his eyes and not look at the carnage. There was no room in his mind for more scenes of violent death.

That night, like a sign of God's displeasure, there was a complete eclipse of the moon, and for a short period of time, complete darkness covered the land.

Volumnius tugged at the leather strap he used to hold the stump of his right arm flat against his side. From the elbow down, his arm had been amputated. The upper arm that remained hung uselessly, uncontrollable due to the damage his shoulder had sustained. He could not stand for the stump to dangle and flop like a dying fish. Viciously, he gave the strap one more tug before he bent his head and used his teeth to help tie the securing knot.

Like the leather strap, Bitterness wound itself more securely around his soul, constantly chanting its mantra of recriminations. "You have been unfairly discarded. You should still be the commander of Herod's palace regiment. Just because you have been injured, he demotes you to commander of his dungeon and nursemaid to Antipater, the imprisoned heir to the throne! Herod does not appreciate what a valuable man you are."

With his left hand, the ex-commander of Herod's palace regiment lifted the heavy ring of iron keys from its hanging place on the stone wall and then turned. With a nod of his head, he indicated that he was ready to escort the servant who had just arrived, carrying a tray of food prepared by the palace kitchen for the eldest living son of Herod.

"Let me see what the pampered prince has today." Volumnius removed the linen cloth that covered the tray and used the point of his knife to poke through the various portions of food to see if they contained anything that the young man might use as a weapon. He did this out of habit and duty. Antipater had been raised in the palace, educated in Rome. He was not a warrior like his father. Volumnius doubted that he would know what to do with a sword even if the cook was clever enough to hide it in a leg of lamb.

Satisfied that the tray of food contained no unusual objects, Volumnius led the way to the cells reserved for those of noble birth who fell into the great chasm of the king's paranoid displeasure.

The servant entered the cell and placed the tray on a table. Antipater, a man close to thirty, looked up from the letter he was writing. "My father?" he asked as he rose to meet the servant and place a coin in his hand.

The servant responded, "He has returned from treatments both at the warm springs in Jericho and in the mineral-filled mud and water of the Dead Sea. Nothing has helped."

The prince is a clever man, even if he is not a warrior, Volumnius mused. He is keeping abreast of the situation and hoping his father, the king, will die before he can give the order to execute him.

"There is no hope for you to regain your post, and there is no hope for Antipater to return to the favor of his father," Bitterness whispered.

"What do the physicians say?" Antipater pressed the servant for details.

"It is whispered that the king will die soon. He is in constant pain. His skin is covered with sores, and worms crawl in and out of his body."

"Has impending death brought any softening to his stony heart?" Antipater asked with a touch of sarcasm. "Has it brought him any clarity of thought? Does my father still believe I sent a vial of poison all the way from Rome to his brother so his brother would slip it into his food?"

"There has been no change in the king's state of mind," the servant responded. "Other servants have told me he knows death is near, and he fears that his subjects will rejoice instead of mourn when he takes his last breath. He has called his sister, Salome, to his side and made her promise to give the order for a great massacre to take place when he dies."

"Massacre?" Antipater asked a little fearfully.

"Right now, in each town, the heads of all the observant families are being ordered to gather in the hippodrome at Jericho. They are being held there until the king dies."

Volumnius saw the king's son let out a long slow sigh. Obviously, he was relieved that the king intended to kill prominent Jews instead of members of the royal family.

"Eat your food, sir, and enjoy it. I have tasted each dish, and you have nothing to fear from this meal," the servant offered.

Shouts, shrieks, and wails suddenly filled the dungeon corridors. Volumnius took a couple of steps out into the main corridor to hear someone shout, "The king is dead! He killed himself!"

Antipater heard the shouts also and started to run out of the open door of his cell. With his body, Volumnius blocked his escape. "When I receive orders for your release, then you will be released!" With his left arm, he shoved Herod's son back into the cell, motioned the servant out, and locked the door.

Antipater came to the barred window and pressed his face against the bars. "Commander!" he called Volumnius.

Volumnius paused and turned.

"Do this country a favor. Prevent unrest and uprisings by releasing me. I can assume the throne without disrupting the country," Antipater begged. "I can restore you to the post of commander of the palace regiment."

Misplaced Loyalty countered, "Who is this man who thinks he deserves the throne his father won with the sword? You, a warrior, are more deserving than he is! Do not be fooled into helping him obtain the throne. Only the emperor can make him King of Judea. Your loyalty must not be questioned. You are loyal to Rome!"

Volumnius turned his back and started to walk away. It was noble to win the throne in battle, but to gain it by political maneuvering and bribery? He had been at the court long enough to know that politics could be more deadly than battle. If the emperor thought he was trying to place someone on the throne—

"I'll make you a wealthy man!" Antipater called after him. "I'll give you a villa near the Great Sea!"

"This is your opportunity," Bitterness shouted. "Antipater is promising to give you the recognition your faithful service deserves."

Misplaced Loyalty pushed Bitterness aside. "Go to Corinthus. You may receive greater rewards by remaining loyal to the emperor and those he has put in high places. Show them you are worthy of greater responsibilities."

Unaffected by the attempted bribe, Volumnius hurried on out of the dungeon and to the offices of Corinthus, the chamberlain who guarded the royal chambers of the monarch.

Slowly, Herod opened his eyes to see a room full of people all staring at him. *What? How? I must have blacked out.*

Then he remembered. He had been sharing a meal with his cousin, Achiabus. As was his custom, he had picked up an apple and a knife when suddenly he had been overcome with the misery of his life. He had wanted to die right then and there, to thrust the blade through his own heart. His courage had not failed him. He had lifted the knife and begun its fatal descent, but Achiabus had grabbed his wrist and wrestled the blade from his hand. At that moment, he must have passed out.

And now… "Clear the room!" he bellowed. "I will not be the object of your pity!" His face turned red as he struggled to raise himself up on one elbow.

There was an immediate scurrying.

"You want to pity someone?" His breathing became labored, but he continued to rant, "Go look at the beggars who sit at the gates to the Temple. Go to the Pool of Bethesda, where fools wait for angels to stir the water. Don't pity me! Don't stand by my bed like vultures waiting for me to die!"

Everyone but Corinthus and Herod's physician made a hasty exit.

"Sire, you had a moment of madness," Corinthus cautiously approached the raving king with placating words.

"It wasn't a moment of madness," Herod countered as he fell back onto his couch. "It was a moment of sanity! Is this any way for a warrior to die?" He gestured toward the open sores on his legs. "Worms even crawl in and out of my bowels! And you can't do anything about it!" He pointed accusingly at his physician. At that moment, a movement behind the curtained entrance to his chambers caught his attention. "Who's out there?" he growled.

Corinthus, the chamberlain, hurried to pull one of the curtains aside. Voluminus stood there. "You should not be here," Corinthus warned.

"I came to honor my monarch," Volumnius responded.

"Do you honor me dead or alive?" Herod questioned from his couch.

"Thanks be to the gods, I honor you alive," Volumnius responded as he dropped down on one knee.

"Rise and approach." Herod struggled once more to raise himself up on one elbow. "And my son Antipater, does he honor me alive?"

"I'm afraid the news that you still live and rule will be a great disappointment to him," Volumnius disclosed. "When word of your death reached his cell, he attempted to bribe me into giving him his freedom." Volumnius quickly added, "You can be sure he remains in his cell alive and in good health."

"Again! Before my body lies on its bier, he tries to take my throne!" Herod ground his teeth. "Execute him! Execute him!" A rage overtook the monarch, and he beat his head with his fists as he screamed, "He will not live to see another sunset!" Herod then went into a fit of coughing and fell back onto his couch. His physician hurried to his side while his chamberlain motioned the commander of the dungeon out of the room.

"Prepare to transport the king back to the mineral springs of Jericho. It is his only hope," the physician ordered.

"Don't go!" Mary's mother pleaded.

"Do you want me to be killed on my own doorstep?" Heli asked as he gestured toward the small contingency of soldiers sent to the towns in the region of Galilee to bring representatives from each town to the hippodrome in Jericho.

"What does Herod want with you? What does he want with the other elders of the towns?" Mary's mother wrung her hands in agitation.

"According to the soldiers, he wants us to pray for him," Heli responded as he gathered his things.

"I'll give you a prayer to say for that son of Satan," Mary's mother raised her voice. "May his body and soul burn in the fires of Sheol!"

"Be quiet, woman. Your voice can be heard in the street," Heli firmly warned.

"That man is a murderer," Heli's wife continued in hushed tones. "He killed all the babies in Bethlehem, and our grandson nearly died with them! I don't trust him." She paced the room. "I may never see you again!"

"My life is not in the hands of Herod," Heli reassured his wife. "God holds my life in his hands. If it is his time for me to die, then I die. If not, then I live. Remember, our grandson escaped because it was not God's time for him to die."

Heli could see tears forming in his wife's eyes. He came over to comfort her. For as long as he dared, he held her. Their life together had been good.

"You will need food for the journey." Heli's wife pushed herself away and busied herself with the necessary preparations. "And please be back for Salome's wedding?" she asked as she worked.

Heli heard the pain in his wife's last request. For a long moment, he watched as she tried to focus on the task of packing food. The wedding was nearly a year away. Still, how could he assure her he would return to see their youngest daughter escorted to the home of Zebedee the fisherman? Without voicing the reassurances she wanted to hear, he turned away.

All too soon the moment of parting arrived. In the town square, soldiers stood guard over the leading men from other towns, all wearing their prayer shawls, some with phylacteries, small leather boxes containing scriptures, strapped to their foreheads and leather wrapped around their arms. It was the time of prayer, the time when the evening sacrifice was being offered in the Temple in Jerusalem. The men covered their heads and bowed toward their holy city. A lone voice began an ancient Hebrew prayer, "*The* L*ORD* *is King for ever and ever.*"

Other voices joined in, "*The nations will perish from his land.*"[7] There was no danger that the soldiers would be incited by this prayer, for only the scribes and very educated Jewish men could read and understand Hebrew.

Heli stepped into the group of davening men, adding his voice to theirs, "*You hear, O* L*ORD*, *the desire of the afflicted; you encourage them, and you listen to their cry, defending the fatherless and the oppressed, in order that man, who is of the earth, may terrify no more.*"[8]

With patient restraint, the soldiers waited until the prayers ended, then they escorted the men out of the town toward Jericho. As they moved from town to town, their ranks continued to swell until they arrived at the hippodrome; the number of Jewish prisoners was over two hundred.

Carrying a change of clothing and the food his wife had packed, Heli entered the giant stone edifice to Roman decadence. The arena was a place no observant Jew would willingly enter. He looked around. The stone seats were filled with scribes and scholars of the Law of Moses, all forced here at the point of a spear. Nearby, a richly dressed scribe moved over on a stone bench and indicated a space for Heli to sit.

With deference to the obvious status of the man, Heli bowed and politely thanked him before taking the offered seat.

"Do not bow, my friend. We are all equal here," the wealthy scribe commented.

"Indeed, the king has gathered high and low into one place for his perverted pleasure," responded Heli.

"You sound like a man from the area of Galilee?"

"Heli, scribe from Nazareth."

"Hillel, scribe from Jerusalem."

Heli sucked in his breath. He was sitting next to one of the most influential Pharisees in the land, head of the Sanhedrin, founder of his own school. The simple scribe from Nazareth was speechless.

"Don't look so impressed," Hillel advised. "If we are to die, I will be the second person killed." He pointed to another well-dressed Pharisee. "Shammai, will be the first. Herod hates him even more than he hates me."

"Since you are from Jerusalem, I assume you may know why we have been gathered in this heathen place?" Heli asked.

"I believe we are here for the last act of a madman, and only God can deliver us from his perverted plan," Hillel replied.

"Our king is capable of great cruelty," Heli agreed. "He had the young children of Bethlehem slaughtered. Only my grandson escaped because his father was warned by the angel of the Lord."

"It is a comfort to know that the angel of the Lord still visits the land and rescues," Hillel fervently stated. "Where is your grandson now?"

"Egypt," Heli answered. "I have never seen him, but my son-in-law sends messages through his family."

"The king is dying." Herod's physician advised Corinthus in hushed tones, "Gather the family, bring them to the royal residence at Jericho. They will want to hear Herod's will as soon as he takes his last breath."

Herod's chamberlain glanced at the monarch who labored for every breath. Nodding his head in agreement, he added, "I'll also need to send a messenger to Varus, the governor of Syria. It is his duty to make sure there is a peaceful transition of power."

Over the next two days, the family gathered. The royal sleeping chamber was never empty. Like buzzards waiting to feast on the monarch's will, no one seemed especially troubled by the king's impending death, except his sister, Salome.

"Salome?"

The regal woman, dressed for mourning, gave another troubled glance around the room. Those voices were in her head again. "My brother, my brother, what evil have you brought upon me?" she asked as she moved closer to the failing monarch. "All because you made me promise to execute the elders of this land, I am being tormented." She looked down at Herod's equally tormented face. "I believe you are slipping through the Gates of Sheol already and that you want to take me there to suffer with you!"

There was no response from the man on the couch. Salome stared hard at his face. She wanted to be sure that her brother was really dying, that he could not return from the grave to vent his wrath on her.

"Why are you afraid to break your promise to your brother?" the Spirit of God asked. "He cannot force you to carry out his dying wishes. If you give the order to execute the men who are imprisoned in the hippodrome in Jericho, the responsibility rests with you."

Salome shivered. Suddenly, she felt as cold as death.

Again the Holy Spirit cautioned, "To kill those men would be a crime that a righteous God would have to avenge."

Agitated and torn between her duty to her brother and her duty to God, Salome threw her mantle over her head and strolled out into the warmth of the garden.

"You promised!" Satan urged. "Your brother would not have made the request if he had not felt it was necessary to remove these men who incite the people to rebellion."

"Old scribes do not incite the people to rebellion," the Holy Spirit countered. "They urge the people to be productive and to deal with each other according to the Law of Moses. They bless the nation."

Salome's husband met her in the garden. "Your brother has finally taken his last breath."

"Are you sure?" Salome asked.

"He is dead!" her husband replied with finality.

There was a heavy silence while Salome considered her next duty. Her husband had been privy to Herod's request. He knew the decision she must make. For a moment, they locked eyes.

Finally, Salome spoke, "Have a scribe and a messenger sent to me."

"Are you sure?" Her husband seemed reluctant to take the next step.

"I am sure I will never sleep again if I carry out my brother's wishes," Salome replied. "I am sending the men back to their homes."

Nodding his agreement, he hurried to carry out her wishes.

On the docks in Alexandria, Joseph worked at a makeshift bench, refinishing the oars from a Cretan galley. He concentrated on shaving them down and smoothing their splintered edges. He planned to complete this job in two days, leaving for himself the daylight hours of the thirteenth of Nissan to prepare for the Feasts of Passover and Unleavened Bread. He would go to the pool of fresh water at the synagogue and wash, then at sundown, he would light a taper, and with a feather in his hand, he would search his home for leaven. There would be prayers and readings in the synagogue and a special meal at home. He looked forward to those special days God had set aside.

Ignoring the ceaseless activity of the wharf, Joseph bent to his task, keeping up a steady rhythm as oar after oar was examined and repaired. An unfamiliar voice broke through the shouts of sailors and the haggling of merchants, "Carpenter? Are you Joseph the carpenter?"

Joseph paused and looked up into the face of a Roman officer, captain of a troop transport. He took a deep steadying breath before answering, "You have found me."

"Your work has been recommended. I need two additional berths in the officer's quarters of my ship. I need this job done quickly, for I must sail for Caesarea within a week."

"The work you are requesting would take a week. This job that I am now doing will be completed in two days. I could not begin your job until after the Jewish Feasts of Passover and Unleavened Bread." Thinking he had given an answer that would send the Roman looking for another carpenter, Joseph returned to the task at hand.

"You do not understand the urgency," the Roman captain persisted. "Herod is expected to die! I must take my troops to Caesarea and then be prepared to transport Herod's successor to Caesar so he can be confirmed and Herod's will can be approved! My orders have come from Varus, the governor of Syria and the entire region."

Joseph stopped shaving the wood in midstroke. "Herod, the king in Jerusalem, is really dying?" he repeated while he tried to comprehend what that might mean.

"Yes. Additional troops are being summoned to maintain stability in the area while the throne is transitioning, but what is of greater importance is I have orders to transport the royal family to Rome and there are not enough berths on my ship."

"Will Antipater inherit his father's throne?" Joseph had now taken a keen interest in what this Roman had to say.

"No. When I received word to make preparations and come with haste, I also received the news that Herod had ordered Antipater executed." Joseph's face must have expressed the shock and horror he felt when he understood that the king had killed his own son because the Roman captain added, "It does seem unnaturally brutal, doesn't it!"

Afraid to respond one way or the other, Joseph just pressed for more information. "Which of Herod's sons will succeed him?" he asked.

"It is expected that Archelaus will take the throne upon Herod's death," the Roman answered. "Of course, this is subject to the approval of Caesar, so you can see it is imperative that I prepare my ship and then set sail as soon as possible." He ended in an imploring tone.

"Further down the docks is an Egyptian carpenter," Joseph replied. "He is a fine craftsman. He may be able to meet your time requirements."

Joseph watched as the Roman ship's captain made his way along the docks. Over and over in his mind, he pondered the information he had just received. How would this political change affect his family here in Egypt? And what about his loved ones back home in the land, how would they fare?

Mary moved the last of the grains out of her storage area. She had been cleaning for two days in preparation for the Feast of Passover, which is followed by the seven-day Feast of Unleavened Bread. She was just about ready for the final sweeping of her cooking area, the final search for anything that might contain or be used as leaven. She picked up a bunch of stiff feathers bound securely together and began to brush out her oven. Preparation for the spring feasts was extremely time-consuming. But when the house was totally clean and the family had gathered at the synagogue for services and then returned home to have a meal together, it felt so good. Only one thing was missing—a real Passover lamb. Passover lambs were only sacrificed in the Temple, and the Seder meal was only eaten within the confines of the expanded limits of the city of Jerusalem.

Pausing from her work, she rested her arm and wondered if both of her parents would go to Jerusalem this year and whether they would camp out or stay with friends.

> *I rejoiced with those who said to me,*
> *"Let us go to the house of the Lord."*

Without hesitation, the women answered,

> *Our feet are standing in your gates, O Jerusalem.*

The group of men and women from Nazareth rounded a bend in the road, and the city was suddenly before them.

> *Jerusalem is built like a city that is closely compacted together.*

The men sang with their eyes fixed on the city. From that point, they could see the white walls and the houses crowded together on the mountain that was originally David's citadel. It was a soul-stirring sight.

> *That is where the tribes go up,*
> *the tribes of the Lord,*
> *to praise the name of the Lord according*
> *to the statute given to Israel.*

The women danced as they sang. Even Mary's mother felt young as a virgin and danced with a vigor she did not normally possess. There was something about going to Jerusalem, about rounding a bend in the road and seeing the city set before you like a precious gem. It stirred the blood and lifted everyone's spirits.

There the thrones for judgment stand,
the thrones of the house of David.

The men in the delegation bowed toward the holy city as they sang. In their hearts, they wondered what kind of judgment they would be living under now that Herod was dead and his son Archelaus had inherited the throne.

Pray for the peace of Jerusalem.

Men and women joined together.

May those who love you be secure.
May there be peace within your walls
and security within your citadels.
For the sake of my brothers and friends,
I will say, 'Peace be within you.'
For the sake of the house of the LORD *our God.*⁹

The last notes of the song faded away.

"Peace? Heli, do you think there will be peace now that Herod is dead?" one of the men asked.

"I do not know," Heli responded, "but some things have not changed." He pointed ahead toward the city. A legion of soldiers was entering the gates. "The son evidently needs as many reinforcements as his father."

A coldness, like the hand of the death angel, passed over the men. In their lifetimes, they had all seen the brutality of Rome. It was a never-ending plague throughout the land.

Heli changed and lightened the subject. "I've been invited to share the Passover meal with the famous Hillel."

"No!" his friends jested.

"I have his invitation in my pocket." Heli pulled out a small parchment scroll. "He's not an unapproachable man. He and I discussed the scriptures for days while we sat in the hippodrome and waited for Herod to die."

"I do not care about the tedious discussions of the men," Mary's mother spoke to her friends. "I want to see his home. It is in the Upper City." She paused to read the envy in each woman's eye. "Of course I'll meet his wife and eat with the women. I promise to return to camp and tell every detail!"

Like maidens, her friends giggled in anticipation of such an intimate glimpse into the lives of the rich and famous.

Heli continued to talk to the men walking beside him. "Since I am a guest, I will not actually be going to the Temple to sacrifice a Passover lamb, but later in the week, I will go up to the Temple and sacrifice to the Lord."

"We also plan to see my aunt Elizabeth." Mary's mother was still elaborating on her plans for the week. "She and her husband will come to the camp. They know where the people from Nazareth always camp. Elizabeth's husband is a priest, and a few years ago, she had a little boy. He should be about four years old, close to the age of Mary's oldest son." Mary's mother sighed. "How I wish Mary and Joseph could be here. I have never even seen their children."

"Mary, you are a wonderful cook." Joseph rubbed his full stomach as he lay down to sleep. "This Passover meal could only have been better if we had eaten it in Jerusalem."

"I hope we will return one day," Mary responded as she stretched out beside her husband. "I want Jesus to see the Temple."

"In time," Joseph mumbled. He was falling asleep. "The work here is good. I have never had…" He never finished his sentence.

By the light of a single lamp, Mary could see that her husband was already asleep. She blew out the flame and laid her head on his shoulder.

Chapter 15

RETURN TO NAZARETH

*After Herod died, an angel of the Lord appeared in a dream
to Joseph in Egypt and said, "Get up, take the child and his
mother and go to the land of Israel, for those who were trying
to take the child's life are dead."*

—Matthew 2:19–20

"Justice! Reparations! We want to see the king!" A small mob
stood outside the palace gates, demanding to be heard by
Archelaus, the son of Herod who had been named in Herod's will
as the heir to his father's throne.

At the entrance to the king's private chambers, the commander
of the regiment stationed at the Fortress of Antonia waited for an
audience. Through the heavy drapes that curtained off the royal
chambers he could hear this son of Herod. "The people demand
more and more of me!" Archelaus paced the chamber. "Now they
want me to pay reparations for the forty young men my father
executed! What right do they have to ask me to open my coffers
to pay for the actions of my father?" The men were guilty. They
did pull the Roman eagle from the Temple gate and smash it!"

"These Jews are just taking their measure of you," Corinthus
responded. "They want to know if you will be as strong a ruler as
your father. You can be sure the people of this land will continue
to demand as long as you give in to their demands. It is only when
they fear even whispering your name that you will live in peace."

For a moment, the young man who expected to be king stopped his pacing, considering the words of the chamberlain he had inherited from his father. "A week ago, I fantasized that Caesar would confirm my father's will. I would officially be king of the Jews, and my people would love me. But now I can see, if I am to have any peace, they will have to fear me more than they feared my father!"

"Good!" Satan exclaimed. "You will be an effective weapon in my hands."

With one hand, Corinthus pulled aside the drapery, and a Roman commander entered as the chamberlain exited.

Settling himself behind a table covered with scrolls, Archelaus asked, "What is your report?"

"The Temple is filled to capacity. At least ten thousand are within its gates at all times. The city is overrun with pilgrims for Passover. All the way to Bethany, there is not a square cubit of ground that is unoccupied," the commander stated.

"And what about the mood of the crowd?" Archelaus inquired.

"Hostile," the commander replied. "Small pockets of dissenters are gathering throughout the city, very much like the group at your gates. Within the Temple, a group has gathered that is loudly mourning the deaths of the young men who pulled down the eagle of Rome. It appears they plan to mourn conspicuously until their demands for reparations are met."

"I have reached the end of my patience with these people!" The new king shoved the scrolls onto the floor as he stood. "My father's body has been in its grave less than two weeks, and I have spent the entire time trying to secure my throne through appeasement! If I allow these fanatical Jews to continue with their public outcry, Jerusalem and then the nation could revolt. I would then have to call on Varus, the governor of Syria, to send more troops."

"If you expect Caesar to confirm your father's will and allow you to rule Judea, you cannot appear to need assistance governing these people," Satan advised. "Think! What would your father do in this situation?"

"I must demonstrate that I can control these people!" Archelaus, the son of Herod, brought his fist down on the table with a stroke that split the wood. "Corinthus!" he called at the top of his lungs.

In response, the experienced chamberlain hastily burst through the drapes.

"Tell the commander of the palace guard to put every demonstrator at my gates in my dungeon. Every one of those ungrateful Jews is to feel the whip, and they are not to be released until Jerusalem becomes submissive." The new monarch turned quickly to face the commander from the Fortress of Antonia. "You are charged with putting a decisive end to every demonstration in the Temple area. Use whatever methods you find necessary."

Still reveling in the honor of being a guest for the first night of Passover in the home of the famous Hillel, Heli hurried to the market on the lower slopes of the Mount of Olives where animals suitable for sacrificial services were sold. He looked at the sun and shook his head in dismay. One evening with the rich and famous, and he had slept so late that one would think he had servants to send to the market. Now it was already past noon! "God, be merciful to your foolish servant," Heli breathed a short prayer as he continued to thread his way between campsites and clusters of people. Only with the help of God Almighty would he get his thank offering to the Temple before the regular evening sacrifice was offered.

As he neared the market, Heli saw that a mass of people filled the area. Close to the animal pens, they pressed shoulder to shoulder. Closer to the road, they milled about as if they did not know where the animal pens were located. "God," Heli groaned his unspoken petition, then he resigned himself to a long wait.

"Go out through the Sheep Gate, to the animal market on the Mount of Olives. The Temple market is too crowded and too expensive," the Holy Spirit continued to urge the faithful to purchase sacrificial animals at the market that was not on the Temple grounds. He continued even after the hillside was too congested for more than a few business transactions to take place. Satisfied, the Spirit of God looked over the mass of frustrated buyers. They were jostling each other, shouting and pushing.

With a mere thought, the Spirit summoned two angels. "Keep my faithful engaged in a fruitless attempt to buy. No one is to leave this mountainside and go to the Temple."

The Holy Spirit then moved on, across the small valley and into the Temple courts, speaking urgently to everyone who would listen, "Leave! Go back to your camping place. Do not stay in the Temple courts!" He spoke to each person. "Your business is finished here. Find your wife. You are hungry. Go home and eat."

Ophaniel, with a legion of angels dispatched by Michael, reported to the Spirit, "Satan and his troops are riding with the commander of the fortress."

"I have seen them, and I know their plans," the Holy Spirit sadly replied.

"Can we do something?" Ophaniel asked.

"I am presently doing all that can be done," the Spirit of God responded, "so now, prepare to visit the Place of the Dead."

Haughtily, the commander of the Fortress of Antonia rode his horse up the steps of the Eastern Gate. Only a small contingent of soldiers accompanied him. It will be enough, he smugly assured himself as he urged his horse forward. Like the Red Sea, the mass of humanity at the main entrance to the Court of the Gentiles parted to make way for the Roman commander and his squad.

Only a small group of Jewish men remained where they were. Some were wailing and mourning at the top of their lungs while others chanted their demand that Archelaus pay reparations to the families of those young men Herod had executed just weeks before his death.

"Disperse! Go to your places of lodging. Return to your villages." Sitting high on his mount, the Roman commander looked down on the small knot of rebellious men. "The king will not listen to your demands. He has ordered that all demonstrations cease!"

At that moment, a stone sailed through the air, striking the commander on the cheek. Suddenly, the air was full of stones. The commander's horse reared, and the commander fell, striking his head on the stone pavement.

"Draw swords! Attack!" Satan issued the orders for the fallen commander.

Instantly, every Roman soldier in the squad drew his sword and thrust it indiscriminately into the nearest Jew. Men and women began falling, running, screaming. Every exit was suddenly jammed with people escaping the inevitable carnage.

"Reinforcements!" Satan relayed his orders to the lookout on the walls of the fortress adjacent to the Temple.

Drawn swords in hand, hundreds of Roman soldiers ran down the stairs into the Court of the Gentiles. Every Jew in their path was chopped down. Blood ran across the flagstones. The slaughter extended into the Court of the Israelites, past the altar where ministering priests were slain as they performed their duties. Swords were not returned to their sheaths until every Jew who could not escape the Temple compound was dead or dying.

Slowly, the Gates of Sheol opened. The spirit named Death supervised. One by one, angels delivered the spirit forms of the deceased. Most went into chambers on the side reserved for those who hoped for the promised Deliverer.

"My enemy has done this!" The anguished cry of the Eternal Father shattered the tranquility of the heavenly Temple. Anthems and praises ceased. For a time, only the sobs of the heartbroken Father of mankind were heard.

"How long?" the souls within the labyrinth of chambers in the Place of the Dead moaned. Their voices were heard by a grieving Father God

He answered, "For now, my enemy has the right to hold mankind in the bowels of Sheol. He won the keys of Death in the garden. But I have sent my son, Yeshua, to conquer Satan and to eradicate death. Do not despair! He will take the keys. "Yeshua will prevail! Do not despair!"

On the Mount of Olives, panic spread from one person to the next as the stampeding crowd escaped the Temple grounds. They surged through the small valley and up the hillside. Heli found himself pressed into running, moving with the screaming mass of terrified people. They trampled campsites and market stalls while scurrying for the safety of the countryside.

"My wife!" The people from Nazareth always camped in a grove of olive trees on the mountain's terraced slope. He feared for her safety. As the crowd moved, Heli tried to push himself in a direction that would take him to his campsite. He had to find his wife so they could leave the city together.

Around him, the panicked crowd continued to flow away from the gates of the city. Heli had no choice but to move with them, skirting the perimeter of the wall and on to the road that led to Nazareth.

At last, after rounding the last bend in the road from which the walls of the city could be seen, he was able to make his way to the side of the road. There he stopped, exhausted and worried. "God, help your servant." Heli dropped to the ground, gasping for breath. "I am no longer a young man. I do not have the strength to push back into the city and search for my wife."

For the tenth time, Mary's mother described the silver goblets, the linen napkins, and the gold-edged platters used for the Passover Seder that had been held in the home of Hillel. Such a story she had to tell, and it was fun to be the center of attention.

The last group of women she had shared her experience with moved on to their own campsites, and for the first time since she had sent Heli off to the animal market, Mary's mother found herself alone with nothing to do but straighten up her own campsite. But she wasn't ready to return to the mundane. Instead, she leaned against the trunk of a nearby olive tree reliving the extravagant evening.

A sound like distant thunder interrupted her thoughts. It came from the valley between the Temple and the Mount of Olives, and it puzzled her.

"Leave everything and climb the tree," the Holy Spirit urgently pressed this thought into her mind.

Mary's mother looked around, trying to make sense out of the situation and her own thoughts.

"Climb the tree?"

The voice in her head persisted, but Mary's mother argued with it, "I am an old woman. I have not climbed a tree since before I was married. No, I will put such foolishness out of my mind. I will roll up our bedding and straighten up the campsite."

By the time she finished rolling up the woolen blankets she and Heli had slept on, she could tell the roar that she was still hearing was not thunder but running feet, and above the running feet, she could hear screams. Turning toward the Temple, her own scream caught in her throat. At the foot of the mountain, she saw a mass of humanity rushing toward her.

"Climb the tree!" the Holy Spirit was insistent.

This time, Mary's mother obeyed the voice in her head, hiking up her robes and pulling her body up from one limb to another until she perched on a sturdy branch well above the frenzied sea of humanity that trampled everything in its path.

"Heli?" Mary's mother scanned the contorted faces of the men and women as they ran past her place of safety. "Oh God, where is my husband?"

"Was the prominence of the home where you celebrated last night's Seder really significant?" The Spirit of God took this opportunity to ask a question.

Repentance filled her. "Oh, God, forgive an old lady for being so foolishly impressed by the wealth of the famous. I am satisfied with my home and my husband. Do not take my husband from me. Do not separate us and never bring us back together again. Return my family to me—my husband, my daughter, her children, and her husband."

"Return to your campsite. Pack up what remains and then take the road to Nazareth. Your husband will find you there," the Holy Spirit directed.

When most of the fleeing crowd had surged past the olive tree where she had found refuge, Mary's mother climbed stiffly to the ground. "I am no longer young," she muttered as she picked her way through her trampled campsite. All that was left to salvage were a few articles of clothing. She pulled them out of the dirt, shook them hard, and then rolled them into a bundle. She slung it over her shoulder.

Standing on the side of the road, Heli scanned the faces of the fleeing people. Jerusalem was emptying. Passover week was coming to an abrupt end. He could not see every face, so he called over and over, "Is anyone from Nazareth?"

Carried along by the fleeing crowd, Mary's mother could do nothing else but move with her terrified countrymen. "Heli?" From time to time, she called her husband's name, but the effort seemed futile.

"Move to the side of the road." The Holy Spirit pressed the thought into her mind while Ophaniel broke a path through the crowd.

Without being urged, Mary's mother skirted to the side of the road, threw her bundle of clothes to the ground, and sat on top of it. For a long time, she just sat there, catching her breath and watching the faces of the people as they streamed by.

Very faintly, she heard a familiar voice. "Is anyone from Nazareth?

Mary's mother jumped to her feet and looked back toward Jerusalem. She saw a very familiar figure. She couldn't see his face, but she didn't need to. "Heli!" she yelled. "Here I am!"

The figure turned and then began running toward her.

"Praise God!" She had never been so happy to see her beloved Heli.

With a crude oath, Volumnius looked up from his meal of bread and wine to see Corinthus entering the dungeon. "Corinthus," Volumnius began his complaint, "I don't have room for one more prisoner. Every jail cell is holding twice the number of traitorous Jews that it was built for. When am I going to receive orders to execute some of them? It is the only way to solve this overcrowding problem."

With a wave of his hand, the politically powerful Arabian brushed aside the concerns of the commander of the dungeon. "The entire royal family has gone to Rome to secure the throne. No one is here to withstand an attack on the king's treasury!"

"An attack on the king's treasury!" Volumnius rose to his feet ready to use his one good arm to defend the family of Herod.

"Sabinus, the assistant governor under Varus, has come to the palace, and he is demanding to audit Herod's treasury."

"This is a political matter," Volumnius responded. "Why do you come to me?"

From beneath his robes, Herod's chamberlain pulled out a ring of keys. "Guard these, and set your men at the doors to the treasury."

For a long moment, the commander of the dungeon stared at Corinthus, leveling the chamberlain's status down to his own. "And what do I get for this service?"

"Death warrants," Corinthus responded. "You can empty half of this prison."

"Jesus?" Joseph pointed to the notched sticks that he had lined up on the floor of the courtyard. "How many weeks has it been since Passover?"

Intently interested in accuracy, the little boy counted each of the seven notches on each of the seven sticks.

"It has been six weeks and six days," Jesus answered with a certain amount of satisfaction in his ability to count.

"And what happens seven weeks after Passover?" Joseph asked.

"We have another feast," Jesus shouted. "The Feast of Weeks!"

From near the water jars where Mary was washing the dirt from baby James, she looked up and smiled proudly at her oldest son. Not even four years old, and he could count.

"Joseph?" Mary spoke thoughtfully. "It will soon be time to enroll Jesus in the synagogue school. When he is five years old, he should, like all the other Jewish boys, begin studying the third book of Moses. I do hope we are back in the land by then. The schools here do not teach exactly like the schools in Israel. Some of the scribes do not even read Hebrew! They use the Greek translation. My father—"

Joseph cut into Mary's comments with a rueful laugh. "Say no more. I will not disappoint Heli. If the angel of the Lord has not instructed me to leave Egypt and return to Israel before the boy turns five, I will obtain a Hebrew tutor for him."

"Toma?" Uncle Shaul absentmindedly scratched the shaggy camel as he stood beside Kheti's caravan, which was preparing to leave Bethlehem and travel to Jerusalem. "In two days, it will be the Feast of Weeks. Wait in the city just two days and worship in the Temple with me."

"Uncle Shaul, I do not know…"

"Toma, do not say you no longer believe in God. Your mind struggles because of your experiences, but your heart will always believe. You are a son of the covenant."

"Kheti?" Uncle Shaul called. "How long will you be in the city?"

"Several days," the Egyptian merchant answered.

"See? We can meet on the bridge between the Upper City and the western gate to the Temple grounds at the third hour of the day," Uncle Shaul pressed.

Not knowing what else to say, Toma replied, "I will be there."

Gloating over the ease with which he manipulated men to do his bidding, Satan glanced at the pile of timbers in the courtyard of the Roman guard. He estimated there was enough wood to construct twenty crosses. Twenty men at a time, he would begin killing off the descendants of Abraham. He would continue killing the descendants of Abraham until not one son or daughter of the covenant lived in any region of the earth. He laughed to himself sadistically,. "Then what becomes of God's promise to Abraham, '*I will make you into a great nation*?'"[1]

Transforming to his eagle face, Satan then soared into the center of the Roman soldiers' barracks to stand behind the eagle on the shrine to the emperor.

Volumnius approached the golden eagle mounted on the wall above the bronze bust of Caesar. Bowing, he placed his offering, a cup of wine and a loaf of bread, before the two supreme gods of

Rome. "I pray for a successful day, a day that brings honor to the empire." From behind the emblem of the eagle, Satan nodded in satisfied acceptance. "I grant you the lives of twenty Jewish men today and many more in the future," he declared.

Omnipotently observing the actions of his enemy, God stood up in his throne room and announced, "Are not the sons of Abraham my dear children? Even though I have often spoken against them, still I love them. My heart has great compassion for them. I will not allow Satan to destroy these twenty men. I have not granted to an angel, especially a rebellious angel, the power to declare life and death. Stir up the men of Israel. Call them to arms, and I will free these men."

Immediately, the Holy Spirit knew the intent of God, and he called Michael to prepare the heavenly and earthly warriors.

With his left hand, Volumnius saluted fist to chest before leaving the shrine. Above all else, he was a dedicated follower of the emperor and the evil power behind that Roman ruler. Stepping into the courtyard, he gave the first order of the day, "Bring the prisoners."

Twenty Jewish men beaten beyond resistance slowly shuffled into the courtyard.

With heartless aloofness, the commander of the dungeon supervised as each man was given the crossbeam of his own cross to carry.

Above the dungeon courtyard, Satan and his demonic horde gathered. Agitated and excited, they shouted, *"Our hand has triumphed; the LORD has not done this!"*[2]

On the bridge that spanned the valley between the elite residences of the Upper City and the Temple complex, Toma waited for his uncle. He tried to remember the last time he had come to the Temple to take part in the services. It had been years.

Curiously, he looked around. Something was different. He saw very few women or old men. Mostly young men strolled the bridge, seemingly without a specific direction. He noted that some carried weapons. Walking a few paces away from the gate, he observed that a large group of men had gathered not far from the Palace of Herod. Picking up his pace, Toma hurried in the direction of that group.

"Go ahead. Join them, Toma," the Holy Spirit urged. "These are the men I have called to battle to carry out my vengeance on the followers of my enemy."

Running as fast as he could, Toma joined the band of angry men just as the palace gates opened and Roman guards led twenty men out toward the place of crucifixion. Breathless and horrified, Toma watched until a one-armed commander on horseback exited the palace and the gates closed behind him.

"Throw the first stone, Toma. The honor is yours."

A shofar blast was heard as the heavenly host swept in from the east.

Toma picked up a fist-sized stone and hurled it with all his might at the Roman commander as he rode past.

The stone struck the commander's horse squarely on the nose, causing him to suddenly rear. Volumnius was thrown to the ground.

"The sword and the righteous vengeance of the Lord!" the Archangel Michael shouted.

"The sword and the righteous vengeance of the Lord!" the men shouted as, with raised swords, they charged down the slope toward the prisoners and troops on the road. Toma ran with them, picking up stones and hurling them with all his might at the outnumbered soldiers, who now crouched under raised shields with swords ready for the attack. Suddenly, with a clash of blades and a clatter of stones, the two groups met.

Brave men rushed forward and released the prisoners, tossing the heavy timbers they had been forced to carry at the overpowered soldiers. One of the timbers landed squarely on the head of the one-armed commander of Herod's dungeon.

Once more, the shofar sounded as a legion of heavenly warriors descended on the Temple.

Without warning, fighting erupted on the Temple grounds. Roman soldiers from the Fortress of Antonia poured through the gates into the Temple, only to find themselves surrounded by angry Jewish men who had prepared for this battle. From the top of the portico, the Jews threw darts into the ranks of the Roman fighting men, cheering over each soldier who fell.

"Fight back! Do not retreat!" Satan issued orders to the commanders of the Roman troops in the Temple. "Set fire to the portico!"

Immediately, soldiers with flaming torches ran forward. Most fell under the barrage of darts, but one made it to the cedar columns that supported the roof. Flames leaped into the air while those men on top leaped, many to their deaths.

Angels continued to carry the fallen through the Gates of Sheol. Many were laid to rest on the side of hope. At that same gate, others were transferred into the shackles of Satan.

Before fleeing from the scene, Toma took one last look at the carnage around him. At least twelve Roman soldiers were dead on the road, including the one-armed Roman commander. One of the timbers that had been carried by a prisoner lay on top of his crushed head.

It was sundown, the beginning of the ninth day of the summer month of Av. In Nazareth, Heli, along with the rest of the men, sat on the floor of the synagogue. As one man, they each placed one hand over their hearts and grasped a portion of their garment, tearing a ragged hole, and then throwing the dust from the floor on their covered heads, they began to daven, swaying back and forth as they wailed, "My God, my God, have you forsaken your people? Two thousand Jewish men hang on crosses that line the roads to Jerusalem. Our neighboring city of Sepphoris has been burned and all its population sold into slavery. Emmaus has also been burned."

"My servant, Varus, the governor of Syria, has proven an effective tool," Satan commented as the mournful cries of all the men of Israel were heard throughout the land. Taunting the Spirit of God, he continued, "You liberated twenty men, allowing me to kill thousands. Your small victory resulted in catastrophic retribution. In my kingdom, I cannot be defeated!"

"God is not deaf," the Holy Spirit responded to the taunts of Satan. "He hears the cries of his people. He has promised a Deliverer."

"You mean Yeshua the Creator in the body of a child? That little boy hiding in Egypt?" Satan laughed derisively.

"Do not scoff at what you do not comprehend," the Holy Spirit warned. "God's ways are not your ways. He thinks and plans on a plane that you can never attain. Be assured that God has prepared your torment and your destruction. This slaughter will not go unpunished!"

On heavenly Mount Zion, God stood and announced, "It is time to prepare my son for battle. Call Yeshua to come out of Egypt. He is to return to the land I gave to Abraham and his descendants."

Immediately, Ophaniel responded, flying with a warrior escort through the void of space to the home of Mary and Joseph in Alexandria, Egypt.

"Joseph? Joseph?" Blazing white, with skin like burning bronze, Ophaniel, the same angel of the Lord who had sent Joseph and Mary with the child to the safety of Egypt, spoke to Joseph in his dream. "It is time. '*Get up, take the child and his mother and return to the land of Israel, for those who were trying to take the child's life are dead.*'"[3]

Joseph suddenly woke up, remembering his dream in vivid detail. He glanced at his wife and knew she would be glad to know that this very morning, he would begin making the preparations for their return to the land.

The planning and providence of God, the father of Jesus, was obvious, for Kheti and Toma had arrived in Alexandria on the previous day.

"Joseph, here are all the waterskins." Mary struggled to carry a pile of empty waterskins to the stable where Joseph was getting ready to load the cart. She dropped them on the floor and then noticed that her husband was slowly walking Lily in circles while he watched her left rear leg. "Is something wrong with Lily?" Mary asked.

"She seems to be limping a bit," Joseph replied. "We cannot start this journey with a lame animal. In the heat of the summer, it is going to be a hard trip."

Standing by and watching with big brown eyes, three-year-old Jesus followed every move his parents made.

Joseph paused and handed the halter rope to the little boy. "Walk her for me, son." Obediently, Jesus took the rope and led the docile donkey back and forth while Joseph squatted down to study her gait. As he watched, he slowly shook his head. "I'm afraid we are going to have to sell Lily and buy another donkey."

"Oh no!" Mary exclaimed. "There could not be another donkey as sweet as Lily! Isn't there something we can do for her leg?"

"Rest might heal her," Joseph answered, "but we don't have time. Kheti and Toma are buying and selling on the wharves right now. They are going to want to leave within two days. That doesn't give me much time to sell her and buy another animal."

Jesus had stopped walking the donkey. He just stood there listening to his parents, comprehending their problem as best he could. "Is Lily hurt?" he asked.

"I'm afraid her leg is injured," Joseph gently answered.

"Rub your hand over her leg," the Holy Spirit spoke to Jesus as one of Michael's guarding angels placed a restraining hand on the animal's hindquarters.

Immediately, Jesus walked close to the donkey's back hooves and placed his little hand on her left leg. The young boy shivered as a tingling surge of healing power rushed through his little body.

"Son!" Joseph cried in alarm. "Stay away from the donkey's hind legs!" He ran and frantically snatched Jesus up, away from the danger of being kicked. "You know better! I have taught you to never walk close enough for an animal to kick you!" Joseph scolded.

"Walk Lily again," Jesus said.

"No, it's no use," Joseph responded as he placed Jesus on the floor a safe distance from the donkey.

"Walk Lily again," Mary repeated her son's words as she recalled the time when she had found Jesus holding baby James, who had suddenly gotten well.

Shrugging his shoulders at the uselessness of the task, Joseph complied.

"Look," Mary squealed, "she is not limping!"

Joseph turned his head and watched the movements of his faithful work animal as she displayed a normal sure-footed gait. Joseph stopped walking Lily and looked first at Jesus, then at Mary. "You don't think?" He didn't have to finish his question.

Mary knew exactly what was on her husband's mind. "I don't know. I just make a memory of each unusual event and store it away in my mind."

"He is only three years old." Joseph couldn't take his eyes off the little boy, who had now forgotten all about the donkey and was busy arranging small scraps of wood into a childish construction.

"My father used to say one way we would know the Messiah had come was by the miracles that he would be able to do. According to the prophet Isaiah, our Deliverer would open the eyes of the blind and the ears of the deaf. He would make the lame leap like deer and the dumb shout for joy."

"Do you think Isaiah was talking about a donkey?" Joseph asked incredulously.

"I stopped trying to figure it out after I was visited by the angel," Mary responded. Still bewildered, Joseph nodded his head in agreement. So much was beyond their comprehension.

"Once more they will cross the desert," Satan and Raziel, his second in command, sat on a nearby rooftop and contemplated the opportunities this journey might present.

"They will be well guarded," Raziel pointed out.

"I know," Satan growled. From his perch, he could see the glow of warrior angels standing shoulder to shoulder around the house and stable Mary and Joseph had been renting for nearly two years.

"Still, we can make them miserable," Raziel suggested. "Allow no cloud cover, let the sun blister their faces and the sand bite through their clothing."

"Let them suffer thirst," Satan pondered the possibilities. "In the midst of all that misery, they may speak a word against God."

"Mary and Joseph are only human. In the midst of all that discomfort, they may become abusive toward their son," Raziel added. "We may be prevented from doing the child any harm, but his parents still have free choice."

From their perch, Satan and Raziel watched as Joseph put his donkey into her stall for the night. With hate in their eyes, the Prince of Darkness and his lieutenant studied Joseph as he hoisted his three-year-old son high on his shoulders and carried him into the house for their evening meal.

"It will be a long miserable journey," Raziel commented. "There will be many opportunities to disrupt the nauseating harmony of Joseph's family."

"I feel like my ancestors who said to Moses, 'Have you brought us into the desert to die?'" Mary commented as she tried unsuccessfully to shake off the dust. It seemed to be continually blowing across the road that traversed the Northern Sinai Peninsula. "Our food is filled with sand. My skin is constantly gritty," she complained to no one in particular as she reached into a basket in the back of the cart and brought out three pieces of flat bread. She handed one to her husband, divided a second one between her two sons, and kept the third for herself. Her unusually lifeless brown eyes met her husband's travel-weary eyes. "We are running out of food," she flatly stated.

Before Joseph could respond, she turned away and sat down beside the road to eat her morning meal with her two sons. Joseph did not need a spiritual eye to see that discouragement and hopelessness draped themselves over her weary body.

For a moment, Joseph considered possible responses, but what could he say? They had been walking for three long weeks. At first, they had been scorched by the sun, then as they traversed the marshlands, they had been plagued by bloodsucking insects. Now the stinging sand of the desert was taking its toll.

Turning away, he decided silence was the best reply. For the past several days, one word had led to another until he and Mary hardly had a civilized word left in their vocabulary. Listlessly, he bit into the dry bread, forcing himself to chew and swallow. A wave of shame suddenly washed over him. He had been so consumed by misery that he had forgotten to bless the bread he was now chewing. Between bites, he began chanting, "Blessed are you, O Lord our God, who brings forth bread from the earth."

Slowly Joseph moved to the back of his cart and picked up a full waterskin. He allowed himself just one swallow to wash the dry bread down his throat. Then he counted the waterskins in his cart, six empty and four full. He scratched his sand-encrusted beard and wondered how far it was to the next settlement where water would be available. Toma walked by, checking the lines of camels interspersed with donkeys. "Do you have any extra water?" Joseph called to his cousin.

Toma paused and slowly shook his head. "I have never been on such a difficult trek. The heat, the blowing sand, our water supplies are also terribly low. The camels have not had water in more than a week. Have you seen how their humps are sagging?"

"How much farther?" Joseph asked. His eyes were on Lily. He knew that a donkey could not go on as limited a water ration as a camel.

"Under these conditions, at least three more days before we reach Gaza." Toma put his hand out and scratched Lily's head. "We're all worried about the animals."

"I'm afraid we will run out of water before then," Joseph admitted his concern.

"If you run out, let us know" Toma offered, "but use what you have very sparingly."

"Thanks," Joseph was deeply appreciative of the safety that Kheti's caravan had provided on their journey.

Toma moved on, and Joseph picked up a waterskin and carried it over to Mary and the boys. "Two swallows each," he said as he held the waterskin for each of them to have a drink. Then without further conversation, he returned the waterskin to the cart.

"You have certainly failed at taking care of your family." A Condemning spirit took advantage of the situation.

Joseph looked at his wife with their two sons. Mary was holding James. Jesus was standing beside her. He could not argue with the condemning voice in his head. His family was covered with dust, underfed, tired, and thirsty. A little gust suddenly threw a cloud of flying sand into the air completely blocking his family from view. "God, bring us safely through this desert and back into the land," Joseph prayed.

The Spirit of God looked down at the forlorn family and then toward the interior of the peninsula, where the enemy of God and all mankind kept a constant wind gusting. "It is enough!" His voice penetrated the desolate wastelands where Satan prowled.

With a thought, he summoned Michael, the commander of the heavenly armies. "Engage our enemy," the Spirit ordered. "He is to be forced out of those waste places where he is hiding and manipulating the weather."

Immediately, the shofar sounded, and legions of angel warriors unsheathed their fiery swords as they flew directly toward the high desert to seek out and engage the enemy of their Creator.

Suddenly, the dust settled, and the caravan began to move under a cloudless blue sky. Joseph took a deep breath, finally able to fill his lungs with clean air. Running from the side of the road, Jesus caught up with his father and began walking beside him, imitating his manly stride. After a while, Toma and Kheti came back to walk with them.

"At last," Kheti commented, "we can cover a day's journey in a day." He gestured toward the clear sky. "The day after tomorrow, we will see the walls of Gaza, and before sunset, we will drink from the wells of the city."

A sound like thunder in the interior startled the men and caused them to look inland. Kheti stopped walking and stared at the sky. Huge thunderclouds appeared to race toward each other and clash.

"I have never seen a sky like this," Toma commented in awed tones.

"There is never a cloud in the summer," Kheti remarked almost fearfully.

For a time, the entire caravan stopped moving. All eyes were fixed on the unusual cloud formations and their violent rolling clashes.

After a time, the thunder ceased, and all but one of the clouds disappeared. Except for that one cloud, which seemed to move with them, the sky was clear and blue as the caravan moved forward.

All morning, they walked. At noon, they stopped. Joseph gave the donkey and each member of his family some water. Now, only three skins full of water remained.

The caravan moved on. Kheti and Toma went forward to check on the lead animals, while Joseph and his family continued moving through the dust that rose from the feet of the animals that walked before them. Unexpectedly, the caravan halted again. Eager to break away from their place near the end of the line, Joseph, with Jesus following close behind, hurried along beside the standing animals to see what was causing this new delay.

Near the front of the caravan, they found Kheti standing beside a camel that had dropped to its knees. Toma was removing the animal's load. "He's an old camel," Kheti muttered to himself, "the first camel I ever purchased."

"Maybe he can continue without a load," Joseph suggested.

Kheti shook his head doubtfully. "If he had water, maybe, but I have to save all of my water for the donkeys, or we will not arrive at Gaza."

Kheti and Joseph considered the situation while Toma and the other drovers redistributed the loads.

Drawn to the collapsed animal, Jesus moved close to the camel, rubbing his little hands on its rough fur, speaking childish comfort to the shaggy beast.

"Yeshua!"

Jesus stopped stroking the camel and looked around. Someone was calling him by his Hebrew name.

"Dig a hole in the sand in front of the camel and say to the earth, 'Bring forth water.'"

Immediately, Jesus knelt down in front of the kneeling camel, his little hands scooping and tossing the dirt aside. When the hole was as big as his mother's kneading trough, he placed his hands in the dusty hole and obediently said, "Earth, bring forth water!"

Suddenly, muddy water began bubbling up from the ground, filling the hole, running out over the hard earth. The camel bent its head and began to drink. Jesus squealed and began to splash in the water that was overflowing, turning the dust into mud.

Kheti and Joseph suddenly stopped talking. Joseph looked down. His feet were wet! Kheti's mouth dropped open in amazement, and then all eyes turned toward the little boy splashing in the muddy water.

"A spring! A spring in the desert!" Kheti exclaimed. "Bring shovels! Dig a trough for the animals to drink!" Kheti began shouting orders, but Toma and Joseph did not move. They continued to stare at the little boy and wonder, What kind of child is this?

"*The poor and needy search for water, but there is none; their tongues are parched with thirst. But I the* LORD *will answer them; I, the God of Israel, will not forsake them.*"[4] The Spirit of God broke into joyous laughter. "*I will turn the desert into pools of water, and the parched ground into springs.*[5] Smiling at Jesus as he played in the water bubbling from the sandy ground, the Spirit proclaimed, "I have made pools of water to spring from parched ground, and I have brought the Living Water to all mankind. It will be life to everyone who believes, and they will thirst no more!"

Above the melee of flight and pursuit, Satan heard the Holy Spirit's proclamation of victory. He shook his fist in the wind and shouted back, "Just let me meet Yeshua on my own terms without his legions." As the last word flew from his mouth, he felt the heat of Michael's sword close to his back. Immediately, he spread his wings like an eagle and soared away toward the distant mountaintops.

Two weeks later, Kheti's caravan entered the little town of Bethlehem, going directly to the market to tempt the local merchants with exotic goods from the port city of Alexandria.

Walking through the familiar maze of blankets covered with merchandise and baskets overflowing with trade goods, Mary fell into step beside Joseph. "I want to see our home," she said so softly that he almost didn't hear her.

"It's being rented you know," Joseph replied. "Another family is living there."

"I know."

Joseph looked into Mary's eyes and asked, "Do you want to live here again?"

"Part of me does," Mary answered. As she spoke, her eyes caught sight of an old friend coming to the market. "It's Jabek's wife! Mary called to her, and the woman raised the stump of her right arm to return the greeting. Mary's excited greeting caught in her throat. As the woman hurried over to welcome them back into the town, Mary found it hard to pull her eyes away from the place where a hand should have been. Confronted with the evidence of the tragedy that both she and her son had escaped, she felt the uncomfortable guilt of being spared while others suffered great loss.

Joseph carried the conversation, catching up on their lives, avoiding any mention of her missing hand or the son she had lost. Mary couldn't speak. In her mind, gratefulness warred with guilt. She was relieved when Jabek's wife moved on to look at the Egyptian linen Kheti was unloading.

"Let's go to the other side of town. We'll visit Uncle Shaul," Joseph whispered into Mary's ear as he lifted both Jesus and James into the cart. At the well, they stopped to water the donkey. From there, they could see the spot where Toma's house had stood. Every stone had been removed. For a long time, Joseph and Mary just stood and stared at the bare earth where they had spent so many happy hours with Sarah, baby Avrahm, and Toma's mother, Leah. Their minds could find no words to express the pain in their hearts.

"Joseph? Is that you?" A familiar voice broke into their painful thoughts.

Joseph looked up to see Oved, one of the shepherds who had come to the stable the night of Jesus's birth. Greeting the man with a hug, he asked, "And how is Ehud?"

"Dead!"

"What?" Joseph recoiled. He could not believe his ears. Had everyone he had been associated with met tragedy?

"He was in the Temple during Passover when Archelaus ordered the slaughter, then fifty days later, Nahum was killed in another Temple riot."

"Toma told me about the uprising during the Feast of Weeks and how Varus has punished the land. So much blood has been shed!" Joseph covered his face with his hands and leaned back heavily onto his cart.

Oved responded, "The emperor has officially proclaimed Archelaus king of Judea, and this son of Herod is as wicked as his father."

Joseph shook his head in dismay. "I will not live under such an evil tyrant."

"Then you cannot live in Judea," Oved replied. "His spies infiltrate the country, and his troops are everywhere."

"We will go to Nazareth," Joseph stated with finality.

"Antipas, another son of Herod, rules there," Oved cautioned.

In a gesture of helplessness, Joseph raised his hands and exclaimed, "Lord, where can a man and his family live in safety?"

"Deliver an answer to my faithful servant Joseph," the Spirit instructed Ophaniel. "Tonight as he sleeps, tell him to take his family to Nazareth and make his home there."

One week later, without Kheti's trading caravan, Joseph and Mary, with their two boys, approached the Galilean town of Nazareth.

"Joseph, look! There is a wedding procession coming out of Nazareth!" Mary pointed to a group of maidens who were dancing in front of a bride carried on a sedan chair. Joseph, with Jesus walking beside him, maintained his steady pace toward the town they had left more than three years earlier, but Mary became excited. As fast as she could, with James in her arms, she hurried forward. "I see my father!" She called back to Joseph, "Hurry!"

Joseph urged Lily to walk a little faster until he caught up with his wife. "That's Zebedee, the fisherman!" He pointed to the bridegroom.

"This must be Salome's wedding!" Mary squealed as she pressed James into Joseph's free hand and broke into a run.

"Where is Mama going?" Jesus asked, concern and puzzlement all over his face.

"She is going to see her sister." Joseph pointed to the veiled woman seated on the fabric-draped chair carried on the shoulders of four strong fishermen.

Jesus still looked puzzled, his little-boy face a sea of unasked questions.

"Come on," Joseph urged. "Let's catch up with them so you can meet your relatives."

"Salome!" Mary called. She ran straight toward the bride who lifted her veil and peeked out.

"Mary!" Salome nearly fell off the chair as she reached for her sister's hand. "I hoped you would come for my wedding." She lifted her veil again and looked around. "Where are Joseph and the children?"

"I just shoved James into Joseph's arms and ran ahead," Mary confessed as she looked around.

"Oh, Mary, how could you?" Salome exclaimed.

"It's all right." Mary giggled as she realized she had not shown much deference to her husband. "Look"—she pointed to the back of the procession—"Joseph just caught up with father, and mother has taken James. She is showing him to her friends."

"And where is Jesus?" Salome asked. "I can't wiggle around to see, or I will fall off this chair!"

"He is leading the donkey," Mary answered proudly. "He is holding that rope like such a little man."

"Oh, he couldn't be big enough!" Salome exclaimed.

"He'll be four next Passover," Mary answered. "He is the sturdiest, most dependable little fellow, and Lily is a very gentle animal. Don't worry, Joseph is keeping an eye on him."

"I am so happy you are here." Salome bent over and tried unsuccessfully to kiss her sister's cheek.

"We're going to live in Nazareth," Mary announced.

"Oh, but I'll be in Capernaum," Salome moaned.

"That's not so far," Mary answered. "I have walked all the way from Egypt! A trip to Capernaum is nothing. We are going all the way to Zebedee's house with you now.

"Is marriage good?" Salome asked a little apprehensively.

"Very good!" Mary answered. She looked back at her husband and her two sons. She was blessed. "We'll talk. I'll tell you everything, but right now, I had better go see mother and father."

Mary left the front of the procession and ran back to where Heli and Joseph were walking together deep in conversation. Home! She was home! She found her mother walking beside Jesus as he led the donkey and cart. Already, the two had a conversation going. Mary hugged her mom and fell in step.

Joseph looked back and caught her eye, sending a big satisfied smile her way.

Like a wedding canopy, the Holy Spirit spread himself over the length of the procession. He breathed his blessing on all the families, but especially he blessed the family of Joseph and Mary to whom he had entrusted Yeshua the Creator.

Index of Characters

Biblical Characters

Adam   The first man (Genesis 2–3)

Anna   A prophetess who lived in the Temple (Luke 2:36–38)

Elizabeth   The wife of Zechariah and mother of John the Baptist (Luke 1:5–24)

Eve   The first woman (Genesis 2–3)

Father God   A name for God

Gabriel   An angel messenger (Daniel 8:6, Luke 1:19, 26)

Heli   Grandfather of Jesus, one theory is that the genealogy in Luke is actually the genealogy of Mary (Luke 3:23)

Holy Spirit   Part of the triune Godhead: Spirit of God, Spirit of Father God, or Spirit

Joseph   The earthly father of Jesus (Matthew 1–2, Luke 1–2)

Lucifer — A name for Satan or the devil while he lived in the perfection of heaven (Isaiah 12:14, KJV)

Magi — Men from east of Israel who brought gifts to the baby Jesus, there are many theories and traditions about the identity of these men, where they came from, and when they arrived in Bethlehem; nothing factual is known (Matthew 2)

Michael — A prince of angels who often contends with the forces of evil (Daniel 10:13, Jude 9, Revelation. 12:7)

Salome — The sister of Mary and the wife of Zebedee, this relationship is theorized by comparing the two scriptural passages about the women who were with Mary at the cross (Mark 15:40, Matthew 27:55–56)

Satan — The devil, the fallen angel once called Lucifer

Simeon — A man who prophesied over baby Jesus (Luke 2:25–35)

Yeshua	The Hebrew name for Jesus in this story, Yeshua refers to Jesus in his role as part of the triune Godhead
Zebedee	A fisherman, the father of James and John, husband of Salome (Matthew 4:21)
Zechariah	A priest, the father of John the Baptist, the husband of Elizabeth (Luke 1:5–22)

Historical Characters

Abgar	King of Edessa from 4 BC–AD 7 and AD 13– AD 50. In the writings of the church historian Eusebius, there is a letter to Jesus from this king asking him to come to Edessa and heal him. Jesus replied that he would send a disciple after he returned to heaven. Thaddeus was sent; King Abgar was healed. This king from Northeast of Jerusalem, Edessa in Parthia, which used to be part of the Medo-Persian Empire, had a documented conviction regarding the divinity of Jesus.
Antipas	A son of Herod who inherited rulership of Galilee
Antipater	A son of Herod who was executed days before Herod's death

Archelaus	A son of Herod who inherited rulership of Judea
Arsinoe	A Jewish woman who lived near the Jewish Temple in Egypt. The inscription on her tomb tells of her death during childbirth
Caesar Augustus	Emperor of the Roman Empire
Corinthus	An Arabian man who was a chamberlain for Herod the Great
Herod the Great	Vassal king of Judea under Rome from about 37 BC–4 BC. Historians are not certain that these dates are accurate.
Hillel	This famous Jew lived from 75 BC–AD 15. He founded the rabbinical school of Hillel in Jerusalem.
Manu III	King of Edessa from 23 BC–4 BC
Phabeis	According to the inscription on her tomb, the husband of Arsinoe
Salome	The sister of Herod the Great and ruler over a few small city-states
Sabinus	Assistant to the Roman governor of Syria

Shammai	Jewish scribe, the head of a rabbinical school in Jerusalem
Varus	The Roman governor of Syria
Volumnius	A Roman commander in the Court of Herod the Great, it is not known whether or not he took part in killing the babies of Bethlehem or the uprisings during the feasts
Zarbin	A military commander from Edessa, this information comes from the inscription on his tombstone

Fictional Characters

Abdu	One of the magi, a Zoroastrian priest
Abigail	A woman in Nazareth
Avrahm	The son of Toma and Sarah
Ehud	One of the Temple shepherds
Elisheva	Joseph's aunt
Ezra son of Samuel	A man of Nazareth
Hadassah	Mother-in-law of Joram, a friend of Elizabeth, woman who lived in Carem

Hur	Silversmith from Nazareth
Jabek	A man of Bethlehem
Jabek's wife	A woman of Bethlehem
Jethro	Man of Nazareth, friend of Joseph
Joram	Priest from Carem, married to Rivkah
Kefa	Son of Jabek
Kheti	Egyptian merchant
Leah	Mother of Toma
Malachi	Tax collector for Bethlehem
Moshe	Man of Nazareth, friend of Joseph
Nahum	One of the Temple shepherds
Oved	One of the Temple shepherds
Rivkah	Wife of Joram, woman of Carem, friend of Elizabeth
Sarah	Wife of Toma, mother of Avrahm, friend of Mary
Shammah	Old shepherd who owned the stable where Jesus was born

Toma	Joseph's cousin
Toviah	One of the Templeshepherds
Uncle Shaul	Joseph's uncle
Zepporah	An old shepherdess who helped Mary give birth, wife of Shammah

Traditional Characters

Ophaniel	A heavenly angel
Raziel	An angel of the occult

Biblical References

Prologue Part 1

1. Exodus 20:11

Prologue Part 2

1. Genesis 2:17
2. Genesis 3:10
3. Genesis 3:11
4. Genesis 3:12
5. Genesis 3:15
6. Genesis 3:15

Chapter 1

1. Luke 1:28
2. Luke 1:30
3. Deuteronomy 22:23–24
4. Luke 1:31
5. Luke 1:32–33
6. Luke 1:35
7. Luke 1:38
8. Luke 1:36–37
9. Luke 1:30
10. Luke 1:35
11. Exodus 20:16
12. Luke 1:30
13. Psalm 84:11

Chapter 2

1. Luke 1:32–33
2. Deuteronomy 22:24
3. Isaiah 7:14
4. Psalm 118:1–4
5. Psalm 118:5–8
6. Jeremiah 33:14–16

Chapter 3

1. Luke 1:42
2. Luke 1:43–45
3. Luke 1:46-47
4. Luke 1:48–49
5. Luke 1:50–51
6. Luke 1:54–55

Chapter 4

1. Micah 6:8
2. Psalm 119:105–107
3. Psalm 139:1–3
4. Genesis 15:5
5. Matthew 1:20
6. Matthew 1:21
7. Matthew 1:23
8. Luke 1:63
9. Luke 1:68
10. Luke 1:70–72
11. Genesis 3:16
12. Luke 1:76–78
13. Deuteronomy 22:23–24
14. Numbers 30:1–2

15. Luke 1:28
16. Luke 1:30
17. Luke 1:31–33
18. 1 Chronicles 17:13

Chapter 5

1. Micah 5:2
2. Psalm 91:1–2
3. Psalm 91:7–11
4. Exodus 20:17
5. Isaiah 45:22–23
6. Psalm 2:2
7. Psalm 2:4–7
8. Psalm 22:19
9. Psalm 27:14
10. Luke 1:30
11. Psalm 150:2–3

Chapter 6

1. Genesis 3:15
2. Genesis 3:16
3. Isaiah 12:2
4. Isaiah 12:3–4
5. Genesis 49:10
6. Isaiah 9:6–7
7. Luke 2:12
8. Luke 2:10–12
9. Luke 2:14
10. Isaiah 9:6
11. Jeremiah 23:5–6

Chapter 7

1. Song of Solomon 1:15
2. Song of Solomon 1:16
3. Song of Solomon 4:10–11
4. Isaiah 54:1
5. Isaiah 54:4
6. Deuteronomy 32:43
7. Numbers 6:24–26
8. Exodus 13:1
9. Psalm 34:1–4

Chapter 8

1. Numbers 24:17–18
2. Deuteronomy 4:19
3. Amos 5:26
4. Numbers 24:17
5. Micah 5:1–5

Chapter 11

1. Proverbs 15:1
2. Genesis 12:3
3. Psalm 10:2–3
4. Psalm 10:8–11
5. Psalm 10:12
6. Psalm 11:5

Chapter 12

1. Leviticus 19:34

Chapter 13

1. Psalm 18:2–3
2. Psalm 91:1–2,4

Chapter 14

1. Exodus 20:3–4
2. Deuteronomy 6:5
3. Deuteronomy 6:6
4. Deuteronomy 6:7
5. Deuteronomy 6:8
6. Psalm 119:11
7. Psalms 10:16
8. Psalm 10:17–18
9. Psalm 122:1–9

Chapter 15

1. Genesis 12:2
2. Deuteronomy 32:27
3. Matthew 2:20
4. Isaiah 41:17
5. Isaiah 41:18